Novels by Elliott Arnold

THE CAMP GRANT MASSACRE
PROVING GROUND
CODE OF CONDUCT
FORESTS OF THE NIGHT
A NIGHT OF WATCHING
FLIGHT FROM ASHIYA
THE TIME OF THE GRINGO
WALK WITH THE DEVIL
EVERYBODY SLEPT HERE
BLOOD BROTHER
TOMORROW WILL SING
THE COMMANDOS
ONLY THE YOUNG
PERSONAL COMBAT
TWO LOVES

The
Camp Grant
Massacre

A NOVEL BY **Elliott Arnold**

SIMON AND SCHUSTER △ NEW YORK

Library of Congress Cataloging in Publication Data

Arnold, Elliott. 1912–
    The Camp Grant massacre.

    1.   Apache Indians—Wars—Fiction.   I.   Title.
PZ3.A7535Cam [PS3501.R5933]   813'.5'2   75-25995
ISBN 0-671-22193-0

FOR JEANNE

The Apache kills and robs as a means of livelihood. It is his normal condition.

—Gen. Irvin McDowell
Com. Dept. of California,
Annual Report, 1867

It is useless to try to negotiate with these Apache Indians. They will observe no treaties, agreements or truces. With them there is no alternative but active vigorous war, till they are completely destroyed or forced to surrender as prisoners of war.

—Gen. H. W. Halleck
Com. Div. of the Pacific,
September, 1868

Troops to capture and root out Apaches by every means and to hunt them as they would wild animals.

—Gen. E.O.C. Ord, successor
to Gen. McDowell, 1868

The settlers and emigrants must be protected, even if the extermination of every Indian tribe was necessary to secure such a result.

—Ulysses S. Grant
President of
the United States, 1868

This is a true story.

The names of every one of the major characters are the names of real people.

Although some of the dialogue and details have been invented the events related are actual events.

They took place just a little over a hundred years ago.

ELLIOTT ARNOLD

Part One

△ △ △ ONE

△ 1

The thin autumn rain had come and gone and the dirt streets had turned into mud on that afternoon late in November, 1870, when First Lieutenant Royal Emerson Whitman, 3rd Cavalry, led a column of seven second lieutenants and one hundred raw recruits into the walled settlement of Tucson, Arizona Territory.

People in the streets, Mexican and American, watched with interest as the desert-grimed cavalrymen, bone-weary from the long haul from San Diego, picked their way carefully on the greasy alkali. Dogs barked and small children jumped up and down and clapped their hands. A Mexican took off his big hat and waved it and shouted, *"Bienvenida, soldados!"* A priest, hurrying to the cathedral church of San Augustin, blessed the troopers with the sign of the cross without breaking stride. A young woman, her face half hidden by a red shawl, looked up at Whitman from large, dark eyes as he passed her. He touched the brim of his hat.

Lieutenant Whitman wiped the sweat from his face and looked at the adobe houses and the piles of garbage and he sniffed the smells of Mexican cooking. He was a tall, spare man of thirty-seven. His face was covered with a three-day stubble. After the days and nights on the desert on the journey from the Pacific coast he was glad to have reached any place, even Tucson.

"Lieutenant!" It was Sergeant Clarrity.

Whitman twisted in his saddle. He saw that something had happened in the rear of the column. He raised his gloved hand and called a halt. He wiped the sweat from his face again with his neckerchief and rode back to see what it was.

He heard a horse neighing loudly and saw that people had collected and then he saw that the horse had slipped into an abandoned wellhole and had thrown its rider. The horse was struggling to get its forelegs out of the hole. The eyes were glaring and the head whipped from side to side and made terrible sounds. The hapless trooper was back on his feet. He was covered with mud from face to boots. Children pointed at him and laughed.

The trooper came to attention and saluted Whitman, and that looked even funnier to the children, the way the trooper was, and they laughed harder. The trooper wiped his face. Whitman saw that he was very young.

"Well, get that mount out," Whitman said. He was exhausted and his hip ached.

The trooper saluted again and grabbed the horse's reins and tried to pull the animal out. The horse screamed in agony.

"Clarrity," Whitman said.

Sergeant Clarrity dropped off his horse and he and the trooper got the horse out of the hole and Whitman saw that the animal's right foreleg was broken.

"Shoot him," he said to the trooper.

The young soldier looked at the animal that had supported him all the way from California.

"Shoot him," Whitman said again.

The boy wiped more mud off his face. He looked as though he wanted to cry.

"The lieutenant gave you an order!" Clarrity said.

The trooper looked at the horse and at the children who were hopping around in the mud and laughing. He looked at Sergeant Clarrity and at Lieutenant Whitman. He backed away, shaking his head.

Whitman pulled his gun out of its holster and shot the horse between the eyes. The horse flinched when the bullet struck him, and fell. The trooper flinched more.

Whitman looked around. He saw carcasses of horses and mules on the street. He started back to the head of the column, leaving the dead cavalry mount with its civilian companions in the open-air graveyard.

"What's that trooper's name, Sergeant?" Whitman asked.

"Duncan, sir. Trooper Colin Duncan. Shall I put him on report?" Clarrity said.

"No." Whitman wondered what Trooper Duncan was doing here. He wondered how long Trooper Duncan would keep himself alive.

The column moved on through the Tucson streets toward Camp Lowell on the edge of town. Trooper Colin Duncan marched behind the last horse, the dead horse's saddle on his back. The rear horses kicked mud on him. The children followed and laughed.

Before the troops reached Camp Lowell, the sun was full out again and the sky was stainless and the mud had dried. Now the rear horses kicked alkali on Trooper Duncan. The children had lost interest by then and were not there and no one laughed at him.

The throats of all the men were filled with grit from the sheeting desert winds. They coughed and tried to spit out alkali. The tents of Camp Lowell became a small miracle, as the first sight of Tucson had been a miracle when seen from the desert.

Lieutenant Whitman saw to it that the men were quartered and fed. He cleaned himself and shaved and put on a fresh uniform.

△ 2

The newly arrived officers were made to feel right at home by Charlie Brown in his Congress Hall, the most celebrated saloon in Arizona. Charlie Brown brought up the good whiskey from beneath the bar and made it clear that the drinks were on him.

Some of the notables of the Old Pueblo, as the inhabitants called Tucson, came over to have a look at the officers who soon would be defending them against the Apaches. William Sanders Oury, rancher and businessman, part owner of the weekly *Arizonan*, who had served as the first American mayor of Tucson, looked the officers over closely, the way he might look over horses or cattle he was thinking of buying. The Spanish aristocrat Don Jesús María Elías, whose family once ran cattle on 250,000 acres of royal Spanish land grants, whose father had been the last Mexican *alcalde* of Tucson, smoked a thin cigar and contemplated the officers languidly. Merchants Hiram Stevens, who spoke in thunderclaps, and Bill Zeckendorf, whose German accent had trailed him from the Fatherland, walked over. Sammy Hughes, the Adjutant General of the Territory, who also was a leading Tucson butcher, looked on.

These pillars of Tucson shook hands with the officers and exchanged names. They liked what they saw. The officers all looked trim and brave and put down whiskey well.

John Wasson, editor of the rival weekly, the *Citizen*, was interested most of all in Lieutenant Whitman, who was assigned to Camp Grant, fifty-five miles northeast of Tucson, astride the Apache incursion route. Whitman obviously was more mature than the other officers and Wasson was pleased that he was going to Camp Grant, Tucson's field station against the Apaches.

The newspaperman nosed around among the young shavetails and learned that Whitman had been a full colonel of Maine Volunteers during the Civil War, that he had been wounded in action and brevetted for bravery, and that he had a lead ball lodged in his hip, a battle souvenir. He reckoned Whitman must have a rough time of it in the saddle.

Wasson observed as well that Whitman alone was clean-shaven, without the almost mandatory cavalry mustaches sported by the other officers. He guessed that Whitman was conscious of his age and did not want to look more than his years. The face, Wasson saw, was a strong face. It was a type of face not uncommon in Maine, where Whitman came from, a stubborn face. It was the kind of face every man in Charlie Brown's saloon wanted up there in Camp Grant.

Whitman puffed on the fine Havana presented to him by Bill Oury and answered questions put to him with the thriftiness of a New Englander.

"Royal Emerson Whitman," Wasson said slowly, enunciating each syllable of each name. "That's quite a collection, Lieutenant."

Whitman nodded. He had been through this kind of thing before. On this night he was feeling good. The ache in his hip, which had tormented him during the days in the saddle, was gone and the whiskey was as good as he had ever tasted and the cigar was first class.

The corners of his eyes crinkled. "My father's name was Royal. When I was a boy down East I developed muscles on that name."

"And the Emerson?" Wasson asked.

"My mother and father were devoted to his work. I am too."

Bill Oury closed in a little bit. Bill Oury didn't give a damn about Whitman's names. "What do you think about those feed stations for Apaches, Lieutenant?" Oury asked.

Oury's voice was low and gravelly. His face was grizzled. He was not much above middle height. He was in his early fifties, but some of the early years might have been accounted double years, and he looked older. His body was flat-bellied and wiry and he moved quickly and his eyes were sharp.

"Feed stations?" Whitman repeated. "What are they, Mr. Oury?"

"Places at Army posts. The Government feeds Indians. Mostly Apaches." Oury spat.

"To what purpose, sir?" Whitman asked.

"Supposed to keep them peaceable. Anyway that's the general idea."

Lieutenant Whitman finished the whiskey in his glass and considered the question. "I come from the State of Maine," he said, as though that were an answer.

"So you said, Lieutenant," Oury said.

"We are accounted prudent folk, Mr. Oury," Whitman said. "We don't usually hold with giving away anything for nothing."

Bill Oury beamed and looked around.

Whitman held up his empty glass. "Certain exceptions permitted, of course."

Bill Oury chuckled in his beard. Oury had done a considerable amount of soldiering in his time. He liked the company of soldierly men, and while, as a loyal and unrelenting Southerner from Virginia, he didn't have much use for the Yankee military leaders, he respected the younger officers and the men who had to do the fighting against Apaches. Whitman looked to him as though he had learned to handle himself and he didn't smile too much and Oury liked that. Bill Oury suspected men who smiled a lot.

"What about General Stoneman?" Wasson asked, as Oury refilled Whitman's glass from his own private stock.

"What about General Stoneman, sir?" Whitman asked.

"What do you think of him?"

Whitman fixed his eyes on Wasson. He thought the editor looked like a curious squirrel, a curious squirrel with a goatee. "What do I think about General Stoneman?"

"That's what I put to you, Lieutenant."

"Have you ever been in the service, sir?" Whitman asked.

"No."

Whitman nodded. "And obviously, sir, you have never heard that Military Regulation Number One expressly forbids a lieutenant to possess any thoughts about a general, particularly when that general happens to be his commanding officer."

The chuckles rumbled again behind Bill Oury's beard. Hiram Stevens' laughter could be heard in the street. All the men had a laugh. Even Don Jesús stroked his graying imperial and allowed a small smile to appear on his lips, something Don Jesús rarely permitted now.

"Welcome to the Territory, Lieutenant," Bill Oury said, raising his glass. If it had been necessary that would have served as official blessing.

Whitman raised his own glass. "Thank you, sir."

Oury liked the way Whitman looked him in the eye. Bill Oury always looked a man in the eye. He had fought more than one duel in Tucson and had killed two or three men. He always looked them in the eye when he pulled the trigger.

The officers and men rested for several days in the Old Pueblo and then departed for the various outposts in Arizona

Territory. When Lieutenant Whitman arrived at Camp Grant it was to learn that the commanding officer, Captain Frank Stanwood, was away on leave, and that he was in command of the post.

"All these officers are fine-appearing gentlemen," John Wasson wrote in the *Citizen*, *"and we believe will prove efficient in public affairs."*

△ △ △ TWO

△ 1

Navidad was alway celebrated emotionally in Tucson by Mexicans and Americans alike but this year the spirit of Christmas could be found only in the hearts of small children.

On a blustery Saturday in the middle of December a large number of the adult population of the Old Pueblo was gathered in front of the office of the *Citizen,* a small adobe building on the corner of Congress and Main streets. The crowd was so large it almost blocked the entrance to Zeckendorf's store next door. Bill Zeckendorf didn't protest about that. He was out in the crowd with everybody else.

John Wasson's paper was selling as fast as the press could turn it out. Men read the story on page one and then read it again.

GENERAL STONEMAN LEAVES
THE TERRITORY

Your correspondent has learned that General George Stoneman, Commander of the Department of Arizona, has vacated Fort Whipple and is moving his Headquarters to Drum Barracks, in Wilmington, California.

From this time on the general will direct his campaigns against the Apache Indians from the Pacific Ocean.

The move, the report went on to say, *"made it possible for the general to spend the Holidays with his family at his new ranch in San Gabriel Valley."*

△ 2

It was late at night but the Congress Hall was full. Nobody felt like sleeping. The smoke lay like a cloud bank. Everybody was talking at the same time and all about the same thing.

Bill Oury and Jesús María Elías were sitting at the table regarded by all citizens at Bill Oury's table. Bill Oury always took the same table at the Congress Hall and the only other men who sat there with him were men Oury invited to join him.

Don Jesús fingered his glass. Don Jesús looked old and weary. His eyes were dark recesses in his face. "In the old days, Don Guillermo, the Americans used to laugh at Mexicans in this part of the country. They used to say Mexican generals always stayed far down in Mexico where they were in no danger of running across Apaches."

"It's your turn to laugh now," Oury said. "Don Jesús, what is going to happen to us here?"

Part Two

△ △ △ ONE

△ 1

After a while the shaking subsided and he thought he might
again try to read the report from Washington. But he wanted
to be sure the seizure had ended. He'd had to put the paper
down twice now because his hands had twiddled too much and
he didn't want to be cozened again. Lieutenant Whitman
waited another moment or two and then had another go at
the document that had just come in.

CAMP GRANT, ARIZONA TERRITORY
INFORMATION FURNISHED BY
ASSISTANT SURGEON CHARLES SMART, UNITED STATES ARMY

Camp Grant is situated at the junction of the
Aravaipa with the San Pedro River. Its elevation above
the sea is about 2,500 feet. It is distant north from
Tucson 55 miles.

The prevailing winds are from the southeast
down along the course of the San Pedro, carrying with
them the malaria from the marshes along its banks
exposing the troops stationed on the knoll to its dele-
terious influence.

Well, well, so that was it. He had been astonished at the
malaria in Arizona. He had always associated the fever with
hot, wet places—India, Burma, Africa. Arizona was supposed
to be so dry. But, as it turned out, it had its own little wet
place, the old San Pedro, and it was wet now, in February.

He lit a cigar. He complimented himself on the steadiness
of his hand. It was a small victory. At Camp Grant one learned
to tick off all victories, large, small, and even very small.

He drew on the cigar and wiped his forehead with the back of his hand. He never knew these days whether the sweat was from the heat or from the fever. Or perhaps both.

And what more did the learned doctor, so aptly named, have to say about Camp Grant and the poor benighted denizens thereof?

The camp is composed of adobe, stockade and reed buildings, supplemented by tents. All the roofs are liable to leak in rainy weather. There are three sets of soldiers' quarters; one is adobe, 120 by 24 feet, with the usual mud roof, earthen floor, and open fireplaces ventilated by the doors and windows, and affording its average occupation 400 cubic feet per man; two are rather open stockades, thatched with cane and reeds, and freely ventilated by the interstices in the walls.

The august Assistant Surgeon might have been an anthropologist describing the habitations of primitive people in the darkest part of Africa.

The walls were freely ventilated all right and the men didn't call those gaps in the walls interstices, and that splendid ventilation opened the quarters to scorpions and spiders and the vinegarroons that stunk like stale vinegar when they were squashed and the rattlers that occasionally were gentlemanly enough to give warning they were there, and all the other small and poisonous creatures that seemed to prefer shelter, even that kind of aboriginal shelter, to the Arizona desert.

Lieutenant Whitman had been in command at Camp Grant for more than two months now, from the time of his arrival in the early part of December, the previous year. In that time he had become acquainted with a number of truths about that military stronghold. One of these truths was that if a person connected himself with Camp Grant during the winter months the chances were that very soon afterward he woke up with malaria, and usually around three o'clock in the morning.

He learned, too, not to be disconcerted by sudden shaking, anywhere, any time. If men did not during the winter months often appear to be practicing voodoo, they were looked upon with suspicion, as though they were inhuman, or at the very least found themselves better whiskey than anybody else.

> The officers' quarters, adobe, consist of four sets
> of two rooms, each room 15 by 18 feet. There were six
> officers at the post during the year; two of them had
> their families with them.

That must have been downright pleasant. Six officers and two of them with their families. Camp Grant must have been a merry place the year before, although the report did not make it clear whether all those officers were there at the same time. As far as officers were concerned this present year, the number was exactly two, and neither with family.

Whitman broke off the ash of his cigar. He felt rotten. The post surgeon had recommended that he remain in the infirmary for another day or two but he felt worse there. And the only thing the surgeon did was dose him with quinine and douse him with whiskey and hope that one or the other or both did the trick. He didn't have to remain in the sick house for that.

His head was spinning slightly now and he felt airy. He didn't know whether *that* was from the considerable temperature he was running or from the drink of booze the surgeon had given him. A fine point. He didn't object to either remedy but together they often had a peculiar effect. Sometimes the quinine made the alcohol work very fast. It was the cheapest drunk around. If word got out about that, half the saloons would be put out of business.

> The diseases are all malarial and prevail to such
> an extent during the autumn and winter months as to
> unfit the garrison from any active service.

A bit of hyperbole, excusable perhaps. Still, there were twenty-three men in the infirmary right now. One man, Carr, had had his right leg amputated that day—gangrene from an

Indian arrow. Some of the men insisted the Apaches frequently poisoned the tips of their arrows. And where the devil was Duncan? He had sent him over to check on Carr half an hour ago. The other twenty-two men were down with malaria. The surgeon liked to call it the ague.

In 1868 intermittents were so general that the affected troops had to be moved from the post to a temporary convalescent camp, 28 miles south, on the road to Tucson. This was the nearest place which could be found at the same time supplied with water, accessible to wagons, and thoroughly free from miasmatic influences.

Whitman looked up as Colin Duncan came into the office. The young trooper now was serving as his striker.

"Corporal Carr is dead, sir," Duncan said.

Duncan's face was white. He was young and he was not used to death, not even ordinary death at the hands of a surgeon.

"See to it they bury Carr's leg with him," Whitman said.

Whitman gazed thoughtfully at the door after Duncan closed it behind him. Over the years a great many Duncans had passed under his orders. He had witnessed the precarious hesitancy of recruits like Duncan and had seen them forced to accept their own death long before they learned to tolerate the death of others.

He tossed the report aside. He supposed he should be proud. It wasn't every military post that was so miserable that the Assistant Surgeon of the Army felt constrained to write a special report about it. And just where was that splendid oasis only twenty-eight miles away where everything combined for the comfort of man and why didn't they just move the post down there?

He felt the shaking coming on again, an old friend now that couldn't leave him long alone. He had never joggled like that in a Maine winter. Well, in any event, Corporal Bernard Carr now was thoroughly free from miasmatic influences for all time.

"Trouble, Señor Teniente," the Puma said.

Whitman looked up with a start. "You'll have to teach me how to move around that way." He got up.

The Puma smiled. "Cochise taught me, Teniente. Would you like me to ask him to teach you too?"

The Mexican came in off the Tucson Road and staggered across the parade ground. There was blood over his white shirt. He was hatless under the savage sun. His sandals were in shreds. His feet bled and left a trail on the pebbles on the parade ground. His trousers hung in tatters, ripped by cactus. One hand clutched his chest where the blood was coming out. Halfway down the parade ground as soldiers started running toward him, even those rookies who had been looking for the first time at one of the wonders of Camp Grant, the six toes on the feet of Oscar Hutton, the Mexican stumbled and fell. He tried to get up. He clawed at the ground and then he was still.

Whitman ran out of his office buttoning his tunic. "Clarrity!"

"Sir!"

"Horses."

Sergeant Clarrity lumbered off. The horses were kept saddled, loosely cinched, behind the grooming stables.

The post surgeon, Dr. Sumner, was kneeling at the Mexican's side, peeling away a bit of the man's shirt. "Deep one, Royal. More like a hunting arrow. Maybe a spear." He straightened. "Well, get him inside and we'll see what can be done."

The Mexican opened his eyes. "Apaches."

"Move him," Sumner said.

Two men bent over to pick up the Mexican. The Mexican raised his hand and said something. The Puma knelt and the Mexican said something else.

"He wants to say what happened," the Puma said to Whitman.

"Get him some water," Whitman said.

The Mexican drank a little water from a canteen and spoke to the Puma. The Mexican's voice was weak and kept trailing away. The Puma held his ear close to the Mexican's mouth.

Oscar Hutton was there by then and he bent his head to listen too.

"This man says there were about forty Mexicans," the Puma said. "This man says there were women and children. This man says they left Tucson and rode north to work on a *rancho* belonging to a *compañero*. They were guarded by *vaqueros*."

The Mexican whispered again.

"Apaches attacked them in an arroyo," the Puma said. "The men held off the Apaches until the women and the children could run away. This man started off for the fort to get help. An Apache on a horse chased him and speared him and went away believing he was dead. This man got up afterward and walked all night."

"There are a thousand arroyos between here and Tucson," Whitman said.

The Puma spoke to the Mexican. The Mexican nodded. The Mexican waved his hand and said something.

"What did he say?" Whitman asked.

"He asked God to forgive him for his sins."

"Ask him to describe where the Apaches jumped him."

"I cannot, Señor Teniente," the Puma said. "This man is dead."

△ 2

Whitman led the troops across the San Pedro and into a deep, walled canyon. It was the middle of the day and the heat between the steep escarps of the canyon made men gasp and the foam and spittle flecked back from the horses and the horses' sides slavered in sweat.

There is something I have to ask Doc Sumner, Whitman thought. Why does that hospitable hip bother me more when I'm enjoying one of the fever attacks? One thing, he thought, jouncing in the saddle, if I were attacked by the shakes now nobody would ever know.

They cleared the canyon and struck scrub that was broken and hilly and pocked with gullies and the air was more open and men breathed. Whitman waved down the pace. There were soft patches, he had learned, where a horse could sink a leg to its fetlock. The horse could go down and stop as though it had hit a stone wall and might break its leg and hurl its rider into cactus bursting with more needles than a porcupine and break the rider's neck as well.

They came upon hardpan again and Whitman stepped up the gait. The Puma was riding on one side of him and Oscar Hutton on the other. The Puma moved like a big cat on his feet and when he got into a saddle it was as though he became part of the horse. Hutton bounced up and down like a sack of potatoes, his boots, with their famous six-toed feet, jammed into the stirrups. Oscar Hutton didn't look graceful but he could ride all day and nothing, absolutely nothing, escaped the little eyes that squinted, shiny as rubbed buttons, from under brows as bushy as a second lieutenant's mustache, whitened by age and sun.

I'm a lucky man, Whitman thought. He was damned lucky to have found the Puma and Oscar Hutton waiting for him when he rode into an unexpected command at Camp Grant. They probably were the best guides in Arizona and Arizona was like nothing he had ever encountered and it was a stroke of fortune that he had those two men to keep him from making too many mistakes.

They rode into another gulch that was like a saber slash made by a distraught god. A saguaro stuck out of one side as though it might have been what the god had aimed at and had missed. The arms of the giant plant were twisted in contortion to scare something more than crows, something that might have flown over the land in prehistory. Perhaps its original design was to warn off wayward pterodactyls. In the trunk of the saguaro was an arrow.

What Indian had galloped by, Whitman wondered, and had whipped an arrow out of the quiver on his back and had struck at his friend. The saguaro was a faithful ally to the Apache, the Puma had explained. The saguaro could supply water when there was water nowhere else. What had made the Indian wound his friend? Was it grief not to be contained, that could be vented in no other way?

Out of the long, narrow slit in the ground Whitman spread his men to cover as much land as possible. He glanced at the Puma. The Puma looked half asleep. The Puma always looked half asleep and he spoke that way too. Whitman turned his head to have a look at Hutton. Hutton, who had wandered over as much of the desert as any man alive, the desert in California as well as in Arizona, who unfolded wild tales of his adventures that were entirely true, was twisting his own head to the right and to the left, his eyes sparkling.

Which one of them had the quickest eyes? Whitman wondered. He would have settled for either and he had been blessed with both.

Whitman looked over his men. Sergeant Clarrity was riding in the van as usual. Duncan was near him. There was excitement on Duncan's face. Whitman was pleased to see that. He had made it a point to order Duncan on this expedition. He had to make Duncan lose some of that baby fat before Duncan got into trouble.

The excitement was on the other men whom he could see. Any one of them could be killed at any moment but the excitement was there. The men were always as saddled as the horses and the cinches were never quite as loose.

Would they find their victims? The Apaches were long gone and the trail was cold. There had been a sharp and unexpected rain and whatever tracks the Apaches had left were probably scrubbed away. But there might still be something that could be done for the victims if they could be found. The Mexican had given no specifics before he died but if the group had gone from Tucson northward to a ranch this was where to look for them.

The plunge of the horses flushed coveys of quail. There was a distant call. Coyotes? Whitman looked at the sky. There was not a cloud. The baleful sun had the place all to itself. A flock of crows, disturbed in conference, squawked and spattered the impeccable sky and vanished.

Whitman saw something else. A puff of smoke from a distant rise and then another. Apache chitchat. The number of troops, their direction. And how is Aunt Moonbeam? As good as the telegraph. The Apaches were smart. They made use of every feature of the country, the spaces, the clarity. The settlers hated them and few admitted how smart they were. Apaches, the settlers hold, were not smart, they were just sneaky.

There was something new in the air, something that didn't belong in that immaculate air. Whitman raised a gloved hand and the troop drew rein. Hutton's nose went up like a setter's. Hutton sniffed. "I smell something burning."

"No," the Puma said, whispering as though he were talking to himself. "Not burning, burned out."

"No wonder there were no damned buzzards!" Hutton shouted, angry, as though personally affronted by that treachery.

The Puma didn't make a move or say anything but his horse understood something and sprang forward and turned left and the others followed. About five hundred yards away they found what they had gone to find.

The Apaches had been neat. They had killed the Mexicans, stripped them, collected all the wagons, put the dead people on them, and then set the whole thing on fire. There was only one pile, one fire. It was tidy.

The wagons were still smoldering as the men dismounted and this close there was the smell of burned flesh. Some of the newer troops turned away their heads. Duncan walked a few steps and retched.

"Those unholy bastards," Sergeant Clarrity said, crossing himself.

"Pick a burial detail," Whitman said.

"They're never altogether dead," Clarrity said. "There are always some of them burned alive."

Whitman watched Duncan. Duncan was still gagging. "Use him," Whitman said. "Use all of them who couldn't look at this."

"And who made you bite that first bullet?" Hutton asked Whitman.

The burial detail cut a large, single grave and the dead

were carried from the smoking wagons and put into it. All of the dead, there were twelve, had been shot by both bullets and arrows and the parts of the arrows that had stuck out of the bodies had been burned away. One man's head was smashed in. Apaches didn't scalp, Whitman had learned, but they liked to bash in skulls with big rocks.

Another's heart had been cut out of his body and had been put on the man's face. The face had been covered by another body and had not been burned and the red muscle was resting on the man's lips.

"That one must have fought bravely," the Puma said.

"Is that what that means?" Whitman asked.

"The Apache wanted to touch the heart to steal some of its power," the Puma said.

Duncan and another soldier picked up the body and started for the grave. Both men looked up and away from what they were carrying.

"Duncan," Whitman said.

"Yes, sir."

"The man's heart fell off."

"Sir?"

"The man has to be buried all together, like Corporal Carr and his leg."

"Yes, sir," Duncan said. He didn't move. He held on to the dead man's feet.

"Duncan, put down the body and get the man's heart," Whitman said.

After a moment Duncan and the other soldier lowered the body and Duncan returned to the pyre. He looked down at the heart. He looked at Whitman and then he picked up the heart and walked back to the body and put the heart gently and carefully on the dead man's chest and then he and the other soldier lifted the body again and carried it slowly to the common grave and when they lowered the body into the pit the heart still was on the chest.

When the last body was deposited in the mass grave, the desert clay and alkali and shale was shoveled into the hole and then the grave was covered with rocks to keep the scavengers away. The fire and smoke had held them off so far but it would not be long before the buzzards and coyotes would be along for their share of the spoils.

Whitman looked up as Hutton ambled up to him. For the last fifteen minutes or so Hutton and the Puma had been snooping around. Hutton shook his head.

"They broke up. Looks like they went off in twos and threes every which way, meeting someplace else. Wouldn't have made much difference anyway. The rain made the ground nice and clean."

The men gathered around the grave. They removed their hats.

" 'Enter into His gates with thanksgiving, and into His courts with praise,' " Hutton said, " 'be thankful unto Him, and bless His name.' "

The troopers said "Amen." Duncan and some of the new recruits stood staring at the grave.

After a few moments Whitman said, "Do you all want to get sunstroke? Put on your hats."

It was late in the day then.

△ 3

The sentries had been posted and the men had seen to their horses and then they lay down and some of them slept and some of them talked quietly of what they had found that day and how it must have happened. The sky lit up with stars, so bright, so many, men could recognize one another without speech.

Whitman took out his watch and tried to read the dial but the stars were not quite bright enough for that. He struck a match and shielded it. It was a little after nine. Where the devil were the wagons? He had left the usual orders before they set out from the camp.

"They will be here, Teniente," the Puma said.

"Yes."

"They are always late but they always arrive," the Puma said.

"Yes."

"It was something Cochise could never understand," the Puma said. "He could not understand how the wagons always found the troops."

Whitman lit a cigar. He eased himself on the ground. His hip was aching from the hard ride. But the fever seemed under control and that was something.

"Do you think this was done by Cochise?" he asked.

The Puma shrugged. "It could be any one of them, Cochise, Eskiminzin. It could be anyone."

"You knew Cochise."

"Yes, Señor Teniente, I knew Cochise."

"You were kidnapped in Mexico."

"Yes. I was stolen from my family when I was a child and I was raised by the Chiricahuas."

"What kind of a man is Cochise?"

"I respect him, Teniente."

Whitman looked up sharply at the sound of rumbling wagons and then horses and he heard a sentry challenge and the reply and a few moments later the second detachment from Camp Grant pulled up in the bivouac. There were water wagons, food, and ambulances, in this instance unnecessary.

The horses were given water first and then water was issued to men who had none left or who had neglected to fill their canteens before they left the post. Once Whitman had thought perhaps men who were so heedless should be punished in some way but it happened only to the new men and seldom more than once and Whitman had concluded that the men had a difficult enough time of it without his adding his own petty pennies to their lot.

Sergeant Clarrity strode over to where Whitman was sitting with Hutton and the Puma. The sergeant saluted. The sergeant was more than six feet tall and his arms were long. Clarrity's salute was more than an act of military courtesy. It was a confirmation of the existence of the Army as an act of God.

"The men are fed and bedded down, sir," Clarrity said.

"Did you tuck them in, Sergeant?"

"With my own hands, sir."

"Good."

"I've assigned men for guard duty. I will take the first corporal's tour myself."

"Thank you, Sergeant."

Clarrity marched away. Whitman lit another cigar. The Puma rolled a cigarette. Hutton stuffed a battered, curved pipe. The horses stirred a little and then were quiet. The whole camp was quiet.

Whitman recalled how, during the war, men had to be careful lighting up their smokes. But there was no point in trying to hide from the enemy here. He had no doubts the Apaches knew exactly where they were and how many there were and what they had had for supper. Out of old habit he was shielding his cigar but that surely was unnecessary here.

"There were no dead Apaches anywhere?" Whitman asked. "No bodies lying around?"

"When they have time the Apaches take care of their dead same as we do," Hutton said.

"They had time," Whitman said.

Hutton peered at him in the dark. "Couldn't have got here no faster, Lieutenant," he insisted, as though again aggrieved. "We came here on a crow line. And all of this happened yesterday."

"The *teniente* believes we have failed," the Puma said.

"Sure we failed," Hutton said, puffing comfortably now. "And next time we'll kill Apaches and when the ones that get away get back home they'll say that time they failed."

It was true, Whitman agreed, but there was one small fallacy in the equation. They would all go out and try to hunt down the Apaches who had killed these Mexicans and sooner or later they would find Apaches and they would kill some of them and they might by chance be some of the ones who did this or they might be other Apaches altogether. In the end, he supposed, it all evened off. All Apaches were guilty of some killing or other and he supposed it didn't much matter how or when they were made to pay off.

But there was something that nagged at his orderly New England nature. How much more fitting it would be if the inevitable reprisals were more precise.

Hutton was snoring. Whitman took a closer look at the guide to make sure his pipe was out, or at least out of his mouth. There was a story once that Hutton had set his beard on fire. The pipe was in Hutton's hand and the hand sprawled away from his clothing and his beard.

Whitman stood up and rubbed his hip. It didn't feel too bad. He was tired from the ride but his hip didn't hurt very much at all. He made a final turn around the camp. In the bright night the cactus all around looked like lost freakery, something left over in a kind of historic joke.

Clarrity, making his rounds, assured him that all was in order. Whitman walked back to where his blanket was spread on the ground. He lay down and stretched his legs. The night had turned cold. He rolled the blanket around him. He breathed deeply. The air seemed unused. He smelled the earth smells. He heard coyotes howling off somewhere, so far away he thought he could hear echoes. He felt fit and soon he was sleeping soundly.

△ 4

The troop returned to Camp Grant shortly after noon the next day. At the sight of the clutter of buildings on the low knoll Whitman shook his head. No matter how often he came upon them he shook his head.

Camp Grant resembled no other military establishment, it was said, and it could be true. There was nothing military in the appearance of Camp Grant. With its squat adobe buildings and the *jacal* sheds, constructed of upright logs chinked with mud, the roofs of small branches and more mud, Camp Grant looked more like the remains of a Mexican village abandoned when its inhabitants regained their sanity.

The men and wagons crossed the dry wash off the Tucson Road and moved onto the parade ground. They entered the camp from the south because they happened to be coming from that direction. They could have gone into the camp from any other direction. Around Camp Grant there was no wall, no stockade, no palisade of any kind.

The troop formed on the parade ground almost smothered in its own dust. Whitman ordered the men dismissed. He dismounted and handed the reins to a soldier and went into his quarters.

He stripped and washed himself. Outside of robbing scavengers of a meal, the scout had been for nothing. Perhaps not. The Apaches had seen them go out. Next time perhaps it would work out better.

He dried himself and was moist again almost immediately. He shaved, looking at himself in a mirror sold by the post sutler to an officer who had occupied the quarters earlier. The mirror had been touted as a genuine French looking-glass. Scraping the razor on his chin Whitman reckoned he would look odd to the French.

He thought about lying down. He decided against it. What was it his father had once said? That one had to protect one's self against the easy weaknesses, the weaknesses one slid into until they became the way of living. He had taken that at the time as typical father talk, typical down East father talk. He had since come to understand what his father meant.

If one got the outside disciplined then the inside could feel safe, then nothing had to go wrong there. He had known officers who were hard all the way through and he had believed that was because they had gotten hard inside first and it had worked its way out. Most of them were proud of themselves. Whitman thought perhaps it was better to keep something sheltered inside. He could be wrong. He could be wrong about what he had done to Duncan. He had told Duncan not to come round for the rest of the day. He had calculated that Duncan needed a little time to himself to sort out a few things and that he could be most completely alone among a hundred other men.

He put on a clean uniform. How the toilers on Suds Row kept uniforms clean with what they had to work with he would never know. He looked at himself in the mirror. If he could believe his reflection the fever had cost him a few pounds, but then that might just be French fickleness.

He finished dressing and went into his other room and sat down on a rocker. He lit a cigar and addressed himself to the suit of armor hanging on the wall. The armor, the fey mirror, a chromo of the majestic Hudson River, plainly far from Arizona, a quiver of Apache arrows, a lance, some Navajo blankets draped on the walls, and, on a shelf, a row of bottles filled with specimens of tarantulas, scorpions, spiders, rattlesnakes and other lodgers of the country were each the legacy of some officer who had passed through Camp Grant before him, an accretion of months and years from men who had come, paused, were either slain or moved on. It was continuity, a passing of greetings. He wondered, on occasion, what it would be that he would leave behind to verify for others in the future that he, too, had been here for a little while.

Of all the mementos it was, of course, the suit of Spanish armor that fascinated Whitman the most. The origin was obscure. The legend was that it had been found somewhere in Texas and had been brought to Arizona and that at one time it provided housing for a Spanish warrior bringing God and seeking gold. Whitman, as had every officer before him, had imagined what it must have been like riding under the Southwest sun encased in steel. By tradition, the armor was kept polished—back and breastplates, gorget and helmet. Each small brass button gleamed. In all, Whitman assured himself, the iron gave back a better image of himself than the French mirror.

He had given the armor a name, Lieutenant Rodriguez Gonzáles, and he had silent conversations with him and the Spanish officer informed him of many things.

He thought about staying in his quarters for a little while. Nothing outside was pressing. He could take a little time, finish the cigar, read a few pages of Emerson from the small volume that never was far from him. He decided against that enticement. He would go to his office, make a report on the scout, General Stoneman was a demon for reports, complete reports, and after that he would finish a letter to his wife, Lucretia.

He got up and tossed a salute to Lieutenant Gonzáles, who was patently disappointed at his leaving, having anticipated some small talk, and left his quarters. He crossed the parade ground in the direction of his office. Some of the men who had been on the scout were clustered in front of the sutler's store going over their adventure with those who had remained behind. From the wide eyes and open mouths of some of the rookies Whitman understood the story was being enriched a wee bit. As he passed he saw that Oscar Hutton now had taken over the narration. Hutton would do his own things to the account. What he would relate would be factual enough; if he did not bend the truth he managed to coat it with his own special flavor. And when he ran out of words there were always those toes to hold his audience.

As Whitman approached his headquarters he saw three Mexicans standing under the *ramada*. One of them was dressed in black and wore a shining, varnished, flat-topped black Spanish hat tilted on his head. His face was half hidden by the hat brim and by his mustache and imperial. He appeared to Whitman to be a man in his late middle age. The other two men were *vaqueros*. They flanked the man in black and flicked quirts back and forth against their boots and looked impatient.

The man in the black broadcloth suit stepped forward. "Lieutenant Whitman," he said. His English was almost unaccented.

The man's voice was younger than his face; the man was altogether younger than Whitman had thought.

"You have the advantage of me, sir," Whitman said.

"I am Jesús María Elías. I had the pleasure of meeting you when you passed through Tucson."

Whitman gazed at Elías' face. The Mexican was not much older than he was he saw now. But the face had been worked over and its features were exhausted. The deeply set eyes were calm. The eyes disturbed Whitman.

"I am at your service, sir," the officer said.

Elías stepped back and then followed Whitman into his office. The *vaqueros* remained under the *ramada*. As Whitman and Elías entered the building one of the *vaqueros* ground a scorpion under the heel of his boot.

△ 5

On the way to Camp Grant that day Don Jesús and the two *vaqueros* rode a little out of their way to visit an abandoned farm. One of Don Jesús' two surviving brothers, Juan, once had owned the farm. Juan had been wounded there and two of his helpers had been killed by Apaches. Juan, permanently crippled, was forced to abandon his home.

Don Jesús and the *vaqueros* dismounted and they looked around for the displaced crosses from the helpers' graves and put them back into place. Don Jesús had restored the crosses many times. The Apaches were superstitious about marking graves. They buried their own dead secretly. They believed designating a grave was an offense, even the grave of an enemy, even the grave of someone they had killed.

Don Jesús looked around. The adobe house Juan had built with the help of the rest of the family was almost eroded away now by winds and rain. What was left looked like a giant's tooth, broken and jagged, sticking out of the ground.

The *vaqueros* hunkered down and remained with the horses as Don Jesús walked to the ruined house. The *vaqueros* had come often to this place with their master and they knew the deserted house and the land had come to have the meaning of a shrine for Don Jesús and that he preferred to visit the shrine alone.

Don Jesús put his hand on the adobe wall. The wall was exactly the same as the earth it rested on and it was smooth and warm in the sun and it still had the feeling of having been part of a dwelling where once there was laughter and talk and food and love and some tears and many prayers. One day it would all again be with the earth and none of that would be in it then but now it still held it, that time when it had been borrowed from the earth and molded into a house.

He poked around the house. In a corner he saw what was left of a quirt. He picked it up. It was half rotted and the braided rawhide lash had been gnawed on. He remembered when Ramón had made that quirt. Ramón had given it to him and he had given it to Juan.

Don Jesús removed his hat and he felt the sun on his face. He closed his eyes and said a few words in memory and in plea.

△ 6

Don Jesús and the *vaqueros* continued on to Camp Grant, alert always for roving Apaches. When they came within sight of the camp the men drew rein again and surveyed the outpost. Don Jesús remembered when the Government built Camp Grant in 1859. It was called Fort Aravaipa then because that was the name of the creek and of the canyon beyond the creek.

The American military had sought out Jesús Elías for assistance in selecting the location. He thought then that was unbecoming and without tact. The Americans had taken over that part of Mexico less than three years earlier under the terms of the Gadsden Purchase and now the gringos were asking a Mexican to help them spread their military power over more of the land. And they were not talking about safeguarding settlers against the Apaches, which would have mitigated the indiscretion. No, they were talking about plans to build a railroad and about establishing an outpost to protect the line.

They had come to Jesús Elías because he had a wide reputation as an Indian fighter who knew the land as did few others and who knew the tricky ways of Apaches and the trails they followed. At first Elías was affronted by the request and was prepared to refuse aiding the conquerors in any way but then he saw past the railroad, which, as it turned out, never was built there. Elías saw the possibilities of the fort and of the troops that would be stationed there. Officially they might be sent out to protect railroad tracks against Apaches. Once there they could not refuse to protect people from those same Apaches. The location he helped the American military select was a natural one. The confluence of the San Pedro River and the Aravaipa Creek was the hub for four routes of Apache travel. To the south and west went the road to Tucson. Ten miles up the valley to the north lay the Gila River, along which Kearny had marched from the Rio Grande to California. Eastward the Aravaipa Canyon made its way through the Galiuro Mountains, opening on to the upper Gila and the Sulphur Spring Valley. And to the south the San Pedro Valley led into Sonora and was a main thoroughfare for Apache raids into Mexico.

It was obviously a strategic place to construct a military strongpoint. The sole objection to the location was adjudged a minor one. Military doctors declared the place unhealthful. They predicted chronic malaria that seasonally could reach epidemic proportions. Their warnings were filed and ignored.

Bill Oury and other ranchers and businessmen were delighted with the site chosen on the delta. Oury agreed heartily with his friend Don Jesús that soldiers stationed anywhere for any purpose had to be good.

"Hell, chances are they'll never build that damned railroad through there," Oury said. "More than likely when the time comes they'll put it right through Tucson. But the main thing is we'll get some soldiers up there. Good for development. There's a lot of fine land in the San Pedro. And even if they do go ahead and build their railroad up there that'll help scare off Apaches too."

Fort Aravaipa looked old the day it was completed. Nobody appeared to have any overall plan and nobody appeared to care much.

It looks the same way today, Don Jesús thought, leaning on his saddle horn, looking across the land at the hodgepodge on the delta. What he had done more than eleven years earlier had been wise. The railroad never was built and the soldiers had the mission to protect settlers. And for a little while the San

Pedro and other valleys had prospered. Until the bloodiest of all Apache wars erupted.

There was, despite everything, no sense of permanence about the outpost, Don Jesús thought. But how could there be? The Americans were a restless and impermanent people. They kept changing the name of the outpost, so it could never develop tradition. From Fort Aravaipa to Fort Breckinridge to Fort Stanford. And always "Fort," as though the title itself could give the miserable place some dignity. And now it was called Grant because there was a man in the White House with that name.

At least it was called Camp Grant.

△ 7

"What can I do for you, Mr. Elías?" Whitman asked.

From across Whitman's desk Elías thought he caught the smell of whiskey. He saw the patina of sweat on Whitman's lips. An occupational disease for the American military. Explained away as the result of the isolation, the loneliness, the lack of other diversion. More truly, Elías thought, it is due to the insubstantiality of the breed. What values did most gringos possess?

"We have not seen much of you in Tucson, Lieutenant," Elías said courteously. It was nothing that concerned him and he knew that Americans had little interest in civilized amenities anyway.

"No," Whitman said.

"I know you are very busy," Elías said. "I have come to ask you something about the attack by the Apaches on the Mexican ranch workers and something of the Mexican who brought you the word."

"Why are you interested, Mr. Elías?"

"That man who brought that word was Manuel Ortega."

"And?"

"He is a cousin to my wife."

"I am sorry, Mr. Elías."

Elías caught the sound of sympathy in Whitman's voice. He was, doubtless, a good man. "Thank you, Mr. Whitman. It is not an unaccustomed event in our family."

Whitman gave Elías a brief account of the attack as he knew it and what they had found.

"They were all dead?" Elías asked.

"Yes."

"And Manuel Ortega?"

"He died too. Here at the fort. There was nothing we could do for him. He was a brave man, Mr. Elías. He was lanced badly and he walked here and gave the word before he died."

"All the Apaches escaped?"

"I don't know how many Apaches your people killed. There were no Apache bodies around when we arrived."

"There was no trail to follow?"

"When we reached the arroyo where the attack took place more than twenty-four hours had passed."

"A trail does not vanish in twenty-four hours, Mr. Whitman," Elías said.

Whitman glanced sharply at Elías. He was about to say he resented the implication of incompetence. He recalled at that moment that Elías had a name as an Indian fighter and he guessed Elías was putting forth a professional posture.

"It seems they broke up and left in small groups. The trails went in every direction."

"And none could be followed?"

"There was a rain, Mr. Elías."

"Yes, I remember. There was a small rain."

Elías took out a leather cigar case and offered it to Whitman. "How is it all to end, Lieutenant?" Elías asked.

Whitman thought that Elías was suddenly very Spanish, very somber and very Spanish. And he thought, too, that the Mexican had a natural elegance and he wondered how he had ridden all those miles in that black suit and showed no dust. Did those *vaqueros* dust him off? Expertly, with their quirts?

"Does something amuse you, Mr. Whitman?"

"No."

"I thought I saw a small smile."

"No." Whitman said. He drew on the cigar. It was an excellent cigar.

"It has been a bad year thus far, Mr. Whitman," Elías said. "I have not been able to smile. So many of my friends have been killed, just since the start of this year. Jim Pennington, chasing Apaches who stole his cattle, shot and killed just three miles from Tucson."

"I know about that," Whitman said.

"The mail rider from Tubac, a distant relative of mine." Elías leaned forward and his dark eyes glowed. "Our family has been here for many years, Mr. Whitman. I have many relatives. This one, the mail rider, was murdered just two miles from Tucson. Almost within calling distance."

Elías' eyes were burning now. Whitman frowned.

"Simms, Sam Brown, good friends, killed near Tres Alamos while they were hauling a load of timber to use on their farm." Elías spoke in a cadenced manner, reciting a litany with no expectation of response. "There is no end, Mr. Whitman. There is no end." He leaned forward slightly. "Do you believe people die for each other, Mr. Whitman?"

Whitman looked at Elías thoughtfully. "I have seen men sacrifice themselves for other men in battle."

Elías shook his head patiently. "No, I do not mean that, Mr. Whitman," he said in the voice of explaining to a child. "I mean people dying in place of each other. I mean people being selected to die—so that other persons will not die."

"I have never given that any thought," Whitman said.

"Two of my brothers were killed by Apaches," Elías said. His eyes burned and then the fire flickered out. "And my father's brother, Ramón, as well. And my father died with an Apache bullet in his skull."

"I regret to hear that."

"I have thought more than once they died in my place," Elías said. "Has General Stoneman said when he will return to Arizona?"

The new tack did not catch Whitman by surprise. He was prepared to hear anything from Elías now. "No, Mr. Elías. But I believe he is due shortly."

"It must be difficult for the general to fight a war in Arizona when he is sitting on the Pacific coast." Elías' voice now was sympathetic, as though he commiserated with the general for his unfortunate predicament. "Don't you agree, Mr. Whitman?"

"I believe that is something for General Stoneman to decide," Whitman said.

"How can he possibly manage it?" Elías asked.

Whitman picked up some papers. "Mr. Elías—"

"How can he do it, Lieutenant Whitman?" Elías' voice rose suddenly and sharply.

Whitman looked up. Elías slapped his hand on the desk. "How can any general manage that! I demand as a citizen that you explain that to me!"

Elías' face was in a knot. His eyes glared.

"Mr. Elías, I am not in a position to explain the determinations of the commanding general. And I must inform you that I have a great deal of work to do."

After a moment Elías nodded slowly. His body relaxed. His eyes closed and when he opened them they again were reposed. He rose slowly and gracefully to his feet.

"Thank you for the time and information you have granted me, Mr. Whitman. May I ask what disposition was made of the body of Manuel Ortega?" His tone was quite normal.

"He was buried on the post."

"Do I have the lieutenant's permission to visit the grave?"

"Certainly."

"I will say a few words over it. I should have brought two of my sons with me for this occasion instead of hired help. But I could not take the risk of endangering such a large portion of my family at one time."

Elías again was composed and again very Spanish and elegant and grave, Whitman thought, and he spoke as a reasonable man. But Whitman knew now what it was that had bothered him about the man's eyes. It was what they had been disciplined to cover. It was the prisoner they kept hidden, except for those unavoidable moments when the prisoner defeated them and escaped.

"In what was my wife's cousin buried, Mr. Whitman?" Elías asked with exquisite politeness. He was wholly relaxed now. He might have been asking the time of day, and as a point of very little interest.

"I don't know, Mr. Elías," Whitman said. He smiled. It was an expression that rarely set his lips. It broke apart the dark lines. "We have no lumber here. We use what we can, packing boxes, cracker boxes, anything. And if there is nothing around at the moment, nothing is used." Whitman stood up. "It is of little importance, Mr. Elías. Your wife's cousin was a man and he died performing a brave act and he did not have to be put into a fancy wooden box to journey to his Maker."

Elías looked down. He bit his mustache.

"If you would prefer, Mr. Elías, I will order the body exhumed and sent on to you so that you may give it Catholic burial."

Elías raised his eyes. His face was more Spanish than ever. He looked oddly younger. "A thousand thanks, Mr. Whitman." He stroked his imperial. His voice was indifferent. "As you have said, Manuel Ortega met death as a brave man and perhaps it is fitting that he lie in the earth where he died."

As Whitman accompanied Elías to the door the thought passed through his mind that this man could not be very much different from the man who had occupied the bright armor in his quarters.

"Do not be such a stranger, Lieutenant," Elías said presently. "You have friends in Tucson."

Outside, the *vaqueros*, who had been hunkering down in the shade of the *ramada*, sprang to their feet. They came to attention, Whitman noted, as smartly as any soldier. Whitman summoned Duncan and told him to find out where Ortega had been buried and to take Elías and his men to the grave.

Whitman turned to bid Elías farewell. The Mexican was staring at something on the parade ground. Whitman saw that whatever it was that was imprisoned behind the eyes had escaped again.

He swung his eyes to see what it was the Mexican had seen. He saw walking slowly across the pebbled parade ground five Apache women. One of the women held up a small branch to which had been attached a dirty white rag. She waved the peace sign slowly as they walked and her eyes moved from side to side to assure herself the banner was being respected.

Whitman saw the hands of the two *vaqueros* move slowly to their pistols. He stepped between the men and the women, unsnapping the flap of his holster.

"Don't," he said, pulling out his own gun.

The *vaqueros* stared at him, their eyes going hard, and then they looked at Elías and their hands fell to their sides. Whitman slipped his gun back into the holster and glanced at Elías.

He saw in the Mexican's face the glow of hatred so pure it made for religious ecstasy.

△ 8

Clarrity waved his arms and shouted at the women. The women stood silent and grouped tightly and the woman with the torn cloth held it up as though it were a talisman that would protect her from all devils, even white ones. Other soldiers joined Clarrity and gawked at the women. The men separated to make way for Whitman.

Whitman looked at the women closely. It was the first time he had ever laid eyes on wild Apache women. He had heard about the Apache women. Oscar Hutton said they were worse than the men. Hutton said the men generally were satisfied to kill you and mutilate you after you were dead but that the Apache hags specialized in torturing you while you were alive. Hutton said if you got yourself into a fight with Apaches, get yourself killed, don't let the women get their hands on you.

These women appeared to be old, although Whitman could not be certain of that. The Indians he had seen, men and women both, were like Orientals. It was always hard to fix their age. And the faces of these women were covered with dust from their march over the desert.

They looked to him like a collection of scarecrows. They were half naked. Their clothing, what there was of it, was torn. The clothing was interesting. It was assembled from many sources. There was calico and cotton manta and heavy drill, and nothing of it native to aboriginal Indians. One of the women wore men's shoes, Army brogans, Whitman would have guessed.

Four of the women kept their eyes on the ground. The fifth, the one with the white rag, stood erect. There was in her face a fierceness, a defiance of her enemies, that Whitman found appealing.

"Sir!" Clarrity bellowed.

"Yes, Sergeant," Whitman said. He looked from one crone's face to the other. He came back to the ancient with the flag of peace and the face of challenge. He saw the set of her jaw and he rubbed his own jaw.

"Shall I have them thrown off the post?" Clarrity inquired.

"Let mules drag them off by their hair," Oscar Hutton suggested.

Hutton looked at the women with vast disgust. Hutton had had a friend whose eyes had been gouged out by Apache women and who was tied down and left for the ants. There was rarely a time there was no twinkle in Hutton's eyes. There was none now.

"Get the Puma," Whitman said.

Lieutenant William Robinson, Whitman's second in command, the only other commissioned officer on the post, coming out of his quarters, heard Whitman's order and looked at Whitman curiously. Whitman noticed that Jesús Elías had moved closer and that the Mexican was contemplating him as well.

"Damn it to hell, Clarrity, I gave you an order!"

Whitman wondered why he was angry, and at what. He saw that some of the soldiers were crowding up to have a closer look at the women and that some of the women were not as old as he had thought at first and that the soldiers were ogling their breasts and were making comments about them.

"Clear the area," Whitman said.

The soldiers moved away reluctantly. Hutton remained. Elías remained. Lieutenant Robinson remained. The Puma appeared.

"Teniente," the Puma said.

"Ask them why they came here," Whitman said. He looked at the woman with the flag. Her chin jutted like the prow of a ship.

The Puma spoke to them rapidly. At the sound of their own tongue all the women raised their heads. It was as though their language reminded them they were human. They straightened and seemed for the first time to realize how they must appear. They made an effort to drag their patchwork clothing around them.

When the Puma finished there was a silence. The soldiers had backed off to the sutler's store. They stood there watching. No one spoke.

Whitman looked at the Puma impatiently. A change had come over the Puma, too. The Puma's face had become as Indian as the words that had come from his mouth. The Puma was in a state of quietude. His eyes were distant and he appeared to be waiting for something he did not regard as imminent.

"Don't they understand you?" Whitman asked.

"They understand." The Puma's voice was as remote as his eyes.

"Then why don't they answer?"

"They are on Indian time, Teniente."

"What the devil does that mean?"

"They are never in any hurry, Teniente."

"Not even when they're building a fire under you," Hutton commented.

Whitman waited for a few moments. He had the sense that he was being made to look ridiculous and that the Puma was on Indian time too and he was about to order the women off the post when Lieutenant Robinson spoke up.

"Get rid of those old bitches, Royal," Robinson said.

"With a load of buckshot," Hutton said.

"Perhaps the lieutenant enjoys to stand in the sun waiting for Apache women to make up their minds to speak to him," Jesús Elías said.

There were a number of Whitmans who would have recognized the expression that passed over Whitman's face. "Ask them again," he directed the Puma.

Before the Puma could repeat his query the woman with the white flag and the granite chin began to speak. She spoke slowly. She had all the time in the world. Her words fell from her mouth like small cinders. The other women listened and nodded. The woman stopped speaking and waved the stick with the rag to remind everyone it was still there and she lifted her chin and was silent.

"She says they are Aravaipa Apaches," the Puma said. Whitman saw Jesús Elías spit on the ground.

"She says one of the boys in the tribe is missing," the Puma said. "She says he is the son of one of these women. She says in the tribe it is said the boy was killed by soldiers. She says the boy's mother wants to know if he is dead so that she can bury his belongings. She says it would be bad for him to be dead and without the things he owns."

"Clarrity!" Whitman called out.

"Sir!"

"Do you know anything about an Apache boy being killed recently?"

"Not recently, sir!"

"Tell the woman we know nothing about a boy having been shot," Whitman said to the Puma.

The Puma spoke and after a normal interval the woman with the flag replied. When she finished she held her eyes on Whitman.

"What did she say?" Whitman asked.

The Puma hesitated. Then when he saw Whitman's face tightening he said softly, "The *teniente's* pardon, but this woman wants to know if you are speaking the truth."

"Jesus Christ!" Robinson said.

"Yes," Elías said.

Whitman's lips twitched and as Hutton was about to add his own wisdom to the discussion he held up his hand and stayed him. "Tell this woman that from what information has been given to me, I am telling her the truth."

The Puma looked at Whitman for a longish time, not long as Indian time, but long. Then he started to speak to the old woman. He was interrupted when Oscar Hutton snapped his fingers, a sound like a small pistol shot.

"Wait a minute," Hutton said. "Maybe she means that Apache kid who is helping Fred Austin in the store."

"Get the boy," Whitman said to Clarrity. He said to the Puma, "Tell the women they may sit down."

The women made themselves comfortable on the parade ground and drifted off into their own place of being. The woman who had spoken stuck the branch with the white rag into the ground and sat next to it. She folded her hands in her lap and withdrew with the four other women.

Clarrity returned. "No sign of that boy, sir."

"I saw him just a little while ago," Hutton said. "He was unloading some goods behind the sutler's store."

"He probably unloaded the stuff all the way back to the Apache camp," Lieutenant Robinson observed.

"You'll have them crows hanging round till doomsday, Royal," Hutton said.

Whitman looked once more at the old woman sitting next to the stick with the dirty rag. He wanted her to believe that he was telling the truth. He could not have explained why but he wanted her to believe that.

He was about to order the Puma to tell the women they could not find the boy around the camp but that no Apache youth had been killed, not recently anyway, when he heard a small to-do and he looked around to see the sutler, Austin, walking toward them, holding the hand of a young boy who was dressed in American clothing but who, Whitman saw, was an Indian, about twelve. The boy was trying to break away but the trader pulled him along.

One of the women squatting on the ground let out a little cry and got to her feet and ran to the boy. Austin released him. The woman embraced the boy and spoke to him. The boy remained silent, his hands at his sides. He gave no response to the woman's words or caresses.

Whitman wondered why he felt surprise to see an Apache woman show affection for her son. "That is the right boy, isn't he?" he asked the Puma.

"He is the son of that woman. His name is Naco."

The boy's mother now was pleading with the boy, her hands clasped at her breast. He stood there, his arms hanging, and when she finished he replied, shaking his head. She spoke again and Whitman saw that her eyes were wet. The boy replied again, still shaking his head.

"What are they talking about?" Whitman asked the Puma. "She has her son. Why doesn't she take him and clear out?"

"The mother is asking him to return to the tribe with her but he does not want to go," the Puma said. "He says he is fed here and clothed and that he sleeps nights in the same place and that he is not afraid he will be killed by soldiers because there are many soldiers here and no one has tried to kill him."

"Well," Whitman said. "Well." He glanced at Jesús Elías. The Mexican's face was frozen.

The boy's mother returned to the other four women and spoke to them in a low voice. The women bent their heads together. Their hair fell over their faces like curtains.

The woman with the flag spoke to the Puma. "She asks the *nantan's* permission to remain here overnight," the Puma said.

"Overnight!" Lieutenant Robinson exploded.

"What is a '*nantan*'?" Whitman asked the Puma.

"It means captain," the Puma said. "It means boss."

"It means promotion," Whitman said.

"The woman says the boy's mother would like to have her son think on it and that she would like to speak to him again tomorrow and that maybe by then he would change his mind and go back with them."

"What do they think this place is?" Lieutenant Robinson demanded. "A hotel in the desert for Apaches?"

"No need to let them stay on here, Lieutenant," Oscar Hutton said. "They see the boy's okay and that's what they came to find out. Fact he don't want to go back to being an Apache ain't nothing to exercise us."

Whitman looked at the men around him. He looked at the Apache women. He looked again at Lieutenant Robinson. His second-in-command was about ten years younger than he was. Lieutenant Robinson had had a great deal of experience fighting Indians in California. He was only recently transferred to Arizona. But he had landed at Camp Grant before Whitman.

"They came here to talk," Whitman said to Robinson.

"They talked," Lieutenant Robinson said.

Whitman contemplated his junior officer. He knew very little about Bill Robinson. He could see he was plump and placid and he knew he was competent. He had listened to Bill Robinson talk about food and wine and he seemed to know a great deal about both. And Bill Robinson was not entirely at home in Arizona. There were no niceties and he was familiar with niceties.

"Bill, would you walk into an Apache *ranchería?*"

"Any day of the week," Robinson said heartily. "And you can include Sundays and holidays." He stood with his hands behind his back as though to keep them as far removed as possible from the Apache women.

"That's what I mean, Bill," Whitman said. "They came here."

"They knew they were safe in doing that."

"Did they?"

"They knew perfectly well we would do nothing to them except perhaps kick them out."

"Did they, Bill?" Whitman looked at him intently. "Did they know that?"

"They damned well knew it."

"How could they be so sure?"

"We're just not that way. We're civilized."

Whitman wiped sweat from his upper lip. He hoped the fever would not choose this time to pay one of its tedious visits.

"Have we never killed Apache women?" Whitman asked.

"Not this way. Not when they come in under a white flag."

"Do you believe they were certain of that?"

"Yes."

Whitman felt the sweat on his back. The sun was burning hard. He wet his lips and straightened. "I don't believe they were certain of that at all."

"What are you trying to prove, Royal?"

"That mother wanted her child back so badly she came here without knowing what would happen to her. And she persuaded four other Apache women to come with her."

"And what does that prove?"

"I don't know. I don't know what it proves. I don't know if it proves anything." He paused. "Bill, could you call it human?"

Hutton snorted. Jesús Elías watched silently.

"Clarrity," Whitman said.

"Sir!"

"Get these women some food from the mess."

"Yes, sir."

"Fred."

"Yes, Royal."

"Scrounge around that store of yours and dig up a few yards of manta and some tobacco."

Austin, a short man with a homely, friendly face framed by a beard with no mustache, asked, "You reckon you know what you're doing, Royal?"

"No."

"You never can go wrong not doing."

"No, I don't know that either." Whitman turned to the Puma. "Tell these women they can stay here the night. Tell them they will be given food and tobacco and manta. Tell the boy, Naco, to stay with them while they are here. Tell them if Naco chooses to go with them he is free to do so."

Whitman saw that Surgeon Sumner had joined the group and that the doctor was looking at him. He wanted to tell Sumner he was fine now. He wanted to tell Sumner that for a little while he thought there was going to be trouble but that he felt fine now. He felt splendid.

Jesús Elías, who had smoked and listened with a face as impassive as any Indian's, spoke for the second time. "With permission, Lieutenant."

"Gladly, Mr. Elías," Whitman said.

"I admit I do not understand why you are being hospitable to these women. But I understand least why you have ordered the boy to remain with them."

"To give the mother as much time as possible to get him back."

"So that he may grow to manhood and learn how to be a true Apache?"

"That is not my present affair, Mr. Elías."

"Nor will it ever be." Elías studied Naco. "I would say he is between twelve and fourteen. He will need a few more years of seasoning. He will not learn all the Apache ways of murder and robbery for perhaps five or six years." Elías turned slowly to Whitman and looked at him directly. "We will still be here, Mr. Whitman. Where will you be stationed six years from now?"

"Have you finished, Mr. Elías?" Whitman asked.

"But for one thing. Has it occurred to you that any or even all of these women may be the wives or mothers of the savages who attacked the wagon train?" Don Jesús tossed away his cigar. "With your permission, Lieutenant, will your orderly now conduct me to the grave of Manuel Ortega?"

Whitman returned to his office. He looked out the window. He saw that the Apache women had found shade under the *ramada* outside the post bakery. He saw Austin speaking to the boy, Naco. He saw Austin give the boy a little push and then the boy walked slowly toward the women.

After a little while Whitman got started on his report to the general. He heard hoofbeats on the pebbles outside and he raised his head. He saw Elías and the two *vaqueros* leaving the post. The three Mexicans looked at the women for several moments and then continued down the parade ground.

When Whitman finished his papers it was still light. He stood up and stretched. He walked to the window. The women were sitting under the *ramada* eating the food Clarrity had produced for them. One of the women, Whitman thought it might be the boy's mother but he could not be sure at that distance, made a cigarette and lit up.

Naco was not eating. Naco was standing there stiffly, as though undergoing punishment.

The hours the women spent with Naco accomplished nothing. They failed to persuade him to return to his people. The five women departed the next morning. Naco's mother embraced him and then the five women walked off the post. Whitman no longer thought they looked like scarecrows.

The old woman with the flag held it high as they walked the length of the parade ground. She held the stick above her head long after they were off the post.

△ 9

Whitman reread the letter from his wife for the fourth or fifth time. It was Lucretia's Christmas letter and it had reached him two or three days before. He tried to imagine Christmas in Maine. He could no longer quite remember it. Oh, he could remember it, yes, with his mind. But he could not feel it, the way it was.

It was as though in coming out to Arizona, in passing through the miles that separated it from the East, he had passed not into a new land alone but into a new sensibility. He had heard, before coming to the territory, that men who served there were never quite the same afterward. He had taken that with a New England grain of salt. Arizona was still in the present. He did not know how he would be afterward. But he knew that after only a couple of months he was not the same.

So, quickly now, he thought, closing his eyes against the glare, against the heat, quickly now, snow and blue spruce and the lash of the sea against the rocks, the cold wind and fires blazing in hearths and hot rum and snowmen and snow fights and Christmas bells on the sleighs and the carols.

They had sung carols on the post on Christmas Eve. They sounded sad and incongruous until some of the Mexicans working on the post sang their own carols in Spanish and they sounded right.

The children were well, his wife wrote, and they all sent their love and she was teaching English in a Portland high school.

He put down the letter. He found a sheet of paper and dipped his pen into the inkwell and started to write.

"How can I describe this place to you? I look out my office window and what I see is so strange, so unreal, that gazing directly on it one's eyes want not to be credited."

He raised his eyes. The parade ground was empty. The post flag drooped in exhaustion. The desert lay beyond.

He scratched the pen on the paper again. The nib was bone-dry. It was something he had to keep remembering. The ink dried on the nib almost as soon as it was out of the inkwell.

"It is the spring of the year here and to make everything even more incredible the cactus has blossomed. One would have as readily expected a stone cairn to flower. The ocotillo has scarlet flowers and the Spanish dagger is demurely white. All of the different cactus growths have produced flowers in extraordinary colors. They are all grouchy old men, ready to tear at one's clothing and rip gashes in the sides of horses, and here they are now as adorned as young ladies attending a debutante's ball."

He looked up as Duncan entered the office. Duncan had never spoken to him about the burned wagon train and the burial. He wondered what that had done to Duncan and whether it was good or bad and whether he should have ordered it. Perhaps one day Duncan would let him know.

"What is it, Duncan?" he asked.

"Those five Apache women who were here last week," Duncan said.

"What about them?"

"They're back."

"Good Lord, what for?"

"They brought some baskets and some other things to trade, sir."

"Oh? Well, that's all right. Get someone to tell them I give my permission for that. And get Clarrity to stay with them and see there's no trouble."

Whitman dipped the pen into the inkwell.

"There is something else, sir," Duncan said.

"What's that?"

"The old woman with the flag asked to speak with you."

"About what?"

"She didn't say, sir."

"Find Lieutenant Robinson and tell him to have a word with her."

"Yes, sir."

As Duncan started out, Whitman stopped him.

"Never mind. I'll see her."

The women were squatting under the same *ramada* outside the bakery, as though that was the portion of Camp Grant they had come to know and had some rights to, as though they felt safest there or perhaps least intrusive. As Whitman walked toward them he saw that the Puma was there and that Lieutenant Robinson was talking to the women.

"Would you like me to bring them to you, sir?" Duncan asked.

"No." Whitman wished as he had wished before that he had not been born in Maine, that he had not been given, unasked, a persistent New England conscience that evidenced itself in all things, large and small, and even, as in this case, trivial.

When Whitman reached them the women looked up and he thought he discerned relief in their faces. Relief from what? And their faces, he saw, had become faces. The first time he would have said that he probably would never have recognized them again, with the exception, perhaps, of the woman with the flag and the chin. But he recognized all of them now.

The woman with the flag was the oldest of the lot, he guessed. Naco's mother was much younger, he could see now, and two of the women were quite young and not unattractive by any standard. One of them was downright comely.

He saw that they had cut and sewed the coarse cotton cloth he had given them into decent garments. The manta was clean and neat and the women appeared less ravaged by the desert dust. And the flag that the old woman had planted in the ground of what now was obviously her terrain was a small cutting of the manta, which Whitman considered a very nice touch indeed.

It was curious, he thought, how they had emerged from anonymity and that he could never again think of them as five Apache women, any five Apache women.

"What is it now?" Whitman asked.

"I don't know," Robinson said. He looked irritated.

"Haven't you been talking to them?"

"I've been trying to talk to them. They won't talk to me."

"They will speak only to the *nantan*," the Puma said.

"All right, tell them they may speak now."

The Puma questioned the woman with the flag again and after a passage of Indian time the woman took the flag out of the ground and held it aloft as she replied, as though the banner, having warded off ghosts and others who would do them harm, now would serve another purpose, that of giving validity and substance to her words.

As she spoke, Whitman saw that the Puma's eyes widened slightly and that he shook his head, although whether in denial or disbelief Whitman could not know. He smelled Oscar Hutton's pipe behind him.

"This rubbish back here again?" Oscar Hutton inquired.

The woman finished. The Puma hesitated.

"Well?" Whitman asked.

"This woman says their chief would like to have a meeting with the *nantan* at Camp Grant," the Puma said.

Hutton snorted. Robinson started to say something. Whitman touched his arm lightly.

"To what purpose?" Whitman asked the Puma.

"To talk of peace," the Puma said.

"Bullshit," Oscar Hutton said.

"Well," Whitman said. "Bill, what do you make of that?"

"I make it to be wonderful."

"You do?" Whitman looked at Robinson in some surprise.

"If I could believe it."

"I see," Whitman said.

"But in any case, Royal, it's no concern of yours," Robinson said. "First lieutenants are not authorized to make peace treaties with hostile Indians. The regulations are not written that way."

"Hm. But it would be a pleasant prospect, wouldn't it?"

"So's pie in the sky, Royal, and snow in July," Oscar Hutton observed.

Whitman looked at the Puma. The Puma's face might

have been a mask fashioned for an ancestor, designed to show a god's total indifference to human fate.

"Have you a comment as well?" Whitman asked.

"No, Teniente," the Puma said.

Whitman pursed his lips. He looked at the old woman. She had lowered her flag now. She had gone away as the Puma had gone away.

"It is official Government policy," Whitman said. "We are supposed to encourage the Apaches to come to peace, are we not?"

"That was last year." Robinson said. "As far as I understand it, policy has changed. This year we are heavy on Apaches."

"It may not be policy," Whitman said. "It might be decency."

"You ain't asked my opinion yet, Royal," Oscar Hutton said.

"I was coming to that, Oscar," Whitman said. "You may believe I was coming to that."

"Keep your ass out of this," Hutton said.

"Is that your advice, Oscar?"

"You heard it."

"I'm new here," Whitman said in a low voice. "I'm new here and I don't know much about Apaches yet and I'm just a first lieutenant, albeit a little aged in grade, and I ought to allow policy matters to be dealt with by my superiors. Most of all I don't know a damned thing about Apaches. Is that what you are telling me, Oscar?"

"Forget it, Lieutenant."

"The wise old veteran and the dude from the East?"

"I said forget it." Oscar Hutton started off.

"Oscar."

"Don't try to make a damned fool out of me."

"I wasn't. I'm confused, Oscar, and sometimes when I get confused, I run off a little at the mouth."

Hutton grunted. Whitman turned to the Puma.

"What is the name of this chief?" Whitman asked.

"Eskiminzin," the Puma said.

The old woman raised her head at the sound of the name. Hutton spat.

"This woman is his mother," the Puma said.

Whitman looked at the old woman with even more interest. "What do you know about Eskiminzin?" he asked the Puma.

"He is an Apache. He kills."

"You respect Cochise. Do you respect him?"

"I have never met Eskiminzin."

Oscar Hutton spat again.

"I didn't hear what you said, Oscar," Whitman said.

"Eskiminzin's one of the worst," Hutton said.

"Have you met him?"

"Ain't many white men who have and who are walking around talking about it."

"That bad," Whitman said.

"It's not a question of good or bad, Royal," Robinson said. "These are primitive people. Their standards—if you can call them that—are completely different from ours."

"It ain't that Apaches want to be bad," Hutton said. "It ain't as though that's what they went out and chose for themselves. Maybe if they had a choice it'd be different. But they ain't had that choice. It's the way they was born, to be a certain way and do certain things. They can't change that."

"No more than a leopard can change its spots."

"Exactly, Royal," Hutton said. "You put it exactly right."

"Different standards, different standards," Robinson said.

"To want to make peace," Whitman said slowly. "That doesn't seem such a barbaric standard."

"Just long enough to lick their wounds and fill their bellies," Hutton said. "Them feed stations never worked and never will."

Whitman looked at the women again as though they might inform him of something he did not yet know. Not one of them appeared to be taking an interest in what was going on. Of course none of them could understand a word of what was being said but it must have been plain to them that there was opposition to Eskiminzin's request. And yet they all seemed to be half asleep, to be vegetating in a kind of remote and unassailable apathy, as though apart from trading the woven baskets they brought with them there was no real reason for them to be there, and whatever the result of the discussion it would for them be meaningless.

"You believe it would be improper for me simply to listen to this Eskiminzin?" Whitman asked.

"Listening's dealing," Hutton said.

"Which I have no warrant to do."

"Not lieutenants, not lieutenants," Robinson reminded him cheerily. "With all due respect, Royal, those pretty birds have long since flown from your shoulders. That was another time and another place and another war."

Presently Whitman said, "I don't want to meet with this Apache."

"Well, that's a relief." Robinson clapped his hand on Whitman's back. "Puma, just pass the word to that old bat that it's no dice."

"But I must," Whitman said.

Hutton snorted like an old spavined horse and Robinson backed away a few paces and clasped his hands behind his back.

"I'm opposed to it, Royal," Robinson said stiffly. "I want to go on record."

"You are on record."

"Nothing personal."

"Of course."

"And, Royal—a suggestion."

"Yes?"

"Notify General Stoneman. Get his official endorsement. In writing."

Whitman's lips tightened in anger. "Endorsement for what! I don't know how this is going to turn out. Do you expect me to run puling to the general for his blanket sanction for anything?" He breathed out hard. "Damn it to hell, Bill, we are supposed to make decisions," he said quietly. "We are men."

Whitman glanced at Hutton. The guide was shaking his head in disgust. Whitman turned to the Puma.

"Tell the old woman to inform her son that I will listen to him."

"Yes, Teniente."

Whitman thought he could detect a slightly different tone in the Puma's voice but the interpreter's face did not acquaint him with what it was.

"Tell Fred Austin to have a look at those baskets and tell him I said not to cheat the women too much."

"Yes, Teniente."

"And get hold of Naco. Tell him his mother is here."

Whitman started across the parade ground. He saw that the soldiers were keeping their distance from the five women, possibly because they were now fully clothed and less intriguing.

Duncan caught up with him. Whitman had forgotten about his striker. Duncan had listened to everything that had been said. Whitman wondered what he was thinking. Duncan's face looked as it always did, very young, unformed.

Whitman felt good. What he had done was undoubtedly wrong and against regulations and, worse, probably stupid as well. But he was reasonably certain that what he had done was something his father would have done. And if that did not make it altogether right, he knew damned well it was not altogether wrong either.

△ △ △ TWO

△ 1

"... *The Apache nation in this region as compared to what I knew it to be more than 20 years ago is nearly harmless ...*"
General George Stoneman, John Wasson considered, was not only a sniveling coward, he was an idiot.

When Americans started to drift into the little Mexican settlement of Tucson, and for a long time afterward, quarrels, personal feuds, arguments, political differences, jealousies, and most other ferments were settled by guns, knives, fists, rifles, and occasionally by a noose tied to a strong limb of a tree. Words rarely were employed in such matters since there often were differences in language, and even if there were not, the majority of men who found in Tucson a safe haven knew very few words. What with natural difficulties and alcohol it was always simpler to pull a gun.

What Tucson desperately needed, although not a person realized it, was a spokesman, a conscience, a champion who would take on windmills, an artisan of words who could construct a soul for the community and give that soul expression. In the latter part of 1870 a man fashioned by nature to fit this bill settled in the Old Pueblo.

At the age of thirty-eight John Wasson had not yet discovered exactly what he was meant to do in this life. From Ohio, he had at various times taught school, prospected for precious metals, clumped over the land as a surveyor. Some inner voice instructed him that all these activities were merely peripheral, but what was at the true core of existence continued to elude him. But somewhere in this world, he was certain, there was a role for him.

He was a smallish man with bright-blue eyes and a mustache and a pointed beard and soon after alighting in Tucson he established a weekly newspaper, the *Citizen*. This in itself might have seemed foolhardy in a town not noted for its devotion to the printed word. What was more curious was the fact that the *Citizen* proclaimed itself as pugnaciously Republican. This in a community that had been a hotbed of rabid Southern intrigue during the recent War Between the States, and where the still predominant political passions were already served by Bill Oury's Democratic *Arizonan*.

But Tucson had not yet come to know what it had on its hands in John Wasson. His politics were only a minor aberration. John Wasson was a zealot.

In the first issue of the *Citizen*, Wasson demanded that the streets of Tucson be cleared of garbage and the bodies of horses, mules, dogs, cats, rats and anything else rotting about town. This preposterous suggestion was so out of tune with the mores of the community that at first people thought he must be referring to some other place entirely. When they realized John Wasson was talking about Tucson and that he was in earnest they decided he must be mad.

Those piles of garbage, those dead animals, were not only hallowed landmarks, the flavor and smell of the Old Pueblo, eternal as the mountains and the deserts, but they served a useful practical purpose as well. How else could one citizen direct another to a residence or a store or a saloon or any other place if he could not explain that the location in question was five garbage piles down that street and then turn left past the dead burro?

Instead of dealing with that reasonable justification, John Wasson went on smiting right and left. Next he demanded that the open wellholes be boarded up. Then he demanded that streetlights be erected to illuminate the town at night. He demanded that more schools be built. He demanded many things and when he could think of nothing new he went back to old demands.

Bill Oury could always spot a straight man. One evening in the Congress Hall, Oury spoke up. "John," he said, while the room quieted down somewhat, "John, supposing for the sake of argument you're right. How would you go about paying for all those things? How would you raise the money?"

The question did not faze John Wasson one bit. He emptied the glass of special whiskey he had been served because he was in the company of Uncle Billy Oury, and he said calmly, "Tax every gambling hall and saloon in town."

That, of course, set a new standard in Wasson imbecilities.

When the patrons of the Congress Hall recovered their senses and looked for Wasson to separate him from some of his skin, they discovered that the editor, knowing a good curtain line when he heard it, even if it fell from his own lips, had taken his leave.

After that the inhabitants of Tucson looked upon John Wasson in varying ways. His friends defended him as a visionary and explained that all visionaries were a little odd. Others looked upon him as a kind of nut, or a common scold, a gadfly, good for a laugh, entertaining enough, always full of those crazy ideas. But obviously not to be taken seriously.

When he walked down a street still adorned with that garbage and those carcasses, his nose sniffing around like a bird dog, smelling the garbage and trying to smell out stories, some people crossed the street to avoid him and there were Mexicans who believed this wild man with his wild ideas had been affected either by God or the sun and when they passed him they lowered their eyes and crossed themselves.

A new facet of John Wasson's personality was revealed, however, in that same Congress Hall, where he was still welcome because of his inventive and unexpected talk. One evening when the spirits, good and bad, were flowing, he discoursed on his hates. He hated many things, he announced, which was no news to anyone, every man there could have listed Wasson hatreds one by one, but more than anything else, Wasson went on, he hated Apache Indians. He hated them coldly, intellectually, and, as he disclosed, from a typically original Wasson point of view.

"Apaches," he stated, and now he had an audience, "Apaches are a racial defect, like a vicious strain in dogs."

The burning reformer of Tucson could see no reformation of Apaches.

"There is no cure," he stated, "except extermination."

On that instant John Wasson became a sage.

For the first time men now heard their innermost feelings explained in a manner that was almost scientific. Those were not reprehensible prejudices seething inside their hearts, not at all. What was there was the perfectly normal and decent rejection by the healthy of the diseased.

And on that instant, too, John Wasson had at last come upon his true vocation. No need ever again to beat his breast and question the heavens. He had been given his answer.

Bill Oury pronounced the judgment. "Let John Wasson rave about garbage and putting lights on streets. A man's got the God-given privilege to believe in anything, even the Republican Party. But what I want to say is that while John Wasson's newspaper is hurting my newspaper, on the main issues, he thinks right."

A racial defect. That was a new theory for Jesús María Elías as well. *Santa Madre de Dios!* It set the whole concept of Apaches in a new dimension.

△ 2

John Wasson lit a fresh cigar and tugged at the point of his beard and checked over the long sheet of proof. He had come across the story by chance. Well, not wholly by chance, nothing was wholly by chance, but there was luck involved.

General George Stoneman had spent a little time in Arizona in the fall of 1870 after he was given the command of the new Department and on October 31 of that year he had written a report on the conditions in the Territory. The report was written in the quiet and peace and safety of Drum Barracks but was datelined Fort Whipple, Arizona Territory, the general's proper and official headquarters, and John Wasson, when he heard about that, had wondered who the general thought he was fooling by that gross deception. Even his superiors in San Francisco, to whom the intelligence was directed, knew that Stoneman was not where he was saying he was.

From the time the people of Arizona heard about this report they waited anxiously to see what it contained. The general's ideas, however superficial, however quickly formed, quite simply would determine their future, their prosperity or poverty, in many cases their living or their dying. What they hoped for, of course, was that Stoneman would propose an all-out war against the Apaches. Nothing they had heard about the general supported any such dream, but they would settle for far less. They would settle for an honest and reasonable protection against their enemies.

There were many rumors about the contents of the general's communication and all were negative and frightening. But no one knew for certain and everyone hoped, if not for the best, not for the worst either, and some people prayed.

And everyone was embittered that this military stranger, who had made such a perfunctory examination of their situation, held their fate in his hands.

One of the first steps John Wasson had taken when he started publishing the *Citizen* was to subscribe to newspapers from other parts of the country. These always arrived in a batch whenever mail riders succeeded in running the Apache gauntlet. Normally he went over them quickly and tossed them away. There was little that happened in Chicago or San Francisco or New York that was of any interest to *Citizen* readers.

On a wet evening in February he glanced through the latest assortment of these newspapers even more rapidly than usual. He had worked hard that day, the weather was miserable, the Congress Hall, where he was a hero now, beckoned to him. He always got the good whiskey now, whether he was with Bill Oury or not.

He riffled through the newest issue of the New York *World* and was about to dump it into his wastebasket when his eye caught the name "Stoneman." He read on. A newspaperman's excitement began to fill his blood and warm his bones more than any of Charlie Brown's whiskey.

For the New York *World* had in some way gotten hold of General Stoneman's report, written almost four months before and not yet officially made public. Matters in Arizona were not of blazing interest in the city of New York and the *World* had printed only excerpts from it. But that was enough. The excerpts contained the heart of the report and John Wasson saw that the ugliest fears of the people of the Territory were realized and he saw, too, that he had the hottest news story of the year.

He reread the story and read it a third time and put down the paper carefully. He sat back and set his feet on the desk and thought. He thought how he was going to handle this windfall. He wanted to make the greatest impact possible on his readers and he had to work that out.

He gambled that he had the time. He was reasonably certain no one else had that particular issue of the New York *World*. Of course Jake Mansfeld got out-of-town newspapers for his Pioneer News Depot sometimes but the chances that he would get this issue of this paper were fairly remote. He thought he could count on his having an exclusive.

He was very quiet at the Congress Hall that night, quite unlike himself. People were used to his making pronouncements on every subject. He sat alone and nursed his drink and thought. Bill Oury had the notion that Wasson had come on to some piece of news but he knew it would be useless for him to try to wheedle it out of his competitor.

In the end, what John Wasson elected to do was to run the short excerpts from Stoneman's report in one column, interspersing commentaries of his own, and at the same time in an adjoining column list some of the latest Apache atrocities.

△ 3

And now everything was ready. The front page of the next issue of the *Citizen* was laid out. All that remained to be done was for him to correct the proofs of the Stoneman report and his remarks about it and then go to press. He wiped his glasses, picked up a pencil, cornered the cigar in his mouth so the smoke would not get into his eyes, and he went over the general's words. What words. What a general.

For starters General Stoneman had recommended that of the eighteen military posts and quartermaster depots in the Territory, seven of the posts be deactivated and three of the quartermaster depots broken up and the civilian employees discharged.

When he first had read it, this last item brought a puckish grin to the lips of Wasson. Wait, he had thought, until the boys of the Ring read that!

The general had written further:

> "The posts and depots recommended to be discarded are exorbitant and can be disposed with advantageously to the Government without detriment other than a pecuniary one to the people of the Territory in their immediate vicinity who will of course object, as they will be unable, as heretofore, to dispose of their hay, grain, etc. to the Government at the usual excessive profits."

At this point John Wasson interjected:

> Is it strange corn, wheat or barley is 6¢ or 7¢ a pound, beans 10¢–12¢, hay $30 a ton, when men who produce and furnish these articles do work with one hand—carrying a weapon for defense with the other? Not only will people who supply lose, but that is not important. Settlers will have to leave, because of defenselessness.

Then came a section of the Stoneman recommendations that enraged Wasson:

> "The all-absorbing topic in Arizona—the irrepressible Indians—is approached with no little reluctance, fearing that the authorities at HQ in San Francisco as well as Washington may

have already been surfeited and wearied with
its consideration."

John Wasson stormed:

When within the memory of man did any man
before him in high military position apologize
to his superiors for making his report on the
circumstances and conditions of the enemy he
was sent out to fight?

And then came the most dishonest Stoneman conclusion
of them all:

"The Apache nation in this region as compared
to what I knew it to be more than 20 years ago
is nearly harmless and their destitution is great
in extreme. They must either starve, steal or be
fed. As they are unwilling to do the former,
it becomes simply a question as to which is the
best policy: feed them or continue to endeavor
to prevent them from stealing."

"Feed them . . . or prevent them from stealing." The good
general had lowered himself comfortably on both sides of the
fence. John Wasson looked over the parallel column listing
the latest tabulation of those robbed and killed at the hands
of Apaches. There was almost no call to run any other kind
of obituary column, he thought. There were few deaths in Arizona from natural causes.

He reviewed his own final words:

Reduce the forts in Arizona by half! And after
that "feed the Apaches or prevent them from
stealing." And in the latter event—with just
half the number of the military posts which in
their present strength have never been able to
keep the Apaches off the backs of helpless
settlers.

John Wasson handed the proofs to his printer and told him to lock up the page after he made the corrections. He sat back in his chair. In a very little while he heard the sound he now most loved, the press in action, and he fancied that each thud was a blow against General George "Economy" Stoneman. He wondered what the weather was like in Southern California. He wondered how General Stoneman was enjoying it.

△ 4

Doña Inez poured more coffee and then left the room.

"Way I heard it down at the depot," Bill Oury said, "was that a lot of these enlistments, the soldiers' enlistments, are running out, their time is coming to an end. And they tell me that nothing is being done about it."

Jesús María Elías nodded. "I have heard something about that."

"They tell me there are about sixteen hundred troopers stationed out here," Oury said. "That doesn't seem like very much to me as it is, but the way they tell it, it's going to be less."

Elías nodded again. He knew that his friend's sources of information at the Tucson Quartermaster Depot at Camp Lowell were excellent. Until the year before, Captain Gilbert Cole Smith, who was married to Oury's daughter Lola, had been in charge and Oury spent a lot of time at the place, talking about this and that, and listening. Oury was always looking around for any information that might help him turn a few pennies but he picked up military news as well. Captain Smith had been transferred but Bill Oury still had his connections.

"Why do you suppose they treat us this way, Don Jesús?" Oury asked. He finished his coffee and poured some whiskey.

There was no need to define "they." "They" were the high Army officials and the politicians, the people far away in San Francisco or Washington. "They" were men who were at worst malignant, at best stupid. "They" were the ones who seemed to be writing Arizona off the map of the United States.

Elías knew that his friend's question, posed many, many times, was largely rhetorical and need not be answered, not even if he had known the answer.

Doña Inez entered the room again and asked the men if they wanted more coffee. They thanked her and said they were drinking whiskey now. She nodded and left the room. There was no need for her to remain and listen to her husband and his friend. She was welcome to stay, she knew, but there was no need. Her husband and Don Jesús talked often and always about the same thing. When they were in the Oury house she did not bother to listen and when they were in the Elías house Doña Teresa did not bother to listen. She, too, had heard it all many times.

That was not to say the two women did not share the feelings of their husbands. Doña Inez felt exactly as her husband did. But it was not necessary, *gracias a Dios*, to replenish herself so constantly.

A son had been born to Lola and Captain Smith and had been taken in an Army ambulance to San Xavier Mission and had been baptized there by Bishop Salpointe, the first American child to be so honored, it was said. That was a new soul given by God to replace the soul of the child lost on the *rancho* that night. The boy, Cornelius, named after a brother of Don Jesús who had been killed by Apaches, soon would be two and he was healthy and strong, and some of the loss in Doña Inez's heart had been restored.

Doña Inez hated Apaches, yes. True, the good Señor Cristo adjured against hatred, but in this instance she felt strongly that He would make an exception. Yes, she hated Apaches and with reason, but she had prayer and if her husband were a believer he, too, would have prayer and his own soul would not be so corroded. But then Don Jesús was of the faith and he hated even more than her husband. It was more than Doña Inez could understand. All she knew was that it was unnecessary for her to listen to the words spoken by Don Jesús and her husband.

The two men spoke in low tones. They talked about people who had been robbed and people who had been wounded and people who had been killed. They named the names. The names were names both of them knew well and they could have communicated with each other silently, simply by looking at each other. But they named the names as though those names and the savageries with which they were connected formed a personal liturgy, and no name and no event could be overlooked on the pain of committing a cardinal sin.

"Today is Marius' birthday," Oury said. "He would have been fifty. I can never think of Marius as fifty." He pulled on his cigar and let the smoke drift out of his lips. "It's strange. I can't even think of Marius the way he was when he came out here. Whenever I think about him I think of him as the kid I left back in Virginia." Oury looked at Don Jesús. "My God, that was a long time ago."

One of the Papago hands, Pacho, came into the ranch house at Tanque Verde and told Bill he smelled Apaches and Bill and his brother, Marius, who had come out West because Bill was there, got shotguns and went out to the corral. Doña Inez was in the house with their newborn baby, their first son. The baby was only a week old and still unnamed and was not strong but Bill knew the good ranch air would soon fix him up.

Bill and Marius and Pacho settled down at the corral, their shotguns loaded and in their hands. "Beats a duck blind any time," Bill said to Marius. Then he said to Pacho, "You sure your nose is working all right?" Pacho said he was sure.

They waited for about a half an hour and Bill had just about made up his mind that Pacho's nose had failed them that night when they heard the sound of an owl hooting. Bill stiffened. His own nose began to sniff. "Apaches," he whispered to his brother. "We'll let them kill a steer. While they're butchering it they'll be close together and they'll make us a nice target."

A few moments later they saw three Apaches walking toward the corral. Bill put a warning hand on his brother's arm. Marius was new to the West and he had no idea of the kind of ears Apaches wore. The Apaches went inside the corral and looked around cautiously and then one of them tossed a rope around one of the steers and led it off to a place about twenty-five feet from where Bill and Marius and Pacho were hunkered down. One of the Apaches pulled out a long knife and slit the steer's throat. Then the three Apaches set to work.

Bill touched Marius' arm again and both men stood up and fired at the same time. Then Bill and Marius and Pacho walked over to the Apaches. The Apaches were mostly in little pieces. Bill booted the largest piece. "Bury them," he said to Pacho, "before they begin to stink."

Bill heard a low whine and a soft thud and a small human sound and then the soft pounding of unshod hooves and when he turned his head Marius was already slumping to the ground. Bill caught him. The Apache arrow was through his neck. The obsidian point was out the other side. Marius tried to say something. He shook his head and closed his eyes and got heavy.

"Guillermo!" It was Doña Inez, calling from the house. Bill stared at his dead brother. Three or four Papago workers came up. They took off their hats and crossed themselves.

"Guillermo!" It was Doña Inez again. Bill took Marius in his arms and carried him to the house. He saw Doña Inez standing in the doorway. She was holding his newborn son the way he was holding his brother.

"When you fired your guns he cried and I went to him," Doña Inez said. Her tears fell on the baby's face. "Guillermo, your son is dead."

She did not seem to see Marius.

Bill Oury talked about that time. He could hear the wind blowing outside and he talked about that night. He had talked about it before and Don Jesús could repeat the story in every detail, but those memories were no different from prayers for the dead, and could not be told often enough.

Don Jesús listened gravely to his friend and it passed through his mind, as it had often before, how, in all the years of their friendship, in all their talking together of the things that had wracked their lives, Don Guillermo had kept so much of his past private. It was as though Don Guillermo's existence had begun on that spring day in 1856 when he and Doña Inez and their two little girls arrived in Tucson, just a short time before the Old Pueblo officially changed from Mexican to American hands. Very little of Don Guillermo's life before that time ever crossed his lips.

But Doña Inez had related some of those early events to her friend Doña Teresa, Don Jesús' wife, and Don Jesús knew of them, and he knew, too, why Don Guillermo remained silent about them.

Don Jesús knew about the years Bill Oury had fought Mexicans in Texas and in Mexico. He knew that Don Guillermo had been one of the Americans trapped in the Alamo and that the gringo Colonel Travis had sent out eleven men to get help for the beleaguered garrison. Don Guillermo was the twelfth and he managed to slip through the Mexican lines but he could get no help from anyone. Six days later the Americans in the Alamo were killed to the last man. But Don Guillermo never spoke of that.

And Don Jesús had learned how Don Guillermo had been captured in Mexico with 169 other Americans, and how Santa Anna, the Mexican president, had ordered them all to be shot, and then relented and said that only one in ten had to die. The Mexican *coronel* had an *olla* filled with beans, white beans and seventeen black beans, and the Americans who drew the black beans were lined up against a wall and the rest of the gringo prisoners watched them go down under a firing squad.

After that the survivors were all marched down to Mexico City and were thrown into dungeons, and when Don Guillermo was released, eighteen months later, the light almost blinded him. Don Guillermo never talked about that either. The only event of that part of his life that Don Guillermo ever talked about was how he had found Inez García in Durango just as she was about to enter a convent and how he had won her heart and how that was the most important thing that had ever happened to him.

No, Don Guillermo never talked about the days when his life was dedicated to killing Mexicans, and Don Jesús could understand his silence and the reasons for it. The hatred and the suffering of those days had run deep on both sides, and Don Guillermo had closed that book and Don Jesús respected that.

When Bill Oury finished his account of that night when both his brother and his only son died, the two men talked of other things the Apaches had done. They talked without anger. They talked about Apache Indians as gravely as other men in other places might discuss the Koran or the cabala or Hindu prescripts. They talked unhurriedly. Each word had value.

And when they finished their devotions and their whiskey they rose, refreshed in body and mind and soul, and departed from the house to visit the Congress Hall. This was Saturday and the saloon was not to be missed.

As they stepped onto Main Street in the oncoming twilight they heard a shot fired from the direction of the *Citizen* building. That did not alarm them. It was not unusual for someone to shoot at someone else, particularly on Saturday. As they walked closer to the newspaper office they saw some men gathered there and they saw that the shooting was being done by a man holding a copy of the newspaper in one hand and his gun in the other. He was firing bullets into the sky.

When they reached the corner half a dozen men began to shout at Bill Oury at the same time. Hiram Stevens, a leader in the community, called out, "Bill, goddamn it all, we just have to do something about this!"

He shoved the latest issue of the *Citizen* into Oury's hand, and as the man continued to make war on the heavens, Oury and Don Jesús read the lead story John Wasson had fashioned. By the time they were finished, the man had sent off his last shot and was looking at the ground despondently, his empty gun dangling from his hand.

Bill Oury raised his eyes from the newspaper and said to Don Jesús, "And you were disturbed because that fool officer let five squaws spend the night in his camp. Won't be long now before the whole damned tribe can move in."

△ △ △ THREE

△ 1

Before taking himself to the New World in search of fortune or at the very least fame, and finding neither in the Army, Sergeant Francis Xavier Clarrity had studied for one year at Trinity College in Dublin, which quite possibly made him the most highly educated man in uniform at Camp Grant. He kept this background secret, as though it were a blood taint; he feared that if it ever came to public attention he might be commissioned a second lieutenant. Sergeant Clarrity could easily see himself as a captain or even a major. Second lieutenancy was a purgatory he had no inclination to endure.

He detested, too, the common clichés about the Irish. He drank only moderately and when imbibing did not sing sentimental songs about the Ould Sod and he discouraged others from doing so. He also did not believe in leprechauns.

He looked somewhat Irish, with a fair skin and blue eyes and a longish upper lip, and he had an Irish cadence to his speech. He considered himself a practical, down-to-earth, no-nonsense noncom, but for a brief time on that bright, sunny, windy day toward the end of February, Sergeant Clarrity almost was persuaded to believe in black magic.

He was making his rounds, inspecting the guard late that morning. Lieutenant Robinson and a small party were on scout. Lieutenant Whitman was in his office working on the report he was required to forward to General Stoneman on exactly the last day of every month.

Sergeant Clarrity paused to watch off-duty men sporting in the San Pedro River at the rear of the enlisted men's quarters.

"Stop horsing around and get yourselves soaped and

cleaned," Sergeant Clarrity commanded. "Cleanliness is next to godliness, which is as close as any of you muckers will ever get."

He checked to make sure there were sufficient armed men guarding the bathers—it would be humiliating for a man to be shot down by an Apache when he was naked and with soap in his eyes—and he continued his tour. He was at the far end of the parade ground, just about where it debouched onto the Tucson Road, when he first saw them.

He was looking down the barrel of a guard's carbine, found it reasonably clean and tossed it back. He raised his eyes. One moment they were not there and the next moment they were. They had not been there that moment before, Sergeant Clarrity henceforth would swear.

There had been dust, blowing the stinging way dust blew on the infernal, godforsaken Arizona desert, and then they were there, about fifty of them, mounted on ponies, armed with guns and bows and arrows, feathers fluttering on their lances.

"Holy Mother of God," Sergeant Clarrity said. He was about to sound the general alarm when he saw that one of the Apaches, seated erect on the bare back of his pony in the forefront of the band, was holding up a white flag.

"Notify Lieutenant Whitman," Sergeant Clarrity instructed the guard, his eyes still on the Apaches on the other side of the Aravaipa Creek.

When the guard did not spring into action, Clarrity looked at him. The youth, hardly more than eighteen or nineteen, was as though transfixed. His eyes stared. His mouth was open.

"Move!" Sergeant Clarrity roared. He gave the man a push that sent him reeling. Then the man caught his balance and started running toward headquarters.

"Men!" Sergeant Clarrity called out in a voice that now was not loud but which penetrated halfway down the parade ground. "Men! To me!"

In a moment he had a dozen troopers at his side, all of them with rifles at the ready. Sergeant Clarrity did not draw his own revolver. He stood in front of his soldiers, arms akimbo, as though he would fight off an invasion of the post with his bare hands.

The Apaches made no attempt to come closer. They sat in stillness, their legs in the high Apache moccasins dangling against the sides of their ponies. The ponies were still as well, and the men and the animals, having emerged from nowhere, as though formed on the instant from alkali, now became part of that alkali, as rooted and inhered as other desert growth.

Sergeant Clarrity, who regarded wild flights of fancy as a deplorable Irish ethnic indulgence, had the weird feeling that it was not impossible that the Indians and their ponies and their lances with the waggling feathers could become as much a fixed part of the world outside the fort as the giant saguaros standing as sentinels next to them.

△ 2

Little Captain looked at the soldiers in the fort. He said, "Those men have guns."

Eskiminzin said, "They are soldiers. Soldiers have guns."

Santo said, "When will they use the guns on us?"

Eskiminzin said, "They will not, I think."

Little Captain said, "It is not an easy thing for soldiers to have guns and not use them on us."

Eskiminzin said, "We have the white cloth. They respect that."

Santo said, "They did not respect the white cloth with Mangas Coloradas. And there were others."

Eskiminzin said, "That is the truth."

Santo said, "Then why do we put trust in it here?"

Eskiminzin said, "They have not shot at us yet and now there are many of them there. They will not, I think."

Little Captain said, "And if they do?"

Eskiminzin said, "Then we will shoot back. But they will not, I think."

Little Captain said, "Why do you have faith in this, *nantan?*"

Eskiminzin said, "He sent the word with my mother for us to come here and talk."

Little Captain said, "Once we deliver ourselves to the soldiers they won't want to talk, maybe."

Santo said, "This man is right."

Eskiminzin said, "The women had good feelings about him."

Little Captain said, "He treated them well and then used them as bait."

Eskiminzin said, "My mother said this *nantan* has a good face."

Little Captain said, "Daya is an old woman. The sun has made her eyes tired, maybe."

Eskiminzin said, "Leave then. You are free to leave."

Santo said, "I will stay."

Little Captain said, "I will stay. I will see whether this *nantan* makes me feel good too."

△ 3

Lieutenant Whitman buckled on his cavalry sword.

"You could be making a mistake," Oscar Hutton observed.

"Always."

"Want me to go out there with you?"

"No."

"Could get a mite hairy out there."

Lieutenant Whitman straightened his tunic and put on his cap. "That's what Uncle is paying us for, isn't it?" He looked across the office at the Puma. The Puma was leaning against a wall. His eyes were half closed. "Ready?" Whitman asked.

The Puma stretched and started for the door.

"Might be smarter to wait until Lieutenant Robinson gets back," Hutton said.

"Tired men who spent hours scouring the desert for Apaches? And then finding them waiting for them here?" Whitman shook his head. "That damned well could blow the whole thing sky high."

"Where it belongs."

Whitman gazed at the guide intently. "Oscar, I have to give this a try. You're with me there, aren't you?"

"No."

"Oscar, if an Apache leader wants to talk peace I have to listen to him, don't I?"

"No."

"I know. Listening's dealing and I have no authority to deal. I know."

"Maybe they're just fixing to shoot you and then skedaddle, ever think about that? Maybe they know Lieutenant Robinson's out with a lot of men and the best horses. Maybe they figure they've got a cheap shot."

"In that event, Oscar, when Lieutenant Robinson returns, give him my compliments and tell him he is in command of Camp Grant."

△ 4

Little Captain said, "Two horsemen are coming."

Eskiminzin said, "One of them is the *nantan*."

Santo said, "How do you know that?"

Eskiminzin said, "My mother has said the face of the chief *nantan* is without hair."

Little Captain said, "The Mexican with the *nantan* carries a white cloth. No soldiers come with them."

Santo said, "The *nantan* is brave."

Eskiminzin said, "I will be as brave."

He kicked the sides of his pony. A nervousness like the trembling of leaves on quaking aspens passed over the Apaches as their chief rode away from them.

Eskiminzin and Lieutenant Whitman met almost in the dead center of Aravaipa Creek and almost equally distant from their men.

The Apaches now sat motionless on their ponies. The nervousness was contained now. Some of them clutched their lances and their guns more tightly but none of them shook.

Fifty or more soldiers were gathered at the foot of the parade ground. Clarrity had formed them into two lines and had ordered them to stand at attention. No man could understand why; showing that kind of respect to Apaches was peculiar. But each man obeyed. Clarrity stood in front of them in a brace. His gun was still in its holster.

Whitman was grateful for the Indian custom of not hurrying into discussions. It gave him time to size up the Apache.

He saw a stocky man with a dark face that held its even, strong features together compactly. The eyes were dark and somber and full on Whitman and unwavering. He appeared to Whitman to be in his forties, but Whitman could not be certain of that. He wore deerskin and moccasins that reached to his thighs and turned up in points at the toes. His hair was in two long braids and was streaked with gray and he wore a red turban around his head. There was a string of silver coins and little shells around his neck. There were turquoise bracelets on his wrists and the signs of Sun and Lightning were painted on his shirt.

Presently Whitman said to the Puma, "Speak to him."

The Puma spoke and the Apache replied in a voice that was low and quiet.

"He says his name is Eskiminzin," the Puma said.

"Tell him I am Lieutenant Whitman."

When the Puma spoke, Eskiminzin looked puzzled and he frowned and he turned and looked nervously at his men. When he spoke again his voice was harsh.

"This man says he can see that the *nantan* is a white man," the Puma said. "This man says that he gave his own true name to the *nantan*. This man asks why the *nantan* keeps his own true name from him."

"I never thought of that," Whitman said. "Explain to him that Whitman is my own true name."

Eskiminzin relaxed a little but he still seemed nervous.

"Ask him why he is here," Whitman said.

"He says he is here to talk peace."

"Tell him I welcome that. Tell him we will go to my headquarters and talk."

Eskiminzin raised his head sharply, like a deer scenting danger, when the Puma translated that. He spoke quickly.

"He says he will talk here," the Puma said.

"Tell him he will be safe in my headquarters. Tell him if we start walking toward peace we must begin with some trust." Whitman had the uncomfortable feeling that Eskiminzin's eyes were looking right into his head. When the Puma finished, Eskiminzin kicked his pony and rode back to his men.

"He will talk it over with them, Teniente," the Puma said.

Whitman shifted in his saddle to ease the ache in his hip. He felt the sun, dead weight on his head. He felt sweat starting to crawl down his back. He wondered what the hell he was doing out here.

He felt like a sitting duck. He had exposed himself before in his military life but never like this. He had never before felt quite so alone. He felt a thin line of fear stirring in him and he knew what one might do, unplanned and without will, from nerves. He hoped he would do nothing and that his men would do nothing. He had given orders to Clarrity for the men to hold tight unless the Apaches started something. He wondered what orders Eskiminzin had given to his fighting men.

And he wondered why he was sticking out his neck this way. Perhaps his father could have told him, or perhaps he already had.

"He gave you his name, Teniente," the Puma said. "That was a big thing." The Puma was leaning on his saddle horn. He looked sleepy.

"Why was that a big thing?" Whitman asked.

"Apaches do not give out their names. They believe when they give their name to someone they give that person power over them."

"And that's why he made such a fuss about my name."

"He believed he gave something important to you and that you were trying to fool him."

"Whitman . . White man," Whitman said. "Well."

Eskiminzin said, "The *nantan* wants to go into the fort to talk."

Little Captain raised his head sharply.

Santo said, "It is good to talk here."

Little Captain said, "I think it is foolish. Let us go away."

Eskiminzin said, "And what of the peace talk?"

Santo said, "He is right. We can talk another day."

Eskiminzin said, "The *nantan* says we must start with trust."

Little Captain said, "Shall I repeat the names? Cochise. Mangas Coloradas. Juan José. They all trusted and now two of them are dead and Cochise lives only to kill the white men who betrayed him and hanged his brothers and two nephews."

Some of Little Captain's words were overheard by the nearest Apache warriors and they began to tremble again but not from nerves.

After a while, Eskiminzin said, "I remember what the boy, Naco, told his mother. I remember each word because the words burned into my head when she repeated them to me. The boy said he was given food here and clothing and that he sleeps nights in the same place and he no longer is afraid he will be killed by soldiers when he sleeps. All of our children should be able to sleep that way, and their parents, too."

Whitman looked at Eskiminzin and then at the two men who returned with him. One was old, with white hair and a thin, ascetic face and eyes that seemed to have seen everything and were tired. The other man was small and young and coiled like a spring and his eyes sparkled with hostility and he kept his lips tight to hold back the anger behind them.

"These men will go onto the post to talk with the *nantan*," the Puma said.

"Clarrity!" Whitman did not turn his head.

The sergeant strode to the edge of the stream. "Sir!"

Whitman did not move his eyes from Eskiminzin. He knew it would be smarter to watch the small man with the baleful face but the chief's face held him.

"These three men are going onto the post with me for peace talks," Whitman called out to Clarrity.

"Sir!"

"The others will wait out here. Lieutenant Robinson is out somewhere in the direction of the Galiuros. Send out two couriers to find him and inform him of what is taking place here. I don't want him to come on these Apaches by surprise."

"Sir!"

"Then keep a sharp lookout for Lieutenant Robinson. As soon as you see him coming in send two more riders out to intercept him in the event the first two men failed to find him."

"Yes, sir!"

"Puma, repeat to these men the orders I have just given."

When the Puma finished, Eskiminzin spoke.

"This man agrees that what you have done is wise, and he will tell it to his warriors," the Puma said. "This man says that the other *nantan* is not scouting in the direction of the Galiuros. This man says Lieutenant Robinson is looking for Apaches near the Gila River."

Whitman looked at Eskiminzin. The Apache's face was impassive. "Clarrity!"

"Sir!"

"Tell the couriers to ride north. I have it on reliable authority now that Lieutenant Robinson is somewhere near the Gila River."

A few minutes later Clarrity bellowed: "Attention! Present arms!" Clarrity turned and saluted.

Whitman and the Puma and the three Apaches rode by the line of soldiers. As he touched his fingers to his cap Whitman wondered at the unsuspected reserve of grace that had caused Clarrity to consider it necessary, or even appropriate, to bring all the troops into the act, to enhance Whitman's stature, or that of the Apaches, or both.

He looked at the Apaches to see whether they were in any way conscious of the salute. The Apaches were not. The Apaches all were like uneasy animals now, their eyes darting everywhere, their heads twisting back and forth. They looked at everything and they saw everything. They were as restive as the half-wild ponies they sat on, sniffing the air suspiciously, ready to spook at an unexpected sound or sight, even the flying of a stray pebble. Even the old one, Whitman noticed, even the old one suddenly looked younger and alert and his eyes no longer were tired.

Whitman saw soldiers standing in front of buildings looking on curiously. He had ordered that the men keep their distance. There always was the chance of a drunk who might get careless. And there were civilians working on the post, many of them Mexicans, many of them with old grievances and long memories.

He saw Fred Austin and Oscar Hutton standing in front of the sutler's store. Hutton had just finished whittling a piece of wood to a sharp point. He stuck the knife back into its sheath and started picking his teeth, rocking back and forth on his heels.

△ 5

Inside the adobe building it seemed almost cool and, after the brutal glare of the sun, pleasantly dark. The three Apaches made two very quick circuits of the small office, their eyes scouring everywhere, as though seeking out possible assassins, and then, satisfied they were in no danger for the moment at least, they moved around more slowly, examining everything in the room.

Whitman ordered Duncan to set up three piles of folded blankets with one in the middle slightly higher than the other two, as the Puma had suggested to him earlier. Then Whitman turned to see Eskiminzin standing in front of a large wall map of the Arizona Territory. The Indian looked at it and moved on and then returned to it and looked at it again.

"That is a map of this land," Whitman said, walking over to the Apache.

The Puma had a little difficulty translating the word. He settled for "picture writing."

Whitman pointed. "This is Camp Grant, where we are. This is the Aravaipa Creek and the San Pedro."

As Whitman spoke he saw something cross over Eskiminzin's face. It was something more than nervousness. Now the other two men moved over to the map.

Eskiminzin pointed to a place on the map. Whitman noticed the Apache brought his finger close to the map but was careful not to touch it.

"That is Aravaipa Canyon," Whitman said.

When the Puma translated that the three Apaches looked at one another and their eyes became troubled and frightened.

Again Eskiminzin pointed.

"That is the Sulphur Spring Valley," Whitman said.

Eskiminzin moved his finger.

"Those are the Galiuros."

Eskiminzin moved his finger.

"That is Sonora, in Mexico."

By now the three Apaches were in a state of fear that appeared to be so profound that it went beyond the fear for their lives. Eskiminzin muttered something and Little Captain nodded and Santo, who appeared more disturbed even than the other two, stared at the map and his lips moved silently as though he were fortifying himself with prayer.

Whitman looked at the Puma questioningly.

"It is the map," the Puma said.

"I can see that."

"They are saying that this picture writing must give you power."

"Well."

"The old one just said that the markings on the map, the military symbols, are something like the markings on the sacred shirts of the shamans."

"Well," Whitman said again.

"Eskiminzin just said that the picture writing must give you power to destroy your enemies."

"I wish he'd spread that word around," Whitman said. "I wish he'd spread it around in a lot of places."

He looked at the three Apaches. They were still staring at the map. Whitman had the weird sense that if the Apaches were Catholics they would by now be crossing themselves.

"I will try to set them straight," the Puma said.

"You will do nothing of the kind," Whitman said. He saw that Duncan had set up the blankets. "Puma, tell these men that it is time to sit down and talk."

"Sir," Duncan said.

"Yes, Duncan?"

"Do you want me to remain here?"

Whitman paused in the act of unbuckling his saber. "Do you want to stay?"

"Yes, sir."

Whitman handed him the saber. "Fine."

The three Apaches sat down on the blankets. Eskiminzin saw the one pile higher than the others and took it. Whitman gave Duncan cigarettes to pass around. He sat down at his desk and lit a cigar and waited. He kept his tunic buttoned to the neck although the room, cooler than the outside, was very warm. The regimental posture was intended not so much to impress the Indians as to keep himself in hand. And for that same reason he sat flat down on the wooden seat of the chair although he often sat with more weight on the left hip to give the other rest. He once had had the thought to put a cushion on the seat. He had dismissed it immediately.

Whitman smoked his cigar and watched the Indians smoke several cigarettes. From time to time one or the other of the Apaches looked at the wall map.

"Who are these two other men?" Whitman asked.

The Puma spoke to Eskiminzin. "The old one is Santo," the Puma said. "He is an important shaman."

"What is that?"

"He's an Apache holy man. He is related to one of Eskiminzin's wives."

"How many wives has Eskiminzin got?"

"Two, only two."

"Two mothers-in-law?"

"Apaches have a very good arrangement with their mothers-in-law."

"What's that?"

"They never speak to them. It is forbidden."

"That is clever. Does it go both ways?"

"Yes."

"Hm. And the other one, the one who looks daggers at me?"

"He is Little Captain. He is the war chief to Eskiminzin."

"And the chief gave you those names freely?"

"It is not the same thing when one's name is given over by someone else. That does not give away any power."

"You know a great many things, Puma."

"A half of me is Apache."

"Which half?"

"The smart half, Teniente, I can tell you that."

Eskiminzin looked up. He raised his hand. Whitman peered at him closely. The Indian, he saw, had not just marked time while he sat there. He had reorganized himself. He had readied himself for his talk. When he spoke, his voice was deeper and more sonorous.

"I am the chief of the Aravaipas," Eskiminzin said. "I have been at war with the white people for many years, since that day when the boy lieutenant killed Cochise's brothers and two nephews."

He paused to allow the Puma to translate. While he waited he stared at the wall map. Little Captain and Santo kept their eyes on Whitman. When the Puma finished, Eskiminzin again looked directly at the officer.

"For many years my people have been running like dogs," Eskiminzin went on. His eyes were strong and unblinking. "We have no homes. We are chased by troops. We cannot put down our heads at night without fear that we will be killed. We cannot plant grain. We cannot make a *rancheria* where we can live for a season. We are hungry and sick of fighting and sick of killing. I am tired of that kind of life. I have done things the white man calls bad. I do not call them bad but the white man calls them bad. It is our way. It has always been our way. But now the time has come to change our way, I think. That is why I wanted to meet with the white father at this fort and talk to him. I want our children to be taught to live in peace and to raise cattle and live like white people."

Whitman considered the words. "Why doesn't the chief of the Aravaipas take his people to the White Mountain Reservation? They would be cared for there and they could live in the peace he desires."

Eskiminzin was silent after the Puma translated the words. The three Apaches continued to gaze at Whitman.

Whitman knew that as he was attempting to assess the Indians he himself was being judged. He knew that every move he made, every gesture, the sound of his voice as well as what he said, were being taken in in a slow and ancient process and were being evaluated and understood or misunderstood not only in another world but in another millennium.

"The White Mountain Reservation is not our country," Eskiminzin said. "Neither are they our people. We are at peace with them but we have never mixed with them. Our fathers and their fathers before them have lived in these mountains and have raised corn in this valley. We are taught to make mescal our principal article of food, and in summer and winter here we have a supply that never fails us. At the White Mountain Reservation there is none and without it we get sick. We have been in the White Mountains but the people were not content there. They said, 'Let us go to the Aravaipa and make a final peace and never break it.' "

"Why should I believe that to be true?" Whitman asked bluntly. It was the way his father, cannier than he, would have put the question.

"You have said before that the road to peace had to start with trust," Eskiminzin said. "The *nantan* spoke those words himself. I have trusted you. I am trusting you now. I am in your fort surrounded by your soldiers. Would the *nantan* have come into my camp without warriors?"

Presently Whitman said, "I am a lieutenant in the Army. I have no authority to make a treaty of peace."

He saw a stillness pass over Eskiminzin's face and he saw the Indian retreat into himself as though to compose himself for death. Santo stared off at a private vision, the last he might ever have. Little Captain looked from Eskiminzin to Santo and then he leaped to his feet brandishing his gun.

"Then why are we here!" he shouted.

"I cannot make a treaty of peace," Whitman said quietly,

feeling for his pistol. "But that does not mean I can do nothing."

Eskiminzin came back slowly over a small portion of the endless distance he had traversed. Santo turned away slightly from his vision. Little Captain held on to his gun but he lowered the muzzle to the floor and sat down again.

"If you cannot make a treaty of peace what is it you can do?" Eskiminzin asked.

"I have thought about this since your five women were here," Whitman said. "I do not want to promise anything I cannot do. What I can do is this: if you bring your people to the post and surrender as prisoners of war and deliver all your weapons to me, then I will locate you just outside the post and I will feed you and clothe you as best I can, and my soldiers will protect you until I can get instructions from my superiors."

When the Puma changed the words Whitman could see that instant when the interpreter came to the part about surrendering arms. The three Apaches raised their heads at the same time and Little Captain raised his gun a bit and Eskiminzin reached for his own gun. Santo made no other move. Santo was an old man again and had seen too much and listened to too much and he was too tired to go for a weapon.

As the Puma went on, Whitman believed he could see something more in Eskiminzin's face, something that once again went back across centuries, a memory, as though some ancestral wisdom had been tapped. There was fear in his eyes and a tiredness as well, as though he was weary of being tricked, of being betrayed, and, in the end, killed.

Whitman wondered whether he had blundered. Should he have persuaded Eskiminzin to agree to bring in his people before he told him that the weapons would have to be turned in? Would that have been smarter? Or tricky?

Santo spoke to Whitman for the first time. "Mangas Coloradas, the chief of the Mescaleros, believed the words of a white *nantan*. He was a star *nantan*. Mangas Coloradas believed him and went to the star *nantan*'s camp to talk peace and that night he was shot to death."

"I don't know anything about that." Whitman's side was

hurting badly now. He would have liked to get up and walk around.

Little Captain said, "Cochise believed the soldier boy *nantan*. The boy soldier hanged two of Cochise's brothers and nephews."

"If it was my intention to kill you, I would have done it without wasting time in talk," Whitman said. "I have told you of the only way I have the power to bring you to peace—to bring peace to you. You have heard me. Now you are free to leave here and return unharmed to your people."

Little Captain asked, "Why does the *nantan* not kill us?"

"I am tired of the killing as your chief is tired of it," Whitman said.

Santo said, "The white man brought together many Apaches and told them they would all be brothers and to celebrate he gave them a pinole party and in the pinole there was white man's poison and the Indians died. It was a special poison that left smiles on the faces after the men were dead. We were told after that never to trust."

"Then why are you here?" Whitman asked. It was like peeling off layers of skin. There was always something behind something else and perhaps it was late in the day to try to find a way to the bottom. The events that had produced the hatreds went back so far they were as fixed and eternal as the rocks.

Eskiminzin rose to his feet. He walked over to the wall map and studied it for a long time. Then he turned to Whitman and looked at him for a long time. The Indian's face seemed as fixed and eternal as the rocks as well.

Eskiminzin said, "I will think."

"Good."

Eskiminzin said, "I will talk to others and I will think."

Whitman stood up slowly. His side felt as though it were caught in a vise. "Think carefully. These may be the most important thoughts of your life."

Santo and Little Captain were on their feet by then and the three Indians looked at Whitman as though they expected something. He nodded to Duncan and the trooper opened the door. The Indians glanced at one another and then filed past Whitman out of the office.

As Whitman followed them he had a look at Duncan. He thought he discerned in Duncan's eyes a glimmering of something trying to emerge and make a mark on the unblemished landscape.

Outside the sun pounced on them all. The Indians climbed onto their ponies and Whitman lifted his boot to the stirrup. Duncan came running out of the office bearing his saber. He snapped it on and mounted. He thought his right hip was going to snap as well. Duncan sprang to attention and whipped a salute. Whitman returned the courtesy. The Puma slipped onto his horse and the five men rode slowly down the hot parade ground.

When they were about halfway down Whitman raised his head as he saw a clutter of dust outside the post and then he saw Lieutenant Robinson and his men riding past Eskiminzin's braves. The Indians were standing alongside their ponies, their weapons in their hands. A lance bearing a white flag was stuck into the ground.

Robinson and his men, dripping with sweat and covered with desert grime, halted outside the post to allow Whitman and the Apaches to pass by them. Robinson and the troopers straightened in their saddles and saluted and Whitman touched the visor of his cap. The three Apaches looked straight ahead.

Little Captain and Santo rode across the creek and joined the other Indians. Eskiminzin drew rein.

"This man who speaks our language," he said, pointing with his rifle at the Puma. "He speaks it well."

"He was kidnapped by Cochise from his village in Sonora when he was a child," Whitman said. "He lived with Cochise's people for many years before he escaped."

"He knows the customs."

"I believe he does."

The Puma exchanged the words tonelessly and indifferently, showing no interest in the fact that he was the object of discussion.

"He knows that after we sit down and talk to the white man it is the custom to give presents."

"He knows that."

"Has he told you of that?"

"I did not need to be told. When the five women came here I gave them cloth and tobacco."

"You gave nothing to us."

"Is that what you came here for?"

"Then we do not part as friends."

"Time will tell that. But that is not why I did not give the chief of the Aravaipas presents."

"Why did you not?"

Whitman pushed back his cap and wiped his forehead. The sun always seemed to loose its greatest anger before it made its departure for the day.

"Presents are for children and sometimes for women," Whitman said. "Presents are for bribery."

Eskiminzin raised his head slightly. The sun seemed to have no effect on him, on his bare head. But then they belong here, Whitman thought, and we don't.

"If anything is to be done," Whitman said, "what we must find, you and I, is wisdom."

The Indian stared at him again and again Whitman felt that he was seeing into his head and he felt he must not say anything that was not true as he understood it to be true. He thought again of his father and what his father had taught him, what had come from the harsh and unyielding earth where they had been born.

"It will mean something only if it is made with difficulty," Whitman said. It was hanging on him, his own albatross, the New England ethos that taught that anything that came easy was worthless.

After what seemed a very long time, even for Indian time, Eskiminzin said, "Heaven is above. Arizona is below."

The Apache kicked his pony's sides and the animal leaped forward as though stabbed. When Eskiminzin reached his warriors they were already mounted and they started off at once. Eskiminzin looked back. For a moment it seemed to Whitman that he was going to raise his rifle in farewell but the Indian trotted off without doing so.

"Well," Whitman said.

He looked at the Puma. The Puma never changed. The

Puma looked always as though he was just wakening or just falling asleep.

"What did you think of all that?" Whitman asked.

The Puma shrugged.

"What do you think of Eskiminzin?"

"He is not like Cochise."

"Is that good or bad?"

"When you look at Cochise you know right away he is
strong," the Puma said. "With Eskiminzin it takes a little time."

△ 6

"The sun eating at your skull, Royal?" Oscar Hutton inquired.
"Sitting in a room with three armed Apaches?"

"I don't imagine even Apaches would think they could kill
me and then shoot their way out of a fort full of soldiers," Whitman said dryly.

"That's where you just don't know Apaches," Hutton said.
"They generally do something and then the thinking, which
ain't much, comes afterward."

Whitman, Hutton and Lieutenant Robinson were sitting in
Whitman's quarters. There was an evening breeze and Whitman felt better. He felt quite good. He had reviewed in his
mind the meeting with Eskiminzin, going over it carefully, step
by step, and while he wouldn't have put down a bet, one way or
another, he thought it probably had come off about as well as
it could. He thought Eskiminzin might have a genuine concern
for the security of his tribe. He knew he would not like to have
Little Captain get the jump on him in the dark or at any other
time for that matter.

Lieutenant Robinson poured himself another drink from
Whitman's bottle. Lieutenant Robinson had had a good bath
in the San Pedro and was shaved and in clean uniform and he
was content with himself, a man who had done a hard day's
work and had earned a day's pay.

"In the end it may not be the Apaches who will gun you

down, Royal," Robinson said. "In this army it's safer to draw and quarter your great-aunt than to break regulations."

Whitman held his glass between two hands. He leaned forward in his chair. "How can anybody object to it, Bill? If I list them as prisoners of war?"

"I never try to fathom the powers above us," Robinson said. "Especially when one of them is named General George Stoneman."

"Amen," Oscar Hutton said.

"If we had a fight with them somewhere out on the desert," Whitman said, "and we brought them in, nobody could say that was wrong, could they? Nobody could say that was breaking any regulations, could they?"

Lieutenant Robinson emptied his glass and clicked his tongue. "When was the last time you heard of anybody taking a whole tribe of Apaches prisoners of war?"

Whitman sat back. He felt almost as alone as when he was in the middle of the creek talking to Eskiminzin.

Robinson refilled his glass and offered the bottle to Hutton, who accepted it. Robinson contemplated Whitman judiciously. "No, Royal, I think you have been very foolish. But in any case, I suggest again that you sit down immediately and write to the old man and get his official authorization for what you are doing, and, as I said before, in writing."

"But nothing's happened yet," Whitman said. "And Eskiminzin may never come back here."

Hutton drained his glass in a single swallow. "Pray for that, Royal, pray for that."

Δ 7

In the small hours of the next morning the fever, which had held off for several days, returned suddenly for new combat. Whitman tossed on his cot, drenched with sweat. His bones felt pummeled. He got up, shaking, and took a quinine tablet and washed it down with whiskey.

He looked at his watch. It was almost 3:30. He knew that

further sleep that night was out. He bathed his face and poured another drink and wrapped himself in his blanket and sat down shivering.

Maybe Bill Robinson and Oscar Hutton were dead right. Was he doing the proper thing? Why was he crawling out there on that limb? He had made over his whole life to get back into the Army and why was he jeopardizing his career and for what?

He drank some of the whiskey. His hand shook and he spilled some of it on his chin and it dribbled down his neck. He wiped his neck and wiped the sweat from his face and wrapped the blanket around him more tightly. His body burned and he was freezing and his bones hurt so much he wanted to cry out.

His mind spun like a whirlpool. His thoughts ricocheted inside his skull like spent slugs. He wiped his face again and he shivered and his thoughts went inevitably to the doctor-missionary Marcus Whitman.

As a child in Maine on his father's farm in Turner near the Androscoggin River, he had been taught by his parents to appreciate the writings of Ralph Waldo Emerson and to look with wonder and respect on the life and career of a distant cousin, Marcus Whitman. Marcus Whitman was a legend throughout the vast, sprawled-out Whitman clan. It was in 1835, when Royal Whitman was just two, that Marcus Whitman journeyed to unknown land in Oregon and established a mission for the Cayuse Indians and cared for them and worked for them and taught them for more than ten years.

Marcus Whitman wrote letters to the family and the letters were copied and recopied and sent from one Whitman to another and Royal Whitman read them until he knew them by heart, and sitting alongside the Androscoggin, he could look on the water and dream of a day when somehow, in some way, he would join Marcus Whitman in the West.

Other white people followed Marcus Whitman out there before Royal was quite old enough to do that. And in 1847 white pioneers brought with them, among other belongings of the white man, a white man's disease, measles. The disease spread in an epidemic among the Cayuse children.

Dr. Whitman worked tirelessly. But the terrible truth was

that the white man's medicine worked only for the white man's children. The white man's medicine proved useless for Indian children, exposed to the disease for the first time in their history. As their parents looked on in horror, the Indian children fell dead like flies.

And even after all the good years the Indians thought it was Marcus Whitman's doing, that it was a white man's trick, and they rose up against their benefactors.

And now, alone in the small morning hours in his quarters in Camp Grant in another part of the aboriginal West, Royal Whitman shook with fever and thought how Marcus Whitman had put faith in Indians and how he had fought for them all those years and for their rights and how for twelve years until that final catastrophe he had saved many of their lives and the lives of their children. Marcus Whitman trusted those Indians.

And what could he, Marcus Whitman's untutored, inexperienced cousin, what could he possibly know about the Indian mind and the way the Indian mind worked that Marcus Whitman had not known? And what was the last thought that passed through Marcus Whitman's mind when the Indian who was his friend clubbed him to death and broke open his head and killed his wife, and that was not enough for the others, who had to hack the bodies into little pieces and the bodies of twelve other white mission workers before they had enough?

Royal Whitman leaned back in his chair. The thing that had flailed his bones had fled as sneakily as it had attacked. He felt drained. But the ache was gone.

He finished his whiskey and looked at Rodriguez Gonzáles, burnished and gleaming in the moonlight. Rodriguez Gonzáles, along with Marcus Whitman, knew the answers but neither of them was saying.

△ △ △ FOUR

△ 1

Place wasn't the same since Gil was gone. Looked the same, of course, and sure enough smelled the same but wasn't the same at all. Oh, Jim Lee was a good enough officer and knew his business but he wasn't the same as Gil neither and he was brand-new to the West.

Bill Oury watched the wagon train move slowly into the Quartermaster Depot at Camp Lowell. The line of wagons drawn by six-mule teams was strung out and the end of it could not be seen and not just because of the dust. Bill Oury was not a fanciful man particularly but it wasn't hard at all for him to imagine that the wagons were not separate things but were instead different segments of a single creature, jointed, meandering, another laboring anachronism abandoned to eternity at some remote time along with the Gila monster and other leftovers. It made its own world of dust and shouting and cursing and smells and balky mules and whip cracks like rifle shots, and its head was already at Camp Lowell while its body twisted and twitched and humped outside the walls of Tucson and its tail lumbered along miles south on the open desert that gave it its sustenance and passage.

There were more than one hundred wagons in the train and they carried more than four hundred tons of Government supplies to feed and clothe and arm and treat and cure the troops who manned the outposts of the Territory. The stores had started their journey thousands of miles away in the East and had been freighted and shipped to the Mexican port of Guaymas, in Sonora, and then had been loaded onto the wagons and hauled up to Tucson on a trail that was so vulnerable to Apache attack that permanent arrangements had been made with the

Government of Mexico to provide military escorts to the border, where the task of guarding against the hostiles was taken over by American soldiers.

And now the wanderyear of this caravan was ended and the wagons were disgorging themselves and the drivers were complimenting themselves that once again they had beaten the odds and were still alive.

Uncle Billy Oury leaned on his saddle horn, his hat pulled low over his eyes, the smoke from his stogie drifting upward in the windless air, and he watched the crates and boxes and cartons being unloaded by men almost drowning in their own sweat. He listened to the sweet music made by the infinite and sometimes original blasphemies of the mule skinners and he saw a mule take a casual and disinterested kick at a man who wandered too close to its rump and he listened to the orders shouted by lieutenants and sergeants and civilians of importance.

It was a heady scene and he never tired of smelling and listening and watching. He had very little love even now for Yankee soldiers, although his daughter was married to one who had until the year before commanded this depot, but he was always pleasured and gratified and reassured by this scene. Because each box, each cardboard carton, whether it contained guns or crackers or canned peaches, testified to the existence of uniformed men who would continue to need guns and crackers and canned peaches, and clothing and boots.

And this was only a part of it, this beast that had dragged itself up the miles from Mexico. This was what had come in this day, though it would be many days before the final wagon found its destination and the last package was taken down. But there was more, there always was more. Other wagon trains loaded with goods came in from California through Yuma City, and that would be for another day, and more mules and shouts and glorious confusion.

And all together that was only a part of it, too. Because while much of the furnishing and stocking and equipping of the troops had by necessity to come from the Government and from the outside—no guns or bullets or artillery pieces were manufactured in Tucson and there was no factory there to can beans—still there was plenty left for the local merchants to sell for the nourishment and well-being of the uniformed men.

The two channels were bound together, were inextricable, and the size and proportions of this tired train marked the size and proportion of the Tucson end of the business, the local goods, the fresh food and hay and barley and grain and beef, that was supplied to those same uniformed men in their isolated fortresses.

The end of the Civil War—or as Bill Oury, the unreconstructed rebel, insisted on calling it, the War Between the States—had brought prosperity to Tucson, and it was all there before him, to look at and to listen to and to smell.

The cavalry was returned to the Territory and posts and forts and camps were built. Tucson was named as the Quartermaster Depot for the Territory, supplying the outlying posts, Cameron, Wallen, Bowie, Grant, Apache, Crittenden and others. The Quartermaster Department, with its limitless contracts and bottomless purse, was greeted as beneficence from heaven for worthy pioneers.

The men who were advantaged by the military largess worked hard for that. They came to be known as the Ring but only among those excluded from the privileged circle. These Ring members were the solidest men in the Territory and the Army dealt almost exclusively with them and with certain ranchers and farmers. They had all worked like hell for what they had gotten and the hell with those who were too weak or who came along too late to climb aboard.

And the more savage Apache warfare became the more soldiers were sent to Arizona—at least up to now—and the more supplies were needed and the busier the chosen merchants and the ranchers and the farmers were and the wealthier they became.

"Funny thing," Bill Oury had once commented to Don Jesús, "whatever we think about Apaches, those pirates are making us rich."

"Very funny, yes, Don Guillermo," Don Jesús had replied.

Oury quickly recollected himself. "I didn't mean that, Don Jesús. You know what I mean."

Bill Oury smoked out his cigar and then rode over to the office of Colonel James Lee. He had gone to the depot that day for a reason. The arrival of a new train always made holiday enough but this time there was something else and something that wasn't nearly as heartening. The whole town was talking about nothing else but General Stoneman's report, the one the *Citizen* had printed in good part, and Bill Oury figured he might be able to find out a little more about it. If his son-in-law were still there he sure as hell would have turned up an extra fact or two but he wanted to see what he could find out anyway. And he could let off a little steam.

△ 2

Colonel Lee pushed over a box of cigars. The box was one of the first items taken off one of the first wagons to be unloaded. Colonels have their perquisites and quartermaster colonels have particular perquisites in their own depots.

Colonel Lee was a large, expansive man, who, as Bill Oury had noted before, knew his job. The colonel did not greatly relish the way that job had to be performed in Tucson nor did he much appreciate the local merchants he had to deal with. But he was a soldier and he obeyed orders. When things seemed to him to get a little too raw, he reminded himself that he was in raw country.

"Quite a load out there," Oury said, lighting up.

"I've got another train, eight wagons, due in any day now from Fort Yuma," Colonel Lee said. "It's going to be close, unloading this outfit before the other one pulls in."

Oury listened to the yelling and swearing outside and the braying of mules. It was the best music he knew.

"It's good, Jim," he said, cocking his head. "It has a good sound, all that noise out there." He got up and walked to the window. The air was blue with dust and cursing. "It's alive, Jim. Tucson's come a long ways. Ten years after Inez and I pulled in here there were still only six hundred people in Tucson. Now, they tell me, there's more than three thousand."

He walked back to the desk and sat down. "I know how busy you are, Jim, but I'm not just beating my gums. I'm worried. I'm worried about what might happen here."

"You're referring to that newspaper story," Lee said.

"How true is it, Jim, that report by Stoneman?"

"I don't know. I read the story in the *Citizen*, that's all."

"No talk inside the Army?"

"I've heard some."

"Like what?"

"More or less what the paper said."

"Damn!" Oury hit the desk with his fist. "Christ Almighty, Jim, that man must be a blistering idiot." He waved his hand. "Of course you can't say anything against him, Jim, I know that, and I wouldn't respect you if you did. But, Jim, if he closes down all those forts and depots what's going to happen to the poor souls in the Territory?"

"I can't answer that, Bill."

"It's just that Stoneman doesn't know this country. And he sure as hell doesn't know Apaches. He talks about them being worse off now than they were twenty years ago. What the hell does he know about that? He didn't see any service out here twenty years ago. He just passed through a couple of times. Where the hell does that give him any right to pass judgments?"

"I cannot speak for General Stoneman, Bill."

"You think Apaches are harmless?"

"Obviously not."

Oury nodded and rubbed his beard. "Everybody knows they're worse now than they ever were. That bastard Cochise does just about what he damn pleases. All the rest of them, they all do as they please. And there's one thing about Apaches that your General Stoneman doesn't understand at all. Whenever the Army quits, quits anything, quits a fort, quits a depot, quits an area, the Apaches think it's because they drove the soldiers away."

Colonel Lee leaned forward. "Go on, Bill."

"You see, Jim, when the fighting started between the states —what you Yankees call the Civil War—all the troops were pulled out of here and sent back East. I was here then. I was the local agent for the Butterfield Stage people.

"And you got to understand, Jim, that the Apaches didn't know anything about the war going on back there. They didn't know the soldiers were taken away so they could fight in that war. No, the way the Apaches worked it out was that they had whipped the soldiers good and proper, that they had beat the hell out of them and had driven them out of the country. And then the Apaches took over.

"Cochise put everything together. His own Chiricahuas and the Mescaleros with their murderous chief Mangas Coloradas. Mangas is dead now, thank the Lord. The soldiers were smart enough to get him inside a military post and shoot him. Do you know what his name meant, Mangas Coloradas? It meant Red Sleeves. You know why they called him that? Every time he killed somebody he rubbed his arms in the blood. That's the kind of animals they are, Jim, all of them, the Tontos and the Pinals and the White Mountain Apaches and the Aravaipas, with their chief, the worst devil of them all, Eskiminzin."

The voicing of the Apache's name brought about the automatic reflex and Bill Oury turned his head to spit. He realized where he was and swallowed the saliva. He almost gagged on it.

He was silent for a little while and Colonel Lee saw it all in his face, all the things Oury had said and the things he had not said, all there, burning inside of him, pinching his face with hate.

Oury let out his breath slowly. "And that's what they're going to think now, Jim, that the Army is closing down those forts because the soldiers were whipped. And then all hell is going to break loose. If you think it's been bad up to now, you just wait and see what will happen then."

He slumped in his chair and listened to the sounds outside, as though those sounds gave him assurance that it would not happen just yet. Colonel Lee smoked his cigar silently. He was a busy man and he was especially busy that day, but although he could not openly take a stand against the commanding general, he thought Bill Oury made sense, and if he did not like Oury very much personally he believed Oury also was making sense for all the other people who lived in Arizona.

"Who can get to this man, Jim?" Oury asked. "Can anyone

sit down and talk to him? Is he so damned hidebound and stiff-necked that he won't listen to anybody? Far as I can find out he hasn't talked to one single settler here. He holed up in Fort Whipple for a couple of months with his yes-men all around him and then he took off for his little hideaway in California and he's handed down recommendations for this and for that as though he was some kind of a tin god. It's scary, Jim. You can't even reach the man."

"He's due back in Arizona," Colonel Lee said. "I know that."

"For a fact?"

"Yes."

"Well, maybe that's something. Maybe if he spends a little time here and sees what's going on, maybe he'll change his mind. Only an idiot pure and simple could spend any time moving around the Territory and then go on record saying the Apaches are harmless. And whatever else he is, I really don't suppose he's an idiot, I really don't believe that. So maybe there's a prayer."

He stood up. "I'm sorry to have taken so much of your time, Jim, and I'm grateful to you for listening to me. I'm just so damned worried. You know, generals like Stoneman, they just pass through here. Whatever length of time they serve, a year, more, less, they're just passing through. None of them take any root here; my own son-in-law has moved out with my daughter. All of them, the generals and the colonels and the rest of the officers and the men, they're just passing through.

"They're our own Army, but they're like an army of occupation. It's like they were sent out to Arizona by some foreign power, to serve their time and then to move on. But this is my home, Jim, and it's the home for a hell of a lot of good people, and the Army and the Government have to understand it that way. We're not a foreign colony. We're part of the United States, just like any other place in the country. Isn't there some way we can get this through to Stoneman or anybody else?"

He held up his hand as though to ward off an answer or possibly to stop himself.

"I'm shooting off again." He picked up his hat and his

face darkened and tightened hard. "Goddamn it to hell, Jim, why does a stranger like George Stoneman have the right to pass sentence on us?" He paused. "Stop by and have a drink with me soon."

"I'll do that, Bill." Lee stood up and extended his hand. "If I find out any more I'll let you know."

Oury shook the hand. "I'd appreciate that, Jim."

"Take a couple of cigars."

"Thanks." Oury shook his head.

"There are more where they came from, Bill."

Oury grinned and took three or four cigars and shoved them into his pocket. "Thanks," he said again. "Sorry to have taken all this time."

"Anytime, Bill," Lee said. He was not being hypocritical. It was one of his functions to know what was going on among the civilians and if anybody could tell him about that it was Uncle Bill Oury.

He watched Oury walk to the door. Oury opened the door and the noise from the outside poured in. Oury stood at the threshold for a moment or two as though he would say more but then he walked out and shut the door behind him.

Army of occupation . . . Colonel Lee shook his head. He had heard that Bill Oury had been one of the most fanatical of Rebs during the late war and maybe Federal troops did strike him as an army of occupation.

△ 3

"You must be getting old, you old mountain bear, you take everything so damned seriously."

Leslie Wooster laughed. He was a big man, a bear of a man himself, and he had a big laugh that filled a room and made everybody else want to laugh with him. His wife, Trinidad, seemed small next to him. She was small, the way most Mexican women were small, but she appeared even smaller next to him, and she was always watching him and listening to him as though she were afraid that because he was so big he would do something unexpected. She was always afraid that when he did things ordinary-sized people did something terrible would happen. As when he sat down or pounded a table or clapped a man on the back.

"You old horse thief," Bill Oury said. "You old horse thief."

"Look at your face," Wooster commanded. He had a voice that sounded as though it came out of the earth itself. "If it was any longer you'd trip on your chin."

"You old horse thief," Bill Oury said again. "Don't know why you're so damned happy." Then he said, "Congratulations to you both."

"It is not correct to congratulate the bride, Guillermo," Doña Inez said. "It is always the groom who is the fortunate one and in this case that is especially so."

Bill Oury had found his friend, a young rancher from near Tubac, in the house when he returned from the depot. Wooster and Trinidad Aguirre had lived together for three or four years but her religion and a priest or two finally had caught up with her.

"You old horse thief, what are you doing up here?" Oury asked.

"We're on our honeymoon," Wooster replied.

"What?"

"A honeymoon. Isn't that what you're supposed to do after you get married?"

"Honeymoon!" Bill Oury started to laugh. He didn't know why it struck him so funny. Maybe it was just that after the visit to Colonel Lee he either had to laugh or go out and shoot somebody.

"What the hell is so funny about that?" Wooster asked.

"Honeymoon . . ." Oury laughed so hard he had to sit down. He laughed sitting down and the chair shook.

"What is so funny about that, Guillermo?" Doña Inez said. "And that reminds me, we never had a honeymoon."

Bill Oury was laughing so hard now his eyes were tearing. He wiped them and snorted a couple of times and shook his head.

"After all these years a honeymoon is pretty funny all by

itself," he said. "But to come to Tucson . . ." He shook his head and started to laugh again. "Tucson, for a honeymoon . . ."

Bill Oury breathed out heavily and for a moment his face grew somber but then he scratched his beard and made himself smile and he started to pour drinks.

"How'd you get her to marry you, you old horse thief?" he asked Wooster, knowing all about how the priests down in Tubac had been after Wooster for a long time to regularize his household. "Wait, maybe I better ask Trinidad. How come you decided to make an honest man out of this bum?"

Doña Trinidad laughed. She was hardly more than twenty-one or twenty-two and she looked younger than that. Her laughter was a series of tinklings, like small bells, and she had the habit of covering her mouth with her hand when she laughed, the way Oriental women did. She was pretty and Oury thought that right now she looked prettier than ever, and why not?

"How'd you do it?" he asked again.

"Guillermo," Doña Inez said softly.

When Oury returned from the depot he had found his wife and Doña Trinidad chirping away in Spanish but he knew that Wooster, after all this time, still didn't know the language much and so he kept the conversation this side of the border.

"Never mind," Oury said, passing out the drinks, whiskey for Wooster and himself, wine for the ladies. "Never mind. It's over and done with." He raised his glass. "Well, God bless you both, God bless you."

After a while Oury asked, "Things quiet down your way?"

"If you can call it that," Wooster said.

"You going to stay down there?" It was an old question and Oury knew what the answer would be because Wooster was a stubborn man.

"It's our home," Wooster said.

"You ought to move up here."

"It is our home," Doña Trinidad said.

Oury looked at her and then at his wife. He loved to listen to them. Their voices were always so soft, like velvet. Their voices were soft even when they spoke in English. He remembered the sounds of some of the voices when he had been marched down the length of Mexico tied by rope to another man. Even then there were voices soft and filled with compassion and which bade God have mercy on the poor gringos.

"What are you going to do up here?" Oury asked. "I mean what's going to make this into a honeymoon instead of just another old trip to Tucson?"

"We're going to buy things," Wooster said. "We're going to buy some pretty nothings for Trinidad and she says it's about time I had a new suit. We're going to buy things and eat some food and have fun."

"You make him spend, Trinidad," Oury said.

He looked at Wooster. Wooster was about twenty-eight or so, he reckoned. He still shaved his face clean. He was the kind of twenty-eight-year-old Oury would have relished to have had as a son. He wondered how many more Woosters there were around. Maybe if there were enough Arizona might still stay in the hands of civilized men despite anything the Stonemans would do.

"You make him spend," Oury said again. "He's known to be a snug man with the *dinero* but you make him spend."

"My husband is always generous," Doña Trinidad said.

"And any time he starts beating up on you, you remember you have a home here in Tucson," Oury said. "You hear?"

"Thank you, Guillermo," Doña Trinidad said.

"I love you child," Oury said.

"I love you too, Guillermo."

Doña Inez put down her wineglass and stood up. "I think it is better to have something to eat before this fierce old man starts to weep."

She slipped her hand under Doña Trinidad's arm and the two women left the room with their heads together, whispering to each other.

"They sound like a couple of doves," Wooster said.

He got up and poured himself another drink. He sat down again. The chair creaked. He wrapped his hand around the glass. The hand was so big that it hid the glass, and when he lifted the glass to his mouth, it looked as though he were drinking out of a cupped hand.

They could hear the women in the kitchen.

"Like a couple of doves," Wooster said.

△ △ △ FIVE

△ 1

This was daybreak, the best time of day, before the sun got up and ruined it. It was light enough and still cool and the color all around was right, the way it was supposed to be, before the sun bleached it out. A person could breathe and look around and didn't have to squint.

Surveying the men, listening to them announce their identities, Whitman pondered the question of whether to continue the schedule of Reveille and Stable Call and then Breakfast Call, as it normally was done, or whether to try Reveille and then Breakfast and then Stables. One post commander had tried switching things around and he reported the men worked better. Whitman told himself he would have a talk with Sergeant Clarrity.

The men stood Reveille on the parade ground and told off their names into the reborn morning, shouting as though to reach whoever was sitting in judgment, proclaiming they were not sick and not wounded and not drunk and not deserters and were prepared as they had taken an oath to do to fight the day, the little routine fights and the big fights if it happened that way. Having made this renewed oath of fealty to their liege lord, they were dismissed and sent to their quarters to put on their white canvas stable clothes in preparation for Stable Call, the malodorous, ammoniac daily chore that could not make for a good appetite for the first meal of the day, although that perhaps was not altogether a disservice to the men.

It was a question all right. Shoveling horse shit and mule shit and then going in to eat, or the other way round?

After that it would be another routine day: Sick Call at 6:45 A.M.; Fatigue Call at 7; Drill Call at the same time for those not assigned to fatigue duties; Recall from Drill, Adjutant's Call, Guard Mount—all at a fixed hour and a fixed minute, the map of the day, the handholds that gave men order and purpose and perhaps sanity in a place that appeared to have call for none of them. Each man always knew what he would have to do on the post at any given time of any given day and that perhaps reaffirmed to him that he still owned membership in a human race, up to that moment when he might be arbitrarily called upon to relinquish it.

As the men broke ranks, Clarrity looked at Whitman questioningly. Clarrity was a little shaky himself from a tussle with the fever. Whitman nodded to the sergeant, who saluted and marched off, his square back itself an act of defiance, and then in the clear, still light, as yet undamaged by the sun, Whitman saw over the heads of the dispersing men a movement on the desert that crowded in on the far end of the parade ground, movement that was like a wave, as though the land itself were flowing, and he saw that the movement was that of men on ponies, and at the far side of the wash, in the same place they had staked their claim the first time, the Indians came to an abrupt halt, and the dust filtered down and they sat their ponies stiffly, a white flag held aloft, as though awaiting a command.

He came back, Whitman thought. He thought about it and he talked about it and he came back. And this time I am mounted and ready for him.

Whitman heard a movement near him and he saw that the Puma had swung into a saddle and was joining him. The Puma's face told him nothing, not whether the return of Eskiminzin and his warriors was good or bad.

Lieutenant Robinson came out of his quarters smoking an early-morning cigar. "Look what we have here," he said. "Get rid of them, Royal."

"I don't believe I can do that."

"Send them packing."

"I gave him my word."

"Your word—to an Apache?"

Whitman rode slowly down the parade ground past men who had arrested themselves in their stroll to the stables, who speculated that an unexpected miracle might keep them from there that day. When Whitman reached the end of the parade ground he saw Oscar Hutton standing there, picking his teeth.

"You didn't pray hard enough, son," Hutton said. As Whitman moved on toward the creek, Hutton said, "Maybe you didn't pray at all."

△ 2

As Whitman rode toward the creek he saw Eskiminzin detach himself from his men and ride to meet him. He stopped his horse in the middle of the stream. The Puma reined in alongside him.

Eskiminzin rode into the stream. He looked at Whitman for a long time and then he frowned. "It is not the same as when we last met," Eskiminzin said.

Whitman said, "I don't know."

"The *nantan* has had time to think," Eskiminzin said.

"Yes."

"The trust has gone."

"It is not that simple."

"It never was simple," Eskiminzin said.

"No." He stared at the Apache. "You have not changed?"

"I am here."

"Do you still want to surrender yourselves?"

"I came here to do that. Now I am not sure."

"I understand. And yet, we cannot avoid this."

Whitman waited for a sign he knew never would come. The Apache sat on his pony placidly. He gave Whitman nothing. And yet, and yet, the officer thought, he had not taken anything away, backed off a little, yes, but no more than that.

"I have thought about this, Eskiminzin," Whitman said, calling the Apache by his name for the first time. "I have thought about it as you have thought about it. I have talked about it as you have talked."

"And you have been told it is stupid."

"Yes, I have been told that."

"You are alone in wanting this."

"Yes."

"And I am alone among my people."

"I'm sure of that."

"Your people do not trust, my people do not trust," Eskiminzin said. He gazed at Whitman. "Now we must decide. Do we do what our people believe is wise or what we believe is wise?"

After a moment, Whitman said, "I wish I had as much as that. I wish I had wisdom." He was silent for several moments. "I know that it is wrong to kill without cause. We have both had cause. I think perhaps that cause can be removed or, at the least, reduced. I do not believe it is necessary that we go on killing one another."

"And the others, there in the fort?"

"I am in command here."

Eskiminzin looked into Whitman's eyes. "There are no laws to tell us what to do. There are no rules. White men have betrayed Indians. Indians have betrayed white men. There is nothing to tell us what to do. There is nobody to say but you and me."

"Do you believe you can trust me?"

"I think you are not bad. I do not know yet whether you are good but I believe you are not bad."

"I think it will be difficult, Eskiminzin. I have many doubts. I think things will happen that we will wish did not happen."

"The *nantan* speaks as though he is certain we will try."

"We must try. That part is quite simple. There was a reason you came here. There was a reason I was here to listen to you. We must try."

Eskiminzin looked back at his warriors and then he gazed at the soldiers who were clustered at the entrance to the fort and then he looked at Whitman.

"If we deliver ourselves to you as prisoners and surrender our weapons we will be protected," Eskiminzin said. His eyes were troubled and uncertain and it seemed that just voicing the question warned him of the peril.

"Your people will be safe."

"Our women and our children?"

"They will sleep at night as safely as my own men in their quarters."

Eskiminzin stared at Whitman in a kind of agony and Whitman took the pain as his own and he had a profound sense that something had stopped and that something had started and that nothing again would be the same.

In the start of that new time Eskiminzin raised his rifle and tossed it to Whitman. There was a cry from the Apache men as Whitman caught it. The agony was in Eskiminzin's eyes still and Whitman saw that it was something that could almost not be borne.

"Kill me," Eskiminzin said. "If you are going to kill, kill me now."

"I am not going to kill you."

"Do not lie to me. If you are going to kill me, do it now."

"I do not lie to you, Eskiminzin. I am not going to kill you."

Eskiminzin shivered and lowered his eyes. He looked naked and helpless without his gun. Something was gone from him, Whitman knew. In the end, if they were lucky, it might be reckoned as only a small sacrifice, but now it was a castration.

He wondered if he could have done what Eskiminzin had done. He wondered what if, ultimately, it proved useless.

Eskiminzin raised his head and touched the sides of his pony and rode across the rest of the stream to the fort. He looked for a long while at the men gathered there and then he turned and looked back at his men across the Aravaipa. He dropped off his horse.

A soldier ran out of the fort and took the reins of the horse from the Apache, and Whitman, riding up, was surprised to see that the man who performed this act of courtesy was his striker, Colin Duncan.

Eskiminzin picked up a stone and carried it to where the parade ground began. Dismounted, the Apache seemed undersized and even more defenseless. The troopers watched him curiously and some of them looked at him with hatred. Friends had been killed and wounded and what a prize he would be, and no question about it, with him in hand or, better, dead, the odds on any one of them dying of old age would be just that much better. He was so close a man could reach out and kill him with his own bare hands.

Eskiminzin swept his eyes over the men again and his nostrils flared slightly, as though he could smell the loathing all around him, and then he placed the stone on the ground carefully. He remained bent over it for a countable period of time and then he straightened and turned to Whitman. There was something else now in the Indian's eyes and Whitman would have given much to see just a little more light there, just a little more light.

"I and my chiefs have faith in you," Eskiminzin said in a low voice. "You have spoken to us like men and not like dogs. I will bring my people here to you, and so long as this stone shall last, so long shall I keep the peace with you and your people."

Whitman watched Eskiminzin mount his pony and start back across the stream where his men were waiting. The Indian's shoulders were bowed and his empty hands dangled at his sides. The warriors rode off and when the dust dropped they were gone.

Whitman could hear Marcus Whitman now. He could hear Marcus Whitman saying, *"They're Indians, don't trust them; they live by their own code, don't trust them."* He could hear Marcus Whitman saying, *"They're good people; they're simple to our ways but they're good people, have faith in them . . ."*

△ 3

As soon as he returned to his office Whitman sent Duncan out to fetch the Puma. Duncan was going through a change of his own. It was on Whitman's tongue to say something about his running out and holding Eskiminzin's reins, but he decided against pushing it.

The Puma entered the office walking lightly on the balls of his feet. He looked around quickly, searching out every part of the office. It didn't matter where he was, Whitman knew, in an arroyo or in the post commander's office. The Puma had to know what surrounded him, how many living things there were, everything.

Satisfied that he had to deal only with Whitman, that there were no surprises, the Puma took a chair and rolled and lit a cigarette and waited for Whitman to speak.

"What did you think about all that?" Whitman asked.

The Puma breathed out smoke and shrugged.

"What did you think?"

The Puma contemplated his cigarette as though he had never seen one before. "It may be good."

"And it may be very bad?"

"You and Eskiminzin talked. That was good. But the others, the soldiers, the Apache warriors, they have not talked to one another."

"What have the soldiers been saying?"

The Puma shrugged again. He appeared to find it odd that a cigarette, once lit, burned.

"I am not asking you to be an informer," Whitman said. "I don't want names. I just want to have some idea of what the men are saying."

"Soldiers do not love Apaches," the Puma said.

"No, of course not." Whitman sat back and took out a cigar. "And that goes both ways."

"Eskiminzin is strong. His people obey him."

"On that side of the line it's all Eskiminzin, isn't it?"

"There are those subchiefs. Little Captain. Santo, the shaman. Others. But they will probably do what Eskiminzin says. They have their own clans but where the tribe is concerned they probably will do what Eskiminzin says."

"Probably, you say?"

The Puma shrugged again. "There are always men around who will do what they will do."

Whitman lit his cigar. "What a thing that would be," he said to himself.

"What thing, Teniente?"

Whitman smiled. He had forgotten about the Puma's ears. The Puma could hear a fly crawling up a wall.

"I was thinking to myself," Whitman said. "I was thinking what a marvelous thing it would be if I could learn to speak Apache. Even just a little bit of it."

The Puma's eyes widened a little more than was usual and for the moment he forgot about the cigarette.

"It is nothing against you, you understand that, Puma," Whitman said. "But how marvelous it would be if I could understand some of the words out of his mouth, if I could speak to him directly."

"It could be done, Teniente, in time," the Puma said.

"And we might have that time," Whitman said. "We might just have that time." Whitman leaned forward. "Puma."

"Yes, Teniente."

"You are truthful with me."

"I try, Teniente."

"Puma, have I made any mistakes?"

"In what way?"

"With Eskiminzin. There are taboos, wrong things, offensive things to any race of people. If one is dealing with someone as alien as an Apache—an Apache chief—it's easy to say something wrong or to do something wrong. Have I done anything like that so far?"

"I do not believe so, Teniente."

Whitman stood up and began to pace. "I want to know about those things, Puma. It's not that I want to get involved. I don't want to get too involved. I don't want to get in too deep. But I would like to see this work and I don't want to be stupid about anything. You know about these things. You must help me. You must teach me."

The Puma occupied himself rolling another cigarette. "No one ever asked me to do that," he said.

"You told me about the business with mothers-in-law," Whitman said. He paused and looked down at the Puma. "That was amusing, but it's something to know. There are other things not so amusing. The guns, for instance."

"The Apache guns, Teniente?"

"I don't want to send a squad of soldiers out there to demand the guns once these people settle in. Some Apache hothead might just take it the wrong way and that would be the end of it before it started."

"A soldier could have a hot head too, Teniente."

Whitman slapped his desk. "Exactly. As far as Apaches are concerned, you might say, soldiers have been trained to have hot heads."

"Eskiminzin agreed the weapons would be turned in."

"It was the chief condition, Puma. You gave my words to him and his words to me."

"Then he will decide how it will be done. He will have council with his leaders and then he will decide how he will do it."

Whitman shook his head. "I can't wait for that, Puma. I can't wait for Indian time on that." He waved his hand. "You know this place better than I do, Puma. Camp Grant is not a proper fort at all. There is no way to defend it. There are a hundred ways to get inside—between each building. No, Puma, once those Apaches get here they must give up their weapons immediately. They can't keep guns in their hands over the first night. Even if they're really trying to behave themselves there's too much risk. A sentry on duty, men returning from a scout, even stray civilians passing through the area, if there's anything alarming on either side there'll be shooting."

"Eskiminzin knows this as well as you do."

"Do you believe in him?"

The Puma slowly rolled another cigarette. "I think he has honor, Teniente. He respects Cochise. Honor is important to Cochise. I think it may be important to Eskiminzin, too."

Whitman sat back in his chair and rubbed his hip. "We'll find out soon enough."

The Puma lit his cigarette and breathed out smoke. "There is one way you can get those weapons, Teniente, and be certain no soldier will start trouble."

Whitman leaned forward. "How?"

"Collect them yourself."

△ 4

After the Puma left, Whitman sent Duncan to get Fred Austin, the sutler, and Miles Wood, the meat contractor for Camp Grant. Austin represented the Tucson firm of Lord & Williams. Wood bought meat for the troops from nearby ranchers.

The two men did not look happy when they walked into the office. They greeted Whitman and sat down with the air of men expecting more bad news. Having not been dismissed by Whitman, Duncan took a seat in a corner of the office.

Whitman looked from Austin's sour face to Wood's dour face. "I suppose you've both heard about the arrangements I've entered into with the Apache, Eskiminzin.

"Got eyes, ain't I?" Wood asked. He was a stringy, bearded man who wore steel-rimmed spectacles. "Got ears, too."

At the moment Whitman couldn't see those eyes. Wood was sitting in a shaft of light and his glasses looked like pieces of metal. "I can take it you don't approve, Mr. Wood."

"I never was much for having Indians move in on me, Lieutenant," Wood said. "Always found it spoiled the neighborhood. And I haven't had the pleasure of socializing with Apaches yet."

Whitman recalled that Wood had owned a store in California before he came to Camp Grant and that Indians had burned the store down, bankrupting him. And after that it was all laid out. Wood moved from one place to another knowing exactly what he was going to hate and exactly why. It must be a comfort, Whitman thought, not to have to make that decision each time.

"They may be here for a little while," Whitman said. "Perhaps for a long while. I've agreed to issue rations until I receive instructions from General Stoneman."

"Indians'll always settle down for free grub," Wood said. He crossed his legs. The motion must have moved his head a little. He had two gray eyes behind the spectacles now. "In between raids."

"Be that as it may, Mr. Wood," Whitman said. "I have promised to provide that free grub."

"That's your own business, Lieutenant," Wood said. He bent forward and his eyes vanished again behind tiny, shiny shields. "But that meat doesn't belong to you, Lieutenant; it belongs to the Government. You think about that? It ain't yours to give away."

"Those Apaches are surrendering as prisoners of war," Whitman said. "It is military custom, Mr. Wood, to feed prisoners of war."

"Prisoners of war!" Wood spat on the earthen floor. He ground in the spittle with his heel. He pointed a finger at Whitman. "You call them Apaches any damned thing you please, Lieutenant. But calling them prisoners of war don't make them that."

"All right, Mr. Wood," Whitman said.

"You do this, Lieutenant, you're doing it on your holy own."

"Mr. Wood—" Whitman's jaw set.

"It ain't going to be no skin off my ass."

"That's quite enough, Mr. Wood."

"I don't want no part of this." Wood jerked his thumb at Duncan. "That soldier there's my witness—and you, too, Fred. I got no part of this."

"I don't believe you will require witnesses, Mr. Wood," Whitman said very quietly.

"I just want to make it clear where I stand."

"I understand precisely what your position is, Mr. Wood. There is no need to go on about it."

Wood nodded and his eyes came and went like blinkers. "Well, Lieutenant, just so long as you—"

"Goddamn it, I haven't got the whole day to listen to your blubbering!" Whitman jumped to his feet and walked to the window and stared out. Presently he turned around. "My apologies, Mr. Wood."

"Well," Wood said. He looked at Austin. "Well, that's a little better, Lieutenant."

Whitman walked back to his desk and sat down. "Mr. Wood—Fred—we have to work out a schedule to ration food and cloth and whatever else they need to each family—and to make a head count at the same time."

Wood spat again. "You work it out, Lieutenant. I told you I want no part of this and that includes the planning. You work it out and then you give me direct orders what to do."

"In writing?" Whitman asked softly.

"Now that you mention it, Lieutenant, that wouldn't hurt one bit." Wood turned his head and nodded complacently to Austin.

Fred Austin shifted around on his chair like a restless owl on a perch. He cleared his throat.

"Yes, Fred?" Whitman asked.

Austin shook his head.

"He feels the way I do," Wood said comfortably. "Only he's polite."

△ 5

There was shooting outside the fort that night but it was only target practice on the coyotes and skunks that came down at sunset to feed off the piles of garbage to the north of the post. The men had their fun and let off steam and then some of them wandered over to the sutler's store and joined others who were sitting around there, talking, playing cards, writing letters, reading whatever newspapers that had by some inexplicable mistake found their way there from the outside world. And in a very little while the coyotes and skunks returned to their banquet and the coyotes now had carrion as well as garbage for their meal.

It was always pleasant in Austin's store. The place was cool and the water in the *ollas* hanging from the rafters was cool, too, and there was lemon-sugar in cans and there were tumblers and spoons. There was no ice at Camp Grant and there never had been, but the sweating *ollas* worked, as they had worked for the Mexicans for centuries, and if a man had a little whiskey to add to the lemon-sugar and water concoction he was so much ahead of the game. Whiskey or not, being in Fred Austin's store always was a time for celebration. It certified that a man had confounded the percentages and had dodged the Apaches and malaria for another day.

Oscar Hutton sat in a corner with Fred Austin. This was an uncommon evening. Thus far no one had asked Hutton to remove his boots and display his remarkable feet. Austin was telling the scout about the meeting he and Miles Wood had had with Whitman that afternoon.

"Never saw the lieutenant that way," Austin said. "He's got a temper. I never figured the lieutenant for a real temper."

"He's hipped on them Apaches." Hutton looked around the room. He felt he was being slighted.

"His jaw got so hard I thought it was going to bust out of his face," Austin said. "And for a minute his eyes were shooting all kinds of hell." He chuckled. "For a moment there it wouldn't have surprised me if the lieutenant had went over there and took a poke at Miles."

"That Wood's got a mouth," Hutton said. He looked around the store. "Them men've got mouths too, and they're chomping their gums about just everything except what's on their minds."

"Well, you wouldn't expect to hear them talking against the lieutenant right here in public, would you?" Austin asked. "That would be some kind of small treason, wouldn't it?"

"I'd like to hear what they're saying when they get over to their quarters," Hutton said. He stuffed his pipe. "I'd sure like to listen in on that."

△ 6

Whitman finished his inspection of the men's breakfast mess and then in the company of Sergeant Clarrity began a tour of the guard mount. The sentries' noses, he saw right away, were still out of joint. He was getting used to that by now.

The men who had to stand guard were always a little fidgety in their exposed positions and more than one sentry in the history of Camp Grant had been shot down by an Apache who had remained hidden behind a saguaro or in a gully for nobody knew how long and had made his fatal move and then had vanished almost before the body struck the ground.

But for the last few mornings there had been a difference. There was increased tenseness certainly, and Whitman had expected that, but there was something more. The men came to proper military attention and snapped back the answers to the prescribed questions Clarrity shot at them, but there was a tightness around their faces and some of them avoided looking at Whitman altogether and Whitman had often wondered, as Hutton had wondered in the sutler's store, what the men said when they were free to speak their minds.

They were all there to fight the Apache war and Whitman knew that not one of them questioned that. But he was going out of his way, he knew it must appear to them, to bring the trouble home, to bring it right up to the post, more, inside the post, and for a reason few of them could understand or even accept. And as he moved from one sentry station to the next, Whitman asked himself once or twice if perhaps they were not justified in their reaction and possibly even right.

He had been on the point more than once of asking Clarrity's opinion on the step he had taken but he never had, and it was not because he did not want to hear whatever it was Clarrity might have to say. But Miles Wood had emphasized what Whitman already was fully aware of, that he was doing this on his own, without authorization, against all competent advice, and he did not want to get anyone else unnecessarily involved, particularly not anybody in uniform, most particularly not Clarrity. He had the odd notion, perhaps wrongly, that Clarrity might just back him up, and if that limb snapped he wanted to be the only one on it.

And Whitman knew that he was himself not unaffected. He had taken to carrying binoculars with him on his circuits of sentry stations. He had never done this before. He felt self-conscious about it. He saw, too, that the men who shunned his eyes always took a good look at the glasses.

At the end of the parade ground he walked over to the stone Eskiminzin had placed there. The Apache's action had seemed quite moving at the time. In the days that had passed, however, Whitman, despite himself, had come to regard it as theatrics, something the people back in Maine would plain snort at. Maybe if he was smart he'd do a little snorting himself.

"Lieutenant," Clarrity said, and it was in his voice, the thing that had been on the sentries' faces for four days.

Whitman looked out across the sandy wash. As always, with the dust raised, it looked like a moving sea. He put the glasses to his eyes and they rushed in on him almost with a blow. He saw them coming in, coming down from the hills, from out of the canyons, some on foot, some on ponies, in little groups and singly and in large groups, some of the ponies carrying parfleches, some of the ponies dragging travois, some of the men and women pulling travois, some carrying bundles on their backs. There were men and women, and most of the women were in rags like the five women who had come to the post originally, and some of them were half naked as one or two of those had been, and there were children, walking and running, some being carried, babies in baskets on their mothers' backs, and there were dogs. Whitman had never seen so many dogs at one time. The dogs ran straight for the creek, hundreds of them it seemed, and they lapped at the water and yapped and fought to get their share.

Whitman moved the glasses across the field of vision and made out the figure of Eskiminzin. The chief was sitting on the piebald pony Whitman had come to recognize. Eskiminzin sat erect, with the morning sun turning him into a small monument, a desert landmark to guide his people. He sat with his arms folded and watched his people come home.

Whitman saw that some of the people went to work immediately, binding poles and covering them with skins, setting up their dome-shaped wickiups in minutes. He saw that some of the Apaches seemed frightened or confused and went to Eskiminzin and he could see the chief talking to them and whatever it was he said he seemed to reassure them and they went off to erect their own dwellings.

Whitman watched the Apache *rancheria* emerge from the desert earth. It was something he would never forget.

He heard someone walking up to him on the gravel.

"Well, I see our guests have arrived," Lieutenant Robinson said.

Whitman lowered his glasses. The evening before, in his quarters, Robinson had spoken his mind, and not merely for the second or third or even fourth time. Whitman passed the glasses to Robinson. He saw that a score or more of troopers had collected and were looking across the wash.

"How many would you make them to be, Bill?" Whitman asked. "And I would take it as a favor if you didn't reply 'too many.'"

"A couple of hundred, I'd say," Robinson said, the glasses at his eyes. "More. I'd guess about two hundred and fifty or so and more coming in." He moved the binoculars slowly. "And they're damned well armed."

"Yes," Whitman said.

"Rifles, muskets, carbines, lances, bows and arrows—"

"Yes."

"Sir," Clarrity said.

"Yes, Sergeant."

"Is that something I should be concerning myself about?"

"Yes," Whitman said.

"I'm glad to hear you feel that way," Robinson said, still peering through the glasses.

"But not as much as you would if you came upon these people unexpectedly in the hills, Sergeant," Whitman said. He looked toward the Indian camp. Without the glasses the Apaches were reduced to harmlessness.

Robinson lowered the binoculars. "Supposing this was some kind of scheme?"

"What kind of scheme?" Whitman asked.

Robinson hunched his shoulders. "I don't know. Eskiminzin gets his men, armed to the teeth, this close and then old Cochise hits us from another direction and the women and kids and dogs scoot away. Something like that."

Clarrity automatically pivoted and made a 360 degree survey with his eyes. "Shall I double the guard, sir?" he asked Whitman.

"That's why those people are putting up all those wickiups," Whitman said to Robinson.

"Could be to lull us," Robinson said. "To make us drop our guard, that sort of thing."

"I take it you're joking, Bill," Whitman said.

"Only partly. Only partly when I started. But as I listen to myself I like it more and more." Robinson cast his eyes toward the Indian encampment. "Maybe it wouldn't hurt to double the guard at that."

After a moment Whitman nodded. "Clarrity, see to it."

△ 7

Santo asked, "Where is the *nantan?*"

Eskiminzin said, "I do not know."

Little Captain asked, "Why is he not here?"

Santo said, "He is afraid to come here, maybe."

Eskiminzin said, "I believe he is brave."

The day was half over. Almost all the wickiups had been put up and the desert along the bank of the Aravaipa Creek looked as though among the flowering cactus it had suddenly sprouted giant mushrooms. A half dozen or more large fires had been built throughout the village and women were carrying brands into their dwellings to set them into the fire pits for the evening meal. Most of the dogs were sleeping in whatever shade they could find and the children were running around and some of them were splashing in the creek.

Eskiminzin and Santo and Little Captain were hunkered down at the edge of the village nearest the fort. Eskiminzin's two wives had put up the chief's wickiups but they were at the end of the village farthest away from the post. Eskiminzin had ordered it that way so that when Whitman visited him he would have to pass through the entire village. He wanted his people to come to know Whitman and in time, if it worked out well, to trust him. And equally, he wanted Whitman to learn to know the people.

Santo grumbled. "He should have been here with presents. That is the only proper way to do something like this. He should have brought many gifts."

Eskiminzin said, "He spoke to me of that before."

Santo said, "I did not like it then and I like it less now."

"You are back home," Eskiminzin said. "The people are back home. That is present enough."

Little Captain said, "Maybe it is a trick."

"Then we have been tricked," Eskiminzin said. "But I do not believe that."

"Because you trust the *nantan*."

"I do not entirely trust him. But I think a peace will benefit him as much as it will us. For that reason I trust him a little."

Eskiminzin stood up. He filled his chest. "We are home," he said. There was a low ring in his voice. "We are home."

"For how long?" Little Captain asked. "And what will be the manner of our stay here?"

"We will honor my word," Eskiminzin said. "If there is failure it must not be of our doing."

Santo lowered his head.

"What is it?" Eskiminzin asked him.

"Nothing," Santo said.

"You are home," Eskiminzin said, and the ring was in his voice again. "You are home."

"We are home," Santo said. "I should feel better than I feel."

"I too," Little Captain said.

Eskiminzin walked to the edge of the creek and looked into the splattering water. He scooped up a handful and pressed his hand to his lips. He looked upstream and saw the children frolicking in the water. He looked at the village and at the smoke from the fires and at the men and women moving around doing ordinary things. He turned back to Little Captain and Santo.

"When anything happens there is always one side or another side, one door or another door. If you want something to go the wrong way you look on the wrong side or you walk through the wrong door. I do not want this to fail."

He walked closer to the men and looked down at them.

"I said this to you in the mountains and I say it to you here. If I have to die I will die here where I was born. I have sat next to death for many seasons in the mountains and I am tired of that. Our women and children must be allowed to stop scurrying off like frightened rabbits every time they hear cavalry horses. Our old people must be allowed to finish growing old and have the right to lie down at last on their own earth. We have talked about this. But you still have time to change your thoughts. You are leaders in your own right and you can take your clans with you and go back to the mountains. Maybe that would be wise. Maybe what I am doing is foolish."

Eskiminzin turned his eyes to the buildings of the fort, across on the far side of the stream.

Little Captain said after a while, "I will not leave."

Santo said, "I am tired of moving. I will remain here a while before I move again."

Eskiminzin raised his head. He saw something coming out of the post and heading toward the Apache village. "Look," he said.

Little Captain and Santo stood up.

"It is a wagon with mules," Little Captain said.

"A man rides alongside," Santo said. "Maybe it is the *nantan* bringing our presents."

Word of the approaching military wagon spread rapidly through the village and from old habit the people became frightened and the women and children fled to the farthest end of the village and although Eskiminzin had told his warriors there was to be peace many of them picked up their guns and their spears and many slung quivers over their shoulders and gripped their bows.

Whitman rode up to the three Apache leaders. The wagon, drawn by two mules and covered in the back with canvas, pulled up behind him. Clarrity held the reins. The Puma sat at his side. The mules smelled Indians and shuffled nervously and one of them brayed. Whitman marveled at this ancestral wisdom that had so quickly informed them that among life's various maledictions was the melancholy truth that they were to Indians the choicest of foods.

Whitman looked over the village, at the women and children huddled in the distance, at the uneasy fighting men with their arms. It was not a tranquil sight.

In the post Robinson had pleaded with him to take along a platoon of soldiers. When Whitman refused, Robinson asked his pardon and then had called him a damned fool. Oscar Hutton had echoed that conviction without bothering to apply for advance absolution.

Sergeant Clarrity had immediately volunteered to drive the wagon. When Whitman looked at the Puma, the Puma shrugged.

"You didn't hire on for anything like this," Whitman said.

"You and Eskiminzin have become accustomed to me," the Puma said. "Another interpreter would be a strange voice and that would make you and Eskiminzin strangers too."

Now Whitman asked himself whether Robinson and Hutton might not have been exactly correct. Frightened women and children. Nervous men with guns. A hairy combination, Oscar Hutton would have labeled it.

Whitman dismounted and handed the reins to Clarrity, who now was at his side. The Puma dropped lightly from the wagon and padded over to Whitman.

Eskiminzin stepped forward and faced Whitman. The two men studied each other as though they had never before met. When Whitman judged enough Indian time had elapsed he spoke.

"I bring welcome to the chief of the Aravaipas and to his people."

Eskiminzin spread his arms. "My people are happy to be home."

"I hope and pray that the Aravaipa people will remain in their home in peace and will prosper," Whitman said.

Little Captain, looking at the canvas-covered wagon, imagining all manner of delightful surprises, nodded and smiled. It was the first time Whitman had seen him twist around his mouth in this fashion and he thought it would be agreeable if Little Captain did that more often.

"That is my wish," Eskiminzin said. "That is the wish of my people." He looked toward the collection of wickiups and at the smoke drifting up. "It is a long time since I have seen so many fires in my village. It is a long time since there was one fire."

"Light your fires," Whitman said. "I will give you food to cook over them. And in the night your children will sleep safely." He paused. "I have come for your weapons."

The smile vanished from Little Captain's face like a bad thought and it was replaced by something else entirely. Eskiminzin stiffened and his dark eyes darkened more. When the translated words spread among the warriors, those men, who had begun to relax, grew taut again and there were mutterings among them.

Sergeant Clarrity, who knew better than to feel for his pistol, looked one way and then the other, and discovering no miracles, looked back at the fort. The fort seemed quite a distance away.

"The *nantan* is quick," Eskiminzin said.

"You have already surrendered your own weapon," Whitman said. "Have you told your warriors of the terms of our agreement?"

"I have told them."

"Then I will collect the weapons now."

Eskiminzin looked at Whitman steadily. "It is not easy."

"I didn't expect it to be."

"A gun is many things to a warrior. It is his defense and his life and another arm. More than anything else it is his honor."

Several of the Apache men shouted agreement with the words of their chief. One of the men, a man who would be large among white men, waved his rifle in the air and shouted something.

The Puma started to translate what the big man had said.

Whitman stopped him. He said to Eskiminzin, "I don't want to listen to words I'll wish I never heard—and will find hard to forget." Then he said quietly. "This is a difficult time. I know what those guns mean. And I understand the honor. There are different kinds of honor, Eskiminzin. Keeping one's word is honor."

Little Captain went to the rear of the wagon and lifted a canvas flap and looked inside, still hoping to see splendid presents. The wagon, he saw, was empty. He looked at Eskiminzin, his lips pulled down, and he hunched his shoulders.

"I will have those guns, Eskiminzin," Whitman said. "Or everything we have said to each other is wiped away."

"Chiquito Capitán," Eskiminzin said.

Little Captain, still standing at the empty wagon, said nothing.

"Chiquito Capitán," Eskiminzin said again.

Little Captain looked at the wagon and at the mules as though they alone would be gift enough.

"Chiquito Capitán," Eskiminzin said.

Little Captain swung toward his chief. He thrust forward his shoulders as though readying his body for an act of violence. It would not have surprised Whitman to see him leap across the twelve or fifteen feet that separated him from Eskiminzin. Then Little Captain's shoulders sagged and he walked slowly over to where he and Santo and Eskiminzin had talked and he picked up his carbine and walked back to the wagon and flung the weapon inside. It clattered on the floorboard. Little Captain strode to the stream and turned his back on the others and folded his arms and stared off across land that carried his eyes as distantly as would the sea.

Whitman felt the sweat on his back and he knew this time it was neither heat nor fever.

"Santo," Eskiminzin said.

Santo picked up his weapon and walked slowly to the wagon and deposited it inside.

Eskiminzin said to the Apache warriors, "Now will each of you sustain my word."

For a very long time no one moved and Whitman and Clarrity exchanged glances and then one man stepped forward and put his gun inside the wagon and then another and then a third. Eskiminzin spoke no more. He watched in silence.

And Whitman watched in silence. And he saw the change that came over each warrior as he abandoned his manhood. He saw that each Apache walked up to the wagon one man and walked away another.

In the end there were two warriors left, one a very young brave and the other the huge man who had earlier shouted out his defiance. The youth, who had no firing piece, only a bow and a quiver of arrows and a long lance on which there was as yet not a single feather, walked over to the wagon and carefully placed his treasures inside. He walked away from the wagon as dejected as a small boy.

The big man remained where he was, rooted. He stood as though beleaguered. He gripped his rifle in his massive right hand and looked around in every direction as though to solicit support, as though somehow to undo what had been done, as though the tribal emasculation could be undone. He, too, discovered no miracle.

Whitman walked over to the man, who was taller than he was. He looked at the man's face. He saw the anger there and the hatred and the fierce hostility and he saw the wounding.

"Tell your name to the sky," Whitman said. "Do not tell it to me."

The Apache glared at Whitman with the eyes of a distempered bull and he lunged the gun high above his head, out of the reach of the American officer, as far as he could remove it from the American officer, and he held it there, his arm trembling, and a shudder passed through his body, and for a time it seemed that from withholding the weapon from the American officer, from denying it to him, and from denying his chief and the word of his chief, he now would bring the gun crashing down on the American officer's abominated head, and Whitman, the sweat trickling down his back ice-cold, willed Clarrity to make no move.

The warrior held in his isolated, catatonic challenge, and the movement of time stopped and everyone remained arrested, fixed, and the human silence was so total the running of the creek became a large noise, and each man there, at once both spectator and participant, waited, and Whitman knew that it all hung on this, on this man and this moment.

Then when it seemed it could go on no longer, the man's body suddenly tottered, as though the earth had provided for him a private quake, and a sob ripped from his throat as though clawed out, and in his torment and disgrace and shame he turned his agonized face upward.

"Delchan!" he shouted to the air, to the cloudless heavens, to the wind and the cactus and the stones and the black ravens, to coyotes and snakes and lizards, to everything alive and dead, except the white soldier chief.

Whitman held out his hand.

Delchan remained rigid, the rifle held as far away as the length of his arm, and he looked around for the last time for aid, and finding none as he had found none before, he slowly lowered his arm and delivered the weapon to Whitman. There was no expression on Delchan's face but his eyes showed his unmanning and Whitman lowered his own eyes to see no more.

Whitman stepped back and he heard the movement and the breathing behind him, as though the caster of the spell had wearied and had departed, and, as in children's fairy tales, people came back to themselves and again knew who they were, and where.

"It will be necessary to police this village," Whitman said to Eskiminzin, his eyes never leaving Delchan.

When his words were translated there were angry sounds from the warriors. Some of them looked toward the wagon.

"I will need eyes here," Whitman said, watching Delchan. It would not have surprised him to see the Indian topple over dead. "I will need someone to watch the people and see that the things that must be done will be done, and that things that should not be done will not be done."

Eskiminzin said nothing. Whitman saw that something had gone from him, whatever it is a man loses when he enters prison.

Little Captain said, "The *nantan* said nothing before of our having to live with soldiers among us."

Santo said, "That was not spoken before."

Delchan had not moved. He stood, twisted as a saguaro, his eyes gazing off, seeking to find a truth that had escaped him. He was, Whitman thought, very much like the giant cactus, thorny and seamed and harsh on the outside, and, inside, now hollow.

"Will you be my policeman?" Whitman asked Delchan.

When the Puma put the words into Apache there was a soft sound from the men, a low sound, an exhalation like a faltering breeze, and for a little while it was as though alone of all of them Delchan had not heard, or having heard, had not comprehended. Then slowly he lowered his head and his wild and embittered and strayed eyes returned to him.

Whitman tossed the rifle back to Delchan. The Apache caught it without looking, without seeming to try, as though his hand had an animation of its own.

"Your chief and I will decide on the nature of your duties," Whitman said. "Your chief will give you your orders."

Whitman turned on his heel and mounted his horse. Clarity and the Puma climbed back on the wagon. Whitman started back for the fort and the wagon creaked behind him.

Crossing the wash, Whitman turned and looked back toward the village. His hip felt as though hammers were pounding it. He saw the men standing where he had left them and then he saw one move and then another and the tableau fractured and the women and children drifted back and the dogs came out of nowhere and yapped and the children ran back into the creek.

Two Apaches remained motionless. Delchan held his rifle. Eskiminzin watched the departure of Whitman and the Apache guns.

The troops cheered when Whitman rode into the fort. Lieutenant Robinson and Oscar Hutton peered into the wagon and had a look at the Indian weapons. Colin Duncan looked at Whitman in worship.

△ 8

His true Indian name was Hash-ki-ban-zin, which means Angry Men Stand in Line for Him.

"It means control of his warriors," the Puma said quietly in the night. "Apaches are named for what they are and what they do and his name means he is a strong leader and that men obey him even when they may not want to."

"Why is he not known by that name?" Whitman asked.

"It is the way his name came to be pronounced by the white man," the Puma said.

The three men were sitting on the ground at the edge of the village across the stream from the post. The night was cool. There were fires burning in the *ranchería* and the shadows of people moved among them. The wickiups seemed now to have been there a long time. The children and the dogs seemed to have been there for a long time. Although no more than three days had passed since the Apaches had come in, it seemed to Whitman that he could not remember when the village was not there.

He had visited the village briefly two or three times in those three days. He never stayed long. The children ran away when they saw him and the dogs barked and the women looked frightened. He wondered whether the time would ever come when he could pass through the village without terrifying the children and the women and the dogs.

Whitman puffed on his cigar. The Puma and Eskiminzin rolled cigarettes and smoked them one after the other. Whitman felt relaxed and at peace. He was sitting with only a thin blanket between him and the ground and he had been sitting there for a long time. His side was without pain.

"I have done bad things," Eskiminzin said. "I have done many bad things. The things were worse in the eyes of the whites than they were in my eyes but they were bad deeds. I do not blame anything for this or anyone. It happened to us that way."

The Puma never was intrusive and now in the black night his voice was disembodied.

Eskiminzin said, "At the beginning we were not warlike. We never were tame and we always fought when it was necessary. But we also planted corn and lived here by Little Running Water in the Dark Canyon. There were many of our people who planted and lived in one place. That was before the Americans came here. We felt safe and we built strong wickiups because we knew that we didn't have to run all the time. The people were happy."

It is odd, Whitman thought, the peace I feel. He was alone in the night with Apaches. It was true, as Lieutenant Robinson had said, that although they had turned in their guns they still had their knives, and even without knives he was at their mercy. And yet he was experiencing a kind of peace he had never quite known before.

Eskiminzin said, "One day something happened. It was in the hot time of the year, the season called Many Leaves. Three of our women were out finding willow for baskets. Although we did not know it, just a few days before that, some Indians had attacked Mexicans in the Cañada Cocospera and had killed seven Mexicans and had stolen a young Mexican girl. Now the Mexicans were looking for the Indians for revenge and to try to get back the girl, and they came upon our three women in the river bottom and demanded to know where our *ranchería* was.

The women were afraid to lead the Mexicans to our camp because they knew the Mexicans would not ask questions but would start fighting and there were many of the Mexicans and they were well armed, so the three women started to lead them away from Little Running Water, this water here before you, the water you call Aravaipa Creek, and took them toward the Santa Catalina Mountains. The Mexicans became more and more suspicious and they decided that the women were guiding them the wrong way and they lanced the three women and left them for the buzzards and the coyotes."

Eskiminzin made another cigarette. Whitman had offered him a cigar one time and the Apache had taken it and had started to smoke it. He began to cough and choke and then a look appeared in his eyes, a look that said Whitman was trying to do him harm, that he was giving him something a white man could tolerate but which could kill an Indian. And at that moment Whitman had thought about the measles and how that disease had left white children alive and had killed Indian children and how those Indians thought too that Marcus Whitman was doing them harm. He was relieved when Eskiminzin stopped coughing and the look went out of his eyes but he never again would offer him a cigar.

There were so many things to learn.

"That night when the women did not return to our camp we knew something had happened to them and the next morning we sent out searchers and they found the women. Two of them were dead but one of them still breathed and she told what had happened. When the men returned to our camp with the story of what had happened our people were angry."

Again Eskiminzin paused. Whitman could hear the low voices of the people in the village.

Eskiminzin went on. "Santo was the leading chief back then and he was angriest of all and he wanted the men to start attacking on the trail up from Mexico and to kill everybody who passed. But I argued against that. I argued that we could not start killing people on the trail without endangering our women and our children in the Dark Canyon, the place white men call Aravaipa Canyon. I argued that we must kill in revenge, yes, but that our people must be protected while we did that.

"We had corn growing in the fields and soon it would be ready to eat but we left anyway. Something had happened and we had to leave. There was no way not to leave. Even Santo agreed with me. It was that argument that made people listen more and more to me, and afterward, when Santo got older, he was not unhappy for me to become the leading chief.

"We traveled for two days away from Little Running Water. We left our hearts behind us. It was always our home. It is true that much of the desert looks like every other part of the desert and that one canyon and one river are not different from another, but the Dark Canyon and Little Running Water was always our home, here where we now are sitting. I remember it here before the soldier fort was built, when there was nothing of the white man on the land here. The water flowed stronger then.

"We made our new camp in the mountains and from the mountains we made our attacks on the Mexicans and we were very successful because the Mexicans could not follow us back into the mountains, or if they could, they were not brave enough to take the risk. The people saw more and more that I had been right, and while we never forgot Little Running Water, still we were safe.

"That is how it went for some time and then we discovered that new soldiers were in the country and that they were different from Mexican soldiers. They were new here and they did not know the land, and they fought the land and the heat as much as they fought Indians, but they were brave. And then one day we heard that the *nantan* wanted to make peace with the Indians. We did not think much about it because we were used to believing only ourselves, but then we heard that Cochise had visited with the *nantan* at the fort on the Sonoita River in the Sonoita Valley, and we heard that Cochise respected the *nantan* and had made a peace with him and that made us think a great deal.

"Santo did not want to talk to the *nantan*. I spoke to him a great deal about it. I said that if Cochise was satisfied that meant a great deal because Cochise is the greatest of us and the wisest. Finally Santo agreed and some of our men went to see the *nantan* and he seemed to me to be a good man. He told us that the Americans now owned the land and that the Mexicans were gone, except for those who wanted to stay and become Americans. He said the Americans would build forts all over the land and that the killing must stop.

"I asked him if that meant that the white men and the Mexicans would stop killing us. He said that all killing must stop. I told him good, that if that was true, then we could return to our home on Little Running Water, and that it would be up to him to keep our enemies away from us and he said he would do that."

Whitman heard footsteps. He looked up to see the towering figure of Delchan silhouetted against the firelight. Delchan carried his rifle cradled in his arms. He stood there for several moments and then moved on.

"We did what we said we would do," Eskiminzin said. "We gathered our women and our children and brought them down from the mountains to our old home along Little Running Water, and everybody was happy to be here again, and then the soldiers built this fort and we were even happier because we believed that one of the reasons the soldiers built the fort was to protect us. But that is not the way it was. The soldiers drank a lot of whiskey and when they were drunk there were some of them who liked to hunt Indians as though we were animals. They stalked us and shot at us as though we were something to eat. From the time the fort was built until we left again there were more than fifty of our people who were shot by soldiers or prospectors, or by people who started out to hunt for deer and decided to kill one of us instead.

"Then came a big attack by soldiers and Mexicans from Tucson, and it was a big battle and we fought for a long time and we drove them off, but not before many of us were killed, and now Santo spoke up again and said we had to leave the Little Running Water once more and go back into the mountains."

Eskiminzin made another cigarette and when he lit it Whitman could see the austerity in his face. The Apache smoked silently and looked at Little Running Water, tripping by in a thousand reflections from the stars and the moon and the Indian fires.

Whitman tried to fasten the tone of the Indian's voice to the words the Puma gave him, but he could make no pattern. Eskiminzin spoke in a low, harsh monotone. The only quality the throaty sounds possessed was their paced inevitability, as though the words had been spoken before and often and now were being retold and not a single one of them could be changed. It was a minute, fragmented portion of Indian Holy Writ, except the full work never would be assembled, there were no scribes and no disciples, and the story would forever remain fractured in forgotten shards scattered over the land from one coast to the other.

And Whitman knew Eskiminzin was telling the truth as he had known it, remembered it, wanted it to have been. Other men trapped in those events would have different words to describe them. Everyone chewed on the cud of his own racial memories.

Eskiminzin went on. "That is how it was. We lived as wild beasts in the mountains. It seemed that the hand of everyone was against us and that the soldiers who were supposed to protect us, as their *nantan* had said long before, were the ones who hunted us the most. The soldier chief who had given his word to Cochise and to me no longer was there.

"And then it was that Cochise's brothers and members of his family were killed in Apache Pass by the boy *nantan* and were hanged from a tree along with some of my own people who were captured at that time. It was then that Cochise declared his war against the white-eyes and we joined him and we had many fights and we killed many people. We killed them and we tortured them.

"But that was not our way and we did not like it. It was more the way of Cochise and the Chiricahuas. It was not that we were not brave and that we did not fight as well as anyone, but it was not our way. It was not their way to plant corn and that was our way.

"And then we heard there was a new soldier chief here at Camp Grant and we had a council and I said maybe it would be a good thing to talk to the new *nantan* and try to end this living as wild animals and give our women and our children homes they could sleep in for more than just one night or two nights.

"Santo opposed it. Little Captain opposed it. They liked white soldiers less than ever. I listened along with everyone else. I am the leading chief now but Santo still is very respected and he is wise and people listen to him and they respect Little Captain because he is a leading warrior and they listen to him.

"And then I said, 'If we continue to live this way, then we die, one by one we die. Cochise knows that. He has said so and is prepared to do that. In that case, it makes no difference where we die. Let us speak to this *nantan* and try to get back to our home on Little Running Water. And if we are killed there, then we will be killed and we will die on our own earth. I would rather be killed there than sit next to death all the time in strange mountains.' "

Eskiminzin was silent for a long while and Whitman listened to the night and again felt a calmness and he could not have explained why.

"Does this story have interest for you?" Eskiminzin asked.

"Yes." Whitman paused. It is strange, he thought, when the words stop the night rushes in. "I want to know as much as I can about the Aravaipa people. I want to know things beyond the killing and hiding and running and fear. I want to know about the life things of the Aravaipas and your memories and how you believe in God and the things you do and the things you don't do."

Eskiminzin said, "It is the white man who must tell us things and teach us."

"Maybe we can learn something from each other," Whitman said.

When Whitman returned to Camp Grant he saw that Oscar Hutton was talking to the guard on the other side of the wash.

"What did you and that old cutthroat talk about?" Hutton asked as he walked with Whitman toward his quarters.

"A lot of things."

"Did he bend your ear?"

"I suppose so."

"Them Indians are great talkers. Especially at night. Especially if there are enough smokes. Give them the chance and they'll speechify all night."

Whitman usually liked to listen to Hutton, but just then he found him irritating. He wanted to be by himself and sort out the evening and Hutton was getting on his nerves and he was glad his quarters were not far away.

"But then they know something," Hutton said.

"What do you mean?"

Hutton scratched his beard. "I don't know exactly what I mean. But them Indians know things we don't know."

"Do you mean robbing and killing and pillaging?" Whitman asked.

"No, I don't mean them things, Royal, and I don't mean other Indian things like running across the desert longer than a horse can, I don't mean that. It's something else."

They were outside Whitman's quarters now and Hutton waggled his finger and walked on.

"Oscar," Whitman said.

The guide said, "Yes, Royal."

"What do you mean, Oscar? What something else?"

Hutton ambled back. "I don't know. Something private, I guess."

"I wouldn't have thought you felt that way about Indians, Oscar, especially Apache Indians," Whitman said.

Hutton was lighting his pipe then and he raised his eyes to Whitman and Whitman saw something then that astonished him. He saw Hutton go into himself the way he had seen Eskiminzin go into himself, the way he had seen the Apache women go into themselves. It was a bewildering, sudden, impregnable enclosure.

"People say I've killed more Apaches than any white man in Arizona," Hutton said.

"I have heard that," Whitman said. He felt that Hutton was so far away the words could not reach him.

"Maybe so," Hutton said from that distant and sheltered place. "I ain't never kept a particular count. But sometimes I wish there wasn't all that killing. Because those people know something and maybe it wouldn't hurt a body to know a little bit about what that is."

Hutton walked away, leaving behind the pungent smell of his pipe, and what he had said. Whitman stood outside his quarters for several minutes and then he went inside.

He touched the shining metal that was Rodriguez González and he walked to the window and looked out. The post was in darkness. He raised his head at the sudden sound of the bugler sounding Taps. Each lonely note fell into the quiet camp like a dying star.

Δ 9

The next morning, February 28, Whitman wrote a report to General Stoneman disclosing everything that had transpired up to then. He informed the general of the manner of arrival of the five women and what had ensued thereafter. He told the general of the establishment of the Apache village just outside the post and of his having undertaken to issue food and other necessities to the Aravaipa people.

"What the result of all this may be I am entirely unable to

conjecture—beyond the possibilities either way. I think it is quite possible they may be acting in good faith, in which case I was careful not to exaggerate the inducements of life on a reservation. It is also quite possible the movement may be a ruse to obtain temporary relief, in which case I carefully assured them of the vigorous measures to be taken for their extermination should they persist in their hostility to our common government."

Perhaps "extermination" was too strong a word. And yet he had warned Eskiminzin that in the conflict between the soldiers and the Indians in the end there could be only one winner and one loser and that by that time there probably would be very few Apaches left to live or to die, and he supposed that could be defined as extermination.

"I send this by special express via Florence, to intercept the regular mail at Sacaton. Hoping to receive explicit instructions at the earliest moment possible."

He looked up as Duncan entered the office.

"Sir, the dispatch rider is mounted and in waiting," Duncan said.

Whitman signed the letter quickly and addressed it to the Acting Assistant Adjutant General, Department of Arizona. He sealed the paper and gave it to Duncan, who hurried out of the office.

From his window, he saw the rider slip the document into a saddle bag, strap down the flap, wave farewell to Duncan with a gloved hand, and gallop out of the fort.

Lieutenant Whitman felt a weight off his back.

△ 10

The talk all over the post, in the sutler's store, in the men's quarters, in the mess, down at Suds Row where the company laundresses pounded uniforms as though they were destroying enemies, was of nothing but how the commanding officer had gone into the Apache camp and how he had almost single-handedly relieved the wild Indians of their weapons. Even Oscar

Hutton's renowned six-toed feet were forgotten in this new sensation, and Oscar Hutton announced publicly more than once, with vast generosity, that that was only right.

"My feet are here to stay as long as I am," Hutton stated in Fred Austin's store one evening. "But what the lieutenant did doesn't happen very often. I don't mind stating to one and all that I take my hat off to him."

And each time, to make his point clearer, Oscar Hutton removed his hat.

Sergeant Francis X. Clarrity discovered at this relatively mature time of his life that he possessed an ancestral trait he had not before suspected. Sergeant Clarrity, who curled his lip at many of his countrymen's foibles, now found that he had the traditional gift of gab, and that, moreover, he relished it. He held listeners enthralled as he told how the lieutenant demanded the guns and how he got them in the face of a whole tribe of Apaches.

Sergeant Clarrity was at his very best when he described how the lieutenant obtained the last gun from a giant of an Indian. In his telling, the account came to have the imperishable drama of the conflict between David and Goliath.

"There was nothing I could do at that perilous moment," Sergeant Clarrity said. "The lieutenant was between this immense Apache and myself and I could not shoot at the Indian for fear of hitting the lieutenant. But I made up my mind to one thing. If that Indian brained the lieutenant I would shoot the Indian dead, then and there."

The words hung over Camp Grant like strong drink.

The men took to looking curiously at Lieutenant Whitman, with new eyes, as though they had until then been missing something that had been plain to see. They read new things into his quiet manner, the low way he spoke, the way he refused to let the fever get the better of him.

And of all the men, Trooper Duncan was without question the soldier proudest of the post commander. The other troopers, who had looked down on the baby-faced soldier, because of his baby face and because he had hired out to the lieutenant to work as a kind of servant—nobody exactly admired a striker—

now sought him out and asked him questions about his boss. Not terribly personal questions, nobody was trying to snoop, just questions about what Lieutenant Whitman was really like.

Duncan told the men a little bit about the lieutenant but not too much, because Colin Duncan was a Scot and not much addicted to small gossip. But even more than that, Duncan kept his views mostly to himself because his attitude toward Lieutenant Whitman now approached adulation. And he wasn't going to go around telling anybody that. He was not brown-nosing.

But he had to tell somebody about the recent dramatic events at Camp Grant. No one at the post, obviously. Somebody outside. His first thought was to write a letter to his mother in Newfoundland and that had an appeal, because he knew his mother would read the letter to all the other people in the village when they were gathered in the little general store she ran all by herself, after Colin Duncan's father drowned when his fishing boat capsized in a storm. And after that little session in the store, around the potbellied stove—it would be cold there at this time of the year—the low-ceilinged room filled with the good smells, spices and coffee and tea and dried fish, Mrs. Duncan would send the letter along to the rest of the family in Perth, and they, too, would marvel at the adventures of one of their kin in the barbaric land of the Indians.

He started writing the letter but after a while he put down his pen. It was not precisely to his mother he wanted to write. In time, certainly, yes, but right now, no. It would entertain his mother, Lord love her, and her friends and relatives, but right now it was more important that the people in Arizona know what was going on in Camp Grant and what manner of man Lieutenant Whitman was.

He started the letter over again. He had to be careful. He must not be too effusive and he must not include details that might be in violation of military security.

When he finished he read over what he had written. He was reasonably pleased. He started to sign his name but then he realized he could not do that. He could not attach his name to the letter any more than he could tell the men how he idolized Lieutenant Whitman.

John Wasson chewed on the stub of cigar and gazed out the window at the stream of people moving in and out of Bill Zeckendorf's store next door. Bill Zeckendorf was having the biggest sale of his career. Word had just reached Tucson that the Franco-Prussian War had ended in a German victory and Bill Zeckendorf wanted everybody to share his joy.

John Wasson watched the crowds milling around and then he sat down at his desk and threw away the cigar stub and lit a fresh cigar and reread the letter that had come to him in the mail from Camp Grant. The letter was signed "A Soldier."

"*The prospects that your city will not be troubled by the Apaches for some time are very bright indeed,*" the letter read. "*Lt. Whitman, 3rd Cavalry and commanding officer of this Post has just concluded a peace with two of the petty chiefs of the Pinal tribe, who have sent runners out to all their people with the intent that they shall also come in on the reservation. The peace was concluded under the most auspicious circumstances.*

"*A short time since, five women came to this Post under a flag of truce—which I cannot forbear describing. It was a rag that was once white—this you could just discern. It was about ten inches long and about an inch and a quarter wide, and was adjusted to a reed which the most forbidding-looking squaw carried.*

"*The kind treatment those received while here (two days) and the same I have no doubt being unexpected, it soon got noised abroad amongst them.*"

Wasson looked toward the window. There was no question that the news of Bill Zeckendorf's sale soon got noised abroad, too. He put down the letter and walked to the window again. There seemed to be more people trying to push their way into the store than ever. He saw Bill Zeckendorf standing in the street, a stogie in his mouth and a smile on his face. Zeckendorf waved to him and Wasson waved back. Wasson was not altogether certain that he was happy with the Prussian triumph but then that was of very little concern to him. His enemies were neither French nor German.

"We are now in a fair way of having all their folks coming in, and I feel confident in asserting that no matter what other officer comes here, if they are treated with the same kindness and fair dealing as they are receiving at the hands of the now commandant and Commissary, the people of Arizona need be under no further apprehension of an incursion from this portion of the Apache tribe."

John Wasson put down the letter. He pursed his lips and relit his cigar. "A Soldier," whoever he was, was certainly optimistic. He listened to the clamor outside. He wondered whether he should make some editorial comment on the Prussian victory. He decided against it. Nobody in Tucson, with the exception of Bill Zeckendorf, cared a hoot about what happened in France.

"I think that these Indians being left San Pedro and Aravaipa valleys to cultivate, and receiving convincing encouragement by implements, seeds, Etc., in fact everything that could be requisite to start a people on their new career, we will have no more of those Indian atrocities that have so blurred the history of this Territory."

Wasson tossed the letter onto his desk. "No more Indian atrocities . . ." He laughed. It was more of a snort. "A Soldier" was a dreamer, one of those misguided idealists, without a doubt. Then Wasson had another thought: Was it possible that Lieutenant Whitman had written the letter himself or caused someone to write it for him?

John Wasson remembered Lieutenant Whitman. He had been favorably impressed by him. Whitman had been, Wasson remembered now, a senior officer during the Civil War, a colonel, in fact, a man of good sense and experience. No, Wasson decided, Whitman was not the cut of man to have contrived to have someone write something like this.

Then it must be essentially true, at least true as one soldier saw it, a rather silly and romantic soldier, of course, but in any event, the letter had some news value. Anything that dealt with Apache Indians had news value.

John Wasson put a one-column head on the story:

LETTER FROM CAMP GRANT—
PEACE AGREEMENT BY THE PINALS—
DELIGHTFUL HOPES EXPRESSED

He datelined the story "Camp Grant, A.T., March 7, 1871" and sent it to be put into type for the next edition of the *Citizen* on the following Saturday, March 11. Then Wasson took a clean sheet of paper and wrote an editorial to appear on the same page of that same edition.

> Our Grant letter speaks confidently of the value of the peace made with the Pinals. We hope it may be lasting, but no one should trust their person or property where they would not have done so before.

And as for those Apaches?

> They should have been compelled to endure more than one scout from Camp Apache, and still more from Verde, before listening to their peace talks. Even if they have offered peace in good faith, they deserve more punishment, and a most terrible scourging would have made their peaceful professions more worthy of reliance.

John Wasson thought for a moment and then he wrote furiously:

> The Indian must most powerfully feel the government's superiority, ability, and determination to crush him, before his professions of peace are worth listening to by our officers or people.

Wasson reread his editorial, made some corrections and sent that along to be set in type as well. He got up and stretched and walked back to the window. Business at Bill Zeckendorf's was as brisk as before. The people of Tucson appreciated bargains as well as anybody. Wasson chuckled. Good thing the Prussians didn't fight and win every day. Old Bill Zeckendorf would go bankrupt.

△ 2

The page was laid out, John Wasson thought, eminently satisfactorily.

His commentary on the Camp Grant letter from "A Soldier" was in the upper left-hand corner. The letter from the post was also at the top of that page, separated from the commentary by one column. And in that column, sandwiched neatly, was a story with the headline:

ANOTHER INDIAN OUTRAGE—
STAGE ATTACKED—DRIVER SHOT
—HORSES KILLED, &C.

John Wasson considered that a clever bit of placement. The account of the new Indian atrocity underlined his observations of the development at Camp Grant. It was a news story that was in itself an editorial comment, which was the best kind of all.

The entire paper looked good to the editor. He took seriously his self-anointed role as the conscience of Tucson, perhaps of all Arizona, and while he felt duty-bound occasionally to print such idiotic pap as the letter from "A Soldier," he knew his basic responsibility was to give his readers the facts, unadorned. The *Citizen* was the Word, and meanwhile he was kicking the hell out of the opposition paper, the *Arizonan*. Bill Oury was still holding court at the Congress Hall but his newspaper sure as hell was going down the drain.

On that sunny March day there were many choice items to titillate the readers of John Wasson's weekly. There was the always exciting piece of intelligence that a batch of mail had arrived in the Old Pueblo. ". . . *An armed party that went to the scene of the attack on the stage, as described elsewhere,*" found everything destroyed by the stagecoach itself, and were lucky enough to retrieve two bags of mail.

There was another story, less exhilarating:

> A private letter received this morning from Prescott says Headquarters of the Department of Arizona had been permanently established at Wilmington, Cal.; also that some fifty carpenters were there at work building, &c.

"Stoneman!" Wasson said, gripping the paper. Stoneman, Stoneman, always Stoneman. What sin had the settlers of Arizona committed, against whom had they blasphemed, what was their crime and in whose eyes, to have had themselves delivered into the hands of this craven officer?

In another part of the paper that morning there was a comment from the Territorial Governor, A.P.K. Safford, who was one of the loudest, most vocal and most consistent opponents of the feed stations for the Apache Indians. Governor Safford always maintained that he had his ear to the ground and his fingers on the pulse of his constituents and he generally spoke with the zeal of an Old Testament prophet.

> Much dissatisfaction and ill feeling on the part of the settlers on account of the general belief that portions of this tribe on reservations will join with marauding bands against them, and then when their nefarious work is done, return to the reservation for safety.

Not one of Saff's better fire-and-brimstone efforts, to be sure, but still it fit tidily into the scheme of things that day as John Wasson viewed it. And in that same edition, to keep the ball rolling and to give his readers more to chew on, Wasson again struck a blow against the military policy which, he charged, was decimating the ranks of soldiers assigned to protect Arizona. Every single day of the week, he pointed out, the soldiers' enlistments were expiring. From a peak of sixteen hundred men, the military bulwark against the savage Apaches was steadily eroding as men counted their last day, turned in their uniform, and left the Territory to their former comrades and the Apaches.

It was outrageous, Wasson fumed, that as soon as a man was seasoned, trained to do his job properly, he was discharged, and if by lucky chance some other soldier was sent out to fill his shoes, the replacement was always a raw novice who spent his term learning his work, at Government expense, and then, educated at last, saluted the post flag and took his jaunty way homeward.

Some of this scandalous procedure, Wasson emphasized, might in some way be corrected or mitigated by a forceful and dedicated and brave commander of the Department of Arizona. But as his readers could see elsewhere in that same edition that day, the present incumbent was having constructed for himself luxurious quarters in far-off California—also at Government expense.

Having scanned his own newspaper, looking with some satisfaction at the healthy outcrop of advertisements from the local merchants, John Wasson, like any other editor, had a look at what the opposition had done for itself. Bill Oury's paper, he was pleased to see, never looked duller. The *Arizonan* also carried a statement by Governor Safford, who yielded to no man in his desire to keep the people of Arizona informed. Again the Governor inveighed against Apaches who were being fed on military reservations.

> They may go out at any time from their reservation and capture a train on the public highway, and returning again with the blood of the murdered teamsters yet fresh on their lances, can claim and will receive the protection of the

military post at which their reservation is located.

Well, John Wasson thought. That was a little closer to Saff's style and somewhat better than the statement he gave to the *Citizen*. "... *the blood of the murdered teamsters yet fresh on their lances* ..." That was vintage Safford and Wasson felt somewhat short-changed. But all in all, the *Arizonan* was no match.

Wasson stood up, the flower of another week's labor before him, and he strolled over to the window and watched the citizens buy and walk off with his newspaper. It was a very personal thing with him and he was always moved. Some of the men were reading what he considered his own personal letter to Tucson as they went down the street. With the wellholes still uncovered and the garbage piled higher than ever, that was, of course, a hazardous thing to do, and John Wasson took it as a compliment that so many of his readers were willing to risk life and limb to read what he had to say.

Wasson, lighting a fresh cigar, feeling that special enlivenment of an editor who has seen his newspaper come off the presses, wondered what old Saff would have to say about the latest feed station at Camp Grant. He'd have to persuade Saff to give him the choicer statement this time. And Wasson wondered what Bill Oury would have to say about the letter from "A Soldier" and the information it imparted. Whatever it would be, Wasson chuckled, it would be blue.

John Wasson put his big hat on his head and started off for the Congress Hall. He always liked to get there as soon as possible on Saturdays after his paper hit the streets. He liked to see the men reading the *Citizen*. For the Mexicans he always had a few columns in Spanish. Wasson appreciated receiving the compliments of all his readers, Mexicans and Americans alike.

He wondered what the Apaches would say if by some miracle they, too, could read the columns of the *Citizen*. The thought made him chuckle to himself and a Mexican, still remembering the old John Wasson and his crazy campaigns, crossed himself and dodged over to the other side of the street.

Santa Madre de Dios, and what would cause a grown man to laugh to himself while walking down a street in the middle of the day?

The saloon was already full, or perhaps it was just that it was still full. Smoke congealed the air and Wasson wondered whether there ever was a time of the day when this phenomenon, natural as mist and fog, was not present. Since Charlie Brown rarely closed his saloon, probably not.

John Wasson saw Bill Oury at his table surrounded by couriers. Wasson exchanged greetings with friends and admirers and sat down at the nearest vacant table. He didn't have a table of his own but one day, and this was a devout pledge he made to himself, he would.

△ △ △ SEVEN

△ 1

When the coffee started to boil, Child Mother put an iron nail in the clay pot on the small fire in the pit in the middle of the wickiup and Whitman would have liked to have known where she came on that. Child Mother poured the coffee into small clay mugs and gave one to Whitman and one to Eskiminzin and one to the Puma. She set down a basket filled with fresh mescal cakes and then looked to make sure that her husband and his guests were all comfortable, and after that she retired to a far part of the dwelling and sat down and waited in a kind of Oriental patience and solicitude for that moment when her services again would be required.

It was strange, Whitman thought. Child Mother was a typical housewife, with grace and manners, but not until that day when Eskiminzin invited him to visit one of his homes had he been able to think of an Apache woman as a hostess.

The coffee turned out to be uncommonly good, better than that usually served at Camp Grant. The mescal cakes had an odd taste and he found he liked them.

Whitman sipped the coffee and nibbled on the cakes during the obligatory marking of Indian time. Whitman was coming to appreciate the advantages of Indian time. A man could collect his thoughts during Indian time and therefore was perhaps not as apt to blurt out words he did not wholly mean. Whitman used the meditation period now to look around the wickiup at the possessions of an Apache chieftain.

He saw the shields made of skins that once could have deflected arrows and even possibly fended off spears, but which were patently useless against the methods of death the white man had introduced as part of his contribution to social rela-

156

tions. The shields, covered with cabalistic markings, could have value now only in ceremony and memory. He saw a lance flaunting half a dozen feathers. One day, he thought, I would like to know the story each of those feathers could tell. There were arrow quivers, some filled, some empty, and two bows; there were powder horns and belts studded with silver and turquoise, and amulets and heavy silver bracelets, and hanging from one of the shields, with its arcane markings, was a silver chain with a pendant marked with its own private knowledge.

In one part of the round dwelling there were four pallets made of grass covered by blankets, one each for Eskiminzin and Child Mother, and small ones for the children of this branch of the Apache chief's family, the girl, Star, and Ria, a girl child almost two, whom Child Mother was preparing to wean.

In another part of the wickiup were the family parfleches, now flat and stacked neatly against a part of the circular skin wall. Whitman had seen those leather bags fat and filled when the Apaches first arrived and he questioned the Puma about them, among other things, and the Puma told him that everything an Apache owned could be thrown into a parfleche in the event of an alarm and the Indian would be on his way in minutes.

"The parfleche is always open and always ready and the Apache women practice loading them," the Puma said. "There is always talk about how the white people live in terror in Arizona. The Apache lives in terror, too."

Whitman thought he caught an unusual note of remote and old bitterness in the Puma's voice, unusual because the Puma, in training himself to be an interpreter and a good one, had worked hard to keep any personal sounds out of his voice, had striven to make the words he spoke back and forth sterile and uncolored. There was something else there now, and for the first time since he had come to know the Puma, Whitman understood that the Puma with everything else was also a Mexican with a remembered disaffection.

And the thought of an Apache living out of a suitcase, so to speak, was another new vision. Whitman supposed it was funny, in a very sad way. The Apaches and the whites, both in such dread of each other, each thinking the other such demonic monsters, and yet compelled by what unknown command, by whose unknown voice, in what historic joke, to exist together on the same odious land.

As he looked around the wickiup Whitman's eyes fell from time to time on Child Mother and each time he found her staring at him and each time her eyes dropped instantly and he thought, even on her golden skin, he could detect a blush. Child Mother was in a very special state of mind, the Puma had explained to Whitman. It was Apache custom, he told the officer, for husband and wives to remain apart physically while the woman was nursing a child.

"That goes on for about two years," the Puma said. "That is why Apaches have more than one wife, as many as they can feed. Otherwise they pass long, lonely times."

The Puma had not laughed, had not smiled, when he gave Whitman this intelligence. Whitman had thought of the many possibilities of the expansion and development of this bit of lore, of the variations that could be worked up, amid guffaws, in any good American saloon, by any virile American man.

And he wondered, too, how the Puma had picked up this little nugget of news; not the Apache tradition, of course, that would have been learned long before, but of the present schedule in Eskiminzin's household. And the Puma had informed him as well that Eskiminzin's other wife, Small Woman, was pregnant and almost ready to deliver, and Whitman thought Eskiminzin had worked out the timing rather neatly, and he knew that that reflection put him, Whitman, right there with all those other red-blooded American men in that saloon.

To turn his thoughts to a more dignified area, Whitman looked again at Eskiminzin, and there came to his mind immediately the line from Emerson, *"Wherever Macdonald sits, there is the head of the table."*

Until this time Whitman had met with the Apache only in his own office at Camp Grant, with its own symbols, or in the open. Now, sitting cross-legged on several folded blankets, Eskiminzin was in his own home. Whitman had been exposed to some of the different sides of the Apache; he now was in the presence of another. There was a deep gravity on Eskiminzin's face and he had a power Whitman had not discerned before. It came off the Apache like a dark light. Again he was wearing his leathers with their inscriptions and some of his amulets and there were silver and turquoise rings in his braided hair.

Through the open door flap of the wickiup, Whitman saw the titanic figure of Delchan pacing back and forth, guarding the throne room of his chief. Delchan held his rifle cradled in his arms. As the only firing piece in the Apache village it was, of course, now much more than a weapon. Delchan would have died before allowing anyone to touch it.

After the men finished the coffee and cakes, Child Mother rose swiftly and took away the mugs and the cake basket. She brought forth a clay jug and three more clay mugs.

"What's this?" Whitman asked the Puma.

"*Tiswin,* without doubt."

"What is *tiswin?*"

"Beer. A kind of Apache beer."

"Beer," Whitman said. "And will miracles never cease?"

Child Mother poured the *tiswin* into the mugs and then backed away to her place and sat down and somehow seemed to have left the dwelling. Whitman raised his mug and held it out toward Eskiminzin. The Indian looked at him, puzzled.

"Why does the *nantan* do that?" he asked.

"A toast."

The Puma had to think for a moment or two before he could find an appropriate word for "toast," in that sense. He knew that to Eskiminzin the word meant only what was done to the raw mescal to make it palatable. Finally the Puma came up with a "gesture of respect."

That was something Eskiminzin could understand. He lifted his own mug of *tiswin* and held it out.

"I have never quite known why," Whitman said, "but among my people pledges often are made over drink."

"This drink comes from grain that has been given warmth and growth by the sun," Eskiminzin said. "That may have value."

"Perhaps," Whitman said. "In any case, here's to the future—and the hope that we can work out what we have started together."

"It is well," Eskiminzin said.

The two men drank. Whitman found the native beer warm and bitter. After a while, he thought, maybe it gets better.

After another passage of Indian time, Whitman took from his tunic pocket a copy of the letter from "A Soldier" torn from the page of the *Citizen*. He explained to Eskiminzin that this had appeared in the Tucson paper and that the people in Tucson and in other parts of Arizona had undoubtedly read it. He then read the letter, pausing from time to time so that the Puma could turn the words into Apache. When he was finished Eskiminzin said nothing for a little while.

"Read the words again," he said.

Whitman went through the letter again and when he was finished Eskiminzin nodded.

"Those are good words," the Apache said.

"Yes."

"Do you know what soldier sent those words to Tucson?"

"No."

"Will you find out?"

"No."

"Why not?"

"It is not my business."

"What will the people of Tucson think about those words?"

"Some will be glad, others will not."

"Who will be glad?"

"Those who want peace."

"Are there more of those than the others?"

"I don't know."

"I beware the people of Tucson," Eskiminzin said. "They came with soldiers and attacked us."

"Yes."

"There are those who would do it again."

"Yes."

"This is our land and this is our air and you are the interlopers," Eskiminzin said. His voice turned harsh. "Yet there are those who say we have no right to live on the land or breathe the air."

Child Mother raised her eyes anxiously at the anger in her

husband's voice and words. She watched him roll and light a cigarette. He did not look at her.

Whitman availed himself again of the privileges of Indian time. He saw that the fire had just about burned itself out in the small pit. Child Mother had put into it just enough wood coals to do the job, no more.

In the stillness of the wickiup he heard sounds of children outside, running around, calling to one another, laughing. That was another simple verity. Apaches had children and the children played like children and laughed like children and cried like children. In addition to Apache wives who behaved not very differently from housewives, say, in Portland, Maine, Apaches also had children. And the only surprise in all this was that the realization was a surprise.

"I have been told that before your people came here there were other people who lived here," Whitman said at last. "People who scratched pictures on rocks."

"Yes," Eskiminzin said.

"I have been told that when the Apaches came here they fought with these people and those they did not kill they drove away."

"We were stronger than they were," Eskiminzin said.

"Yes."

Eskiminzin nodded slowly. "I understand what you are saying. You are the new Apaches and we are the people who put pictures on rocks."

Whitman leaned forward. "It need not be that way, Eskiminzin. Perhaps we can make it happen in a different way. We must do that. You have no choice. I have told you this before, if your people go on fighting us you all will be destroyed. It will be a fight to the death and we won't be the ones to die, not as a people. I don't say this as a threat, Eskiminzin, but we will not die."

After a while Eskiminzin said, "The letter was written by a very young soldier. His eyes are as unclouded as a child's."

"There is something else," Whitman said. "The man who makes the newspaper made some remarks about the letter."

He read John Wasson's commentary and, as before, the

Apache asked that he read it again. As Whitman interrupted himself and the Puma caught up, Whitman saw that Eskiminzin was chewing on every word, nodding, jutting his lips, narrowing his eyes, shaking his head.

"He says many things in a few words," Eskiminzin said when Whitman was finished. "He questions my honor."

John Wasson would seriously question the use of the word itself, in terms of Apache behavior, Whitman thought. "He speaks in general terms for all Apaches," Whitman said.

"It is my word. My people will do what I say."

"He cannot know that."

"Then he says that even if there is good faith we should be punished more. Is that how good faith is accepted by you?"

Whitman took time to light a fresh cigar. "There is scarcely a white person in this Territory who has not felt the punishment of the Apache. There are no beginnings. We cannot erase what has happened. Whatever you do, however the white people react, whatever we do, however Apaches react, it all is seen through the terrible things that have happened before. You remember the time the soldiers and the Mexicans attacked and killed here. White people remember the times they were attacked and killed by Apaches."

"I have done that," Eskiminzin said. "And more than once."

"Those things cannot be forgotten quickly," Whitman said. "They stay in the air like the smell of smoke after a fire. Whatever you and I may do together we cannot change what has already been done. There will be many who say that you came here not for peace but to fill your bellies and get strong so that you can go out and rob and kill again."

Eskiminzin breathed out a mouthful of smoke slowly. "How do you know that is not what I plan to do?"

"I don't know."

"But you are willing to feed and clothe us."

"It has to start somewhere. Perhaps you will make a fool of me." Whitman paused. "It would have been safer for me not to have taken any chances, Eskiminzin. And yet, if chances never were taken, by me, by you, then nothing would change and the killings would go on."

"It is strange to hear a soldier talking against killings."

"A soldier lives with killing. Perhaps more than any other man he has the knowledge to speak of it."

"What is that other word the man wrote in the paper?"

"What other word?"

The word, by reading all the words slowly, was "scourging."

"What does that mean?" Eskiminzin asked.

"What did the Puma say?"

"He made that into 'punishment.' But the man used the word 'punishment' just before that and since he must know many words he would not repeat himself that way."

Whitman leaned over toward the fire pit and broke off the ash on his cigar. There was a smile on his lips that he did not want Eskiminzin to see. He had not underestimated the Indian's intelligence from the start, but he found he was always making new appraisals.

He sat back. "It means whipping."

Eskiminzin's head raised abruptly and his jaw muscles bulged and there was a sound very close to a whimper from Child Mother.

"Whipping?" The Indian's voice was like a file rasp.

"It is what the word meant originally," Whitman said. "It has a larger, a wider meaning now. It means punishment. The Puma was right."

"Whipping."

The word had an extraordinary effect on Eskiminzin. Whitman wondered whether he had ever been whipped. It was a question he could never ask.

"They whipped Mangas Coloradas," Eskiminzin said in the same grating voice. "Cochise told me of it. He spoke of it after Mangas Coloradas was put to death in the soldier camp."

"You speak often about Mangas Coloradas," Whitman said. "Others do. Who was he? What happened to him?"

Eskiminzin drew himself together. "It was many seasons ago. Mangas Coloradas was the chief of the Mescaleros. They live in the direction where the sun comes from. White men crowded his land looking for white iron in the ground. He wanted those men to go away because. they were driving away all the food animals and they were noisy and they made the land dirty and they tried to force themselves on Mescalero women. Mangas Coloradas told the miners there was more of the white iron in another place, far from his land, and some of the miners went there but other miners said he was trying to trick them and they captured him and tied him to a tree and whipped him.

"There was one of Mangas Coloradas' subchiefs who saw that and when the white miners went away the subchief untied Mangas Coloradas and Mangas Coloradas made him swear he would not tell anyone else what happened to him. Mangas Coloradas said he would rather have been shot to death than whipped. The subchief swore he would not tell anyone and he stayed with Mangas Coloradas until the marks from the whip on his body went away. The subchief kept his pledge and never told anyone of the whipping until after Mangas Coloradas went to the soldier camp under a white flag and was put to death that same night. First the soldiers burned him with hot knives and then when he protested they shot him.

"The subchief who had seen Mangas Coloradas whipped told Cochise about it after Mangas Coloradas was dead. The subchief said that when Mangas Coloradas was whipped he died in a certain way and that the man who lived after that was not the same man."

Eskiminzin stared into his cup of *tiswin*. "I would never allow myself to be whipped, Nantan Whitman. I would kill a man who tried to whip me. I would kill you if you tried to whip me."

Child Mother looked up fearfully again. Whatever it was she wanted to say to her husband she did not say.

It took a little longer this time for Eskiminzin to bring himself under control. He asked at last, "What does it mean? What does the story from the soldier and the reply from the other man mean?"

"Everybody in Tucson, almost everybody in Arizona, will know what is happening here at Camp Grant."

"They would have learned of it anyway," Eskiminzin said indifferently.

Whitman emptied his cup of *tiswin*. It was his third. And the brew, whatever it was, did get to taste a little better. Best of all, warm and bitter as it was, it also was wet, and the inside of the wickiup was warm and he was feeling the heat and his mouth was dry. It was remarkable how much of the outside heat the skin dwelling fobbed off, but there was enough left to go around. And for this first meeting with the Apache chief in his own home, Whitman had dressed with some formality and no matter how much sweat dribbled down his neck he would not loosen his collar.

"I have worked out a plan," Whitman said. "I will give each head of a family a piece of paper and he will take that piece of paper to the beef contractor at the post and to the sutler and he will get food for his family. I will give out the pieces of paper every two days."

"How much food?"

"A pound of beef and a pound of corn or other grain."

"For each person?"

"For each family."

"What will we do for the rest of the food we will need?"

"You must supply yourselves. You gather mescal."

"That will mean people will have to leave the village."

"Mescal is gathered by women, I understand."

"Hunting parties are made of men."

There was a long silence. The outside sounds came in again. Children laughed.

"If there is game, men may go out to find it," Whitman said very slowly. "But only in small parties, very small parties. Do we understand each other, Eskiminzin?"

"We have not attacked white men with bows and arrows in a long time, Nantan Whitman." There was a flicker of a smile on the Apache's lips. "How long will you give us this food?"

"Until I am ordered to stop."

"Have you been ordered to give it to us?"

"No."

"You are doing this without orders?"

"Yes."

"Do you have the power to do this?"

"No."

"You take a risk."

"Yes."

"Have you sent a message to the star *nantan*?"

"I sent a dispatch to General Stoneman. I have heard he may visit Camp Grant before long."

"If he comes here can I meet him?"

"I will try to arrange it."

"Is he the kind of star *nantan* who sits down with Indians?"

"I don't know." Whitman took out a kerchief and wiped his forehead. "Eskiminzin, General Stoneman is important. He can support what I do or reject it. He can approve of my handing out Government beef and supplies or cancel that and punish me for exceeding my authority. General Stoneman is very important—particularly for me. But even more important is the fact that the people in Tucson and elsewhere in Arizona will be watching. They will be watching everything that is done here. We must be very careful. We must make no mistakes. We must do nothing that will give them the chance to say what a lot of them want to say, are burning to say. The head of each family here must show up at the post every two days. I can check on them there but then almost forty-eight hours will pass before I can see them again and I cannot watch over them here at your village. That is something you must do yourselves. In the end, Eskiminzin, it will be you who determines whether we succeed here, you and Little Captain and Santo and Delchan."

"Delchan," Eskiminzin said. "You have made him a head taller. And that was the last thing he needed."

"Then he will see farther and clearer." Whitman leaned closer. "Eskiminzin, listen to me. There will be all kinds of rumors and gossip and accusations from people in Tucson. There will be atrocity stories, and many of them will be true. And white people cannot tell one Apache from another. When Apaches attack they are looked on as Apaches and nobody can say what tribe they belong to. That's why we must be absolutely straight here. We cannot make mistakes. We cannot make one mistake."

Eskiminzin said presently, "I will guarantee my people."

"Totally," Whitman said. He stood up. He waited for Eskiminzin to rise and he stepped back to allow the chief to walk out of the wickiup ahead of him. Whitman turned to Child Mother and bowed. "Thank her," he said to the Puma. "Thank her for me."

Outside, after the semidarkness of the wickiup, he was half blinded for a moment. He blinked his eyes. When he could see clearly he made out Delchan, standing at a powerful attention. Eskiminzin was right. Delchan seemed to have gained height and breadth as well.

Children were playing a game with sticks and a ball made of reeds. When they saw the white officer they stopped. Some of them lowered their eyes shyly. Others stared.

At least they are not running away, Whitman told himself. When he had entered the village that day the children had stopped what they were doing when they saw him, but they had not run away either. Perhaps the day would come when his appearance would have no effect on them. By now the dogs were ignoring him and maybe one day the children would, too.

He saw a young Indian woman outside one of the three wickiups that made up Eskiminzin's compound. She looked familiar. She was on her knees softening a deer hide with deer brains. She worked the heels of her hands into the hide. She looked at him briefly and then returned to her work. Her hands moved faster. She was comely and full-breasted and Whitman recognized her as the most attractive of the five women who had first come to Camp Grant looking for the boy, Naco.

Whitman noticed that the woman wore in her hair a silver barrette in the form of a figure of eight. He asked the Puma if that meant anything.

"It means she is unwed, Teniente," the Puma said. "And that she is ready to be."

Whitman swung into the saddle and felt the hard leather thud against his hip. As he walked his horse slowly through the village he thought all over again that he belonged in that saloon.

△ 2

"Get rid of them," Lieutenant Robinson said. "There's still time to get rid of them."

Dr. Sumner poured cool water onto a cloth and wiped Whitman's forehead. This was one of the bad ones. In his medical diary the doctor had noted that Lieutenant Whitman suffered from one of the severest cases of malaria he had ever treated.

"They're nothing but trouble, Royal," Robinson said. "Get rid of them."

Whitman twisted his head. His eyes were swimming. He set his jaw and tried to speak but was taken by a new seizure. The surgeon poured fresh water from the *olla* and wiped the lieutenant's face and lips.

"I think you'd better leave him be for the time being, Lieutenant," the surgeon said to Robinson.

Whitman shook his head and waved his hand. He wet his lips. "Bill." The word was almost inaudible.

Robinson walked closer to the bed. The window in Whitman's quarters was open but the air stood dead.

"Bill," Whitman said again. He started to speak but compressed his lips against a new spiking pain. He took a deep breath. "You say to get rid of them."

"Absolutely."

"Are you suggesting that I give them back their guns and tell them to go away and start killing?"

"I didn't say anything about giving back their guns," Lieutenant Robinson said.

Whitman pushed himself up on his elbow and waved the surgeon away again. "And what would that make of me?"

Lieutenant Robinson shrugged. "A hero, I'd guess. An officer who disarmed an entire Apache tribe. You'd be decorated and probably even go down in history books."

Whitman nodded. He wiped his face. "Bill, listen to me. I'm giving orders. I want you to instruct every man on this post that when those Indians arrive for their rations there is to be no disturbance of any kind. Is that clear?"

Robinson nodded.

"I want a response," Whitman said.

"Yes, sir," Robinson said.

"No catcalls," Whitman said slowly. His lips tightened again and his body shook. "No heckling, no name-calling, no jokes, no insults from anyone."

"Yes, sir."

"That's an order. From me to every man in Camp Grant. And that goes for the civilians as well. And anyone who violates that order is to be thrown into the guardhouse immediately. There's no question about this, is there?"

"No, sir. But, Royal, I still think—"

"Goddamn it, I don't give a damn what you think!" Whitman dropped back on the bed, his chest rising and falling, his face breaking out in new sweat.

Sumner again wiped the burning face. "Mr. Robinson, this is doing him no good. I am going to suggest that you leave."

Robinson looked at Whitman, still breathing hard, his eyes closed, his hands gripping the sides of the cot, his jaw bulging against the wracking fever.

"Surgeon Sumner, may I speak to you privately?" Robinson asked in a low voice.

Robinson walked into Whitman's sitting room. The surgeon followed. Robinson looked at the suit of Spanish armor.

"Surgeon Sumner, there is a question I am bound by regulations to put to you."

"Yes," Sumner said. "I expect there is."

Robinson glanced toward the other room. "Surgeon Sumner, Lieutenant Whitman appears to be—to be a very sick man."

"He is suffering from the paroxysms usually associated with remittent fever."

"Yes, I have gone through that myself more than once." Robinson hesitated. It seemed to him that there was an expression on the mouthpiece of the helmet on the armor and it was not a pleasant one. "This seizure appears to be of unusual severity," Robinson said.

"What is your question, Lieutenant?"

Robinson turned away from the armor. "Surgeon Sumner, in your medical judgment, is Lieutenant Whitman capable of exercising command?"

Sumner hesitated.

"Why don't you reply, Surgeon?" Whitman asked.

Both men looked up, startled. Whitman was standing in the doorway. He was pale and looked weak but his eyes were clear and in focus and his body no longer shook.

"Surgeon Sumner," Whitman said very distinctly, "Lieutenant Robinson addressed a question to you."

"The question is withdrawn," Robinson said.

"I'll answer it anyway," the surgeon said. "The answer is yes."

"Thank you, Surgeon," Whitman said. "I think I've got myself in hand now. I suggest that you return to the infirmary and have a check on your other patients. I'll drop by later. Bill, will you please stay here."

When the surgeon had gone, Whitman sat down and breathed in deeply and looked at Rodriguez Gonzáles.

"Royal," Robinson said.

Whitman looked up and one of his rare smiles touched his mouth. "Sit down, Bill, sit down. I'm not going to bring you up on charges of attempted mutiny." Whitman nodded slowly. "It was a proper question, Bill. It was your duty to pose it." When Robinson started to speak again, Whitman said, "Pour a couple of drinks, Bill. I'm freezing."

Later, in bed, Whitman started to shake violently again. The Mexican woman cleaning his quarters looked into the room. She wet a cloth and wiped his face.

"*Pobrecito*," she said. "*Pobrecito*."

△ 3

More than anything, Eskiminzin wanted his people to know they were safe. He ordered that a big fire be kept burning at all times in the middle of the village so the people would know they could reveal to the soldiers where they were, and nothing would happen to them. There was a fire blazing now. It was in the middle of the day and the sun was fire enough.

There now were well over three hundred Aravaipas and Pinals in the village and more coming in from the hills and the deserts all the time, and now fifty or sixty or more of the fighting men were collected in the clearing near the bonfire. This was big talk and the children stayed away and kept the dogs away.

Eskiminzin explained how the men would get food for their families from the white men at Camp Grant. There was talking after that and then Little Captain got to his feet. Everybody stopped talking. Little Captain was a notable in the tribe and when he spoke it was well to listen to him.

Little Captain held his spear, with its eagle feathers, and he looked across the faces of the hunkered-down fighting men, who no longer truly were fighting men since the tools for their fighting had been removed from them. Little Captain stood in a half crouch. He looked as though he might spring at any moment, in any direction.

"Does this man say that men must go and collect this food?" Little Captain asked.

Eskiminzin said, "Yes."

"To gather food is women's work," Little Captain said.

There were shouts of agreement. Delchan, marching around the congregation, his rifle in his hand, paused and raised his head and sniffed as though he smelled danger.

"Generally speaking, yes," Eskiminzin agreed. "In this case, no."

"It is undignified," Little Captain said.

"It is undignified to have women and children and to be unable to feed them."

"I would rather go hungry than do something without dignity," Little Captain said.

There were more cries of approval. Delchan surveyed the assemblage as though determining which one he might be forced to shoot first.

"Whether you go hungry or not, whether your family goes hungry or not, that is your choice," Eskiminzin said to Little Captain. "But you will go with the other men so the soldier chief can look at your face."

"Why must he look at my face? He has seen my face."

"I have explained to you that he must look at your face every other sun."

"He does not trust me," Little Captain said.

"Do you trust him?"

Little Captain thought on that and Delchan paused again in his round.

"I trust him a little," Little Captain said finally.

"He trusts you a little," Eskiminzin said. Then he asked, "Does the man think hunting for meat is undignified?"

"No!" Little Captain said strongly. "That is the work for a man!"

"Good. I agree." Eskiminzin looked at his warriors and then back at Little Captain. "Then why do you not look on this as hunting for meat? You leave your village and you go out and you return with beef in your hands to feed your family. What is undignified about that? The beef comes from the same place. The only thing that is different is that the white man has worked for you like a captured slave. He has killed and butchered the meat for you."

Little Captain pondered that and then slowly nodded. By then some of the other men were crying out, and again in approval. Delchan thought that maybe he would not have to shoot anyone after all. He shooed away a dog that had ambled up to see what was going on and then resumed his circuit.

"It is true!" a man shouted, laughing. "It is the same thing as having the white-eyes work for us."

There were a lot of men laughing now, some of them holding their bellies, and Delchan relaxed even more. Little Captain sat down to ponder more and another man rose to his feet. His name meant Bear Skin, commemorating the time when he had slain that animal.

"What the man talks about the beef makes good sense," he said.

There were grunts of agreement and Delchan nodded his own great head.

"But what about the corn?" Bear Skin inquired.

That was a new thought. Men stopped laughing and frowned.

"The corn can be looked on the same as the beef," Eskiminzin said, knowing it was not the same thing at all. He cursed the devil spirit that had put the thought into Bear Skin's head. Bear Skin rarely had an original thought from one end of the year to the next and look at what he had come up with now.

"It is not the same thing at all," Bear Skin said. "With the beef we can pretend to ourselves we killed the animal ourselves. But what can we say to ourselves about the corn? We cannot pretend that we gathered it ourselves because that is something men have never done."

Having dropped that bombshell, Bear Skin sat down, and now there were angry mutterings again and Delchan thought he had been overly optimistic and prematurely so. He would have to shoot Bear Skin, whom he liked personally, chiefly because they gambled often and Bear Skin usually lost, but if it had to be that way Delchan would not fail in his responsibility.

Little Captain felt he had been outflanked by Bear Skin. He felt the distinction between beef and corn was something he should have pointed out. He believed he had lost some face and he stood up again to retrieve it.

"I have thought of a solution to this problem," Little Captain said.

"Listen to the man!" several warriors shouted.

"The men and the women will go to Camp Grant separately," Little Captain said. "The men will collect the beef as though they had hunted it. The women will collect the corn as though they gathered it as they always gathered it."

It was so obviously a wise, more, a brilliant, solution to the dilemma that it was seconded immediately by every man present with the exception of Eskiminzin and, Eskiminzin noted, Santo. Santo would have something to say as well, Eskiminzin knew, but before he dealt with him, he had to settle the present crisis.

"That is impossible," Eskiminzin said.

The men were still shouting out their endorsement of Little Captain's plan and their approbation and most of them did not hear what Eskiminzin said.

"That is impossible," Eskiminzin said again.

This time the men heard him and their happy talking died down.

"Why is it impossible?" Bear Skin inquired. He did not stand up to ask the question so it was plain he had nothing more to say than just that.

"The *nantan* has given me pieces of paper to give to you," Eskiminzin said. "There are only enough pieces of paper for the heads of families. There are not enough pieces of paper for the women. More than that, if the women go to the camp, then who will watch the children? More than that, I do not want our women wandering around the soldier camp. No, the men will get the pieces of paper and the men will go to the camp and the men will collect the beef and the corn. That is the way it will be."

Little Captain stood up again. Little Captain was angry. Little Captain had failed to perceive the difference between beef and corn that Bear Skin had uncovered and that was bad enough; but he had come up with an intelligent solution to the problem Bear Skin had raised, which not only made up for his original obtuseness, but which put him ahead of the game. And now the chief was unceremoniously rejecting it.

"It is in my mind not to do it," Little Captain said.

Now a real tension started to seep across the meeting. Little Captain was a very important man and he was leader of his own clan and could very well have been chief of the whole tribe. He was so important that Delchan knew it would be the most difficult thing in his life to bring himself to shoot Little Captain and he was not certain he could do that.

After a while, Eskiminzin said, "Then you will leave."

Little Captain raised his head a little higher and the men squatting on the ground looked at one another and shifted uneasily.

"This man has been my right arm," Eskiminzin said. "This

man has been my war chief. This man and I have been as
brothers. But if this man does not support my word then we
will look at each other for the last time and he will leave."

"Leave," Little Captain repeated.

"This man will leave here and take his family away and
take whatever followers who want to go with him and they all
never will again return to Little Running Water in Dark Canyon. And if any does return he will be looked upon as an
enemy."

"By whom?" Little Captain demanded.

"By me." Eskiminzin's voice was low. The men on the
farthest edge of the circle heard him. In a still-lower voice, still
heard by every man, Eskiminzin said, "I have given the *nantan*
my word."

Bear Skin shouted, "What is your word to a white-eyes?"

"It is my word," Eskiminzin said. He paused. He was not
certain how it was going to go. In all the time the men had been
sitting there no owl had hooted and that gave him hope.

"You are bound by me," he said. "I tell you this now. All
of you who remain here are bound by me."

His voice grew deeper and took on timbre and the air itself
became silent. There was no sound of birds and the rest of the
village was far away. The gathering near the bonfire became an
encapsulated enclave and the dimensions were the range of
Eskiminzin's voice. There was no world but that world. It was
the power he had. The power spoke through his voice. The men
had heard it before often. It was why he had come to be known
as Hash-ki-ban-zin.

He stood there in the silence and let his power work. He
had to hold these angry men in line.

"Any man who breaks my word is my enemy," he said.
"Any man who breaks my word is an enemy to all of us, to our
children and to our women and to our old people. I have given
my word to Nantan Whitman that I will bring my people to
peace. That peace cannot include men who make me a liar. I
tell you this: those who would break my word, those who would
bring harm to others here, go, go, now, go in safety, go in peace,
go as brothers, but go—and do not return."

The words tumbled around as though the cloud birds were throwing rocks at one another. No one would have been surprised if the sun had suddenly blackened its face and the sky emptied itself of tears.

"Those who walk away will see Little Running Water and the Dark Canyon from the outside," Eskiminzin said. "As soon as you leave this earth you are enemies to all your people. If they see you first on this land they will kill you. If you see them first you will kill them."

The words crashed against one another in the air.

Finally one man spoke. "How can we live without our weapons?"

His words released others from their thralldom and men yelled and roared out the same question.

"We lived with our own weapons for a long time. We killed with our own weapons for a long time," Eskiminzin said. "You can learn again."

The men, sitting on the ground, without moving from their positions, formed little knots, discussing the challenge their chief had delivered, the banishment he had pronounced. Little Captain remained standing, his eyes on Eskiminzin. The Apache chief looked at his war chief as steadily. There was nothing more to be said. The men would chew it out and then maybe some of them would no longer be held in line and would get up and would walk away.

Santo rose to his feet. All talking stopped again, and instantly. Santo held a special respect. He was too old for war but his strength had never lain in fighting but in religion and as a religious leader his white hair added to his wisdom and his prestige.

"I do not worry about dignity," Santo said. His voice was deep, too, and carried, from many years of telling religious truths to people. "Dignity is in the heart. A man with dignity can do nothing undignified."

That was on his side, Eskiminzin reckoned, and that alone might tip the balance. But there would be something else. There always was something else.

"There is something else," Santo said. "This man tells us we must give the white men little pieces of paper to exchange for food." Santo paused for a long time. He had learned in the years to use pauses. "What is it that is put down on the little pieces of paper to make the white man give us food?"

Eskiminzin drew in deeply. He had anticipated this trap, had hoped that by some great gesture of the Everywhere Spirit it could be avoided.

"The names of each head of family," he said.

"Then we are giving our names over to our enemies," Santo said.

Now there was a terrified silence and then a large single outcry. Nobody had thought of that, not even Little Captain. Eskiminzin had thought of it long before, when Whitman had outlined his plan to him. Eskiminzin knew it had to come up in some way before the discussion with his men was ended since miracles never really happen, but he counted it a piece of bad luck that it had to come from the lips of one as revered as Santo. He could not order Santo to pack up and walk away and tell him if he ever showed his face again he would be shot.

"These soldiers no longer are our enemies," Eskiminzin said, knowing the feebleness of that tactic.

"They are always our enemies," Santo said, stating an eternal truth. "Sometimes they are less our enemies than other times but they are always our enemies. And if we give to the white *nantan* at Camp Grant pieces of paper with the names of every warrior in our tribe we are handing this white man power over all of us. We are giving the white man something of ourselves we can never take back. And that white man can use that power over us in any way he wants to use it. And there is nothing even in my power that I could do to stop him."

The men sat cross-legged and transfixed. Santo had reached out and had touched their souls. They stared at Santo as though he was the last living thing in the world.

"To give one's name in speaking is dangerous enough," Santo said. "But the sound of a spoken word flies away quickly in the air and maybe some of the power that has been given away flies away too. But something that is scratched down lasts forever, the way the pictures the ancient people scratched on the rocks has lasted forever."

Santo gripped his lance with both hands and rested on it

as though it were a prophet's staff. Santo looked at no one, not at Eskiminzin, not at the men. Santo spoke to no one, not to Eskiminzin nor the men. Santo spoke to the winds. Santo spoke to the sky. Santo spoke to eternity.

"And what does that mean? It means that the *nantan* has that power over us forever. And what does that mean? This man tells us Nantan Whitman is a good man and can be trusted, but one day a bad soldier chief may get those pieces of paper and then a bad white man would have power over us."

There was an inhalation of breath at the revelation of this ultimate horror and the air in the enclave went away.

Santo raised his head and stared into his private vision. "I do not want to give the white man power over me."

"Nor I!" Little Captain shouted.

"Nor I! Nor I!" The shouts came from everywhere.

"Nor I!" Little Captain shouted again.

Little Captain was on sure ground now. If he had some reservations about walking away from his people on the question of having to accept corn along with the beef, he had no hesitancy on taking an absolute, resolute stand on the cardinal point at issue.

Eskiminzin waited until the clamor subsided and he waited to hear whether Santo had anything more to say and then he waited some more. In the years with Santo he had learned a great deal about the value of pauses.

"He knows your name," he said at last to Santo. "He knows your name," he said to Little Captain.

"I did not give it to him," Santo said bleakly, still staring at nothing. "*You* did. That is a different thing altogether. A name spoken by another yields no power."

"You gave him mine too," Little Captain said.

Eskiminzin nodded in full agreement. He knew that this development, the matter of passing over names, had put the first matter of dignity behind them all. If he could solve this one, he might still have a win.

"Then this is what we will do," Eskiminzin said, and he had learned, too, over the years how to speak in terms of simple practicality, as though what he was ordering was the only sensible thing to do. "When each man steps up to get his ration of beef he will give the white man not his own name but the name of the man behind him. In that way no man will be put in peril. And I will explain it to the *nantan* beforehand."

The men were silent for several moments while that sank through the canonical dread Santo had summoned up, and then one man shouted and then another, and then all of them were on their feet. They danced little steps and waved their arms, and dogs and children were attracted and came closer.

After some more time Little Captain raised his lance, and the men, already licking their chops, stopped dancing and waving their arms, and reluctantly quieted.

"What of the first man in the line?" Little Captain asked. "Who will give his name over to the white-eyes?"

"Yes!" Santo said, turning again to Eskiminzin. "Has the man thought about that?"

"They know my name," Eskiminzin said. "I will be the first in line."

△ 4

"Chiquito Capitán!" Eskiminzin spoke the words clearly.

Even if it were not the triumphant windup to his solution to the problem of handing over personal names to white enemies, Eskiminzin would have led his men into Camp Grant on that day in March when the wind set out to show that when it chose it was irresistible.

The gusts yowled as though they were carrying protests from the dead and the parade-ground pebbles chattered like the rattle of a baby of giants. The dust rose and splattered like surf.

The Apache warriors, now armed with nothing more than the knives tucked into their belts or into the pockets of their moccasins, folded over below their knees, were as nervous as mountain cats. Without their chief to stride in front of them nothing could have made them set foot inside the post.

Eskiminzin walked against the wind and the dust as though he were pushing back endless doors. He looked at nothing, except perhaps the future. His men looked at everything, at the soldiers lounging under the *ramadas*, at the armed guards, at the curious civilians, at the buildings, at the small artillery pieces, at the company washerwomen drifting up from Suds Row, drying their reddened hands on their skirts, squinting against the dust and the wind and the sun to witness the novel spectacle of Apache warriors unengaged in their natural profession.

Even with their chief marching ahead of them with his face raised and looking impervious to anything that the white man or the elements could hurl against it, the men all looked ready to bolt, as Eskiminzin himself and Little Captain and Santo had been again and again at the point of skittering when first they had ridden down the long length of the parade ground.

Whitman was not in sight and Eskiminzin understood that as a gesture not only of tact but of deference as well. It was necessary for the Apache men to know that their chief was capable of providing the fortitude they required to make what seemed to them to be the longest walk of their lives. It would have been wrong and patronizing for the white officer to be there as though he were needed to shepherd them.

In their last meeting, after Eskiminzin had explained the device of the names and Whitman had said he understood and would explain to the beef contractor and the sutler, Whitman had instructed Eskiminzin where to lead his men, and now the Apache chief walked resolutely toward Miles Wood's depot. He was not resolute. He trusted Whitman but he did not know altogether why he trusted him and as he walked he prayed that what he was doing was the right thing to do.

That morning he had stepped outside his wickiup and he had looked upward and he had asked the Everywhere Spirit to give him wisdom and guide him. He had the faith of any Apache in the Everywhere Spirit but he was well aware that sometimes the Everywhere Spirit did things that were not immediately understood. He hoped with all his heart this was not to be one of those times.

The Apache line filed down the length of the parade ground, making a moving shadow that crawled on the pebbles like a monumental centipede, and Eskiminzin presented himself at last at the door of Miles Wood's commissary. Miles

Wood did not look at the Apache chief and at the men behind him with joy. Miles Wood believed it was sinful to give good Government beef to Apache Indians. Miles Wood had to obey the post commander, of course, but that did not mean he had to be happy.

Eskiminzin saw the expression on the beef contractor's face and he understood it so quickly it was as though he had anticipated it would be there. There would be many mouths and eyes like that in the faces of many white men with whom he and his people now would be involved. If he were lucky maybe it would remain just a sign on faces and would get no worse than that.

Eskiminzin stepped up to Miles Wood. He saw Oscar Hutton leaning on the side of the building. Eskiminzin did not know Oscar Hutton's name but he recognized him as a man who was famous for hunting and killing Apaches. Oscar Hutton chewed on a piece of wood and looked quietly at Eskiminzin. The expression on Oscar Hutton's face was different from that that Miles Wood wore. There seemed to be something questioning on Oscar Hutton's face, as though he were sizing up Eskiminzin and was wondering just when, and under just what circumstances, he would have the opportunity to kill him.

"Chiquito Capitán!" Eskiminzin called out.

Miles Wood, clued in by Lieutenant Whitman, handed Eskiminzin a slab of meat. Eskiminzin accepted it and walked on to the sutler's store while Little Captain stepped up to Miles Wood and announced the name of Santo. Eskiminzin was given a small sack of corn meal by Fred Austin. The sutler was no happier about what was transpiring than was Miles Wood or Oscar Hutton. Nature had constructed Fred Austin's face in a kindlier mold, however, so his displeasure was not as grim.

Little Captain proceeded to the sutler's store while Santo presented himself to Miles Wood and called out "Bear Skin." And so it went, without a hitch, each Apache announcing the name of the man behind him, receiving his ration and then walking away, wanting to get off the limits of the post as quickly as possible but refusing to run.

The last man on the line, on Eskiminzin's orders, was

Delchan, who had also been ordered to leave his rifle in the Apache village, and who now looked helpless and confused. He felt helpless without the rifle and he was confused because his name had already been spoken by the man who had stood in front of him.

He had no name to call out, and after standing awkwardly in front of Miles Wood for a moment or two, the contractor handed over his ration and Delchan walked over to Fred Austin and accepted the sack of grain.

Eskiminzin, who had remained throughout the distribution, gave his ration to Delchan and told him to give it to Child Mother.

Eskiminzin watched Delchan walk out of the fort. As he made his way to Lieutenant Whitman's headquarters Eskiminzin heard the soldiers, who had remained silent until then, begin a babble of talk. It was as though the post had wakened from a sleep.

△ 5

Whitman looked at Eskiminzin curiously. "You think it is bad for your people to accept something for nothing," he repeated. "When you attacked wagon trains and took what did not belong to you, when you stole cattle, wasn't that getting something for nothing?"

"We got nothing for nothing."

"You stole, didn't you?"

"We also risked our lives. We often were killed. We paid for our booty in blood."

"Did that make you feel like men?"

"We were men."

"And receiving rations is another thing."

"It is bad for us," Eskiminzin said again.

The Apache finished the coffee that Duncan had brought to Whitman's quarters. He rolled a cigarette.

"Our people are not accustomed to charity," he said. "Charity is dependence. We never were dependent on anything. It was the mark of our people. Whatever we did, whether we grew corn or hunted or robbed or killed, we were dependent only on ourselves. We never had to give out our names and stand in line to be fed. Only old people were fed by others. Only old people who could no longer get food for themselves. And the food was brought to them. They did not have to stand in line."

Whitman poured more coffee. It was not as good as the coffee Child Mother had served to him. He wondered whether he could persuade Duncan to speak to Child Mother about that.

"Are you sorry for what you have done?" Whitman asked.

"No." Eskiminzin smoked the cigarette. "The death had arrived. The only question was what kind of death I would choose for my people. I picked this kind of death. The Apache will have a full belly, maybe, and he will be able to walk around without fear, but he has no weapon and he has died in another way."

"Yes," Whitman said quietly. "I can understand that. And yet there is something to be said for a full belly and an absence of fear."

Eskiminzin nodded as the Puma gave him the words. "Yes, it is good for the women and it is good for the children and the old who cannot fight and find it hard to run. But I did not do this for them. It will not be the men and the women, even the old ones, who benefit from this, and perhaps not even the children. Maybe it will be the children or maybe it will have to be the children of those children."

Eskiminzin stood up and walked past the suit of armor. He looked at the shining metal for a moment and then went on to the window and looked out. He was silent for a long time.

"I suppose what I have done is surrender the souls of the men you saw standing in line there waiting like dogs to be given food to eat. I have given up their souls for those not yet born. And when that time comes, when the children of the children are born, then, by that time, the thing that is in us, the thing that makes us Apaches, the thing that makes us different, then that will have died long before, and it never will have been in those children and it never will be missed." He stared out the window. "I do not deny it, Nantan Whitman. It would have been better if you people never came."

The Apache chief walked slowly around Whitman's quarters looking curiously at everything. Duncan brought more coffee. Eskiminzin watched Duncan until the striker left the room.

"Why do you look at him so closely?" Whitman asked. "You have seen him before."

"His face is being born," Eskiminzin said.

Whitman, lighting a cigar, paused, "You can see that?"

"His face has changed from the first time I saw it."

Whitman blew out the match.

"I think he is learning some things," Eskiminzin said.

Whitman nodded. "I think so too."

"I have another feeling. I have the feeling he may be the soldier who wrote the letter."

"I've thought of that. What makes you think so?"

The Apache shrugged. "He is close to you. He regards you with respect. His eyes are proud when they look at you. And something is coming alive in him. Yes, I think he wrote the letter."

"I don't want to know," Whitman said.

Eskiminzin walked over to the suit of armor. He looked at it with interest. "The grandfathers used to tell of warriors who came here from some distant place to fight, wearing those coverings of iron. They were the Spaniards. They came for yellow iron and they brought shamans who tried to make everybody believe in their god. There were tribes of people here who changed to the Spaniard's god. They always ended up as slaves." Eskiminzin looked at the armor from helmet to metal feet. "I have never seen this before." He reached out to touch the breastplate and then glanced at Whitman, who nodded. Eskiminzin tapped his finger on the iron.

"How foolish to put men in their own prisons," he said. "What must it have been like to be inside one of those things under the desert sun? The warriors must have been cooked before we could get around to killing them."

He turned and looked at Whitman. His face was composed but there was a light in his eyes.

"It seems to me that you people have not learned much from these foolish men. Your soldiers march around on the same desert with enough clothing and blankets to keep them warm on top of a mountain in the snow. They fight the heat and the sun and the desert and when it comes time to fight the Apache the best is gone from them."

"They manage," Whitman said.

Eskiminzin nodded. "Yes, they manage. They manage too well."

"But I will make a report to my superiors. I'm certain they'll appreciate this expert advice from the chief of the Aravaipas."

"They will not," Eskiminzin said. "Those people are not here. They do not have to wear that clothing and carry those things and go out and fight."

Eskiminzin pulled back the curtain that covered the recess where Whitman hung his uniforms. He fingered the uniforms and felt their weight. He strolled around the room, as Whitman smoked and watched silently, and looked at the quiver filled with arrows and at the Apache bow, at the bottles with the preserved specimens of desert denizens, at the colored reproduction of the view of the Hudson River, a kind of river he had never seen, trees he had never seen.

"It is like looking through a small opening," he said.

"Yes. I think the artist would have liked that."

"Do you know that place?"

"More or less."

"Is is far from here?"

"Very far."

"One day you will tell me about places like that, maybe."

"Yes."

He stared at the picture. "A man must have great power to capture a place like that and trap it."

"Yes," Whitman said. "It is surely a kind of power."

Eskiminzin walked over to the washbasin. He raised his eyes and looked for the first time into the mirror above it. He became very still and then an expression of horror crept over his face and he covered his face with both hands to deny his face to the glass and he backed away slowly.

Duncan, who had come in with fresh coffee, started to

laugh and then abruptly stopped himself. The Puma stared morbidly at Eskiminzin, himself not wholly rid of attitudes and superstitions absorbed during his years of captivity. He was in no way surprised at Eskiminzin's terror. He had seen Cochise call off vital meetings with his subchiefs because a tree branch snapped or lightning damaged the sky or an owl hooted.

Presently Eskiminzin brought himself under control. He lowered his hands but kept his face turned away from the mirror. He fingered the amulet hanging from his neck. He looked at Whitman and then at Duncan and then longest at the Puma. He knew that of all of them the Puma understood.

Whitman asked, "Have you never before seen your image?"

Eskiminzin rolled a cigarette. His fingers moved slowly and carefully. "Alone," he said. "In a quiet part of a stream, in a shiny piece of white iron. Men look at their faces. Men look at their faces when they pull out hairs. But always alone. But I have never seen anything that showed me myself like this, and with others seeing it, too."

"Is it the same as giving out the name?" Whitman asked.

Eskiminzin held up his hand as though to ward off the question, and then he nodded.

"You gave me your name in the beginning," Whitman said quietly. "I took nothing from you then. I take nothing from you now."

Eskiminzin fingered the amulet. "Do you look on these things as stupid Indian things?"

"No."

"Our feelings about our names? Our feelings about having our faces caught in glass?"

"No."

"Is it because we are not as clever as you?"

"It has nothing to do with cleverness, Eskiminzin," Whitman said.

The officer thought he could make out what looked very much like embarrassment in Eskiminzin's face and perhaps even some self-disgust. It was suddenly important to Whitman to deal with that.

"It has nothing to do with cleverness," he repeated. "It has nothing to do with differences between Indians and white men. White men have beliefs they cannot explain. At least you make a kind of sense. But, for instance, there are white people who are afraid of certain numbers and they won't do things on the days that have those numbers—and they cannot explain why. There are white people who believe animals of a certain color bring bad luck and they will go out of their way to avoid such an animal—and they cannot explain why."

Eskiminzin nodded and sat down and smoked his cigarette. He looked at Duncan as the trooper filled his cup. He drank the coffee.

Presently Whitman leaned forward and said, "Eskiminzin, this peace that we are trying to work out. That may take something from your people, as you have said, something of the fierce fighting spirit, but perhaps the time for that spirit has passed, perhaps it won't be a bad thing that the children's children will never know of it."

Eskiminzin looked at Whitman for a long time. Then he made another cigarette and this time his fingers worked more quickly.

"You look a great deal on the children in my village," the Apache said.

Whitman's forehead wrinkled. "Is it that plain?"

"You always look at the children. You always look to see how the children look on you."

Whitman nodded slowly.

"You are not accustomed to frightening children."

"I am not."

"But why should the children not be frightened? To our children a white officer has always meant only one thing—death."

Eskiminzin lit his cigarette. For a little while he went away.

"From the beginning our children are taught to hate anything that is not Apache," he said in a low voice, and, it seemed, from some distant place. "That is the way it always has been. That was to save their lives later when they could be faced with danger and would have no time to think out what to do, when they must do the right thing naturally. That is the way it always was. Then they were taught to hate Mexicans above all others. Mexicans pay hunters for Apache scalps. Apaches do not scalp and since Apache scalps are not the easiest thing for men to get their hands on, other Indians have suffered, especially tame Indians. How can the Mexicans tell what Indian head a scalp comes from?

"At first when the Americans came here they were hated because they were strangers, the same as any other enemy tribe, but they were never hated in the beginning as much as the Mexicans. It took a long time, many, many seasons, back to the grandfathers' grandfathers to make a hatred such as the hatred for the Mexicans. In the beginning it even seemed that the Americans and the Apaches could become friends because the Americans fought the Mexicans when they came here and that made the Americans our allies and we would have been happy to fight at their sides against our ancient enemies.

"But then the Americans made friends with the Mexicans. We never understood how people could be enemies one day and friends the next day, and then after that, when the boy *nantan* killed Cochise's people and my people, we decided Americans were not only stupid and unreliable, but that they were treacherous.

"And now when Apache children are given their hatreds, the Americans come first. When Apache children are bad, their mothers quiet them by threatening to give them away to the Americans. That is the way it is."

Whitman shook his head slowly. "It may come as a surprise to you, Eskiminzin, but the same words are used against your people, the same words. American mothers frighten their children by telling them that if they're bad the Apaches will steal them away."

Eskiminzin looked at the glowing butt of his cigarette. "We have done big things against each other. This man wonders whether anything can ever be changed."

"Perhaps not among us altogether," Whitman said. "Perhaps the best we can do is stop killing each other and wait it out and give the unborn children a chance."

Eskiminzin pondered that. Then he shook his head. "I do

not believe it ever will be that way among peoples. Between men, here and there, maybe, but not among peoples."

"Fortunately," Whitman said, "peoples begin with men."

Eskiminzin stood up. "Has the star *nantan* sent a signal to you yet?"

"No."

"Has there been time enough?"

"Yes, I believe so."

"Do you still believe he will visit here?"

"I don't know."

Turning his face to keep it from being reflected in the mirror, Eskiminzin walked past Whitman's writing desk. He saw on it the volume of Ralph Waldo Emerson's works that was never far from Whitman's hand. The Indian stared at the small leather-bound book as though it were yet another piece of white man's magic and then he reached down and picked it up and opened it and looked at the printed words.

"Those are the sayings of a wise man," Whitman said. He wondered what his father would have thought of his book in the hands of an Apache Indian.

"What are some of the words?" Eskiminzin asked. He held out the book.

After a moment Whitman took it. He glanced at the Puma. The Puma, as always, seemed to have vanished into a wall. Was it ridiculous to read something from a book of poetry and essays to an Indian? Perhaps it was. Whitman was glad Duncan was out of the room and he also was a little ashamed at being glad.

Eskiminzin had stepped back and his arms were folded and he gazed at Whitman serenely. He appeared to be taking the moment solemnly, with a total appreciation of its importance.

Whitman looked through the pages. He knew them all almost by heart by now but at this time, when he wanted something uniquely appropriate, especially fitting, nothing he read seemed to do. He glanced at Eskiminzin and wondered what this delay was causing him to think, and he looked back at the book, and then he found something he thought would do.

He looked at Eskiminzin again. Whitman wondered what the words from a book would mean, would they mean more than words from a newspaper? Some of the converted Indians had been exposed to the Bible, but these Apaches surely had not. How, he wondered, would the words jibe with the mystique of the giving of names and reflections in a mirror?

He read slowly, *"The highest compact we can make with our fellow is—'Let there be truth between us two forevermore.'"*

There was nothing in the Puma's voice as he translated, the trained, habitual, sterile monotony, as though the words came from anywhere but from the mouth of a human being.

When the last word was translated Eskiminzin raised his eyes and looked directly at Whitman. Whitman knew it was not ridiculous to read something from a book to an Apache.

△ 6

When the days passed and there still was no word from General Stoneman, Whitman sent out a second letter to the commanding general of the Department of Arizona.

"I have a wonderful family here in the desert," he wrote in part. *"These Aravaipa Apaches, especially their chief, Eskiminzin, have won me completely. The men, though poorly clothed and ignorant, refuse to lie or steal. The women work like slaves to clothe their babies and themselves, and although untaught, hold their virtue above price. They need help to show them the way to higher civilization and I will give them this help as long as they are permitted to stay."*

Part Three

△ △ △ ONE

△ 1

Eskiminzin was hard currency now. In those March days Eskiminzin stories were told in the Congress Hall, in the Quartz
Rock and the Hanging Wall and the Golden West. They were
passed back and forth by shoppers between purchases in the big
busy stores of Tully & Ochoa, Charles T. Hayden, Lord &
Williams, and in the crowded Zeckendorf place next door to
the *Citizen*. They were gone over and over again by bitter men
in front of Jake Mansfeld's News Depot and were discussed in
quiet tones by men elegant enough to patronize Sam Bostick's
Shaving Saloon. In the tiny *tendejónes* in the back streets, the
dark air filled with the bright smells of chili and *carne seca* and
fresh bread, Mexicans whispered what they knew of the Apache
devil. Men dined out on Eskiminzin stories in the famous homes
of Hiram Stevens and Sammy Hughes, and so fascinated were
the guests they almost forgot to look at and comment on what
it was that made those homes famous, the fact that the floors
were not pounded earth but were actually made of wood.

There were those fussy folk who vaguely remembered hearing many of those same stories before, and that the villain then
was not Eskiminzin, but Cochise or Victorio or even Mangas
Coloradas. After having second thoughts those persons thought
they probably were mistaken.

The ghastly, gory stories were recounted most of all at the
Congress Hall because that was where Bill Oury spent his time
and where, more often than not, his close friend Jesús María
Elías joined him.

Elías told the story of Inez Gonzáles. It was a story many
of the men had heard before but, like stories from the Good
Book, it could always be told again.

193

"Inez Gonzáles was a distant relative of mine," Jesús María Elías said. "I was about twenty years old at the time."

The time was the last day of September in 1849 when a beautiful highborn fifteen-year-old girl named Inez Gonzáles departed from her home, the Hacienda La Palma, on the mesa west of the upper Río San Pedro near the small town of Santa Cruz in Sonora. Inez, regarded as one of the great beauties of the area, was setting out to visit a sister in Magdalena to attend the Fiesta de San Francisco and to visit with the nuns who had educated her in one of the convents there. Included in the company were her aunt and uncle, Ramón and Juana Gonzáles, several servants, and many pack mules loaded with presents. All of them were escorted over the seventy-five-mile journey by a detachment of *rurales*.

In Cocospera Canyon, Apaches led by Eskiminzin attacked. Eskiminzin was not then the chief he became but he was a rising war leader, clever in that supreme Apache tactic, the ambush. In no time the Apaches had killed the soldiers, knifing those who had been brought down but not immediately killed. Then Ramón Gonzáles, already wounded, was stripped naked in front of the women and was bound by rawhide thongs to a thorny cactus.

"Normally," Jesús María Elías explained, "they would have used wet thongs, stretched out, and then let the sun dry the thongs and contract them to accomplish their purpose, but they had no time for that leisurely pleasure. Instead, Apaches held the women and forced them to watch as other Apaches, all hideously painted, slowly tightened the thongs, impaling Ramón Gonzáles a thousand times at once. Ramón Gonzáles was a Castilian aristocrat and he fought to keep himself from screaming as the thongs were tightened, and he prayed for forgiveness for his sins, the latest being his indecent exposure, and the women prayed, too, and then their prayers were granted them and Ramón Gonzáles was given peace in death."

The women were then thrown over Indian ponies, Inez on the back of Eskiminzin's pony, and the Apaches started back for their *ranchería*, towing the laden pack mules behind them.

"On the way they jumped a farmer and his two sons in a wagon," Elías went on. "They killed the sons and wounded the father. They located a big ant hill and kicked it to disturb the ants and then they stripped the father and laid him over the mound and weighted down his chest with a heavy rock and watched for a while as the infuriated red ants crawled over the naked body and began eating the father to death."

In the Apache camp high in the mountains, Inez and her aunt and the servants were made into slaves along with other captured Mexican women. They worked from morning to night, carrying water up from a creek far below the camp, hauling food, and the old Apache hags, who went around in nothing but skirts made of strips of bark from trees, and whose empty and flattened breasts flapped against their chests as they moved about, tormented them constantly, beating them, kicking them, pinching them until they drew blood, and at the same time giving them only enough food to keep them alive.

Then Inez Gonzáles learned that something else was in store for her. She had caught the eye of Eskiminzin. Eskiminzin, himself always naked except for a breechclout, was becoming more and more important, and the leading chief, Santo, listened to him. And Eskiminzin looked long and often at Inez Gonzáles, and when her labors were reduced and the hags treated her less severely, the other Mexican women told her what was going to happen to her.

"She was saved from that fate by the goodness of God," Elías said somberly. "There is an old custom among Apaches and the renegades who trade with them. Once a year they all meet on the banks of the Gila River above where it is joined by the San Pedro. There old hatreds are forgotten and the men drink and boast of what they have done in the past year and after that they trade. Juana Gonzáles, Inez's aunt, was sold to a Navajo chief. Inez was sold to three Mexicans." Elías paused again and his face showed even more pain. "These Mexicans unfortunately were not the best of our race, gentlemen. Their plan was to sell Inez back to her family for ransom."

Instead, the Mexicans were intercepted by Captain John R. Bartlett, of the United States Boundary Commission. Captain

Bartlett forced the Mexicans to release the girl and then he saw to it that she was returned to her family.

"Nothing more was ever heard of Juana Gonzáles," Elías concluded.

There was quiet in the Congress Hall as Elías finished. He had cast a spell and each man was experiencing a celebration of hate and no one wanted to be the first to end it.

John Wasson yielded to no man in his abomination of Apache Indians. After all, it was he who had pointed out their racial failing. And yet there was enough of the genuine newspaperman in him to fill his mind now with questions.

"Where is Inez Gonzáles now?" he asked.

"She is married to a Mexican gentleman," Elías said.

"How did she know the Apache was Eskiminzin?" Wasson asked. "It's been my understanding that his true Apache name is something quite different."

Elías, in the act of lighting a long cheroot, looked straight at Wasson. "I do not lie, señor."

Don Jesús' reply struck the newspaperman as something of a *non sequitur*, and in the normal pursuance of his profession he would have rejected it out of hand and demanded something better than that. He had the sense and experience to realize, however, that this was neither the time nor the place—nor, indeed, the subject—for a penetrating cross-interrogation. But Wasson also had in his head the concept of the lustful, uncontrollable, animal-like, wild savage, and Inez Gonzáles had been described as a raving beauty. And she had aroused Eskiminzin or whoever it was, and she was a slave in his camp.

"How long was she held captive?" he asked Elías.

"Eight months, perhaps nine," Don Jesús replied.

"How did she manage to keep her virtue intact during that long period?" Wasson asked.

Elías took a long time to answer. Men leaned closer. Bill Oury raised his grey-bearded face.

"I have already stated, señor, that Inez Gonzáles was my kin," Elías said quietly.

John Wasson considered this response an even greater *non sequitur* than the other. But everybody else appeared to be satisfied with it and Wasson knew he would have to be as well.

He pricked up his ears to catch the details of another Eski-minzin story, related this time by a rancher who had been forced to abandon his property near Tubac after Apaches, led, he said, by Eskiminzin, attacked the place and killed three of his helpers and drove off all his stock.

△ 2

"Well, Don Jesús, there they are, just like the man said."

Bill Oury rested on his saddle horn and stared across Ara-vaipa Creek. It was early in the day and the wind had not yet risen and the Apache village was astir. Smoke from cook fires curled straight up. Women worked. Children played. Dogs barked.

Looking across the wash Bill Oury recalled the first enemy Indians he had fought. They were Comanches, back in Texas, back in 1840, when he was a Texas Ranger. The Comanches had raided a town and the Rangers set out after them and the Rangers were aided in this pursuit by some friendly Indians who had their own scores to settle with the Comanches. One of the friendly Indians was a man named Quatto and Bill Oury was a tough-assed youth of twenty-three then and he liked Quatto and he was damned glad he was riding at his side.

They caught up with the Comanches and there was a bloody fight and Comanches were killed and other Comanches were captured. Then Quatto and the other friendly Indians started doing something that puzzled Oury. They hacked off the hands of the dead Comanches and they fixed the hands on branches of green wood and put them into the fire. Bill guessed this had to be some kind of a religious ceremony.

When the hands were roasted and the skin was crackling, the friendly Indians took them out of the fire and started eating them. Quatto offered a tidbit to his friend Bill. The Indian was mystified when Bill didn't want it, not even a finger.

Bill walked away from the fire then and thought about it. He had never reflected on Indians as people. There were Indians who were friendly and you didn't kill them. There were hostile

Indians and you killed them before they killed you. But he had never sat down to talk to any one of them to find out what they thought about things, not even with his friend Quatto.

But he had always considered them human beings, after a sort. They were human beings, weren't they? Different, a lot different, but human. He had looked on Quatto as human.

He walked back to the fire that day and watched the friendly Indians gnaw on the roasted fingers as though they were chicken legs. It didn't make him feel sick. It was just like watching dogs chew on bones.

Now, in Arizona, a long way away from Texas, a long way away in time, he looked across the wash and he wondered, as he had wondered before, why God had put Indians on earth. What good were they? What was their purpose?

"They look so nice and comfortable and homey there, Don Jesús," Oury said. "They could fool a person. They look almost human."

When Don Jesús did not reply Bill twisted in his saddle and looked at him. Don Jesús was smiling slightly, as though he were gazing at something that pleased him. Bill Oury understood that. He understood that a person could hate something so much it made him feel good to see it.

Don Jesús nodded slowly. He had had his old dream the night before, when he and Don Guillermo had slept at a friend's ranch. It was the dream that sustained him and refreshed him over the years. There were Apaches, so many Apaches they could not be counted, and they crawled over to him like lizards, like snakes, and they begged for their lives and he speared them one by one and he never tired.

The dream had started coming to him in one form or another since he was a child, right after Pilar was killed. Pilar had brought him up at San Ignacio and had taught him to pray and then she married a worker at the *rancho* of Jesús' uncle, Don Ramón, at San Xavier, and on Jesús' sixth birthday his father had taken him to see Pilar. She was in Tucson when he arrived, buying a present for him, and he sat on the corral fence and talked to her husband, Venturo.

It was a bright spring day. The cactus was just coming into

bloom. Venturo was talking to him about God when they heard the shrieks. They looked up to see half a dozen Apaches riding down on a small woman astride a mule. The woman was Pilar. They saw the Apaches lance the woman with such force the lance penetrated her body and more than two feet came out the other side. The mule brayed at the attack and the screaming and the smell of blood and bolted toward the corral. The Apaches kicked the sides of their ponies and galloped off. They were still shrieking.

The mule cast Pilar off at Venturo's feet. The tip of the spear stuck in the ground and for a moment or two Pilar's body was held in the air. Then the body slid down the spear to the ground.

That night Jesús dreamed he captured the six Apaches all by himself. They pleaded with him to spare their lives. But he killed them all. He speared them all to death. He had any number of spears and he left them stuck in the Apache bodies.

The dream always came back to him and he never told anyone about it. That dream was his private experience and he had had it last night and when he woke this morning he was smiling and he knew what he had known for a long time, that he needed Apaches to fill his life, that without them, after all that had happened over the years, there was no reason for him to live.

"They look so peaceful," Bill Oury said. "They sure could fool a man."

"That's the way they've been since they came here."

Oury and Elías turned their heads sharply. They had not noticed that one of the guards from the post had joined them. The trooper leaned on his rifle and looked at the village.

"No trouble?" Bill Oury asked. I must be getting old, he thought, letting that man walk up on me that way. Time was when he could hear a cat walking. Or maybe it wasn't that. Maybe it was just that his feelings were eating on him so much. Don Jesús hadn't heard the soldier either and he had the best ears of anybody.

"No trouble," the trooper said.

"What about the women?" Oury asked.

"What about them?"

"Maybe my eyes aren't what they used to be but I can see some of them walking around half naked. Doesn't that bother you fellows?"

"Wouldn't matter if it did."

"Why not?" Don Jesús asked. It had taken him all that time to get some saliva back into his mouth so he could speak.

"Commanding officer don't allow none of us over there," the guard said. "He's strict about that."

"That's sensible, I suppose," Oury said. "And what about the men? How do you fellows feel about having Apaches parked outside your door?"

The trooper shrugged. He was young and his uniform was a little too big for him. "They're pretty friendly. The chief and the commanding officer get along good. Eskiminzin comes into the post and talks to the lieutenant."

"Is that a fact?" Oury said.

"Eskiminzin even goes to the lieutenant's quarters."

Elías turned his eyes away from the guard. He looked at the Apache village and at the buildings of the post and at the village again.

"Lieutenant Whitman's quarters?" he said.

The guard chuckled. "Colin Duncan, he's the lieutenant's striker, he told me that old Skimmy makes himself right at home there. Pokes around and looks at everything. Even poked around the lieutenant's uniforms, that's how good they get on."

"That's charming," Elías said. "And perhaps Lieutenant Whitman allows the Apache to try on one of his uniforms."

"No, sir, I haven't heard that," the guard said. "But Skimmy feels right at home here and the lieutenant goes right into that Apache village—by himself. He even got the Apaches to turn in their guns—by himself." The trooper shook his head. "More'n I'd do, I can tell you that."

"The Apaches are unarmed?" Elías gazed at the village again.

"All except the policeman."

"Policeman?" Oury asked.

"The lieutenant appointed an Apache policeman, to keep

order over there." The guard shook his head again. "A big Apache, the biggest Apache I ever saw. He keeps things quiet. Not that those people want trouble. Why should they? They got it good now. They're smart, I tell you. They know when they got it good."

"Yes," Elías said in a whisper. "I guess they do."

He raised his head as he saw Apache men leave the village and start across Aravaipa Creek for the post. It was just the way he had dreamed it except they were walking instead of crawling. He could feel the lance in his hand. And he never got tired.

"Feed time," the guard said. "Every other day they come over here and get their grub." The guard chuckled again. "I grew up on a farm in New Jersey. I remember my father tossing out feed for the chickens. They always used to come a-running and a-cackling."

"Is that what those men remind you of?" Oury asked.

The guard hunched his shoulders. "Everything that lives has got to eat."

Jesús María Elías could not bring himself to speak. He had known, of course, that when Apaches attach themselves as bloodsuckers to a military post that they were fed, that's what the places were called, feed stations. But the sight of them walking across the creek for their handout flooded his blood with a surge of execration that made him shiver in his saddle under the burning sun.

Which one, Don Juan Bautista? he asked. Where you are now you could point him out to me. Which one, Ramón? Which one, Cornelio? Which one, Juan? Give me to know. Someone give me to know. *Nombre de Dios*, give me to know.

△ 3

"Is everything all right?" Whitman asked.

"Reckon so," Miles Wood said.

"Any problems?" Whitman had had a bad night. He had

forgotten to take quinine the night before and had wakened shivering and aching. It was still early in the day and he was exhausted.

"No problem, Lieutenant, except doing it in the first place."

"That was not my question, Mr. Wood."

The beef contractor straightened slightly and spoke in more formal tones. "The system's working okay, Lieutenant. The Apaches bring their tickets to me and I issue on them. Afterwards I take the tickets to the office of the assistant commissary of subsistence"—Miles Wood looked up and smiled slyly; he liked to make it sound like an official report; he could have said he took the chits to Lieutenant Robinson but he wanted to separate himself as far as possible from the whole rotten business—"and verify the tickets by the official count of the day. No, Lieutenant, I ain't having any trouble in any way following your detailed orders."

"Thank you, Mr. Wood."

As Whitman started off, Wood called, "Lieutenant."

"Yes, Mr. Wood."

"You receive any authorization yet from the general for all this?" Wood asked.

"No," Whitman said.

Whitman walked away rapidly. There was no reason for him to watch Miles Wood shaking his head and pursing his lips again. Whitman entered Fred Austin's store. It was dark and cool inside. He poured some water from one of the *ollas* and drank it. Would there ever come a time when he would taste cold water again? He questioned the sutler and Austin told him everything was going just fine.

"They're smart, them Apaches," Austin said. He fished around a candy bin and found a lemon drop and popped it into his mouth.

"Are they?" Whitman sat down. He had taken the quinine tablet when he got up and it was not yet time for the next one. He seldom forgot the whiskey he also was under orders to take. Once he had asked Doc Sumner jokingly whether the booze alone wouldn't do the job.

"Some people believe whiskey'll do anything," the post

surgeon had said. "Even cure snakebite. But you'd better take the quinine along with it."

"Why are they smart?" Whitman asked the sutler. What he would have liked right now was a cold beer. An ice-cold beer. There was plenty of beer around but it was as warm as piss, warm as that god-awful Apache brew. He thought about cold drinks, with the ice clinking in the glasses and the glasses beading on the outside.

"I don't rightly know, Lieutenant." Austin sucked on the hard candy. "You know, Royal, I'm not exactly in love with Apache Indians. I've been around here for more than four years and I was attacked by them once on the Tucson Road and only got away by the thin skin of my ass. I got no love for them, but one thing I have to say, I think they're smart."

"How? In what way, Fred?" Steamed lobster and ice-cold beer and the salt smell from the sea.

"I don't know, Royal. They got something."

Hadn't Oscar Hutton said something like that?

"What is it you think they have?" He wanted to know, of course. He really wanted to know. And yet he could not get his mind away from the ocean water off the Maine rocks. It never warmed, not even in the middle of summer, and when you went in you felt as though you exploded inside and then you were numb and you didn't feel anything and then you felt wonderful. Even in August the water never warmed up much.

"I don't know what it is they have," Fred Austin said. With the candy ball bulging his cheek and his forehead puckered and the beard around the outskirts of his face he looked like a troubled gnome. "I just think they're smart."

"How do you think all this is working?"

"You haven't heard from the old man yet, have you?"

"No."

"With his okay I'd say it was working just elegantly."

"Well, Fred, you started all this."

"How do you make that out?"

Whitman remembered a snowman he once built for the kids and how one of his sons, he couldn't remember which one, had seen someone else's snowman with a pipe in his mouth and the boy searched around for a pipe, only Whitman didn't smoke a pipe, and the boy found some of Whitman's fine cigars and shoved one of those into the mouth of the snowman.

"What?" Whitman asked.

"I said how am I responsible, Royal."

"Oh, well, you took on that Apache boy, Naco. If it wasn't for that none of this would have happened."

"Now don't you hold that against me, Royal." Austin grinned. The gnome's burden seemed to have vanished. "Only I don't reckon you making a blame out of that at all, all things taken this way and that."

"I've often wondered about that, Fred. The way you feel about Apaches. Why did you take on Naco in the first place?"

Austin sucked hard on the candy ball and his cheeks collapsed. "Hell, Royal, he isn't a genuine full-grown Apache. He's just a kid."

Whitman nodded. He remembered a snowman his father had once made for his children. My God, how long ago was that? He remembered the snowman lasted all winter and then it started to melt and how he had watched it slowly drip away and finally it wasn't a snowman at all but just a blob, without form or shape, and it was as though a friend was betraying his friendship and he went down to the Androscoggin with his setter, Geoff, and stayed there for a long time. It was the first experience he had with a manner of death.

He realized he had heard the shot before and now he was hearing the crazed whinnies of a horse and shouting and he jumped to his feet and ran out.

He saw that the Apache line had reached Miles Wood's commissary and that it stretched down the length of the parade ground and that there were two mounted civilians on the parade ground and that half a dozen Apaches were trying to pull one of the civilians off his horse and that the horse was rearing and whinnying in panic and that soldiers were trying to separate the Apaches clawing at the civilian and that Sergeant Clarrity had grabbed the arm of the second civilian and was trying to wrestle his revolver away from him and the gun went off again but it was pointed in the air.

The soldiers and the Apaches backed off when Whitman reached them and he saw an Apache on the ground doubled in pain. The man on the spooked horse—Whitman saw now that he was Jesús Elías—was bringing the animal under control. Clarrity had the other man's gun now—Whitman recognized Bill Oury—and Oury, panting and furious, was glaring at the sergeant.

"What the hell is going on here?" Whitman demanded. He knelt down and examined the Indian. The man's face was gray under his dark skin and he was biting his lip so hard he had punctured the skin and there was a dribble of blood running down his chin. "What happened to him?"

"He got kicked by this horse, Lieutenant," Clarrity said.

Whitman stood up. "Mr. Elías. Mr. Oury." He looked at Clarrity. "Sergeant, are you going to tell me what happened?"

"These Indians attacked me," Elías said. He had quieted his horse and he was in control. He had never lost his control even when the horse was trying to unseat him.

"That's exactly right," Oury said. He spat. "Damned savages!"

"What are you gentlemen doing here?" Whitman asked.

"Just having a look, Lieutenant. That's all we were doing, sitting here having a look at Apaches getting their food free, when they broke line and jumped Don Jesús here."

"Did you fire that first shot, Mr. Oury?" Whitman asked. He had not seen Oury since their first meeting in Tucson.

"You're damned right I did, Lieutenant. And I would have hit the mark if that damned sergeant of yours didn't knock my arm. And I'll have my gun back."

Sergeant Clarrity looked at Whitman.

"Do you have business here, Mr. Oury?" Whitman asked.

"This is a free country, Lieutenant, and this is an American military post and I'm an American. I'll tell you what my business is here. We heard about these Apaches being pampered by you and we wanted to have a look for ourselves. And it turned out to be just the way we heard it, another damned feed station at the taxpayers' expense."

By now the Puma had arrived and so had Eskiminzin.

Eskiminzin bent over the injured man and then he straightened and looked at the white men on the horses and when his eyes fell on Elías he went rigid. His neck muscles knotted and Whitman saw him press his arms against his sides to keep his hands from performing an act on their own.

The men who had tried to get at Elías were still milling around angrily and they shouted to the Puma all at once. Oscar Hutton drifted over and listened and nodded.

"Well?" Whitman asked.

The Puma pointed to Elías. "They say that man was the leader of those who attacked their village a few years ago."

"Tell them to get back in line," Whitman said to Eskiminzin. "Tell them if they don't quiet down and get back in line I'll withhold their rations."

"You do that, Lieutenant," Oury said.

When Whitman's orders were translated, Eskiminzin's face turned cold. "You do not have to make threats, Nantan Whitman. My men will do as I order them to do."

He spoke three or four words to the Apaches and they turned and walked back to the line.

"Get that injured man to the infirmary," Whitman said to Clarrity. "Send word to Dr. Sumner to have a look at him and keep him there if he deems it necessary."

Jesús María Elías turned his head. It revolted him to listen to what Whitman was saying.

When Eskiminzin had herded the Apaches back into line and Clarrity had sent off the injured man, Whitman turned to Oury and Elías.

"Mr. Oury," Whitman said, "are you aware these Apaches are my prisoners of war?"

"I heard you put that fancy label on them, Lieutenant."

"There could have been a serious incident here. You know that, too."

"I don't know of any other kind with Apaches."

"You might have killed someone, Mr. Oury."

"That was my intention, Lieutenant."

Whitman felt the sun on his head. "These Indians are under Government protection and you are on Government property. It is well within my authority, Mr. Oury, to place you under arrest."

"Arrest, is it? What was I supposed to do, Lieutenant?" Oury asked gently. "Allow my good friend here to be mauled before my eyes?" He squinted down at Whitman. "How long have you been here, Lieutenant? No, never mind, I remember. I remember when you passed through Tucson. That wasn't much more than three months ago."

"Mr. Oury, if you are suggesting that I am somewhat inexperienced here, I will grant that at once," Whitman said quietly. "But if you are also suggesting that I am unfamiliar with military regulations that cover prisoners of war, and the powers invested in me, I assure you you are quite mistaken."

"May I ask the lieutenant a question?" Jesús María Elías spoke softly. "What punishment do military regulations authorize you to impose on Indians who tried to kill me?"

"Were you involved in the attack on their village?"

"That is not the question."

"That is my question."

"I was."

"Then you just about asked for what happened when you turned up here, didn't you?"

"You still have not answered my question, Mr. Whitman."

"Whoever was involved will be punished."

"How?" Oury asked. "In what way? Will you take away their sugar candy?"

Whitman stepped back. "That is my concern, Mr. Oury. In future, gentlemen, whenever you find it necessary to visit this post, you will before anything else report to me."

"Report?" Elías said, his lips drawing down.

"Of all people, Mr. Elías, you must realize how unwise it is for you to expose yourself to these people without adequate military protection," Whitman said dryly. "Clarrity."

"Sir!"

"Return Mr. Oury's weapon and then escort these gentlemen off the post. Good day, gentlemen," Whitman said.

Oscar Hutton walked along with Whitman toward his headquarters.

"You didn't do yourself a world of good today, Lieutenant," Hutton said. "You know that, don't you?"

△ 4

Whitman clasped his hands behind his back and smoked his cigar and looked across Little Running Water at the Apache village. "Those men must be punished."

It was the third time he had said that to Eskiminzin and he did not know yet whether he was penetrating. The Apache had turned into a slab of granite and Whitman had the feeling his words were beating uselessly against him like spring rain.

"They did what they believed was right," Eskiminzin said, also for the third time.

Whitman had not encountered this degree of stubbornness before. He looked back into the post. The last of the Apaches were collecting their rations. By now the soldiers no longer bothered to watch them.

"It is not what they believe is right, Eskiminzin," Whitman said. "It is what the law says is right. Those men attacked two visitors on this post."

"They had reason."

"They had good reason," Whitman agreed to that. They sure as hell had reason. "But they did not have the right."

"Rights are different things, Nantan Whitman," Eskiminzin said, making a cigarette. "Rights for Americans are one thing. Rights for Mexicans are another thing, maybe. Apache rights are different yet. And that is the way it should be. After all, Americans make the rights." Eskiminzin lit his cigarette. "If we were the conquerors, we would turn it around too."

"That Mexican, Elías—"

Eskiminzin spat. On the ground and not into Little Running Water.

"That man Elías believes he was justified in what he did that time your village was attacked. There are always reasons." Whitman breathed in deeply. The water of the creek sounded cool. "We've got to get rid of those reasons and try to live as though there was no past and no past reasons and no past memories."

"It cannot be done," Eskiminzin said tonelessly.

"It's got to be done. Or else we might as well forget the whole damned thing."

Presently Eskiminzin said, "We will punish these men ourselves, inside the tribe."

"What will you do?"

"I will think on it."

Whitman relit his cigar. "You have no ways of punishing— except to torture or put to death."

"Is that what you would have me do!" Eskiminzin shouted furiously.

"There is no need for that," Whitman said. "But you have no will to do anything at all."

"I will not let you punish those men," Eskiminzin said harshly. He started to walk across the creek.

"I did not take the word of the Aravaipa chief lightly," Whitman said in a quiet voice. "I guess I was wrong."

He put the toe of his boot against the peace stone and slowly dislodged it. The stone rolled over twice and stopped. He strode back to the post. He counted his paces. He counted each one.

"Nantan Whitman."

It was the twelfth step. Whitman paused and turned.

Eskiminzin returned to the bank of the creek. He looked at the overturned stone. "What will the *nantan* do to those men?"

"Let them give their food to their families and then return here."

"Will you shoot them?"

"I have said there is no cause for that. They must go into the guardhouse. For what they did I would give a soldier a month in there, longer. I will give your men five days."

"You do not give those men five days, Nantan Whitman. You take them away." Eskiminzin gazed at Whitman bleakly. "The man who was kicked by the horse?"

"A few bruises. The surgeon says he's a tough bird. It might have killed another man."

Eskiminzin walked to where Whitman had pushed the stone. He looked down at it and then he picked it up and put it back in its place. He straightened and his eyes were on Whitman for a long time.

"It has taken many seasons, from before those times of the grandfathers' grandfathers, but we have learned to survive that which would kill other men."

He turned and waded across the stream. He walked on to his village without looking back. Whitman started back to his office. He was surprised when he realized the Puma was walking at his side. He had forgotten the Puma was there.

△ △ △ TWO

△ 1

There were still little pockets of mist as General Stoneman strolled through the vineyard and the orange grove and smelled the sweet air. It was still early in the year and there was a chill in the air and he walked a little faster than he would have chosen. He preferred to linger. Los Robles spread over more than four hundred acres and he would have liked to have had the time to walk slowly over every foot of every acre. One day perhaps.

Unfortunately, until that time, he had a cross to bear. The Lord had His Gethsemane and he had the Territory of Arizona. He had done what was possible, true. He had put every mile he could between himself and that accursed place, but it was still there.

In the year that now was starting, 1871, General George Stoneman was forty-eight. He was a man of medium size with a somber mien. His hair and mustache and imperial were streaked with gray. His eyes were deeply set, almost sunken under his forehead, and when he pondered on his innumerable and seemingly insoluble problems his expression became even gloomier, and there were those who said he resembled then the martyred Abraham Lincoln.

On this day he sat down on a bench and lit a morning cigar. He was not entirely in the best of moods for many reasons. There was simply no need for his wife, Mary, to have reminded him that morning that he soon would have to return to the Territory. Additionally, Conchita, Manuel's wife, had served liver along with the bacon and eggs for breakfast that morning.

When Conchita offered him the plate he had himself

broken his rule of silence by remarking pointedly, "Liver, no, I never eat deadly organs." And how often had he stated that previously to that ignorant Mexican woman?

"Then just take some of the bacon, George," Mary had said.

"The general could not possibly," Rebecca had rationalized instantly. "The smell of that liver now has permeated the bacon. Conchita, please remove that plate and fry some fresh uncontaminated bacon."

Thank the Lord for his sister, Rebecca. Why couldn't Mary take care of things like that? With all he had on his mind why should he have to concern himself with preparing menus?

He puffed on the cigar and smelled the morning air and cleared his head of the odor of liver.

He saw his aide-de-camp, Captain Gregory Wilson, hovering about nearby. Captain Wilson was a worrier but unfortunately he did not worry about the correct things. Captain Wilson had a file-cabinet mind, which was useful, but he worried about the hours of the day. Captain Wilson's mind worked with engineering precision. He divided the work on hand into hours and minutes, and if it did not all fit together tidily, Captain Wilson fretted. Captain Wilson, despite his thirty-odd years, had a strangely young and uninscribed face, and when he fretted he seemed to pout and he resembled a petulant infant.

The general smoked half his cigar with his back to Captain Wilson, but when he turned around, the miracle, as he had expected, had not occurred. Captain Wilson was still there. General Stoneman knew the day's work would not go away by itself and that Arizona, with its eternal problems, probably never would go away.

The general stood up and walked with his stiff, angular gait toward his office. It had come back to the general that a junior officer had remarked that when the general moved from a fixed position it was as though a statue had come to life. The general had not construed that as a rudeness. After all, statues were ennobling creations.

When he finally reached the little outbuilding in which he had established his office, Captain Wilson was waiting for him at his desk. Captain Wilson looked relieved. The desk was piled high with documents, newspapers, reports, statistical tables, orders from superior headquarters to be sent down through the echelons, and requests from the field to be either ruled on at this level or, when regulations required, sent up to superior headquarters. Unless regulations expressly forbade it—and even then, on many an occasion—the general made his own determinations in his own Department. It was his Department, much as he detested it.

The office actually was the general's third headquarters. The official headquarters, of course, was in Prescott, Arizona Territory, and the supplementary official headquarters was in Drum Barracks. This one, on his ranch, he had located for his own convenience. The proliferation of headquarters brought with it an additional benefit. Mail always was slow between Arizona and California but dispatches that had to go to Prescott and then to Drum Barracks and finally to Los Robles were slowed even more, and sometimes, if he was lucky, when a dispatch reached his hands it already was outdated or else the problem defined in it had already solved itself. True, sometimes overzealous officers by-passed Prescott and sent dispatches to Sacaton to catch the military mail pouch there. General Stoneman resented that. His headquarters at Prescott was simply a fiction and everyone knew that, but still the rules should apply.

"Good morning, Wilson," the general said as he took his seat.

"Good morning, General."

"It's a beautiful morning."

"It most certainly is, General."

The general had often wondered whether Captain Wilson had ever in his life disagreed with a superior officer. It could be raining brimstone and Captain Wilson would agree the weather was beautiful. Well, he would go far.

"What must we deal with today, Wilson?" the general asked.

"There is a confidential directive from Washington, sir."

"And what is it about?"

"According to the brief, sir, Washington has decided to take a stronger position vis-à-vis the Apache Indians."

"Excellent. Then they are going to assign more troops to the Department."

"No, sir. The forces presently under your command will find and pursue Apaches relentlessly."

" 'Find and pursue . . .' Not catch and kill, Wilson?"

"I believe that is implied, sir."

"And what else is in the brief?"

"The new policy has the firm support of the President."

"That is stated?"

"In those words, sir."

"Is there anything else?"

"No, sir."

"Then there is no need for me to read the directive."

"The directive is eight pages long, sir. Some of the writing is not easily intelligible."

The general shook his head. "Eight pages to inform me what a one-paragraph brief can do as well."

"Yes, sir."

"There is no specific action required?"

"No, sir."

The general sat back. The sunlight was slanting through one of the windows in the office. It was most pleasant.

"Would you like to know something, Wilson?"

"I most certainly would, sir."

"I am not a betting man, as you know. Point of fact I disapprove strongly of gambling in any form. But I would not hesitate to make a small wager that at this very moment there is a dispatch en route from Washington with exactly contrary orders."

"Yes, sir."

"By this time the peace people will have found out about the latest policy switch and will get hold of Mr. Grant's ear and persuade him of our moral obligation to serve and feed and perpetuate these savages."

"Yes, sir."

"I tell you, Wilson, if Grant had conducted the war as he is conducting his Indian policy it would have been Lee who would have accepted the surrender at Appomattox."

Captain Wilson remained silent. He was incapable of endorsing a pronouncement such as that about his Commander in Chief.

Nor had General Stoneman expected him to. "What else is there, Wilson?"

"There is a dispatch from Colonel Green, from Camp Apache."

"About what?"

"In the brief the colonel reports on the reaction he is getting for enlisting the services of Coyotero Apaches in cutting hay and wood for him." Wilson picked up Colonel Green's report and extracted the small, condensed synopsis that had accompanied it. "The colonel says that he 'has heard many criticisms from those who made fortunes supplying such things to the military.' The colonel reports that the fury of those merchants was such he deemed it necessary to inform the general."

"What do you think about that, Wilson?"

Captain Wilson considered. "Colonel Green certainly must be the best judge of that, sir."

The general nodded. Captain Wilson undoubtedly had a brilliant staff career ahead of him and the perfect mind for that facet of military operation. Speak intelligently and say nothing. The general liked the officer and he hoped he would not ruin his chances ever by accidentally speaking his mind. But there was little danger of that. The human mind gets trained by time like an espaliered shrub.

Well, back to John Green. The experiment with the Coyoteros was not working out anyway and probably before very long, possibly even now, there would be none of those Apaches around to nibble at the profits of the landed merchants. The businessmen's anger would fade. If this were another one of those lucky times this would be another crisis that self-destructed.

For a brief change from military dispatches, General Stoneman turned to the pile of newspapers. Items that would be of interest to him already were ticked off in red by Captain Wilson. The general pushed aside the California papers and the periodicals from the East and looked over the Tucson *Citizen*, one of his least favorite publications, and saw the article written by "A Soldier" at Camp Grant. He read it through and then read the commentary by the editor, Wasson.

He put down the paper. Had he ever run across Lieutenant Royal Whitman? He thought not. He did remember receiving a dispatch from Whitman earlier telling him something of this development at Camp Grant. The dispatch had been sent directly to Sacaton and not to Prescott, which had irritated the general. He had set Whitman's letter aside for future consideration. He had thought it possible that the Apaches who had wandered over to Camp Grant might just wander away. Apparently they had not.

In the light of Colonel Green's intelligence, the general could easily imagine what the merchants in Tucson—and all the other people in the area—would have to say about Apaches collecting Government rations at Camp Grant. At least this Whitman had not committed the heresy of putting the Indians to work, so those insolent men who formed the Tucson Ring could not squawk about that.

Whitman . . . In one sense the officer certainly had exceeded his authority in accepting the surrender of an Apache tribe, or a portion of that tribe, and designating the Indians prisoners of war. However, the general surmised, in a larger sense Whitman simply was conforming to general Government policy toward the Apaches, or at least what had been general Government policy until this morning. And before long, no doubt, would be again.

He put the Camp Grant matter aside for a moment and looked through other copies of the *Citizen*. He was brought sitting up straight at another marked-off item. The newspaper stated that Whitman *"allowed Indians to run around the camp, enter quarters and disarrange clothing . . ."*

"What the devil do you call that?" General Stoneman demanded.

"I thought it very odd, sir," Captain Wilson said.

"Odd? Is that what you would call that? Odd? I think it's preposterous. Do I have an insane officer in command of one of my posts?"

"The paper is not entirely reliable, sir," Captain Wilson said.

The general agreed with that up to a point. He himself had been savaged more than once by that virulent John Wasson, but always, the general had to admit, with some justification from the newspaper's point of view. Although John Wasson had made him a target of some very nasty attacks, he had never printed an outright lie about him. He presumed he also would not against this Whitman.

He made a note on his diary pad to check on the matter. It was bad enough to have himself and his officers vilified but he was damned if he was going to permit any officer in his command to put himself into a position to be ridiculed.

There were other missives placed before him by Captain Wilson, some from Washington, some from San Francisco, some to be sure from Arizona Territory. He listened attentively to the précis that accompanied each dispatch and earmarked those he would have to read in their entirety.

By noontime the general had gone through his desk work with a concentration that pleased even Captain Wilson. There was at last one bulky dispatch left to be dealt with. The general looked questioningly at Captain Wilson.

"A dispatch from Lieutenant Whitman, sir."

"That same man who permits Apaches to muck around with his clothing?"

"Yes, sir."

"The man must be standing in the sun too much. What's this about?"

"I don't know, sir."

"What the devil do you mean, you don't know, Wilson? What does it state in the brief?"

"There is no brief, sir."

"No brief?" The general looked up. "There has to be a brief. Regulations require a brief."

"There is none, sir."

"God Almighty! Don't they train these new officers properly? Can't they read regulations?"

"Lieutenant Whitman is not an inexperienced officer, sir."

"No? Who is he?"

Captain Wilson tapped the resources of his encyclopedic storehouse of facts. "Lieutenant Whitman is a veteran of the war, sir. I believe he was a colonel and commanded a regiment of volunteers at the time."

Now the general was surprised. "A full colonel during the war. And now a lieutenant?" He frowned. "Whitman, Whitman, Whitman . . . When was he graduated from the Academy? I can't seem to place him."

"Lieutenant Whitman did not attend the Academy, sir. He has come up from the ranks."

"Oh, I see," the general said. "Well, perhaps that explains it all. I could not quite see any graduate of West Point permitting Indians to rummage around his uniforms."

"No, sir," Captain Wilson agreed.

"A full colonel," the general said. "Damn it, Wilson, that simply compounds his oversight. Or perhaps it is insolence, plain and simple. Does this officer think his commanding general has nothing better to do with his time than to pore over whatever voluminous correspondence he takes it into his head to send me?"

"Yes, sir."

"Yes, sir, what, Wilson?

"I mean, no, sir."

The general and his aide looked up at a knocking on the door.

"See who that is, Wilson," the general said, happy for any kind of interruption. He was absolutely scandalized at having been sent a dispatch without the mandatory brief.

Three men walked into the room as Wilson opened the door and they greeted the general warmly. They were three prominent politicians from Los Angeles. The general stood up and shook the hands of each man, giving a specially warm grip to the leader of the group, a heavyset, red-faced man with a hoarse voice.

"That will be all for the time being, Wilson," the general said.

"Yes, sir."

With Wilson out of the office the three men began to talk animatedly. The general sat back in his chair and stretched his legs and smoked his cigar and listened to them. For some time now the men had been telling the general he was a positive asset to the state of California with his renowned name and brilliant military record. At first they had asked the general to consider embarking on a political career after he retired from active service. Today they were urging that he not wait that long.

"Resign your commission now, General," the red-faced man said. "Get out of that uniform and jump in while the water's warm."

△ 2

It rained in the afternoon and, lunch over, the general left the main house and returned to his office. The children were confined to the indoors because of the downpour and he did not want to subject himself to that kind of commotion. Wilson, mercifully, had taken himself off to Drum Barracks on some business or other.

General Stoneman lit his first cigar of the afternoon. He was still in a warmish glow from the complimentary remarks made by the three men from Los Angeles. According to them there were literally no limits to where he might go if he entered state politics. It was all rather heady talk.

The thick letter from Lieutenant Royal Whitman, of Camp Grant, Arizona Territory, lay in the center of the desk and the general regarded it peevishly. It cut into his good feeling like a sour breath.

What kind of officer, he asked himself, would give the freedom of his quarters to Apache Indians and let them handle his clothing? It was absolutely unthinkable. Not even the fact that Whitman climbed up from the cluttered ranks could quite explain that.

He picked up the letter, which had unaccountably arrived without its covering brief, and as the rain spattered on the roof of his office, rain watering his orange trees and grapevines, he started to read it. He read through all of it.

When he finished he set the letter down on the desk. "Good Lord," the general said.

He listened to the rain and thought that Captain Wilson must be getting a good soaking, which would undoubtedly have a salubrious effect on his soul, and then he picked up the communication again and read it over for the second time.

". . . *almost four hundred Apaches and more of them coming in every day. . . . There is a chance of obtaining the voluntary surrender of a large part of the Apache nation. . . . The sender most respectfully but urgently requests that the Commanding General supply him with instructions on what course to follow. . . .*"

"Good Lord!" General Stoneman said again, louder.

He lit the second cigar of the afternoon. The fine Havana tasted like hemp. Emotion seldom played any part in the general's life but on this rainy day he slapped the desk hard. That blasted fool!

The general stood up and began to pace back and forth. Whitman got himself into this mess wholly on his own, without authorization, without consulting anyone, and now he comes around whimpering for "instructions." Why the devil didn't the idiot ask for instructions before he started feeding a tribe of Apaches and allowing them to run around his quarters? Whitman didn't want instructions. The damned fool simply realized that he had blundered badly and now was pleading to be bailed out.

The general sat down again and brought himself under control. He was not given to excess. He puffed on the cigar more slowly to reduce the temperature of the smoke. He tapped Whitman's letter with his square fingertips. He considered the dilemma calmly.

His final directive to his command at the end of the previous year was to mount "a vigorous, persistent, relentless campaign" against the Apaches. And that had brought down on his head all the damned Quakers and missionaries and do-gooders in Washington. Some of them had demanded that the President remove him from his command.

And now, damn it to hell, everything was twisted completely around. Now he was under direct orders to kill Apaches —exactly what he had been pilloried for advocating three months before. Only now he had more than four hundred of the savages on his hands professing to want peace.

If he gave his official endorsement to Whitman's high-handed, unwarranted, egregious undertaking, he would flout all the settlers in Arizona, about whom he did not give a good goddamn, but also, for the time being at least, he would be flouting his superiors in Washington all the way up to the President of the United States, about whom, perforce, he most certainly did.

And if he ordered Whitman to drive off the Apaches and then go out and kill them, he knew as sure as day followed night that when the peace people recovered that same President's ear they would crucify him.

And this was one problem he could not consign to the convenient wastepaper basket of pretermission.

The general broke the ash off his cigar gently and gazed with vast distaste at Lieutenant Whitman's letter. Really, it was quite unseemly. But then how could an officer who had crawled up from the mob below understand the code?

△ △ △ THREE

△ 1

Now on this cool March evening they were sitting around the fire telling Coyote stories. They were telling them and acting them at the same time. Everybody there knew the stories as well as the storytellers but everybody followed the words and watched the mimicking and grimacing and they gasped and laughed and were sad, as though seeing and listening to the stories for the first time.

"You will get to know about Coyote," Eskiminzin said to Whitman. "He is a big thing with us. Everybody understands him and knows why he does what he does. He thinks he is clever and he tricks other animals, and people too. But in the end he is always fooled because he trusts somebody too much."

They were very old stories, Eskiminzin said. The grandfathers' grandfathers told the same stories.

There had been a good meal. Some of the men had located a herd of deer nearby and others had gone out into the hills and had brought back wild turkey. Eskiminzin had spoken to Whitman beforehand about the men leaving the village with bows and arrows.

"There is no risk," Eskiminzin said. He was embarrassed to have to come to Whitman for permission and he showed it. "My pledge is on that."

"There is a risk," Whitman said, seeing and understanding the discomfiture. "Can you speak for every single one of your men?"

"No, there are some bad ones. But there are not many and I will pick the men who will go out."

"They must be back in the village by nightfall."

"Delchan will see that that is so."

Eskiminzin walked away quickly, having degraded himself enough.

Delchan had verified that all of the men had returned and had reported that to Whitman. Delchan seemed a little disappointed. Delchan would not have minded having to go out and kill someone to prove what an excellent policeman he was. Delchan felt that there must be something more positive about his job than just walking around looking important. But then he had the only gun in the village and that was no small thing.

Whitman had eaten with the Apache chief the roast venison and turkey and mescal cakes Eskiminzin's wives had made. The place chosen for the meal was at the exact center of Eskiminzin's three wickiups. The children had watched the white officer for a little while and then had disappeared inside the dwellings. Save for Road Runner. Road Runner was the son of Small Woman and Eskiminzin. He was about six or seven and he had attached himself to Whitman. Small Woman thought Road Runner was annoying Whitman and she told her oldest child, Fawn, a grave girl about twelve, to take the boy inside the wickiup. Whitman asked her to please let the boy remain. Eskiminzin nodded.

The Puma gave Whitman Road Runner's name. "They think he is like that little bird that races along the roads, the one with the crest and brown feathers and the long tail. The bird always scurries and it always looks as though it is going to fly but it almost never flies. These people respect that bird because it attacks and kills rattlesnakes."

Small Woman was Eskiminzin's other wife. She was a few years older than Child Mother. She was pregnant and her eyes had the look of a pregnant woman but she moved around quickly to show that nothing was hampering her. Also in the compound was Eskiminzin's mother, Daya. Whitman recognized her as the fierce, proud old woman who had carried the white flag that first time. The remaining woman was Melana, Child Mother's cousin, who lived in the third wickiup in the compound with Daya. Whitman remembered Melana from that first day in the post and from the time he saw her softening a deer hide.

Eskiminzin told Whitman about Melana. "She stumbled on rocks too soon. There was that time when soldiers and Mexicans in Tucson got together and came up here and attacked our village. She was a very young girl. Some of the attackers held her and made her watch while they killed her mother and her father and her two brothers."

After that Eskiminzin had taken Child Mother's cousin under his protection.

"I could not do much," Eskiminzin told Whitman. "She stumbled on rocks too soon."

Tonight these women were dressed in embroidered skins. The Puma told Whitman that was because of his presence and because of the feast and of the stories that were to be told. Whitman could well believe this was a special event. He had seen the women of the tribe often during the days that had passed. They were still almost all in tatters. It was something Whitman was resolved to work out in some way with Eskiminzin. The manta in the sutler's store was not Government property and could not be issued along with the food rations, not in enough quantity to outfit all the women in the tribe.

Eskiminzin named all the members of his family. Although Whitman had seen Child Mother before and had sat in her wickiup, the Apache chief had never given Whitman her name. When Eskiminzin gave out her on this night she gazed at Whitman as though she had never before laid eyes on him and she lowered her head.

Melana could not look at Whitman very long either, not while he was looking at her. During the meal, she and the two wives of Eskiminzin served the men, but she could not look at Whitman. When he was eating she sat a little way away and looked at him, but only when he did not glance over at her.

"Child Mother still has her early name," Eskiminzin said, gnawing on a deer bone.

The Apache wiped the grease into his mouth with the back of his hand. When he saw Whitman wiping his lips with his kerchief his eyes widened in shock and disbelief.

"Get all the fat inside you," he said. "All of it. What good does it do for you when you put it on that piece of cloth? Are you feeding the cloth to make it strong?"

Road Runner started to giggle. His father stopped him with a look. Then Eskiminzin threw the bone to Road Runner's dog and wiped the greasy palms of his hands on his thighs.

"It makes the legs strong," he explained to Whitman. "It is one of the reasons we can run on the desert for such a long time without tiring. It would be good for you, too, but you would have to take off your boots and pants and you would not be happy to do that with the women watching."

Eskiminzin chuckled at his own humor and the women giggled and Road Runner giggled and this time his father did not stop him. Whitman looked over at Melana. She was giggling, too, but she stopped and lowered her head when he looked her way.

Still amused by himself, Eskiminzin helped himself to another piece of meat. "I took Child Mother as a wife when she was just old enough to be a woman. When she had a child that was the name given to her."

"She had no name before that?"

"Oh, yes, but I forget what it was. Small Woman had another name. She could not be called Small Woman until she was a woman and turned out small. When she was a child she used to run around and dance a lot and she was called Wind Star." Eskiminzin chewed slowly on the meat. "Have you a wife?"

"Yes," Whitman said.

"Where is she?"

"Very far away."

"Why is that?"

"Neither of us wanted her to come here."

"Why is that?"

"Whitman shrugged. "That's the way it was."

"Have you one wife?"

"Yes."

"Why is that? You are an important man. You could feed more than one woman."

"It's not quite that way."

"Don't important white men have more than one wife?"

"Sometimes, but usually one at a time."

Whitman smiled. When Eskiminzin merely looked mildly surprised, Whitman shrugged and helped himself to another piece of venison. The meal was very good. Even the *tiswin* seemed to have something to recommend it. Whitman knew that theoretically the Indians were not allowed to brew their beer on reservations but this was hardly a proper reservation yet, was it? He supposed, in time, he would have to at least state that restriction although he knew very well he could never make it stick.

"There are white men in Utah Territory who take more than one wife," Whitman said. "It has to do with their religion."

Eskiminzin pondered on that for a little while, chewing slowly. "What does the number of wives a man has have to do with religion?"

"I'm not altogether certain about that, but that's what they believe."

"It sounds foolish to me," Eskiminzin said.

"It's not foolish to them. They marched a long way to a new land and experienced many hardships so that they could practice what they believe."

"I can understand that," Eskiminzin said, nodding. "People should live the way they believe. Even if they have to suffer a great deal they should live the way they believe. But what has religion to do with wives? Religion has to do with the Everywhere Spirit. A woman is something else. There is nothing wrong with women but they are not religion. A man takes as many wives as he wants but he does not mix that up with the Everywhere Spirit."

"What are the Apache reasons for taking more than one wife?"

"Many. Men fight and are killed. There always are more women than men. But that is not the only reason. A wife encourages a man to take a second wife. It gives the first wife another woman to share her work and to talk to. And it shows everybody that the man is a brave man and a good hunter. That is the way it used to be. And if a woman gets tired of bearing children and wants to be left alone that way she tells her husband to take someone else. Do you long for your wife?"

Whitman was caught short by the unexpected question. After a while he said, "Sometimes."

"Is that why she is not here? Because you are lonely for her only sometimes?"

"I suppose so."

"Do you have children?"

"Yes."

"Do you feel lonely for them?"

"I think of them often," Whitman said slowly. "Perhaps that is a kind of loneliness."

"You are strange people," Eskiminzin said. "To leave your women and your children and travel a long distance to kill people you do not know."

△ 2

Delchan told a Coyote story about a turkey. He stood in front of the great fire with his gun cradled in his arms. He looked to Whitman like a colossus and his feet were holding down the earth.

"The turkey was up in a tree," Delchan said in a voice that seemed to have deepened with his responsibilities. "Coyote tried to catch the turkey by chopping down the tree. But just as the tree fell the turkey flew to another tree. Coyote kept chopping down trees but the turkey kept flying away until Coyote fell down exhausted."

The people gathered around the fire nodded. The impact of Delchan's story had to rest on his voice and his stature. The rifle, pressed against his chest, prevented his acting out the story. He was impressive enough. He strode out of the firelight. Everything immediately seemed larger.

Little Captain stood up. The people were surprised and then excited. Little Captain was an important man and leaders usually sat and listened to others. That was how the leaders found out what people were thinking. The Coyote stories were valuable. Coyote had many kinds of adventures that told many things.

Little Captain had drunk a lot of *tiswin*. He swayed but not too much and he was graceful.

"Coyote found some rabbits playing with their eyes under a high cliff. The rabbits tossed their eyes high into the air and then the eyes fell down and fell into their places again."

Little Captain made the gesture of scooping his eyes out of his head and tossing them up and catching them in their sockets. Then he shifted slightly and became Coyote, coming on this interesting scene.

" 'That is a wonderful game,' Coyote said. 'Let me play it.'

"The rabbits said, 'Go away, you might lose your eyes.' But Coyote insisted and the rabbits took his eyes and threw them into the air and they fell back into their places.

" 'That is enough for you,' the rabbits said. 'Now go away.'

"But Coyote insisted again, 'Let me play just once more.'

"This time he took out his own eyes and threw them up and while the eyes were up there one of the rabbits said, 'Let the eyes stick to something and never come back.'

"And the eyes did not come back."

As the Puma whispered to Whitman what Little Captain was saying, the officer looked from time to time at Eskiminzin. The chief stared at the ground as Little Captain told the story about the loss of eyes. He reacted in no way.

When Little Captain finished he remained in the light of the fire for a moment or two as though he wanted to say something else. Then Little Captain shook his head and walked into the darkness. The people sat back. The men did not grunt one way or another.

△ 3

There were other Coyote stories but after what Little Captain said the stories were not too interesting. The women went off to sleep finally but the men sat around for a long time talking about Little Captain's fable.

Delchan went over to Eskiminzin and said he thought it might be a good idea to kill Little Captain for disturbing the people this way at this particular time. Eskiminzin said no, this was something he would have to work out.

△ 4

Eskiminzin specified that the sweat bath be built on the edge of the village farthest away from the soldiers' camp. This was an occasion when the sense of being what he was had to remain as uncontaminated as possible.

A bathhouse had to be made each time. It had to be made each time and destroyed each time, as the masks for the mountain dancers could be used only once and then made to disappear. There were special men to make a sweat bath. They were not shamans but they were religious men. Ordinary men would not dare to make a bathhouse.

By the time Eskiminzin and Little Captain got there the bathhouse was already up and the rocks were in the fire just outside. The bathhouse looked pretty much like any wickiup. The entrance had to face east. One of the names the people had for themselves was Hiuhah, Men of the Rising Sun.

Eskiminzin and Little Captain were wearing only loincloths when they met in front of the bathhouse. Little Captain's eyes were red but Eskiminzin did not know whether that was from too much *tiswin* or whether Little Captain had remained awake all night after Eskiminzin told him he wanted to talk to him in a sweat bath.

The morning was still cold. The boss of the sweat bath rubbed the two leaders down hard with powdered juniper and stuck the required sprig of sage into their headbands. Each man drank from a container in which mesquite beans, in the holy number of four, one for each Direction, had been soaked all night. The boss handed each of them sticks to scratch themselves inside the sweat bath. Scratching with fingers was proscribed; a serious infection was certain to result from that.

The four large rocks that had sat on the fire all night were carried into the bathhouse with forked sticks and were dropped into a fire pit that had been dug inside. The sweat-bath boss threw water onto the rocks and Eskiminzin and Little Captain walked into the thick steam. The sweat-bath boss shut the door.

Eskiminzin and Little Captain squatted on their heels. Outside, the sweat-bath boss hunkered down and sang the sacred verses. The words told how the sweat bath purified the mind and cleaned the spirit. The words also spoke of such things as sky and earth and sun. After a while, when the right feeling passed through them, Eskiminzin and Little Captain joined in the singing.

Eskiminzin and Little Captain felt the bad things of living leave their bodies. They felt flushed with truth, so much it hurt. It was impossible to lie.

After the sweat boss finished his singing and they finished with him, Eskiminzin and Little Captain sat quietly. They waited for their minds to be set free and released from their bodies.

Eskiminzin said, "The man spoke words last night."

Little Captain said, "The words were old words."

The steam hissed off the hot stones.

Eskiminzin said, "The man had many old words to choose from. The man chose those words."

"The words had meaning, maybe."

"The words always have meaning."

"The words had special meaning, maybe."

"Let the man speak."

Little Captain was silent for a long time. The steam drifted back and forth across his face so that one time he was there and then he was not. He was careful. Words spoken in a sweat bath never went away. They remained in the air always, ready to be listened to again.

Little Captain said, "The man speaks of what is happening."

Eskiminzin said, "Speak. A single mind is a small thing."

Again Little Captain was silent. Eskiminzin waited with no impatience. He rubbed himself with the end of his stick. His head felt free. He was close to the grandfathers and the grandfathers' grandfathers.

Little Captain said, "Much good is here."

Eskiminzin said, "*Enju.*"

Little Captain said, "The people do not go hungry. They are not chased like dogs by the soldiers on horses."

Eskiminzin said again, "*Enju.*"

"This man does not know if it is good. The man does not know whether it is good to live on charity. The man does not know whether it is good to eat what the white man says we may eat. The man does not know whether people should live on the good will of the enemy. What the enemy gives one day, the enemy may decide not to give the next day."

Eskiminzin considered that. "The soldier chief has pledged that will not happen as long as I keep my pledge."

"Pledge!" Little Captain appeared out of the steam for a moment in his anger and then vanished. "To beg?"

Eskiminzin said harshly, "We do not beg."

Little Captain said, "It is given to us, yes. But we have not taken it with our strength. We receive it because we crawl."

"To start walking toward peace is not the same thing as to crawl."

The men stopped speaking when the stiffened hide door opened and the sweat-bath boss removed the cooled-off rocks and put fresh hot ones down and poured water on them. Eskiminzin had been watching Little Captain closely but now he could not see him at all in the sudden explosion of steam.

Until Little Captain chose to speak again, Eskiminzin occupied himself with digesting what his subchief had said. Some of the things were things he had himself thought, things he had discussed with the white *nantan*. It was useful to listen to them again as spoken by Little Captain.

Little Captain spoke again. His voice was almost spectral, coming through the wet fog. "It is the same as everything else. What a man does not use dies. A muscle that is not used dies. When the nose stops smelling, soon it cannot smell. There is that thing that makes a people what they are. When that is not used the people stop being what they are. It was the way the grandfathers' grandfathers were."

"And you are saying that we should continue that way, even though things are different for us now?"

Little Captain said in a low voice, "I think only about getting lost."

"Lost?"

"The young men do nothing. There is nothing for them to do."

"They will learn new things."

"Only a small time has passed and they are different."

"I have said it, the world here is different. I think they must learn to be different in this different world."

Little Captain asked, "How will they ever know the wonder of themselves?"

Eskiminzin said, "They will learn new things and find new wonder."

Little Captain's face emerged slowly out of the settling steam. It was streaked with sweat and the eyes no longer were red.

Little Captain asked, "How will they know when they become men? How will they know anything of themselves? How will they know of the power in themselves if they never put themselves to the test?"

The words were words that had gone through Eskiminzin's head and he was glad to hear them spoken aloud. Perhaps he could answer the words better than when they were just flying around inside his head.

Eskiminzin said, "There are different kinds of tests, maybe."

Little Captain said, "Our tests are our tests."

The two men were able to see each other now. They had known each other from the time they were children and they had grown up together and as boys had learned warrior ways together and had become warriors together. They had fought and had slain and they respected each other.

Eskiminzin said slowly in a little while, "There are big seasons. Not the seasons we see following one after the other but big seasons. Once there were people who scratched on the rocks. Their season ended. It is said their season ended when we came here. Where are they now? There may have been those among them who wanted to make changes to suit the new time and those among them who counseled that things must stay the way they always had been. I believe it was those people who won and that it was because the rock-scratchers stayed the way they were that we destroyed them.

"Our season has lasted for a long time, longer than anyone can remember, before the grandfathers' grandfathers, and now new people have come here and they are to us as we were to the rock-scratchers. We can remain the way we have always been but then in the end nothing will remain of us, nothing except what the people who defeat us will say and remember about us. We have not even scratched things on rocks."

It was a long while before Little Captain replied. "Some think that would be the better way. To be remembered always as men who knew how to fight and die, and not to live in a way in which a man is no different from a woman." He looked directly at Eskiminzin. His face was agonized. "I am ashamed every time I stand on line and walk up to a little house and a white man who would like to see me dead gives me something to keep me alive. Each time he does that he kills me a little and he knows it and I know it."

Eskiminzin asked, "Do many think as you do?"

"Some."

"Many?"

"Some."

"If enough think that way they can choose another chief and walk another path."

Little Captain said, "No man wants another chief."

"Do you?"

"I said no man."

"Do you?"

"No."

Eskiminzin said, "Listen to me. I have tried to think of what is the best thing for the people. No change is easy. One thing is easy. It is easy to say 'let us die.' It is not easy to sit living next to death but it is easy to die. That is all right for the young men to want to do. But there are many of us here and the young men are fewest of all. And if the young die so that they may be remembered as being brave, what becomes of the others? I am ready to die. You are ready to die, yes. But what becomes of the others? The old people and the women and the children. You have six children. What would become of them? What would become of the women if the warriors allow themselves to die gloriously so they will be famous in the time to come? The women would be taken by the Mexicans and made into prostitutes. The children would be taken by the Mexicans and made into slaves, and when the girl children became women, they would be made into prostitutes, too. By then the warriors would be dead and famous."

As Eskiminzin spoke, Little Captain became more and more agitated. The steam and the heat had drained him and his head was floating, as it was supposed to do.

Eskiminzin said, "It is something new to us. It is something new not to do what is right for just that moment but to try to do something that is right for the moments that have not yet arrived. To stand on line and be fed the way a dog is fed, the way a dog trots up and waits to be thrown a bone, that is a bad thing. But that is how it has to start. To do that silently and to live with that develops another muscle, maybe. It is easy to be proud when you have killed an enemy and won a victory. It is not easy to be proud when you have to stick your hand out for food. And yet if pride could come from that, it would be a stronger pride, maybe."

The sweat-bath boss brought in more rocks and water and the wickiup became opaque again and it was as though Eskiminzin and Little Captain, who had been together for a little while, retreated to their own places and were alone.

Eskiminzin said, "I want to learn. I want us to learn new things. The old ways never can come back no matter how hard we would fight. The white man is too strong and there are too many and we could kill them every day and there would be more. This is the time of the white man and we must bend to that time so that one day we can straighten again and by that time the young men will be the leaders who govern the people and they will know things you and I never will live to know and they will look back at the old days and smile at them and be happy the way they are."

Little Captain said, "It is possible."

Eskiminzin was silent again. He breathed in the hot vapor. It burned his lungs. "Do you want to walk away?"

Little Captain said, "No."

"Any man can walk away. If enough men want to walk away this man will walk away instead."

"No."

"I have pledged my word to the white *nantan*."

Little Captain said, "No one will betray it."

Eskiminzin's voice was hoarse from the steam and from what he felt. "If there is any betrayal it must come from the white man."

Little Captain said, "None of your people will twist your words around."

Eskiminzin nodded. His head was like a cave that had been cleansed by fresh winds.

"When the people ask questions, tell them of what we have spoken and of what you have said and of what I have said. Tell them that I know only a little bit about things but that I believe this is right. Tell them that if this is not right then it will become known clearly to us and if that time comes we can decide to do other things." Eskiminzin felt weariness spreading through his body. This was the final stage. "As long as we remain here in Dark Canyon alongside Little Running Water there is a pledge from me to the white *nantan*. He holds my word in his hand and while it is there it cannot be changed. That is another pride, to keep one's word. It is as great a pride as killing an enemy."

They sat for a while longer. They had finished with what they had to say to each other. They spoke now within themselves. They spoke to Usen and to White Painted Lady. They spoke to Child of the Water, who was born immaculately to White Painted Lady, and who killed Giant and made it possible for the People to come up out of the ground.

When they stepped outside, the sun was high. They were enfeebled and they went to their dwellings to rest.

△ 5

Child Mother was suckling the baby, Ria, when Road Runner burst into the wickiup with his dog. Road Runner ran like any other boy now. He did not flap his arms the way he used to. When he was younger, when he was four, he was positive he could make himself fly. He did not believe that now, although Eskiminzin encouraged him to keep trying.

Eskiminzin was fashioning a small bow when the boy ran into the wickiup. He slipped the bow away. He was making it for Road Runner, the boy's first bow, and he wanted it to be a surprise. Aravaipa men might not have to hunt so much now that the white people were giving them food but Eskiminzin wanted his son to learn how to shoot arrows as soon as possible. It would help Road Runner know who he was.

Road Runner, breathing as hard as his dog, reported an astonishing thing. "The water has gone from Little Running Water," he gasped.

"Sit down," Eskiminzin said. He wondered whether the boy's heavy breathing came from the short run from the creek or from excitement. He thought it might not be a bad idea to have athletic contests for the boys as in the old days. The men enjoyed them and made bets and it was good for the boys.

"Little Running Water has gone away," the boy said.

"Sit down," Eskiminzin said again. "It goes away each season this time." He felt sad that his son and all the other young people had been away from their home for so long they didn't know about the habits of Little Running Water.

"Where does it go?" Road Runner asked. He hunkered down and his dog crouched next to him, panting hard and looking at Road Runner with adoration.

At one time Eskiminzin would not liked to have seen that closeness between his son and a dog. When the Aravaipas ran from one place to another, chased by the soldiers, they often had nothing to eat but their dogs. But those days were ended and, Eskiminzin hoped, for all time, and now a dog could be simply what it was intended to be, a friend, especially a friend to children.

"Where does Little Running Water go?" Eskiminzin shrugged. "Somewhere. Nobody can say exactly."

"Why not?" Road Runner asked.

Eskiminzin pinched his nose and looked over to Child Mother. He did not like it when his son asked him questions he could not answer.

"A person goes to sleep one night and the water is trickling down out there and when the person wakes the next day the water is gone." Eskiminzin knew that was not much of an answer. It was not an answer at all.

"Where does it go?" Road Runner persisted.

"Into the ground, I think."

"Why does it do that?"

"It gets tired, maybe, running down the canyon in all that heat. Maybe it has to have a rest somewhere." Eskiminzin considered that was at least possible. "It only goes away when it gets very hot," he added, to bolster his theory.

"Does it come back?"

"Always. It was here to greet us when we arrived this time."

Road Runner nodded. His forehead was furrowed and it made him look like a little old man. His forehead always crinkled when he learned a new thing. Once he had jumped off a rock and had flapped his arms trying to fly. He had fallen on his face. When he got up his forehead was crinkled.

"What do we drink while it is resting under the ground?" the boy asked.

"Little Running Water still flows farther up Dark Canyon," Eskiminzin said. He said that with full authority. He knew that to be true. He was glad to have finished with the unknown.

"Is that near here?" Road Runner asked.

"Not very far."

Road Runner smiled. He had a grave face like his sister, Fawn, and Eskiminzin liked to see him smile.

Road Runner stood up. "Is what you have just told me secret?"

"Secret?" Eskiminzin asked.

"I want to tell it to the others. They were worried."

"Tell it to them. Tell it to all of them. Tell them it is nothing to worry about." As Road Runner started out of the wickiup, his father called to him. The boy turned around. The dog, already outside, came in again. "I am happy that you think about the others," Eskiminzin said.

Road Runner nodded. His face flushed. He was overwhelmed at receiving a compliment from his father. He could not reply. He ran out and the dog ran after him.

Eskiminzin retrieved the unfinished bow. Child Mother put Ria down and covered her breast. The baby started to crawl on the ground. Child Mother picked her up and put her on a pallet and gave her a small piece of stick with thongs fastened to the end of it and dried berries fastened to the thongs. The baby rattled the dried berries.

"I had forgotten about that myself," Child Mother said.

"Forgotten what?" Eskiminzin was deep in the intricacy of making a proper bow, small size.

"About Little Running Water going away as it does. It has been a long time since I saw Little Running Water go to sleep down here."

Eskiminzin looked at her fondly. He liked Child Mother very much. She had a soft voice and she did not nag. Small Woman spoke quietly and she did not nag either. There had been another wife a long time ago but she died giving birth to a child, which was a waste because the child was dead too. She never nagged either. He was lucky with all his wives. There were men whose wives nagged them all the time. They did not do it in front of people, they would not dare to do that, but they did it inside their dwellings. Eskiminzin knew about that because he could see it on the faces of the men sometimes. Sometimes they looked angry and ashamed and Eskiminzin knew their wives had been at them.

Ria started to wail and Child Mother went to her and picked her up. Child Mother patted Ria on her bottom and the baby stopped crying right away. She put her down again and the baby fell asleep.

Eskiminzin watched his wife with interest. The baby was almost weaned and before long he would be able to enter Child

Mother again. It had been a long time. When he was able to do that with Child Mother he would spend most of the day in Small Woman's wickiup. He had found that balanced things, to spend as much time as he could spare during the day in the dwelling of the woman he could not enter at night. He had thought more than once of taking Melana for a third wife but he knew that Child Mother would not approve of that. She would not mind if he took a third woman but she would not like it to be her own cousin.

With the baby asleep Child Mother started sewing up a rip in one of Eskiminzin's moccasins. Eskiminzin watched her for a moment or two. He thought it was a good thing she could work that way with the baby sleeping on her pallet. He remembered the times when women had to work with the babies in baskets on their backs so they could run away quickly in the event the horse soldiers turned up.

"Are you content?" he asked.

The question surprised Child Mother. Her husband knew she was always content when he was near her and she knew too she could give him the night happiness again before much time passed. She knew from the way her husband looked at her these days that he was thinking about that. That pleased her. It pleased her because it made her feel good but it pleased her more because of the joy it gave to her husband and to know it was her body that gave it to him.

"Am I content? Yes." She lowered her eyes. After all this time she still was shy when her husband asked her a question, especially a question about her feelings.

"Do you think it is a good thing I have done?" Eskiminzin asked. "To surrender this way to the white men?"

Child Mother started to blush. She was embarrassed. She was always embarrassed when her husband asked her opinion. She could never understand why a great leader would want to know what she thought about anything. "My words have no value," she said.

"You are one of our people, as I am one of our people," Eskiminzin said. "Some men say it weakens our people to be dependent on the white man."

"Yes."

"You have heard that?"

"From some of the women."

"What do you think about that?"

Child Mother was more embarrassed than ever. She did not consider herself a thinker. She thought Small Woman was clever and would be able to give their husband an intelligent reply. She thought Melana would be able to give him the wisest answer of all.

She pointed to the child. "She sleeps safely."

Eskiminzin nodded. "That is the true answer."

He stood up and put away the small unfinished bow. He touched her on the shoulder and left the wickiup.

She sat there, her legs doubled under her, and she sewed the torn moccasin and listened to the gurgling of the baby and she felt the touch of Eskiminzin's fingers on her shoulder.

△ 6

Eskiminzin always felt something inside him diminish when he went into Lieutenant Whitman's office. The white soldier chief invariably was pleased to see him and made him welcome. Still, something inside Eskiminzin started losing size when he set foot on the post. By the time he reached Whitman's office he no longer was the same man who left the Apache village.

He was glad when Whitman got up and walked around his desk and held out his hand. Eskiminzin had not at first understood or liked the way white men put their hands together when they met. Then he thought it must be some secret ritual. Whitman had explained that it was not that, that it was merely a manner of greeting. Now Eskiminzin was getting to like that greeting and to depend on it. He put his hand in Whitman's hand and felt the pressure there and he felt a little better.

The men smoked quietly and studied each other while Colin Duncan went to fetch the Puma. Both men were thinking about the same thing. Both men were thinking how much better it would be if they could speak to each other directly. It was as though they were to each other senseless lumps until the Puma came along to animate them and give them speech.

By the time the Puma got there enough Indian time had passed and Eskiminzin spoke up immediately. "Little Running Water is gone."

"I beg your pardon?" For a moment Whitman had the mad impression that Eskiminzin was telling him somebody had stolen the creek.

"The water is gone away," Eskiminzin said. "Little Running Water now is as dry as the land on both sides of it."

"The creek drying up? In the spring? That's ridiculous." Whitman looked at Eskiminzin suspiciously, although he could not have said what it was he was suspicious of.

"It is the season," Eskiminzin said. "In this season the water always goes away. Little Running Water is not fed from the melting mountain snow and it always dries up at this time."

"What the devil can we do about that?" Whitman asked.

"The water still flows farther up the creek."

"How do you know that?"

"It has always been that way. Little Running Water stays alive farther up Dark Canyon."

Again suspicion passed through Whitman's mind but this time he was able to focus on it. "Where the water still flows— it is too far away to haul down here, I suppose."

"Yes." A stillness came upon Eskiminzin's face. He knew the thought that was in the mind of the white *nantan*.

"Then what you are saying is that you want to move your village up the canyon," Whitman said.

"We cannot live without water, Nantan Whitman."

Whitman asked the Puma, "Do you know about this?"

"Yes, Teniente."

"The creek dries out this time of year?"

"Yes, Teniente."

"How far would they have to go?"

"About four miles."

"And this happens every year?"

"Yes, Teniente."

The stillness remained on Eskiminzin's face. He sensed that the *nantan* was questioning his words. He did not blame him. He would have done the same thing. But it was not the same as the placing together of the hands.

Whitman sat back and looked at Eskiminzin. He could see the Indian had retreated. "Well," Whitman said, "this is a new kettle of fish."

The Puma did not know exactly what that meant but he puzzled out the gist of it and somehow made a translation for Eskiminzin. The way he put it was "The *ranchería* has been overrun by ants."

Eskiminzin nodded slowly. He knew all about that. He had gathered what Whitman must have said before the Puma put it into Apache.

"Yes," Eskiminzin agreed.

Whitman stood up and walked to the window. He could see down the length of the parade ground. He could see the dry land outside the post. The banks of Little Running Water sloped down and he could not see the creek, wet or dry. On the other side of the creek he could see the closest of the Apache wickiups.

Four miles up the canyon. Actually, it was not that far. He could ride up every day. And the men still would have to come to the post for their provisions. Still, it was not the same as being able to look out his window and see the edge of the Apache village.

He turned to Eskiminzin. "You will have to make a new village. It must not affect our agreement."

"Our words are the same words," Eskiminzin said. "The words could be broken as easily here as there."

"Yes, I suppose so." Whitman sat down again. "It won't seem exactly that way to the people in Tucson when they hear about it. It was bad enough when you were right on my doorstep. When will you move?"

"Today."

"Fred Austin tells me that Naco has taken to visiting his mother," Whitman said.

"Yes. They play cards together," Eskiminzin said.

"Cards?"

"A Spanish game called monte."

"I'll be damned. What do they use for cards?"

"Cut up pony skins that have been marked and hardened."

"I'll be damned."

"His mother is happy. She is old and his father was killed in a fight with Mexicans."

After a moment Whitman said, "It will be hard for Naco to visit his mother after you move your camp. I will let him use one of the horses."

Eskiminzin raised his eyes and then lowered them.

△ △ △ FOUR

△ 1

The time of greatness was long past but the men of the Elías family, those who had avoided Apache murder, were still the *patróns,* and the five Mexicans who came to the Tucson home of Jesús María Elías on this day in the third week of March stood before Don Jesús in respect and humility as they and their forebears had stood before generations of Elías men.

They stood in the big, cool front room of the house, holding the wide brims of their sombreros against their chests, and their heads were held lowered by a convention now as inwrought a part of their make-up as the color of their hair and the speech on their tongues.

The spokesman was a short, middle-aged Mexican named Facundo Salazar, a man with a mild face and mild eyes and a mustache intended for a dragoon. He told his story in slow, faltering words, spoken so low they might not have been heard if they were not dealing with a subject Don Jesús would have picked up if it were being whispered about on the far side of the moon.

"When did this happen, Facundo?" Don Jesús asked. He was seated on a large chair in the large room. The chair was a relic of the splendid days. It was a chair for the *patrón* of a *hacienda,* for an *alcalde.* Don Jesús sat on it well, his arms resting on the arms of the chair. His manner was fitting. He listened and replied with courtesy.

"The word was received from the *teniente,*" Facundo Salazar said. He was a little frightened that he had come to bother the *patrón,* who, in truth, no longer was his *patrón,* who no longer was anybody's *patrón,* but the habit of bringing one's troubles to an Elías had been too strong to disavow.

"Teniente Whitman?" Elías asked.

"Sí, Don Jesús," Salazar said.

"And what was that word, Facundo? Tell it to me slowly and clearly so that I will understand it with no possibility of error."

Facundo Salazar nodded. "Sí, Don Jesús. The *teniente* sent the word that we no longer were to cut hay and grass for the animals at Camp Grant."

"And who, Facundo, will do this work then?" Don Jesús asked.

"Who will do this work, Don Jesús?" Facundo Salazar repeated. "The Indians, Don Jesús."

"Which Indians, Facundo?"

"The Apache Indians, Don Jesús."

"Which Apaches, Facundo?"

"The Apaches who have made a village near Camp Grant, Don Jesús."

Don Jesús sighed softly.

"Can the *patrón* do anything about this unpleasant turn of events?"

"I will look into this matter, Facundo."

"A thousand thanks, Don Jesús."

"For nothing, *amigo*."

"Don Jesús will please remember that I have a family, a wife and six children, the youngest with less than a year, and that the gathering of hay and grass for the military has been my livelihood." Facundo Salazar released the grip of his right hand on the brim of his hat and waved to the others. "All of my *compañeros* earn their living and support their wives and children by the cutting of the hay and grass that now is denied to us."

"Nothing will be forgotten, Facundo," Don Jesús said.

△ 2

By extension Andy Cargill was hard currency, too. Andrew Cargill, a thin, wiry man with a bald head and a beard and a

Scottish accent, was the auditor for the merchant firm of Lord & Williams and he was just back from Camp Grant where he had looked over Fred Austin's books. On this Saturday afternoon he had quite a crowd around him in the Congress Hall. Andy Cargill didn't mind that at all. He had been invited to sit at Bill Oury's table and he was being presented with all the whiskey he could drink and for free, and Bill Oury's special whiskey at that.

"I'll be damned," Oury said. He had said that three or four times as Andy Cargill relayed bits and pieces of the latest news from the post. "How far up the creek did you say, Andy?"

"Four miles, maybe a little more."

"Four miles, maybe a little more," Oury repeated.

"Closest they could find water," Cargill said. "Aravaipa Creek just dried itself out below there." Cargill poured himself another drink. The stuff was nothing to what was brought over from Glasgow, but then . . . "They all had to move, that was all there was to it."

"With Lieutenant Whitman's permission, of course."

"Oh, yes. The chief, Eskiminzin, asked him properly."

"Tell me, Andy," Oury said, "tell me, just how is Lieutenant Royal Whitman going to keep his royal eye on his good Apache friends if they're going to live all that far away?"

"The Apache men come down for rations. And the lieutenant rides up there almost every day to have a look-see. Everything is being done in a proper manner."

Bill Oury rolled his cigar from one side of his mouth to the other. He watched Andy Cargill empty his whiskey glass. Oury liked good whiskey and he liked to see other men appreciate good whiskey.

"Andy," he said. "Andy, I reckon it would have been a little too hard on those poor Apaches to stay where they were and go up the creek and haul down water. I reckon that would have been asking a mite too much of them, wouldn't it?"

"The squaws do that kind of work, Billy."

"And that would be too much for those poor women. It's much easier to let them just clear out of sight and have the soldiers ride up to see them. Something like somebody once said about the mountain going to Mohammed."

Bill Oury laughed and most of the other men laughed. Bill Oury picked up the bottle and refilled Cargill's glass. He was still laughing and the others were still laughing when Jesús María Elías entered the saloon and sat down at Oury's table.

Oury pushed the bottle and a clean glass over to Don Jesús. "Andy's just in from Grant. Wait'll you hear what he's got to say, Don Jesús."

"I, too, have something to tell, Don Guillermo," Don Jesús said.

"Speak then, friend."

"I will listen first, Don Guillermo." Elías drank some of the whiskey. He detested American whiskey. He drank it because Don Guillermo was his closest friend.

Oury repeated what Cargill had just told them. "The right royal Whitman just gave them his royal permission to break camp and set it up again just about wherever they pleased. How do you like that, Don Jesús?"

"Now, Billy, not exactly where they pleased," Cargill protested. "Just to where they could get water. A human being cannot be denied the fluid of life."

"Never thought you'd name water as being that," a man called out.

Cargill, whose opinion of the product of the local wells was well known, emptied his glass to show he was a good fellow. He held up the empty glass for all to see. The men laughed.

"You do not laugh, Don Jesús," Oury said. "I reckon you don't think letting them Apaches park themselves about five miles away from Camp Grant is anything to laugh about."

"No, Don Guillermo, it is not." Elías toyed with his glass. "How is the lieutenant going to supervise them at that distance?"

"Same question I asked, Don Jesús," Oury said. "Andy here says the lieutenant takes a ride up to see them every day and that the bucks come down for their free food so he gets a look at them anyway." Oury frowned. "What's troubling you, Don Jesús?"

Elías lit a cigar before he replied. He nipped the tip with a gold cigar cutter. He struck a match and held it away from the cigar until the sulphur burned away. He turned the cigar around slowly as he held the flame to it. When he had the cigar burning to his satisfaction he reported on the news given to him by Facundo Salazar.

"They came to me to ask what I could do for them," Elías said bitterly. "And what can I do for these poor men who have been dispossessed of their labors to make possible labors for Apaches, whose families will suffer so that Apache families will not suffer, whose children will hunger so that Apache children, already being fed, will be fed more?"

When Don Jesús finished no one spoke. Few Americans in the saloon cared anything at all about the fate of Mexican laborers, but the circumstances of the distress of the five men who had gone to Don Jesús almost made them martyrs.

Bill Oury glanced at his friend and what he saw in Don Jesús' face caused him to look away. Although Don Jesús tried he could not entirely hide the bitterness that had started in his voice and now was on his face. He could not hide his shame at the way things were now and at how futile and unimportant he was in the present order of things, and at how he could do nothing more than listen to impoverished countrymen who believed from habit that he might still have power.

"I did not tell them I could do nothing," Elías said. "One does not deny hope to the desperate."

Bill Oury almost didn't hear those last few words because something else was on his mind. He scratched his beard and frowned and was about to speak when his friend Hiram Stevens, the merchant, spoke out. Stevens was a portly, successful man and there was not a man in the saloon who did not know there was a wooden floor in his house.

"Indians collect hay for the Army," Stevens said. He had a deep, penetrating bass voice. "Isn't that what that Colonel Green was doing for a while up at Camp Apache?"

No one needed to answer the rhetorical question. What Colonel John Green had attempted to do with the Coyoteros was well known to every man there.

"And how many settlers up there almost starved to death while Colonel Green was trying to make good Christians out of Apache Indians?" Stevens asked.

Again the question remained unanswered. In the conver-

sational orchestration that was going around the table, Stevens'
queries were a kind of obbligato.

"You got Indians working for you at your ranch, ain't you,
Uncle Billy?"

Oury looked up sharply to see Lef Tilson leaning over
Andy Cargill's shoulder. Lef Tilson worked as a clerk at Zeckendorf's and was neither by wealth nor social standing a member of the inner circle.

"Yes," Oury said evenly. "I have Papago Indians working
for me and they're damned good workers and I pay them an
honest wage."

Oury looked at the faces closest to him to see whether
anyone wanted to challenge that statement. No one did. Oury
turned to Elías.

"Don Jesús, did those Mexicans tell you what the royal
Whitman is going to pay those Apaches?"

"No," Don Jesús said.

"Wouldn't be no interest to the lieutenant," Lef Tilson
said. "Whatever it is it's Government money, not out of his
pocket." He looked shrewdly at Bill Oury. He had a pretty good
idea about what Oury was paying his Indians and what Elías
was paying the tame Indians who worked on his ranch, and
just about what all the ranchers who hired Pima Indians and
Papagos and other humble and manageable Indians were paying. Everybody knew a person could hire a tame Indian for
about a tenth of what a white man would want for the job and
for less than half of what even a Mexican would ask. It was
good business.

"Bill," Lef Tilson said again.

Oury looked up. He resented this man calling him by his
first name. He resented Tilson's face with its long, droopy nose.
He resented the little eyes.

"Bill," Lef Tilson said again. "Supposing this Whitman
pays them Apaches something near what the Mexicans got."

Bill Oury said nothing. Other ranchers frowned as the blas-
phemous suggestion hovered in the air. They looked at one
another and wondered.

"Supposing he does that, Billy, and word gets around," Lef

Tilson said. "You know, the Indian smoke signals." Lef Tilson chuckled at his own wit. It wasn't often he didn't have to be sore at not being a rich rancher. "Then all the Indians'd want the same pay, wouldn't they?"

Before anybody could discuss that dreadful possibility or do anything to Lef Tilson for daring to bring it up, John Wasson entered the saloon with the latest edition of his *Citizen* fresh from the press. He gave copies of the newspaper, still smelling of printer's ink, to cronies, the first paper, of course, going to Bill Oury. John Wasson always liked this moment in the week. He felt a little bit like the Roman god Mercury.

Bill Oury, who considered the prospect conjured up by Lef Tilson to be entirely conceivable, and never mind the funny, smart-ass business about smoke signals, looked over the front page of the *Citizen* on this twenty-fifth day of March. His eyes went automatically to the casualty list John Wasson printed each week. The names of the latest Apache victims always were familiar to one degree or another. Andy Cargill asked him something and Oury looked up from the paper and then he looked back at it fast and he sat up straight and he felt something strike him hard below his heart.

It was the last item on the list.

> Murdered on their ranch near Tubac, the well-known rancher L. B. Wooster and his wife, Doña Trinidad.

Bill Oury stood up and people made way for him and he walked out of the saloon into the street. For the first time in his life he went into the San Augustin cathedral without his wife. He walked down the aisle and he knelt and wept.

△ 3

"You see, Les had asked me when I had a moment would I come around and help him fix a broken spring on his wagon and when I finished milking that morning I saddled up and rode over. That's when I found him. We didn't find Trinidad right away but that's when I found Les."

John Smith puffed on his pipe. Bill Oury stirred the thick black coffee. There was no need to stir it because there was no milk or sugar in it but Oury stirred it anyway. Doña Inez sat with her hands in her lap. The three of them were sitting around the table in Leslie Wooster's kitchen. Hester Smith, who had brought over the pot of coffee, was somewhere else in the house, opening windows and airing things out.

"I rode over and I called out but there wasn't any answer and I went to the house and there wasn't anybody there," John Smith said. "Surprised me. Les always told me when he and Trinidad was going anywheres so that I could keep my eye on this place, same as he'd do for me, but he hadn't told me nothing about going nowhere.

"I looked around. I thought maybe he was in the barn where the wagon was and he hadn't heard me so I went there but he wasn't there. The wagon was there and it was on a block on one side ready for work on the broken spring but Les wasn't there. I looked around and finally I went to the corral and that's where I found him. Just inside the corral. All his clothes had been taken off him. He was laying there naked as the day the good Lord put him on earth."

"Dead," Oury said.

"Deader'n dead. Cold dead. His body was full of holes from lances or spears. Big holes."

The coffee was cold now and Bill Oury had not touched it. His face was as gray as his beard. His eyes looked as though they couldn't see.

"Trinidad," Doña Inez said. "Where did you find her?"

"Well, Mrs. Oury, at first I thought either she got away or else maybe them Indians captured her. I looked all over the place and I couldn't find her and then I sent Hester around to get some help and some other people from around here showed up and we searched more. Then we found her. Out there in the woods, three, four hundred yards from the house. Figure she was running away, maybe to get help. The woods is between this place and mine. Maybe she was trying to get to me."

John Smith, a former blacksmith and Wooster's nearest neighbor, a massive, bearded man, got up and walked to the stove. He took one of the plates off and banged his pipe empty. He took the plate off with his bare hand. The stove was out and cold.

"We found Trinidad's body in the woods," he said, his back to Oury and Doña Inez. "She was stripped naked, too. There were only three of them lance wounds in her body but they were plenty enough to kill her. Hester took off one of her petticoats and covered the body."

Smith returned to the table, rubbing the warm bowl of his pipe. "She looked scared, Bill. She looked like she knew what was going to happen to her. Her whole face was all twisted around. Her eyes were still open and they were big and kind of crazy with fear. Her mouth was open, too, like she was yelling when they stuck them spears in her."

Oury breathed out heavily and looked around the room. "Place looks nice and clean."

"Oh, Trinidad kept it spick-and-span. She was house proud, all right. It ain't had time to dirty up." Smith shook his head. "Them Apaches didn't touch the house. They ran off Les's horses and beeves but they didn't do anything to the house. Generally they set a fire but this time they let the place alone."

"Maybe nobody happened to have a match handy," Oury said.

"Plenty of matches in the kitchen here," Smith said. Then he said, "Oh, that was your joke."

"Yes, that was my joke. What's going to happen now?"

"Les's got kin back East," Smith said. "I wrote them a letter. Meanwhile I'll keep an eye on the place like I always did when Les and Trinidad went away."

Oury looked across the table at Doña Inez and she nodded. They both stood up. The coffee was untouched.

"So much Indian killing around here," Smith said, pushing back the chair and rising to his feet. "Just in the last year or two specially. Saunders and Blanchard and a mail rider and three or four Mexicans and Pete Kitchen's kid, one of them, and now Les Wooster and Trinidad. Les was going to have a birthday soon. He was going to be twenty-eight."

"Next Thursday," Oury said.

They went outside. It was a lovely day. The air was fresh and clean and they could see the mountains, pink and brown and green, and the sky lay up there like a blue sea turned upside down, and it was all so good.

"This is the best growing land in southern Arizona," Smith said, his black farmer's boot kicking at the ground like a pawing horse. "But you can't step outdoors without a gun in your hand. Used to be a lot of folk in Tubac, just up to three, four years ago there was more than four hundred living there. Now there's maybe twenty-five, thirty men there and they're just passing through. How's this all going to wind up, Bill?"

"Yeah," Oury said.

Oury and Doña Inez thanked Smith for telling them what had happened and for taking care of things and they said good-bye to Hester Smith, who was standing at the door. They climbed into their wagon and two of Oury's ranch hands, who had been sitting in the shade of a tree, got up on their horses to follow them back to Tucson.

Oury and his wife stopped off at the little cemetery in Tubac. Oury stared at the two mounds of newly turned earth. Doña Inez said a prayer and crossed herself and righted the cross over Doña Trinidad's grave.

"Those graves," Oury said to his wife as they rode home, "they didn't look like places where a man and his wife were buried. They looked more like they were for a grown person and a child."

△ 4

The cartoon was four feet by four feet. It was painted red. It showed an Indian wearing a full set of head feathers beating a white man to death with a tomahawk. The bodies of several other white men were lying around, their heads already split open. The Indian looked more like a Plains Indian than an Apache but that was no inadvertency. Despite the constant, oppressive presence of the Apache and his baleful impact on the life of every person, there were few in Tucson who actually had had a look at an Apache and had lived to remember it. The artist who fashioned the poster deemed it wise to depict an Indian anybody could recognize as an Indian.

Under the imaginative cartoon, lettered in the same lurid paint, was the announcement:

INJUNS   INJUNS   INJUNS
BIG MEETING AT THE COURTHOUSE
TIME FOR ACTION HAS ARRIVED
COME EVERYBODY

The cartoon with its message was nailed to the end of a long pole that was held high for all to see by the local version of a town crier. His fee for his work was free drinks at a saloon of his choosing. In order that no one would happen not to see the message bearer, he was accompanied by a small boy who beat a sharp drum. The boy's fee was five cents.

The man and the boy made their way carefully through the hazardous Tucson streets. From time to time children attached themselves to the pair and followed them for a little while, dancing and jumping to the drum beat.

△ 5

Tom Dunn was shocked when Lieutenant Whitman entered the Shoo Fly and limped toward the table. Not because of the limp—Captain Dunn, commanding officer at Camp Lowell, remembered that Whitman had an old wound from the war, and the ride down from Camp Grant must have been hard—but at the change in Whitman's appearance since the last time he had seen him. There were new lines around Whitman's mouth and a tired grimness in his eyes and his skin was yellowy from quinine. It seemed to Dunn that the four months at Grant had put about four years on his fellow officer's face.

Captain Dunn, a trim, neat man with a trim, neat mustache, rose and shook hands with Whitman. He realized he was staring at him. He averted his eyes and waved to the other chair at the small table and sat down. Whitman sat on the rickety chair and looked around with pleasure.

However he might appear to Dunn, Whitman felt good. The fever had left him alone for some time now and he had enjoyed the ride from Grant, though the hours in the saddle had the usual effect on his hip. After he had made sure the six men who had ridden down with him were being properly seen to at Camp Lowell, he had washed and shaved and put on a clean uniform.

Tucson seemed like a metropolis. Men and women moved about in the streets and children were all over the place. There were stores crowded with shoppers. There were saloons. The Shoo Fly was exotic.

The restaurant had another name but by then no one could remember what it was. Even Mrs. Wallen, the owner, who abhorred the nickname, would have to give herself a moment to think if anyone asked her what the proper designation was.

The restaurant was crowded, as it always was at the dinner hour. The regulars sat at their regular tables, their places marked by their napkins in their own napkin rings. Captain Dunn, who did not qualify as a mealer, had nonetheless managed to wangle from Mrs. Wallen a very decent table commanding a view of the back yard, where a Mexican woman was at the moment engaged in washing dirty clothes.

It was all very exciting to Whitman. He felt like a prisoner let out of jail, or at least temporarily paroled. He turned to Dunn and found him again staring at him.

"Sorry, Royal," Dunn said.

"Funny thing, I feel marvelous."

"What a pesthole that place must be."

Whitman shrugged. "About half the men are down with it."

Dunn shook his head. "Every single year in his annual report the Army Surgeon recommends that Camp Grant be deactivated and every year somebody or other says it certainly will be and every year is the beginning of the same old year at Camp Grant."

The men looked up to see Mrs. Wallen standing at the table. She had already started reporting on the menu for the evening. Mrs. Wallen went through the items just once, naming each thing in the same monotone. The diners had to listen hard and carefully and remember. Mrs. Wallen, a Yankee from Connecticut wasted words no more than she wasted anything else.

The food they remembered when she was finished and they had ordered was excellent. There was shrimp up from Guaymas, having somehow gotten through the Apache gauntlet, some very good beef broth, a beef stew with a strong Mexican accent, fresh tomatoes and crisp lettuce, all followed by oranges, limes and fresh quinces and Mexican figs. The coffee was very good.

To Whitman it was a feast of which Lucullus might not have entirely disapproved. Dunn, observing him with amusement, frowned at one point and asked, "Is there anything wrong, Royal?"

"Wrong? My goodness, what could be wrong with this?"

"You did look slightly concerned for a moment there."

"Did I?" Whitman picked up a fresh, plump, red tomato and looked at it. "I guess I can never forget what my father drilled into all of us—that it's sinful to enjoy anything too much."

Dunn chuckled and relaxed. "It must be difficult to go through life with a New England conscience." As they stirred their coffee and lit cigars, Dunn asked, "Are you still certain you are doing the right thing?"

Whitman watched one of the two white-clad Mexican waiters take a swing at a fly.

"He never gets one, does he?" Whitman asked.

"Never. Never in the memory of living man."

Whitman drew on his cigar. "I don't know whether it's wise or not, Tom. I know it must be done."

After dinner they had brandy at the Congress Hall and then walked to the courthouse. There were a dozen or more youths lounging in front of the courthouse. When the two officers approached the building, a heavily built youngster of about seventeen or eighteen shouted, "There he is!"

The young men collected themselves. Some of them picked up clubs. Dunn and Whitman paused for a moment and then continued to walk toward the courthouse.

"Injun lover!" the heavy youth shouted. It was a signal to the choir.

"Injun lover!" The boys with the clubs waved them in the air. "Injun lover!"

Again Dunn and Whitman paused and looked at each other. They resumed walking to the building.

The young men moved in a body toward the officers. The heavy leader bent down and picked up a stone. Some of the others did the same. Those who had been foresighted enough to provide themselves with the clubs waved them again.

When the youths and the officers were less than five feet apart the heavy youth cocked his arm to throw the stone. A man moved swiftly past Whitman from behind and raised his walking stick and brought it down hard on the leader's hand. The youth howled in pain and dropped the rock. For a moment it appeared that he would attack the man with the cane. The man, elegantly dressed in black with a black, flat-topped hat, leaned on his cane and said nothing.

"Goddamn you!" the heavy youth screamed.

The man said nothing and made no move and the youth raised his fists in despair and then turned and walked away rapidly. The other youths dropped their stones and followed.

The last boy, waving his cudgel, shouted, "Injun lover!" He might have been addressing himself either to Whitman or to the man with the cane, or both.

The civilian waited until the young hoodlums were well on their way and then he turned slowly and inclined his head. "Lieutenant Whitman."

"Mr. Elías," Whitman said.

"Captain Dunn." Jesús María Elías lowered his head slightly again.

"Mr. Elías," Dunn said. "And we're grateful."

"It is a pleasure to see both of you gentlemen here," Elías said. He stepped back to allow the two officers to enter the courthouse before him.

△ 6

Bill Oury, sitting in Judge John Titus' chair, picked up the judge's gavel and banged it on the bench.

"Meeting will come to order," Oury announced.

The talking, which had gone on from the time the men had gathered in the courthouse, which had increased in volume and interest and anger when Whitman and Dunn walked down the center aisle and took seats in the front row, slowly died down.

The room was hot and stuffy and unventilated. Tobacco smoke mixed with fumes from the oil lamps. There was a rich smell of whiskey, stale and fresh.

"Meeting will come to order," Oury repeated, banging the gavel again.

Men made themselves comfortable, spat tobacco juice into cuspidors, lit cigars and cigarettes, relit pipes.

"First order of business is to listen to Lieutenant Royal Whitman, commanding officer of Camp Grant. Lieutenant Whitman got wind of this meeting and asked permission to speak."

Bill Oury sat back in the judge's chair. He did not gesture to Whitman or make any sign. He did not look at Whitman.

After a few moments Whitman realized that Oury was going to say no more and that everybody was waiting for him. He stood up and walked to the witness chair. He glanced up at Oury, sitting on the raised platform that made the judge's dais. Affixed to the wall behind Oury was a large American flag with its thirty-seven stars. On one side of the flag was an engraving of George Washington; on the other, one of Abraham Lincoln.

Oury is in good company, Whitman thought. Still a little shaken by what had taken place outside the courthouse, what had almost taken place, he was relieved that he could isolate even that scantling humor.

(What would have happened outside? The ultimate ignominy of stoning. Plus clubbing. Would he and Dunn have had to draw their revolvers? Would they have fired them? Well, one up for Jesús Elías, where Whitman did not particularly want it to be.)

Whitman turned and faced his audience. The faces behind the smoke merged, it seemed to him, into a single face. Only that face did not remain the same face. First, it was the face of Jesús Elías, long and somber, a cigar between his lips, his hands resting on the silver top of that cane. Then the face seemed to lose itself into the squirrelly face of John Wasson. Except Wasson was not squirrelly. He was just smart.

Whitman would have given a great deal to know which face to speak to. He was not much good at this in any case. If Tom Dunn at that moment had questioned the wisdom of his coming here tonight he could not have given him as positive an answer as he had before.

Some men started murmuring again and then one man shouted, "Get on with it!"

Oury banged the gavel, but gently.

Whitman leaned on the back of the witness chair and began to speak. He told of the manner in which he became involved with the Aravaipa Apaches and Eskiminzin. There was agitation in the room when he spoke the name of the Apache chieftain and he paused while Oury tapped the gavel soothingly.

"I reported what had occurred to General Stoneman and asked for instructions. Until those instructions were received I understood clearly that the responsibility for these people rested solely on me. Therefore I have kept them constantly under my observation. I have come to know many of the faces of the men and women, and of the children, too."

Whitman paused. There was no response from the room. At least the men were silent now. But what kind of silence? He felt the heat in the room and the airlessness and he ran his finger around his collar.

"When these people showed up at Camp Grant they were

in the worst state of poverty," he continued. His voice, nourished by conviction and memory, grew stronger. "Some of them were nearly naked."

There were scattered snigglings in the room.

"They needed food and clothing and some of them needed medical care. I worked out a system by which they gathered hay and grass for the cavalry horses and mules and they received tickets for their work and by means of these tickets were able to obtain manta for clothing. At the beginning the men would not participate in this labor, but under the stern command of their chief they broke with one of their oldest traditions and went out into the fields and worked with the women."

He paused again and again could hear derisive sounds in the room. He was getting nowhere, he knew, and yet he had to go on.

"During this time small parties left the camp to gather mescal. These parties were almost entirely women and children. I checked on these departures. I checked on the amount of the mescal brought in."

He looked at Dunn. The captain was staring at the floor. Was he that unconvincing? He gripped the edge of the chair back. He felt a slight dizziness. What would happen if he asked that some doors be opened?

"From the beginning I was determined to know these people, their hopes and intentions—"

His listeners broke into low mutterings and he heard one man repeat in tones of utter disgust, "Intentions."

"For this purpose I spent hours every day with them explaining the relations they must sustain with the Government. I warned them of what would happen to them in the event of disobedience. I learned from them—and I still am learning—much of their ways and thoughts and the rules that determine their lives. In turn, I made it a rule to answer any questions they asked in as plain and simple and straightforward a manner as possible.

"I am constantly astonished at how smart they are, how quickly they understand. They seem happy and content and they try to show it in every way."

"We damned well know how they show it!" a man shouted from the rear of the room.

Oury tapped the gavel. "We have permitted Lieutenant Whitman to speak here. We will afford him every courtesy."

Whitman turned his head and looked up again at Oury. Just those few feet above the floor and he looked Olympian.

"The ranchers in the vicinity seem friendly to the Aravaipas," Whitman went on. "They have no fears about the large numbers gathered. As a matter of fact, I have sent out some people to speak to some of the nearby ranchers and they have promised to engage the Indians at a fair rate of pay to harvest their barley when it is ripe."

Through the tobacco smoke and the smoke from the oil lamps Whitman could not see the glances exchanged between some of the Tucson merchants at this bit of intelligence.

"I will conclude, gentlemen, by repeating that I make frequent visits to their camp. If they are absent from the count at ration time, I have made it my business to know why. I can say, on my honor, that to the best of my knowledge, to the best of the knowledge of the military and civilians posted at Camp Grant, the Aravaipa men have not engaged in any illegal acts since they have come under my protection."

He went on over the sounds of contention and mockery, trying to remember the words he had written to General Stoneman. "I would like to say as well that I have come to have respect for them, for men, ignorant, who are ashamed to lie or steal, for women who work cheerfully like slaves to clothe themselves and their children and who—untaught by any of our standards—hold their virtue above price."

Again he heard a kind of low chortling around the room. He had gotten nowhere, nowhere, he knew.

"From my first thought, gentlemen," he said in a low voice, "to treat them honestly and justly as an officer of the Army, I have come to feel a strong personal interest in helping to show them the way to a higher civilization." He paused. "Thank you for giving me this time and for listening to me."

He started back to his seat.

"Lieutenant Whitman," Oury said gently.

Whitman paused.

"Pray stay where you are, Lieutenant," Oury said. "It is possible that some of the gentlemen here might have a question or two."

Whitman walked back to the witness chair. Having finished what he had to say, whatever had sustained him was rapidly slipping away. He felt very tired and hot and he wished he had not eaten so much food at the Shoo Fly. After the spartan months at Camp Grant his belly was unused to such variety.

"This expression of Christian zeal cannot fail to make its impression," Oury said in the same mild tones. He looked away as though he were seeing something. "I cannot answer Lieutenant Whitman on those matters on which he alone is expert. Only he can speak of the virtue and industry of Apache women. Only he can testify to how quick and clever the men are, although we, too, can say a word or two about how clever they are—and how quick—to kill."

There were shouts in the room, quite different from the kind of thing Whitman had heard before. Oury tapped the gavel once more. He cocked his head. "Instead of high-minded assurances, I will instead rack my memory for names. Cook on the Sonoita. Saunders and Blanchard at Calabasas. Long, McKenzie and Chapin near their farms on the San Pedro. Wagon train attacked between Florence and Picket Post, three men killed and a large amount of property carried away. John Smith's ranch on the Santa Cruz above Tubac attacked, and although Smith and others were able to drive the Apaches off without loss of life, they lost all their stock, including their plow horses. And as Shakespeare makes Shylock so aptly say, 'You take my life when you do take the means whereby I live.' Oh, I could go on, the Tubac mail rider murdered near Lee's mill, not more than two miles from Tucson, Simms and Sam Brown, murdered near Tres Alamos, I could go on and on . . ."

Other names were yelled out from the gathered men. Whitman, looking into the room, again found the face of Elías, smoking a fresh cigar. Elías' hands still rested on the top of his cane. He stared ahead, removed from everyone in the room.

Oury cleared his throat. "Yes, all those, gentlemen, and many, many, many more, and all of this taking place during that sanctified period Lieutenant Whitman has just told us about, when all he has seen of Apaches is how good and decent and hard-working they are. All of these, gentlemen, yes, and more, ending with the latest—" Oury stopped. Tremors passed over his face. He could hardly bring himself to say the next words. "The latest," he repeated, and then he coughed out the names in a harsh rasp, "the murders of Leslie and Trinidad Wooster."

Everybody in the room knew what the slaying of the Woosters had done to Bill Oury. The room became as silent as a chapel.

After a moment Oury lifted his face. "And all these, mind you, while Lieutenant Royal Whitman was showing those Apaches the way to a higher life."

The commiserating with Oury ended in wild yells and laughter. Whitman raised his hand and for a little while it appeared that the crowd would ignore him. Oury tapped his gavel and the laughter tapered off.

"Mr. Oury," Whitman said, "how can you be so sure it was the Aravaipa Apaches who committed these crimes?"

Oury leaned over the bench. "They're the closest and the fastest and the slickest—and also the strongest with their bellies filled with good Government beef."

"Damned right!" a man shouted.

"I can state that none of the men from Camp Grant have left to go on raids," Whitman said.

"How can you be so sure, Lieutenant?" Oury asked.

"I issue rations."

"How often?"

"At this point, every three days."

"And how is that done?"

"The heads of families come down from the camp and collect it." His dinner and the brandy after it was churning in Whitman's gut. "Also I visit their camp almost every day."

A man cried out, "That don't leave much time for nothing else, does it?"

Oury asked, "Is it not possible, Lieutenant, that some of the men may ride out and do what comes naturally between these feedings?"

"It is possible, but I do not believe it."

"Why not, Lieutenant?"

"I have been given that pledge by Eskiminzin."

"Eskiminzin," Oury repeated slowly, emphasizing each syllable of the name. "You have been given the word of an Apache and you believe it."

"I respect Eskiminzin. I have come to know these people. I respect them."

Lef Tilson stood up. "Specially the women."

"What do you mean by that?" Whitman asked. His voice was lost in the gleeful laughter.

"The whole thing started with them women, didn't it?" Tilson asked. "The women went there first and the way I heard it you treated them so good they went back and brought in the whole tribe."

When a new wave of jollity subsided, Whitman said, "I don't believe that warrants an answer, sir."

"Why not, Lieutenant?" another man asked. "Nothing wrong with Injun women so long as you get them young enough —before they start to smell."

Whitman lowered his head and held himself in control. He knew that he was shaking and he knew it had been a mistake from the start.

"You feeling all right, Lieutenant?" Oury asked.

"I repeat," Whitman said quietly, "I will stand witness for these people. I repeat, none of them has engaged in any raids. For additional proof, I will point out that they have no guns. They turned their guns in to me at the outset. They now possess nothing beyond hunting bows and arrows. The raids listed by Mr. Oury—of course they took place. But the attacks were made by Apaches armed with guns."

Whitman paused. The oppressive feeling persisted that he was talking up an empty chimney, that his words were drifting away unheard or, if heard, unheeded. The malevolence in the room was as thick and impenetrable as the smoke.

"It is easy to lay the blame wherever you want, wherever it suits your book. But there is not the slightest proof that the Aravaipa Apaches are responsible for any of these killings and robberies."

Whitman was astonished to hear for the first time that there were men in the room who were not in total disagreement with him. He heard someone say, "He might be right." Another voice called out, "That's true enough."

Hiram Stevens stood up. He was an impressive man with a heavy gold watch chain making crescents on his vest. He hooked his thumbs in his vest pockets. "Lieutenant, how can you know that all the Aravaipa weapons were turned in to you?" His deep voice rolled through the smoke like claps of distant thunder.

"I was there," Whitman said, encouraged by the support, however scattered, he had heard. "I took the guns. The guns are still under lock and key at Camp Grant."

"There was a story in the paper about soldiers at Camp Apache trading in Army guns and ammunition with Apaches in return for fresh game," Stevens said.

"I know nothing about Camp Apache or what goes on there, sir," Whitman said.

Bill Zeckendorf, with his German accent, shouted, "Maybe some of your soldiers are doing the same thing, Lieutenant."

"Every weapon at my post is registered and accounted for," Whitman said. "I can verify that none is missing."

"Ach, Lieutenant, but there is no way of knowing that to be true except that you say so," Zeckendorf said.

Whitman flushed. He looked toward Captain Dunn. Dunn's eyes were straight on him now. His small mouth was crimped under his mustache.

"If Mr. Whitman says that none of his weapons are missing, I believe that," Jesús María Elías said quietly. It was the first time he had spoken.

Whitman looked at him swiftly.

"And if he says the Aravaipa weapons are in his custody and locked away, I believe that as well," Elías said.

Don Jesús was sitting back in his chair now. His hands

still clasped his cane. His unexpected support of Whitman brought about a new clamor in the courthouse. Whitman saw John Wasson swivel his head to stare at the Mexican.

Bill Oury tapped his gavel. When he could be heard, he said in a moderate voice, "No one questions Lieutenant Whitman's honor."

Now Whitman turned to Oury. It seemed to him at that moment that the world was turning upside down. But that could not be true. There was more to come.

Oury looked down at the officer benignly. "When Lieutenant Whitman knows the facts whereof he speaks, I believe he will relate those facts precisely as he knows them."

The men in the room were arrested in stupefied silence. Tobacco chewers suspended action in their jaws. One man, leaning over to spit a blob of used juice, remained that way, his head at an angle, his startled eyes on Oury.

Whitman waited for the hammer.

"But I do question Lieutenant Whitman when he speaks of things he cannot possibly know about. For example"—Oury paused just long enough, and then he continued in the same temperate voice—"for example, what those Aravaipa men are doing during the long seventy-two hours between Government feedings."

The men, who had thought for a little while that they had been betrayed first by Jesús Elías and then by Uncle Billy Oury, were so relieved they shouted and clapped one another on the back.

"I have attested to that, Mr. Oury," Whitman said.

Oury shook his head and smiled peacefully. "You have not, Lieutenant. What you have attested to, to use your own expression, is that you have Eskiminzin's word that his cutthroats have not gone out on raids. You have nothing more than that, Lieutenant, the word of an Apache. And I'm afraid that does not hold much water in this courtroom, or in any other courtroom in Arizona."

Whitman stared at Oury and was about to reply when Lef Tilson jumped to his feet and introduced something new.

"What about them Injuns going through your clothes,

Lieutenant?" Tilson demanded to know. "Were they planning to sell them secondhand?"

This was taken by the audience as the wittiest remark of the evening and they clapped their hands.

For the hundredth time Whitman would have liked to break Colin Duncan's neck. It could only have started with him. And, for the hundredth time, Whitman conceded to himself that it was only normal for his striker to gossip with the other men.

"It was not 'them Injuns,' " Whitman said. "It was one Indian, Eskiminzin. He was in my quarters and he was naturally curious about everything he saw."

Oury leaned forward. "It's just plain going against your grain, having to explain things, isn't it, Lieutenant?"

"Yes, Mr. Oury, it is going against my grain," Whitman said.

"Why do you feel that way about the likes of us?" Oury asked.

"I don't know what you mean by 'the likes of us,' Mr. Oury. I simply feel that a perfectly ordinary occurrence has been blown entirely out of proportion. The first time I stepped inside Eskiminzin's wickiup I was just as curious about his possessions."

"Did you poke around the Injun's smelly old moccasins and his dirty breechclouts, Lieutenant?" Lef Tilson inquired.

When it became apparent to all that Whitman was not inclined to reply to Tilson, Bill Zeckendorf asked, "You have visited the hut of this Indian often, Lieutenant?"

"Several times," Whitman said.

"*Gemütlich, ja?*"

"I'm afraid I don't understand."

"He means kind of cozy," Oury explained.

Whitman straightened. "Mr. Oury, I came here with the hope of discussing a serious matter. I did not anticipate attending a local vaudeville show. I think enough has been said and that enough jokes have been made. I bid you good evening."

"I agree, Lieutenant," Oury said quickly. "I surely agree." He leaned forward and looked down. "Here's something that ought to be serious enough for you. Is it true that General Stoneman has not officially endorsed your adopting this Indian tribe?"

"That is true, Mr. Oury."

"He's had plenty of time, if he was so minded, hasn't he?"

"He has, Mr. Oury."

"Then those Apaches are there only because you—only you—want them there."

"I have received word that General Stoneman has returned to his headquarters at Prescott," Whitman said.

"That's nice to hear," Oury said.

"Now that he is back in Arizona I look forward to receiving his instructions before very long."

"But meanwhile, you're still on your own, aren't you, Lieutenant?"

"Yes."

"If you wanted to, you could just send those Indians back where they came from, couldn't you?"

"Yes, Mr. Oury, I suppose I could." Whitman could taste his dinner in his throat and the brandy burned there. He ran his finger around his collar again.

"You okay, Lieutenant?" Oury asked again.

"I was not aware that the state of my health was intended to be the subject of discussion this evening." As the words passed his lips Whitman cursed himself as a damned fool. Here he was trying to bring some new understanding to these men, and even if that was a lost cause, he was botching it and had botched it almost from the time he opened his mouth. And now he was engaged in making asinine retorts to Bill Oury, of all people, and it didn't do any good to tell himself that Bill Oury brought that out in him and stiffened an already stiff neck. He glanced at Captain Dunn. That officer was staring at the floor again, shaking his head.

"You look a wee mite tired, Lieutenant." Oury spoke in his kindest voice. "You've been standing a long time. Why don't you just sit down there on that witness chair and rest your bones?"

"Are you quite finished, Mr. Oury?" Whitman asked.

"You could send those Apaches back where they came from, couldn't you now, Lieutenant?" Oury was almost wheedling now.

"Unarmed, of course," Whitman said. "Then all of you could go out and have fun and games. Not on your life, Mr. Oury."

"Send them back, Lieutenant," Oury said softly. "Then there's no problem. Just send them back. We'll care for them."

"He's right, Lieutenant," Hiram Stevens rumbled. "Send them back."

"Send them back," Bill Zeckendorf shouted.

"Send them back!" Lef Tilson yelled.

"Send them back! Send them back!" The men in the room welled up in chorus. "Send them back! Send them back! Send them back!"

Bill Oury half closed his eyes and nodded his head in quiet pleasure, then brought down the gavel several times, although whether it was to stop the male chorus or simply to give it cadence could not be known. The men took it for a beat and they shouted in unison and stamped their boots on the wooden floor of the courthouse, producing a thudding reverberation novel to almost all of them.

"Send them back! Send them back!"

Bill Oury tapped his gavel rhythmically and smiled amiably and the men stomped on the floor and Whitman felt he was inside a drum. He closed his eyes and raised a hand to fend off the noise.

"Send them back! Send them back!"

Whitman felt as if his head were going to burst. He knew he needed something to hold on to, the back of the chair, something to keep him erect. He clenched his fists. His jaw bulged. He would not use the chair.

"*Send them back! Send them back! Send them back! Send them back!*"

Whitman looked at Oury sitting up there between the Great Emancipator and the Father of His Country, pounding his gavel in a kind of syncopation, beaming like any other loving grandfather watching his grandchildren enjoying themselves.

Then Oury, his own eyes on Whitman, put down the gavel and raised his hand and the shouting and stomping dwindled away and then died. It was as though an army had passed by and was gone.

Whitman felt himself go slack and he drew himself up and sucked in his gut and made his shoulders go back.

Oury, watching him, nodding, smiling, asked, "And what do you say to that, Lieutenant?"

Whitman wet his lips. He glanced at Captain Dunn. The captain was shaking his head again, or maybe still. Whitman looked up at Oury.

"What do I say to that sir? Go to hell." Whitman faced the room. "All of you, go to hell," he said slowly and distinctly.

The voices rose again as he started to walk away from the witness stand.

"Lieutenant Whitman." Oury's voice was almost a purring whisper.

Whitman paused without turning. "I think we are quite finished, Mr. Oury."

"Lieutenant Whitman, I understand you hail from the state of Maine."

The irrelevance of the question stopped Whitman dead and blanketed the noise in the room instantly. Every man there wondered what Uncle Billy was up to now.

Whitman turned slowly. "I was born in the state of Maine, Mr. Oury."

"What you would call a Yankee?"

"Yes, Mr. Oury, what I most certainly would call a Yankee."

"Horse traders, Yankees," Oury said musingly. "Shrewd businessmen, always with an eye on the main chance."

Now Whitman understood where Oury was pointing his tongue. "Mr. Oury, I think perhaps the evening has been a long one for you, too. I suggest that you stop right where you are."

Oury pursed his lips and looked at the ceiling. "I've often wondered, Lieutenant, how the average Indian agent with a salary of fifteen hundred dollars a year gets to be a rich man in a couple or three years."

Now both Hiram Stevens and Bill Zeckendorf caught the drift of Oury's questions. They grinned and nodded vigorously. Don Jesús, who had not stomped with the men, who had not shouted with them, stared ahead impassively. He had picked up Oury's line with his old friend's first words and he did not approve. He felt it was improper for Oury to fog the issue with petty vindictiveness. If he were questioned at the moment, he would have said Whitman was not the problem at hand. The problem, as always, was the Apache Indian and the fact that he was allowed to remain alive on earth under any condition. Whether Whitman was a grafter or not was of no importance.

But no one questioned Don Jesús and his thoughts remained with him. As always, when the purity of his hatred was sullied, his lips turned down in disdain.

Whitman took a step closer to the bench. "Mr. Oury, I warn you—"

Oury looked down at Whitman with no anger and, without raising his voice, said, "It couldn't be, Lieutenant, that there is something a little more practical than Christian missionarying that you have inside that smart Yankee head. It couldn't be that you smell a golden opportunity to make a little side money out of putting those poor Indians to work, could it?"

"You son of a bitch," Whitman said, making a rush for the bench.

Captain Dunn leaped to his feet and the men in the room who found at last what it was Uncle Billy was getting at roared their agreement and stomped their feet in pleasure.

"Lieutenant Whitman!" Captain Dunn shouted.

Whitman jumped onto the judge's platform.

"Lieutenant!" Dunn shouted again.

Whitman brought himself to a stop. Oury gazed at him serenely.

"Lieutenant, I order you to step down," Dunn commanded.

After a moment Whitman climbed down to the floor.

Oury peered down at him. "Any man accuse me of that," he said in the mildest of voices, "I'd call him down and settle it—unless it happened to be true, that is."

Dunn strode to the bench and put himself between Oury

and Whitman. "Mr. Oury, you damned well know that Army officers are not permitted to fight duels."

Oury sat back in the judge's chair. "Mighty convenient, as it happens, isn't it, Lieutenant?"

When Whitman made a move to the platform again Dunn grabbed his arm and propelled him away. The two officers walked up the aisle and left the courthouse. The hoots and cat-calls fell on their ears like rotten vegetables.

The air outside was cold and fresh. Whitman sucked it into his lungs.

"What the hell happened to your limp?" Dunn asked.

△ 7

Oury rapped the gavel for order. "Now that that nonsense is over, friends, let's get down to business. I move we raise a volunteer company to wipe out the Apaches."

Every man in the courthouse seconded that motion. For the first time that evening Don Jesús nodded his head and a small smile formed on his lips.

"Opposed?" Bill Oury demanded to know.

The courthouse was heavy with smoke and sweat and silence.

Oury banged the gavel. "Motion passed unanimously."

Hiram Stevens rose to his feet. He thumbed his vest again and his voice rolled out sonorously. "I move that Bill Oury be named captain of the volunteers."

There was no argument about that either. The motion was seconded and passed unanimously as well. The men in the room now came to the reasonable conclusion that the business of the evening was terminated and most successfully so, and they stood up for the third unanimous motion, that to the nearest saloon for their victory over the Apaches. For those Indians were as good as dead.

But Oury had had long experience with the military and certain memories had stayed with him. He knew all about vol-

unteers and how quick they were to volunteer for anything to
get to that saloon, and what happened to many of them when
the call actually came. He smashed down the gavel. "Hold it!
Hold it!"

The men, many of whom were already on the way out,
their mouths parched from the long evening's drought, paused
and turned. What did Uncle Billy want now?

"Before you gentlemen leave the courthouse we have to
draw up a piece of paper," Oury said. When some of the men
waved their hands derisively and continued up the aisle, Bill
Oury delivered himself of a smiting of the gavel that almost
brought down the ceiling.

"It has to be done fit and proper," Oury shouted. "Now
all of you, sit down! Goddamn it, I said, sit down!"

The men took their seats with enormous reluctance and
considerable lapping of tongues over arid lips. They watched as
Oury extracted from the desk of Judge Titus a pad of legal
paper. He spoke the words aloud as he put them down: "The
undersigned have agreed to form themselves into a company of
volunteers, and upon the next occurrence of Apache outrage, to
go out and eat up every Apache in the land."

Oury set down his name first, adding "Captain."

"Now you men line up and sign your names here," he said.
"And after you put down your John Hancocks, you stay right
here in this room. I got one more thing to tell you."

Some of the men groaned.

"If there's any trouble," Oury warned, "I'll appoint a sergeant at arms and keep you here."

There were not too many who understood exactly what a
sergeant at arms was, but it sounded impressive and military.
The men formed a peaceful line and stepped up to the bench
and put their names down on the paper. Don Jesús, disliking
to queue, waited until the end. His name was last, as Oury's
was first.

"It makes a kind of parenthesis, Don Guillermo," he said.

There were, in all, eighty-two signatures.

Bill Oury folded the sheet of paper carefully and put it in
his pocket. "A final word," he said. "Before we go out to any

Apache-killing expedition, there's one thing I have to do first. I have to have a talk with General Stoneman."

There was a stunned silence and then loud shouts of protest. Oury held up his hand and when that did no good he stood up for the first time and in that act quieted the room.

"Now you listen to me, all of you," he said evenly. "We've all heard a lot about this General Stoneman but nobody here's had a chance to listen to him, or even laid eyes on him. This is a country of law. The law says the Army's supposed to protect us against Indians. I want to hear what General Stoneman has to say about that before we take the law into our own hands."

He surveyed the room.

"I know something about vigilantes. I lived in San Francisco when they had vigilante law. Not everything the Vigilantes did would let an honest man sleep at night."

Part Four

△ △ △ ONE

△ 1

Holos was taking his usual good time ambling across the heaven. Now he was resting for a moment on the mountain peak, taking a final look around before dropping off to sleep for the night. It was at just that moment that Santo made his way through the people.

Santo was wearing his holy shirt. He had not put it on for a long time. It was the medicine garment that marked his knowledge and his power. All the important things were painted on it. There were the symbols of the elements, the earth and the sky, the rain and the sun and the wind and Lightning. Under these consequential references were paintings of the snake, the centipede and the tarantula.

Santo carried his medicine cord in his right hand. The cord had four strands, one for each of the Directions. A small painted gourd was attached to each strand. Santo walked to the center of the clearing. The people hardly breathed. Even the children and the dogs were quiet.

Santo paid his respect to each Direction, one after the other, and then he began to swing the cord around his neck. The gourds went round and round his head. Because of the way he used his wrist the gourds never touched one another but remained almost the same distance apart, making the four points, the four Directions, the holy number of four. The gourds went faster and faster. In the bright April twilight they almost became a blur. But they never touched and the people almost forgot how to breathe.

All the power in the world was in Santo. He had led his men in battle when he was young but he always was more than a war chief. He always dealt with things that could not be seen.

Slowly Santo cut down on the momentum of the swinging gourds until by some magic they came together in pairs and one pair fell upon his right shoulder and the other pair upon his left shoulder and now the number of four was in his body and all the power went back into him and the people felt weak.

Santo remained still for a long time and then he moved his hands across his chest and the gourds slipped down and dangled in front of him. He took from under his medicine shirt a small leather pouch containing tule pollen. He walked up to Eskiminzin, who was sitting in the forefront of the people, and he sprinkled a little pollen on Eskiminzin's right foot. He rubbed some pollen on Eskiminzin's forehead. He sprinkled Eskiminzin's left shoulder and left knee and left foot.

Eskiminzin was wearing his skins. There were bracelets on his wrists and amulets hung from his neck. There were two streaks of white paint on his face, starting just to the side of either eye and running almost together on his chin.

Eskiminzin remained motionless. He stared to the west, where there was still a little fire in the sky. As Santo moved about in front of him, Eskiminzin did not see him. He saw through Santo and watched the fire die in the sky.

Lieutenant Whitman did not move either. He had been asked by Eskiminzin to attend the blessing of the new village farther up Little Running Water. Along with the other men and women, and the children, he had been caught in the hypnotic ceremony of the gourds. He knew nothing of the nature or significance of the powder the old shaman had put on Eskiminzin, but throughout the ceremony he had sensed the profound admixture of the Apache and his surroundings and the things the Apache believed in. The earth and the air and Little Running Water and the Apache were all the same family.

Santo made a last obeisance to the Directions and he went away with his shoulders bent, as though he was weary from his dealings with the mysteries, and presently Eskiminzin stirred himself and stood up and there was enough fire left in the sky to brighten the silver he wore and to reveal the signs on his deerskins.

There was a low sigh from the people and the children

began to talk again and dogs barked. Eskiminzin, their chief, had been renewed by life and the times were good and now the people scrambled to their feet and made their way to where they lived and would eat.

Some of the men remained to talk to Eskiminzin. The chief stood with his arms folded and listened to them. His face, with the paint streaks, was a new face to Whitman. Eskiminzin, who was not a large man, seemed now, in the twilight, almost larger than life. Whitman understood why angry men would stand in line for this man who seldom raised his voice.

△ 2

Piled up against the wickiups were neatly bound bundles of hay, gathered that day, to be delivered to Camp Grant the next. Whitman, who had left Eskiminzin to the privacy of his people and who had walked over to Eskiminzin's compound with the Puma and Road Runner, commented on the quantity Child Mother and Small Woman and Melana had brought in. Looking at Small Woman, who appeared ready to deliver her child at any moment, Whitman wondered how she had worked in the fields at all.

"It was not us alone," Child Mother said, giving Whitman a cup of coffee. "He went with us."

Child Mother was making a stew of the Government beef in a pot over the fire. Small Woman had made mescal cakes. Melana helped both of them. Daya, Eskiminzin's mother, supervised everyone and saw that there was no quarreling. Road Runner hunkered down near Whitman and stared at him. When she thought no one was looking, Melana stared at Whitman too.

"It was necessary," Child Mother said.

"Because of the others," Whitman said.

"They did not like it," Child Mother said. "There were those who said it was work for women."

Whitman nodded. "I can understand that."

"There were those who said it was bad enough for men to have to stand in line for food," Small Woman said. "But they said they would not kneel in the fields like Mexican slaves and cut grass."

Whitman sipped the hot strong coffee. "That bad."

"Worse," Child Mother said. "For a little while there was talk and it was not good talk and then he called them before him and he spoke to them."

"He did not speak harshly to them," Small Woman said. She spoke proudly. "Some men shout. He did not. He told them cutting grass was not dishonorable. He said that white men worked in the fields and that they were not women but brave men as everyone knows. He said that if they hated to do it that was good, because it is easy to do what a man wants to do. It takes a full man to do that which he hates to do."

Whitman smiled to himself. Eskiminzin and his father, Royal Whitman. The two of them would have found they had a few things in common. The chief of the Aravaipa Apaches and the Maine farmer.

"He asked then if anybody wanted to walk away," Child Mother said. "He said any man could take his family and his possessions and walk away. Only they could never return."

Child Mother held her pride tightly. Her voice wanted to burst with it but she held it in by pressing her hands against her breasts and by making her speech flatter.

Whitman lit a cigar. He blew out the match and put it down. Road Runner picked up the burned match.

"No one wanted to walk away," Child Mother said. "And then he said that he would lead them into the fields and that he would cut the first grass and make the first bundle and that he would carry that bundle himself to the Army post."

"That was the way it was," Small Woman agreed. "The *nantan* may not think it is much, the gathering of hay."

"It is much," Whitman said.

Daya spoke for the first time. "Does the *nantan* believe that?"

"Yes," Whitman said.

"Then maybe my son is right," Daya said. "Maybe things will be done. I tell you that it would have been easier to make the men go out and fight, even without guns, than it was to make them go into the fields."

"I believe that."

"If you believe that then perhaps the things will be done."

When Eskiminzin joined his family at last Whitman saw he had washed off the paint and that it was the face he had come to know. After everybody had eaten Whitman asked Eskiminzin about the ceremony.

"The Everywhere Spirit knows what goes on in our hearts, but it is a good thing to thank him," Eskiminzin said.

"Where is he?"

Eskiminzin gestured up and around. "Everywhere."

"It is different among white people," Melana said.

She had not spoken all evening. Her voice was low and timid.

Whitman smiled. "I don't know that it's so different. We have a kind of Everywhere Spirit."

"But you put him inside a place," Melana said.

Whitman nodded. "True. There are special places where Americans go to worship God. How do you know about that?"

Melana, whose face was flushing from talking to Whitman, glanced at Daya to see whether the old woman wanted her to become silent. When Eskiminzin's mother said nothing and did nothing, Melana turned back to Whitman.

"There are shamans among your people who go among Indians and try to make them believe in their Spirit," Melana said. "And where they are successful they always build these places and they say that people must go under that roof to find the Spirit."

"That's exactly right," Whitman said. "It sounds a little strange at this moment, but that's right."

"Why must you go to a place?" Melana asked. "Why do you make your Spirit stay in a single place?"

Whitman thought about that. "Well, it's like a ceremonial place."

"But if you have many of these places how can the Spirit be in all of them at the same time?" Melana asked.

"Well," Whitman said, "I suppose one could say that he

is like your Spirit, an Everywhere Spirit. Maybe it's the same Spirit."

Melana considered that. No one spoke. The other women and the chief of the tribe and Eskiminzin's children waited in silence until Melana finished asking what she had to ask and telling what she wanted to tell. It is ordinary courtesy, Whitman thought, and he tucked it away among other things he was learning bit by bit about Apache Indians.

"We believe that Usen is everywhere and cannot be put into one place," Melana said. "He would not like us to make a building and keep him in it. He is everywhere. He is in each tree, in each piece of grass, in each rock. He is in the rain and the thunder and in Lightning and he shines with the sun. At night he sleeps and White Painted Lady helps him out. She keeps an eye open, only one eye, for the stars help her to see. She tries to keep her eye open all the time but she gets sleepy too and her eye closes more and more and finally she dozes off and only the stars are awake, and while she is asleep the stars look around sharper and brighter and then she wakes again slowly and her eye opens more and more and finally it is opened all the way again."

She sat back. She was certain she had spoken much too long before the chief. She lowered her eyes in embarrassment.

"You are wise, child," Eskiminzin said.

She looked up again and her eyes widened at the compliment.

"You spoke of Usen," Whitman said.

"I spoke too much."

"Who is Usen?"

"He is the Everywhere Spirit."

"And who is White Painted Lady?"

"She is his wife and she is the mother of Child of the Water," Road Runner explained.

"That is right," Eskiminzin said.

"Child of the Water?" Whitman repeated.

"The boy can tell you about it," Eskiminzin said. "I have taught him."

Road Runner looked around proudly. "In the old days

the People were kept under the ground by Giant and they could not come up to smell the air and see the sun and the stars. Giant kept them under the ground and there was nothing that could be done about it."

Road Runner looked at his father. Eskiminzin nodded.

"Well, one day White Painted Lady lay down on the ground and she spread her legs apart and it rained hard and Lightning wrote all kinds of things in the sky and then soon White Painted Lady had a baby and he was called Child of the Water because of the way he was made." Road Runner puckered his lips. "Some people believe Lightning had something to do with it too."

Eskiminzin rolled a cigarette and nodded again. He was proud of his son.

"When Child of the Water grew up there were things he had to do," Road Runner went on. "He had to prove he was not the same as other boys. One of the things he had to do was kill Giant, who was still keeping the People down there in the ground. He tried to kill Giant but Giant just stood there with his hands on his hips and laughed. Nothing Child of the Water could do could even hurt Giant."

Road Runner looked at Whitman and grinned. Road Runner was enjoying himself. It wasn't often that he was the center of attention for so long.

"Well, a small bird sat down on Child of the Water's shoulder and whispered to the boy that there was only one way to kill Giant. That was to hit him in the heel. Child of the Water picked up a stone and threw it and it hit Giant's heel and Giant fell over dead and then all of the People came up out of the ground and stood around in the sun."

Road Runner finished triumphantly. He was breathless. A few minutes later he was asleep, leaning against Whitman's side.

In his quarters that night as he prepared for sleep Whitman reflected on the origins of a people who believed in Hercules and Achilles, David and Goliath, a universal, invisible deity— and immaculate conception.

△ 3

"... *It is easy in the world to live after the world's opinion; it is easy in solitude to live after our own; but the great man is he who in the midst of the crowd keeps with perfect sweetness the independence of solitude. . . .*"

He had a long way to go, a long, long way. He could have broken Oury's neck with perfect sweetness, but that was as far as that went. He looked up as Lieutenant Robinson entered the office. He put down the Emerson book.

"You really don't have to read that stuff, do you, Royal? Surely you must know every line by heart," Robinson said.

"Just about."

"Does it do you any good, all those lofty words?"

"If it has, it sure as hell hasn't surfaced as yet. Are you all set?"

Lieutenant Robinson sat down on the edge of Whitman's desk.

"You ought to be ashamed of yourself," Whitman said, sitting back. "It's downright indecent for a man to look so happy."

"Illusion."

"I should think so. Why would any man of sound mind want to go away from Camp Grant?"

"One thing worries me."

"You lost that privilege when I signed your leave papers. Worrying resumes officially when you report back for duty."

"Just how are you going to manage without me?"

"I'll try to survive, if possible."

"Splendid. I'm also disturbed about something else."

Whitman stood up and walked to the window. A light wind was making swirls over the parade ground and off in the distance he could see a dust devil dancing alone like a mad dervish on the open desert.

"So am I," he said.

"No word."

"None."

"He must have his reasons."

"Generals always do. It's one of the perquisites that goes with that star."

"Perhaps now that he's back in Arizona he will do something about it."

"Perhaps."

Robinson slapped the desk. "Goddamn it, Royal! Why doesn't he piss or get off the pot!"

"Wouldn't it be lovely to ask him?"

"Don't quote me." Robinson hesitated. "I suppose that by now he's had word of what happened in Tucson."

Whitman turned from the window and nodded.

"I'm damned sorry it didn't work out, Royal," Robinson said.

"Didn't work out?" Whitman gave a short laugh. "I wish to Christ it was only that it didn't work out. Bill, it was a total fiasco. And it was all my fault."

"I doubt that."

"I let that son of a bitch Oury get under my hide. He dug and he dug and I did just what he wanted me to do. I blew up."

"I think that was understandable, under the circumstances."

Whitman walked back to the desk and sat down. "Don't bullshit me, Bill. I went to that meeting to talk sense to those men."

"Impossible."

"Impossible or not, I went there and they listened to me and then Oury went to work and made mincemeat out of me. Jesus Christ, Bill! I've been under real fire. I should have been able to stand up against that old bastard." Whitman breathed in deeply. "I guess it just takes a different kind of balls. I guess that I don't happen to have them." He tapped the Emerson book. "I guess that reading this is just a waste of time after all."

Whitman's jaw hardened. He stood up and began to walk back and forth, punching the palm of his hand. "I had a chance, Bill. I had a chance and I blew it."

"No chance, Royal. Not with that outfit."

"A chance." Whitman stopped and faced Robinson. "There's always a chance, Bill. If you can get people to listen there's always a chance. I had that chance. But he did it to me.

He dangled bait and I bit. I made a goddamned horse's ass out of myself and he just sat up there and laughed."

"Well, maybe the old man will take over." Then Robinson said, "You could send them all back, you know."

Whitman looked at him.

"No, I guess you couldn't." Robinson stood up. "Any little thing I can bring you from the great cities?"

"A pail of ice."

"Consider it done. Goodbye, Royal." The two officers shook hands. "And good luck."

Whitman nodded. Robinson came to attention and saluted. Whitman returned the courtesy. Robinson started out of the office. At the door he stopped.

"Royal . . ."

"Yes, Bill."

"Those Apaches . . ."

"Yes?"

"Well, for whatever it's worth . . ."

"Yes."

"Well, I would have bet money there wasn't a decent drop of blood in the best one of them."

Whitman watched Robinson and a small patrol ride out of the fort. He sat down and lit a cigar. He was the only officer around now.

△ △ △ TWO

△ 1

The April sunlight pouring through the open window flooded the small glass of brandy. It was as though the general were holding a brilliant amber gemstone in his hand.

"Incredible color, isn't it, Mr. Oury?" the general asked. His voice was very low. It made listeners have to lean a little to hear him.

"We didn't come all the way up here to talk about your brandy, General," Oury said.

General Stoneman slowly lowered the glass of brandy and turned to Bill Oury. His eyes were sad. "I'm certain of that, Mr. Oury. But then we are civilized human beings, or at least we make pretensions in that direction." The general smiled a courtly smile. "We should be able to retain good manners."

The general walked away to talk to his friend Alexander Thompson and left Bill Oury to stare out of the window at the Gila River. Oury took a little time at it. He was there to get something from the general and he had to keep remembering that.

Oury, Sidney DeLong and three others had set out from the Old Pueblo the previous Thursday to find General Stoneman. It was not the simplest thing in the world. The general was reported to be in Arizona but he moved around mysteriously and always with the greatest secrecy. Since the general's subordinates had to know where he was, and since the Apache Indians would have no difficulty in keeping an eye on him, Oury and the others had concluded that Stoneman was making an effort to keep his whereabouts hidden only from decent white settlers with legitimate grievances.

After a couple of days of wandering about with horses and

pack mules, following a couple of false leads, Oury and his party had finally located the general at one of his temporary encampments on the Gila near Florence. It was Saturday by then and the men from Tucson were filthy and tired and riding on the edge of their nerves. They had seen a lot of Indian signs and one of the mules had broken its leg and had to be shot and left behind, to feed Apaches without doubt, and the dead animal's load had to be redistributed among other balky beasts of burden.

The general, immaculate in his blues, his linen impeccable, his hair and imperial neatly trimmed, raised his brows at the sudden appearance of the five travelers, but then asked them to join him in a meal at the home of his friend, Mr. Thompson, where he was staying at the moment. The general suggested that the Tucsonans might like to freshen up. If the general had been playing a game of hide-and-seek and had lost, he was taking it with good grace.

Sidney DeLong now joined Oury at the window. Oury's fingers were wrapped around his own glass of brandy. From the whiteness of the knuckles DeLong feared his friend might squeeze the glass to death.

"I feel like walking right out of here," Oury said.

"Not until the horses and mules get some rest," DeLong said with a smile. Sidney DeLong was a gentle man and he had ideas of being a writing man and Hiram Stevens had sent him along especially to keep Oury cool.

"You know what I keep seeing in that damned river out there?" Oury asked.

"I think I can guess."

"Funny, I don't see faces, Sid. I just see names. Like they were written there on the water. Like they're passing by with the current. Like if you don't grab them and hold on to them they'll be gone forever and nobody'll ever know or remember or give a damn."

"Mr. Oury," the general called out. It was calling out only in relation to the way the general normally spoke.

Oury stared down at the brandy glass buried in his hand. "I'd like to throw this right into his face, with the glass."

"Bill," DeLong said soothingly.

"Yeah."

"Mr. Oury," the general said again.

Oury filled his lungs and took a last look at the names floating down in the river and then he turned around. "Yes, General?"

"Have you tasted that brandy yet?"

"Yes, General," Oury lied.

"And what is your opinion of it?"

"It's mighty fine brandy, General."

"There is none better in California."

"I believe that, General."

DeLong gave Oury a small jab with his elbow and Oury strolled across the room to where the general was talking to Thompson, a plump businessman in Florence who was honored almost beyond containment at having General George Stoneman for a houseguest. Standing at the other side of the general was Captain Wilson, who beamed his pleasant face for the pleasure of anyone who cared to look at it.

"What do you know about oenology, Mr. Oury?" the general asked, gently stroking his imperial.

"I don't know what the word means, General," Oury said.

"Sorry. Simply a technical word for wine making."

"I don't know any more about wine making than I did about that word, General," Oury said. He saw that DeLong was next to him again and he was glad about that. "General, do you have any notion why we are here?"

"I believe I do, Mr. Oury."

"Then can we get down to business?"

"Later."

The general turned to Thompson and Oury felt a door had been shut in his face. Not slammed, but gently and firmly shut.

"Do you believe the vineyards of California will ever rival those of France and other European countries, Mr. Thompson?" the general inquired.

"I never gave that much thought, General Stoneman," Thompson said.

The general pursed his lips and knit his brow. Presently he said, "One day I believe they will, Mr. Thompson."

"It's good to know that, General," Oury said.

Stoneman turned and contemplated Oury. How he would have responded had to remain forever unknown for at that moment a Mexican servant entered the room and announced that the meal was on the table. The general, Mr. Thompson, Captain Wilson and the others went into the dining room and sat down at a huge table.

A very good meal was presented to them by their host, who was beaming now even more than Captain Wilson. There was venison and wild turkey and fresh tomatoes, and, an unexpected surprise, a platter of potatoes, the greatest treat of all. There were several unlabeled bottles of wine placed strategically around the table.

Oury picked up a bottle. "This from your spread, too, General?" he asked politely. He saw DeLong nod almost imperceptibly at this display of courteous interest.

"Yes, Mr. Oury," the general said.

"I know how busy you are, General," Oury said. "Can we start some of the discussing now? You see—"

"The general never talks at mealtime," Captain Wilson said. The luster in his voice made the statement sound very little less than the Eleventh Commandment.

Bill Oury had an old fighting man's attitude to an aide-de-camp and he looked at the general for some amplification or explanation of Captain Wilson's singular pronouncement, but he saw that in a sense General Stoneman had left the room. Upon picking up his knife and fork he retreated into a kind of impregnable privacy. The general could not talk or be talked to because the general no longer was there.

The gelid ambiance created by the general was instantly pervasive. The Commandment was operative. The general did not speak and no one spoke and the only sounds at the table were those of cutting and chewing and swallowing and drinking. This affected neither the serenity nor appetite of Captain Gregory Wilson, who had been long conditioned to what to him now was simple normality, or that of Alex Thompson, whose cup was running over anyway, and to whom conversation might have been too heady to absorb.

It was a new kind of experience for Bill Oury, who had never eaten a meal in company in silence in his life, even if the talk had to be in whispers because the enemy, Mexican or Apache, might be close by. It made him feel now like some kind of dumb animal, sitting with other animals, similarly dumb, around a feed trough. The table was a round one but Oury had the distinct sense, nevertheless, that he and his friends had been somehow seated below the salt.

△ 2

The meal ended abruptly. General Stoneman speared the last neatly cut piece of venison on the tines of his fork and steered it into his mouth. He chewed it carefully and soberly and swallowed it and drank some wine and placed his knife and fork exactly parallel to each other on his plate and surveyed the table. He seemed to emerge back into the room like a figure developing in a darkroom on one of the photographic plates Mathew Brady made during the war.

The general's placement of his eating tools on his plate served as an alarm signal to the Mexican servants who had been poised for that moment. The table was cleared immediately. Anyone who had failed to synchronize his ingestion with that of the general was out of luck.

The general took out a cigar. He clipped one end carefully and put the cigar between his lips. Captain Wilson, who by long practice had cleared his own plate at the precise moment the general was doing the same with his, struck a match and held it out.

The general blew out a cloud of smoke. "A Committee of Public Safety. Is that how you gentlemen designate yourselves?"

"Not exactly, General," DeLong said.

"Have I been misinformed, Mr. DeLong?"

"Not exactly, General," DeLong said again. He had seen the look in Oury's eyes and he knew he had to keep talking for a little while. "Actually, General, the Committee of Public

Safety includes most of the leading men in Tucson. The five of us are just a small part of that committee. A subcommittee, you might say." He smiled uselessly.

"Gentlemen, I know exactly why you are here," the general said.

"Good," Bill Oury said. "Then we don't have to waste any more time." Bill Oury had scarcely touched any of his food or drink, and that was a first for him too.

"I gather you are here first of all to register a complaint about the conduct of my war against the Apaches," Stoneman said.

"I suppose you could start off by saying that, General," Oury said.

"You believe my campaigns against the Apaches have not been pursued with sufficient purpose, Mr. Oury?" the general asked.

"What campaigns?" Oury asked politely.

Stoneman removed the cigar from his mouth and contemplated Oury thoughtfully. DeLong kicked Oury under the table.

"It is my duty, gentlemen," Stoneman resumed presently, "to inform you that the orders I issued at the end of last winter for the prosecution of a vigorous campaign against the Apaches have been severely criticized in Washington."

"What campaign?" Oury asked again.

"It also is my duty to inform you that President Grant has instructed General Sherman to modify my policy toward the Apaches to conform to the present Government policy."

"And what is that present policy, General?" DeLong asked.

"Moral suasion."

"Moral what?" Oury asked.

"Moral suasion, Mr. Oury, and kindness, looking forward to their Christianization."

"Christianization of Apaches?" Oury looked at the general, at Captain Wilson, at DeLong, at anyone, to disabuse him.

"They are better off raising corn than raising scalps, Mr. Oury," the general said.

Captain Wilson chuckled at the general's wit and Thompson nodded and seemed ready to burst with the pride in him.

"Moral suasion," Oury repeated slowly, as though he were tasting new words for the first time. "Kindness. Christianization. To Apaches. General Stoneman, you cannot be serious."

"I am always serious, Mr. Oury."

"Does that moral suasion include Eskiminzin's freeloaders at the Camp Grant feed station?" Oury inquired.

"I have no orders to differentiate, Mr. Oury," the general said, privately reassigning that former enlisted man, Royal E. Whitman, to a new station in the inside of the inside of hell.

Oury leaned over the table and tapped his blunt fingers as he spoke, as calmly as he could manage. "General Stoneman, maybe it's a coincidence and maybe it's not, but since the time the Department of Arizona was established and you were put in command, things here have gotten worse than they have ever been. The Apache has just plain taken over. He kills and he robs as he damn well pleases and little is being done to stop him."

From sour and bitter memory, Oury ticked off the people murdered by Apaches. And as always, he almost choked over the names of Leslie and Trinidad Wooster.

"And there are more, General, many, many more," Oury went on. "And we have reason to believe that most of these crimes were committed by those Apaches you're fattening up in Camp Grant. And we're all asking ourselves what you are going to do. And all we hear about is that you're going to save a little money by cutting down the number of forts in Arizona, and how the hell is that going to help anything? And besides, the enlistments of the men are running out and nothing is being done about that. General, if the United States Army is not going to protect us, who is?"

As Oury was speaking, the general rose slowly to his feet and walked a few stately steps from the table and turned his back. Oury looked at that back and his gorge rose.

"You have made it your business to stay away from Arizona, General," Oury said to the back. "But there are those of us who call Arizona our home. And when things get rough here in Arizona we don't have nice, pretty, safe hideouts in California where we can sit and watch the grapes grow."

Oury, who had started waving a hand at that back, dropped it and slumped in his chair. He felt he had been talking to nothing.

Captain Wilson, appalled, stared at the square, blue back, hoping it could tell him something of what was on the face on the other side. Alexander Thompson looked as though someone had stuck a pin in him and let out air. His hangdog face gazed at a desecrated world.

Presently the general turned around. If Oury's words had had any effect on him he did not show it. The sidelighting from the window illuminated the general's pale, melancholy countenance, with its mustache and spiked imperial, giving it something of a weary, maligned nobility.

He began to speak, still in slow and measured tones, and in a voice that made everyone cock his head to listen. "Last summer, soon after I assumed command of the Arizona Department, I was presented with a memorial that was purported to have been prepared by people living in Tubac and in the Santa Cruz Valley."

The general puffed on his cigar and walked back and forth unhurriedly. Oury and the others from Tucson knew all about that memorial and Oury wondered what the hell it had to do with what he had just said. He was now positive that he had spoken to emptiness. DeLong, knowing what the mention of Tubac did to his friend these days, looked at Oury with worried eyes.

"The memorial," the general continued, as his eyes inspected the beams in the ceiling, "which called upon me to launch a campaign against the Apaches, was signed by two hundred and fifty names, all adult men." His manner now was that of a teacher in a classroom, lecturing to pupils either very young or not very bright. "In a document that accompanied this memorial, it was stated that those two hundred and fifty names were merely half the number that could have been obtained." The general paused in his pedantic ambulation and looked at each member of the committee, ending with Bill Oury. "It appears to me, gentlemen, that a community of five hundred able-bodied men could take care of itself."

Again Oury felt DeLong kick him warningly and just in time, too, because Oury had almost reached that point where he was ready to stand up and tell General Stoneman exactly what he thought of him, clearly and succinctly, and then leave.

The general raised a hand as though someone had raised an objection to what he had just stated, or, at the least, questioned it. He went on, without raising his voice in the slightest. "However, I am convinced there is no such number of genuine American settlers there, in my definition. The people who occupy those lands, in my opinion and from what I have heard, are hardly more than illegal squatters, covered by the so-called Spanish Grants. Their title to the land is dubious, to say the very least. They qualify for no more American military protection than they have already received."

Sidney DeLong turned swiftly to Bill Oury. He knew what Oury, who was married to a Mexican, thought of the Mexican Jesús Elías and of other Mexicans in Arizona, and he was prepared to hold his friend down by force if necessary. What he saw astonished him. Oury did not appear to be angry at all. Stamped on the hoary, weather-beaten face was a mark of supreme exhaustion. Bill Oury, who had survived the Alamo, who had survived that game where his life hung on the color of a bean, who had survived years of battle, who had survived hunger and thirst and cold and heat, who had survived, Bill Oury now looked as though he could not raise the strength to break a matchstick in half. His chin was on his chest and his calloused hands lay without life on the table.

Finally Oury lifted his head and it was as though someone had raised a gravestone. "The land was Spanish originally, General," he said, sapped.

"I am aware of that, Mr. Oury."

"Then what exactly is dubious about titles issued by the Spaniards?"

"There has been a change of ownership of the entire section of country, Mr. Oury."

Oury nodded slowly. "I know that, General." He closed his eyes and shook his head as though he were shaking off a sleep and then his eyes opened suddenly and he pounded the table violently. "Goddamn it, General!" he roared. "What the hell are we talking about!"

He pushed himself away from the table and jumped to his feet, brushing aside DeLong's restraining hand. He strode to the general, his arm extended, his finger pointing. Captain Wilson half rose from his own chair, ready in the event the general needed help. The general clasped his hands behind his back and regarded Oury calmly.

"What are we talking about?" Oury asked again. "We're talking about people living and working on land they've lived and worked on for years, generations, centuries. Who the devil gives a good goddamn where their grants came from? What are you trying to say, General, that in lieu of a good United States title the land really belongs to the Apaches?"

The general unclasped his hands, inspected his cigar, saw that it was consumed and had expired, walked past Oury to the table and deposited the stub in an ashtray.

"Is that all, Mr. Oury?" he asked courteously.

"No, General, it is not all, not by a long shot!" Oury was aware that DeLong was signaling him. "We came up here representing the people of Tucson, more than that, the people of this part of the Territory. All of us have relatives and friends robbed and murdered by Apaches. We came up here as American citizens demanding that you do something."

"Demanding, Mr. Oury?" the general asked. He looked at Oury questioningly, as though the word were unfamiliar to him.

Oury wiped his mouth and took a deep breath. With an effort as mighty as any he had applied in his life, he forced himself back into the general's world. "General Stoneman, your uniform and your rank grant you special privileges in the Army," he said quietly. "We are citizens, General, and we pay taxes and we vote and the way I was brought up to look at it the Army is part of the Government, and the Government belongs to the people. This isn't one of those European countries where the Army runs everything the way it damned pleases and ordinary citizens are stomped on by men in fancy uniforms."

Bill Oury lit a cigar of his own and he took his own time

doing it. The general and all the other men watched him silently. When he had the Havana burning to suit him, Oury said in even more reasonable tones, "What's an army for, General? To protect its citizens against enemies. Now there's no foreign war going on that I know of and since there doesn't seem to be any outside enemies at the moment what you may have to do is settle for Indians."

General Stoneman considered the premise as dispassionately as Oury had presented it. "I have no idea what you have in mind, gentlemen—"

"Then we'll just start from the beginning again," Oury interrupted equably.

"—but it is my duty to inform you that the people in Tucson may not expect anything more than has hitherto been done," the general finished.

"Which has been damned near zero!" Oury exploded again.

The general regarded Oury with distaste. "There is nothing that requires me to give explicit reasons for the statement I have just made," he said quietly, "but I am not unaware of your problems and I will take the time to make my position clear to you."

The general resumed his seat at the table and after a moment Oury sat down. The general arched his fingers and inspected the ceiling beams once more. When he spoke it was in another voice entirely.

"I must inform you gentlemen that I have enough horses to mount only one man in five," he said sadly. "There has been no Government appropriation for remounts. Moreover, the Third Cavalry was sent down from the East with broken-down horses, entirely unfit for mountain service, sent down to replace the Eighth Cavalry, which is admirably mounted on young California horses peculiarly adapted for the work required."

General Stoneman appeared sincerely sorry for himself, and for the tricks and deceptions of a capricious and ungrateful Government.

He held out his hands appealingly. "I regret, gentlemen, that I am too circumscribed to do the work you expect of me. Until now, the Government has expended one hundred and thirty dollars per man in the Territory. That now has been cut to thirty-three dollars."

"We didn't come here to talk money, General," Oury said.

The general nodded with distressed agreement. "No, Mr. Oury, quite obviously you did not. But, unfortunately, I must discuss money with you."

"There just are not enough troops here," Oury said. "It's as simple as that."

"Not that simple at all, Mr. Oury. You may be surprised to learn that fully one-tenth of the entire United States Army is presently stationed in Arizona. One man in every ten in uniform is right here, Mr. Oury. And that is a greater proportion than you have any right to expect."

Oury leaned forward. "You are talking money and you are giving me figures and percentages, General."

"I am."

"I don't know anything about that."

"You do not, Mr. Oury."

"And I don't want to know. There are plenty of places in this country where they don't need the Army."

"That is true," the general agreed. "But if persons hang out their watches on a lamppost at night in New York they might expect to lose them."

Oury worked his way through that. "But they could go to the police. They have police. All over the country people have some kind of authority they can go to for protection—police, sheriffs, marshals. Out here, General, we're stuck with the Army. Nothing but the Army. And we have enemies. And I'm not talking about the chance outlaw, the odd gunslinger, the individual burglar. We manage to take care of that kind of crime ourselves. I'm talking about an organized enemy with a sworn purpose—to drive us away or destroy us. And you sit there and throw out numbers and dollars and tell us we ought to wag our tails like dogs and be grateful for scraps."

The general stood up and the face behind the mustache and the imperial was remote again and the sad eyes were not sad for anything that had been spoken of that day. He straightened until he was almost in the kind of brace enforced upon him in his years at West Point.

"I believe that all that can be said has been said," the general said with an inflection that prohibited argument. "I must caution you that a continuance of your complaints might well have the result to withdraw troops entirely from the Territory. This has been contemplated and may yet be acted on."

The general seemed not displeased at the stupefaction on the faces of the members of the committee. He allowed his words to hover for a few moments and then he reached into the pocket of his tunic and took out a newspaper clipping.

"This item has been brought to my attention, gentlemen. It has been taken from the Tucson *Arizonan*." The general peered at Oury. "I believe that you are a part owner of that publication, Mr. Oury. Although undoubtedly you all have already read this, gentlemen, please allow me the honor to read it to you again." The general removed narrow, oblong spectacles from his pocket and put them on. He peered over the spectacles for a moment at Bill Oury. "In a recent editorial the *Arizonan* recommends as an appropriate policy toward Apache Indians, and I quote, 'To receive them when they apply for peace, and have them grouped together and slaughtered as though they were as many nests of rattlesnakes.' End quote."

The general removed his spectacles and returned them to his pocket. He folded the clipping and put it in another pocket. Again he surveyed the representatives of the Committee of Public Safety.

"You all appear to be healthy men," the general said. "And Tucson is the largest community in the whole Territory. I would think if many others were as fierce and as forceful as Mr. Oury that you could easily take care of matters by yourselves."

The general started for the door. Captain Wilson jumped to his feet and raced to the door and had it opened just as the general reached it. The captain followed the general out of the room and shut the door behind them.

As they started back for Tucson, Bill Oury thought about Colonel James W. Fannin, another West Pointer. Oury's mind went back across the years to the time when men were trapped in the Alamo and Fannin had refused to help them and they had all perished.

△ 3

The next meeting at the courthouse was sparsely attended. Of the eighty-two men who had signed up to devour Apaches, fewer than thirty appeared. The others remained away because of cynicism, boredom or despair, all brought about by a sense of hopelessness. Among those present was John Wasson, pencil and paper in hand.

Bill Oury read a report he had prepared on his meeting with General Stoneman. He concluded, "We can expect nothing more from him than has been done, and if anything further is to be expected, we must depend upon our own efforts for consummation."

Jesús María Elías, his hands resting on the silver top of his cane, nodded his head.

△ △ △ THREE

△ 1

WELCOME CHANGE AT CAMP GRANT
THE "ROYAL" WHITMAN REPLACED

Captain Frank Stanwood, of Third Cavalry, recently arrived from California, will assume command at Camp Grant. We have heard nothing but favorable remarks of Captain Stanwood as a thorough officer, and we believe, unless prevented by absolute orders, he will Christianize the savages on the plan recommended by Henry Ward Beecher, for the border ruffians in Kansas about 15 years ago, i.e., by bullets from Sharp's rifles first and doses of Bible afterwards.

"Filled with the milk of human kindness, isn't he?" Stanwood commented.

"Overflowing," Whitman said.

"And witty as well."

"Very. But then I suppose I'm wide open for that one. And I named one of my sons Royal. I've regretted it ever since."

Captain Stanwood tossed the copy of the *Citizen* onto the desk. He brushed up his mustache with his forefinger. "Well, I'm terribly sorry to disappoint the old fire-eater but I do have those absolute orders."

"Verbal orders."

Stanwood nodded cheerily. "And right from that famous horse's mouth: 'Continue to treat the Aravaipas as prisoners of war.' In other words, maintain the old status quo. Looks like you're off the hook, Royal, old boy."

"Why the devil didn't he make that official?"

"He gave me the orders himself. Face-to-face sort of thing. Couldn't be very much more official than that."

"Why didn't he put it in writing?"

"I have no idea."

"Did you request it?"

"General Stoneman makes you stand at attention when he gives you orders. From that particular position, Royal, I've never been able to get out anything but 'Yes, sir!' "

Whitman shrugged. "Then we'll have to live with that. Damn it, I wrote to him twice, asking for explicit instructions."

"He made no mention of that," Stanwood said. "As a point of fact, he made no mention of you at all. But I must say, Royal, that somehow I gained the impression that he was not in a state of total ecstasy about those Aravaipa Apaches."

Whitman nodded. He rose from the desk that no longer was his desk and walked to the map of Arizona hanging on the wall. Stanwood, sitting on a chair, turned around, resting his folded arms on the chair back, watched him silently.

Captain Stanwood, who had ridden into the post that afternoon early in April, was very regimental. He had blue eyes and ginger hair and a ginger mustache trimmed closer to the mode of the British raj than to the United States Cavalry. The desert winds had stroked his cheeks and had flecked them and now they were a little sandpapered and colored high. He was bright and amiable and came from a wealthy and politically influential family and he was almost ten years younger than Whitman and healthy, and he made Whitman feel old and depressed.

Stanwood was aware of the delicate situation created by his return to Camp Grant. Although he had been commanding officer of record all along, he knew that did not alter the fact that Whitman had run the place for more than four months. He had with great tact made it a point to arrive as quietly as possible and had forbidden any military ceremony to mark his resumption of command.

He knew, too, that Whitman, in addition to being older than he was, and very old in grade, had been a full colonel in the war and that he had been wounded, and that when he was not careful or when he was very tired he limped, and he saw that Whitman was wasted and discolored from quinine, and he knew that none of these things helped matters.

He lit a cigar and sat quietly as Whitman stared at the map.

"It would have had importance, Frank," Whitman said at last, "with that gang in Tucson. Establishing Camp Grant officially as a reservation. And by officially, I mean properly, legally, legitimately, with all the authority of the Army and the Government." He splattered his knuckles against the map. "For those people in Tucson to know about, for that little, irresponsible incendiary, Wasson, to publish in that mess of toilet paper he turns out every Saturday." Whitman turned to Stanwood. "This way we're still a never-never land, Frank. You were given orders by General Stoneman and you passed those orders on to me, but as far as those bastards in Tucson are concerned these Indians out here still do not have any status. It's still open season. When I tell the people in Tucson that the Aravaipas are prisoners of war, they laugh. And General Stoneman could have put a stop to that."

He turned back to the scrolls and meandering lines and the names. "It goes beyond that, Frank." He gripped the sides of the framed map as though his arms were encircling Arizona. "Every Apache in the Territory is waiting to see what happens to the Aravaipas. Cochise and the Chiricahuas. Victorio and his Mimbres. All of them. Watching and waiting. And if it works with Eskiminzin and his people, it can do good. And he could have helped." He gripped the map hard. "Goddamn it to hell, he could have helped."

After a moment his hands fell to his sides and he went back to the desk and sat down heavily. "Frank, what gave you to believe General Stoneman disapproved of my taking in those Indians?"

Stanwood blew out a perfect smoke ring. "I can't say exactly, Royal. It was just the feeling I got. I may be wrong. Perhaps it's just that the general disapproves of almost everything." Stanwood grinned. It made him look younger. He had one of those faces to which a mustache does the odd thing. Instead of causing it to look more mature all it did was emphasize how young the face was. "He's a disapprover, Royal. Except when he's in California, of course. Nothing's wrong for him there. But the moment he steps over the state line and puts his foot into Arizona he undergoes what might be described inappropriately as a sea change." Stanwood raised his eyes and hands. He wished that Whitman did not look so grim.

"Does he have any idea of what's going on in Tucson?" Whitman asked. "The meetings, what the people are threatening to do?"

"If he has, he neglected to inform me."

"Has he been to Tucson at all?"

"He did not apprise me of that fact." Stanwood peered at Whitman. "Royal, have you ever met General Stoneman?"

"No."

Stanwood pursed his lips. "Then your questions are not as outlandish as they sound. Five minutes with the general and you would have known better than to ask them. Royal, the general simply is not given to dispensing bits of information. Particularly not to junior officers. I did hear something from his aide, Captain Wilson. It seems some sort of delegation from Tucson had a conference with the general. I gathered from Wilson that it was not a smashing success. Somebody in the delegation named Loory or Oury did not behave toward the general with suitable respect and the general walked out of the meeting in what I believe is referred to as high dudgeon."

"That should help everything everywhere," Whitman said. He cocked his head. " 'High dudgeon.' 'Sea change.' You're full of those little morsels."

Stanwood waved a generous hand. "Feel free to employ them at will." He stood up and stretched. He walked over to the desk and picked up the *Citizen*. "They drink printer's ink, these people. They drink ink and after a while they think it's blood. Their padded chairs turn into white chargers and their little quill pens become flaming swords. I don't know who this chap Wasson is, but I wonder what would happen if I handed him one of those Sharp's rifles and told him to go ahead and shoot down Apaches in cold blood. I doubt very much whether I could get him to hold that Bible."

He threw down the paper and grinned again. He looked

young and strong and the day's ride seemed to have wearied him not in the least.

"I'm going to get cleaned up, Royal. And then I want you to put me to work. I want to be brought up to date on everything that's going on around here. I want to have a good look at those Indians and I want to meet old pushface, their chief. What's his name again?"

"Eskiminzin," Whitman said.

"Eskiminzin. A name to conjure with." Stanwood jutted a forefinger at Whitman. "You can use that one too."

"I'll put it down," Whitman said.

Stanwood waved his hand genially and left the office. Whitman sat back. His body ached and he felt his years.

△ 2

"Sit down," Whitman said.

"Sir!" Clarrity said.

"Sit down, Clarrity. You look pretty stupid standing in a brace with a burning cigar in your hand."

"Thank you, sir." Clarrity sat down.

"What do you think about all this?"

"Captain Stanwood seems fit, sir. He's a fine officer. Of course a change of command is always a dicey business."

"I'm not talking about Captain Stanwood, Clarrity, and I'm not talking about any change of command. Captain Stanwood has always been in command here."

"Ah, the general, sir. Well, I'm sure you should feel relieved that the general is supporting your policy."

"Yes, I suppose I should."

"And I'm sure you should also feel relieved that Captain Stanwood will take over responsibility."

"Yes."

"But you don't, Lieutenant."

"No."

△ 3

The sweat-bath boss threw water on the hot stones and then padded out of the wickiup, closing the hide door carefully and tightly behind him. Eskiminzin and Little Captain sucked in the scalding vapor. Santo was not there. Santo was too old for steam baths. Santo was sitting outside, helping.

The two men listened to the drumming outside and to the song sung by the holy man.

After a while Little Captain said, "The old *nantan* is being punished because of what he did with us."

Eskiminzin said, "Nantan Whitman explained to me he always was the subchief and that the new *nantan* always was the chief."

Little Captain said, "Nantan Whitman has been here since the beginning of Ghost Face. Why should a new *nantan* be sent here now?"

"He did not say."

"Did he ever tell you before he was not the chief?"

"No."

"Did he ever tell you he was the subchief?"

"No."

Little Captain asked, "Did he ever tell you the real *nantan* would come here and be his boss?"

Eskiminzin said, "No."

Little Captain said, "I think the new *nantan* was sent here to punish the old *nantan* and that the punishment is because of us."

"Nantan Whitman is still here. He said he was not going to go away."

"He no longer is chief. It has no importance whether he is here or not here."

"It is important that he is here."

"And now we are without guns. We are without guns and there is a strange chief here and the chief who gave us his word is no longer chief." Little Captain shifted uneasily.

Eskiminzin said, "Nantan Whitman gave me his word again that there would be no change. He gave me his word that all the things he had pledged to me and the people would remain the same. He said that in front of the new *nantan* and the new *nantan* agreed it was so."

Little Captain pondered on that. "The new *nantan's* head looks like it is on fire. Maybe his brains are on fire, too."

Eskiminzin said, "It is always possible."

"Do you believe in him?"

"Daya says his eyes are good."

"White eyes." Little Captain snorted. "Your mother is getting old."

"The new *nantan* said he was ordered by the star *nantan* not to make changes here. He said that we were still looked on as prisoners of war and that we would be given food and that we would work as we have been doing."

Little Captain asked, "What did this man say?"

Eskiminzin said, "This man said he was happy to hear that. This man said it would have been better if the star *nantan* put his words on paper so they could not be changed. This man said that one day the star *nantan* can say that he never said those words and that since he is a bigger chief he will be believed and the *nantan* with the fiery head will not be."

The men grew silent as the bath boss brought in new rocks and poured water on them. While the bathhouse door was open they could hear Santo singing more clearly and louder. The bath boss left and shut the door and the two men were again shut off from the world.

After several minutes, after he felt his head getting light and the world going even farther away, Eskiminzin said, "But it makes no difference. It makes no real difference whether the star *nantan* puts his words on paper or not. Even if the words are down on paper the paper can be torn and then it is as though the words never were written. It has happened many times before. And that is the way it should be. The strong should be able to do what they want to do. It is the way things are. Nobody listens to the defeated."

△ △ △ FOUR

△ 1

By the second week of April the heat again brought down Tucson by siege. The sun lay over the Old Pueblo as though in punishment for every person for every sin ever committed. The town was airless and small movements made people gasp. They remained as much as possible behind their thick-walled adobe buildings and kept still and persuaded themselves they were cool. The dust settled in the streets. Children were absent and dogs stretched out in the shade and hung out their tongues.

The whiskey and beer were even warmer, and men, particularly men in saloons, were careful not to say angry words or words that could be misconstrued, because the blood was close to the skin now and the scorching air seared men's lungs and withered the inside of their heads. A man could be shot and killed because he looked at another man a certain way, or because he did not look at him a certain way, when the man said something to him.

Thus it was that the clatter of the rider was a loud noise but few men could rouse themselves to listen that morning, or if they did, to heed, other than to wonder perhaps for the briefest moment why anyone would gallop a horse on a day like that.

For a little while the rider had no one to tell his story to because no one stirred to listen. He kicked his flagged horse in the direction of the *Citizen* office but before he reached there Bill Zeckendorf stepped out of his store for a very quick check of his window display and the rider saw him and spoke to him and Zeckendorf did not return to his wares.

Bill Oury and Jesús María Elías were sitting together in Bill Oury's house that stifling morning. After the aborted meeting with General Stoneman, Oury's depression had deepened. He thought more and more these days and nights about military betrayals he had experienced or heard of, and General Stoneman's indifference to the predicament of the people of Arizona had taken its place among the best of them.

The lack of any tangible result from the conference with the general did not affect Don Jesús one way or the other. Don Jesús had never set any hope in it. Don Jesús knew that talks and meetings produced nothing but more talks and more meetings.

The two men were saying their own kind of prayers. They had reached that point in their friendship and their experiences where they hardly had to speak. A single word—a name, a place, a date—was enough to set free their thoughts and they would both become silent and would begin thinking of the same thing.

One thing alone Don Jesús did not share with Bill Oury. Don Jesús' dream of spearing Apaches, endless Apaches, with an arm that never wearied, an arm that avenged a father and brothers and uncles, that avenged family, the dream that sweetened his nights, belonged to him alone. He would not yield the smallest portion of it, not even to his closest friend.

The men were so deep in their reveries that the noise outside the house was there for a little time before they heard it. And then there was the loud pounding on the heavy wooden door and then someone yanked the chain outside and caused the Mexican silver bell with its silver clapper to ring through the house.

Oury and Elías went to the door. There were about fifty men in the street and they were all shouting at the same time, nothing unusual to either Oury or Elías, neither of whom had any doubts as to what this was all about. In the forefront of the crowd was Bill Zeckendorf. He was in shirt sleeves and wore curly garters on the sleeves. The rider was not one of the mob. The rider had given over what he had to give and was himself given immediate succor from the sun and the glare and the heat and a parched throat.

"Apaches!" Zeckendorf shouted unnecessarily.

Oury nodded. It never was a question of who or what, only where. Don Jesús' face set into bleak lines. He looked down at the ground, a lean monk in a hair shirt, ready to undergo a new flagellation.

"They raided down near San Xavier," Zeckendorf said. The sweat streamed down his plump, jolly face. "They ran off a lot of stock."

"Mine," Oury said, unsurprised. The Eastern Shorthorns he had introduced to Arizona had long headed the list of favorite beef for the Apache.

"Yours, all right, Bill," Zeckendorf agreed. "And some beeves belonging to Don Jesús." He waited for Elías to react. Don Jesús did not. "And some horses and cattle belonging to the Papagos. The man said they took off in the direction of Cebadilla Pass."

Don Jesús looked up sharply.

"Let's go after 'em!" a man shouted.

All the men screamed out their desire to draw Apache blood. Several drew guns and began shooting against a defenseless atmosphere.

"Cebadilla Pass," Don Jesús said in the voice of a drained ascetic. "That's on the trail to Camp Grant."

△ 2

The rattlesnakes were holed up against the heat. The facets of the stones and rocks in Cebadilla Pass reflected the sun like thousands of tiny mirrors. The men drew rein and Don Jesús jumped down. Of the fifty or more men who had gathered in front of Bill Oury's house demanding death for the marauders, eleven had agreed to join Oury and Elías in forming a posse.

Bill Zeckendorf, still in gartered shirt sleeves, was one of the eleven. Bill Zeckendorf had not hitherto been regarded as a bloodthirsty man. He was more given to cutting ribbons than throats. But the magnificent Prussian victory over the French the previous year and the capture of the French Emperor Napoleon III at Sedan had inflamed unsuspected martial Teuton blood. With a revolver fresh out of his store's stockroom dangling from a new gun belt, a virgin rifle stuck in a saddle holster from which the price tag had not been removed, Bill Zeckendorf sat on his horse like a dragoon, awaiting his first opportunity to fire a shot in anger.

Don Jesús inspected the ground. The ground told him everything. Don Jesús read the ground as a priest read his breviary, as John Wasson read proofs, Bill Zeckendorf ledgers. Once Bill Oury had remarked that Don Jesús would have made a fine Apache. Far from being offended at what might have been taken as a mortal insult, Don Jesús, who respected professionalism in everything, from an Apache on up, accepted the statement in the sense it was intended, as a profound compliment.

Don Jesús pored over the ground from one end of the pass to another. He poked a broken branch into drying horse droppings. He walked back to his horse and climbed back onto the saddle. The ground had informed him how many animals had passed, how many were cattle and how many were stolen horses and how many were unshod Apache ponies, and how long ago they had made their way over the flinty Cebadilla Pass. He had no requirement to convey these arcane findings to the others. He spurred his horse. He knew the rest would follow without questioning.

A little more than three hours later, as the sun was lowering, following a track that twisted in the general direction of Camp Grant, after Don Jesús had called two or three more halts to reassure himself he was still on the spoor, the posse came upon a single young Apache, armed with a rifle, on a lamed and shambling pony, herding a dozen tired beeves.

Holding on to his rifle, the Apache rolled off his pony and scurried like an outsize lizard to the shelter of a rock. A volley from a blending of thirteen revolvers and rifles stopped him for a moment, flattening him in a posture of frenzied deformity, and then the disjointed body began to move again, now not under its own power, the battering slugs doing it, arms and legs flailing as though unhinged.

The cattle bellowed in fright and scattered, and the Apache

rolled like tumbleweed, jerked and twitched and kicked as the lead plowed into him, and he found himself against the rock he had tried to get behind. He sat up and faced his enemies and he emptied his rifle aimlessly at his enemies and he gave a scream of rage and torment and hatred and he picked up a small stone and flung it and fell over dead. The stone struck Bill Zeckendorf in the face.

The men of the posse continued calmly to empty their guns, jerking the dead body around, chipping pieces off the rock. One by one the weapons were emptied. A last shot was fired at the corpse and then there was a hush.

For a few moments the men remained in their saddles, breathing hard, experiencing the rapture of having committed death, and that death on an Apache Indian, and then Bill Zeckendorf, who had come to know for the first time the sensuous pleasure of a revolver warming in his hand, felt something trickling down his cheek. He put a finger to his face. The stone thrown by the Apache in his last act in life had drawn blood.

Zeckendorf cried out a towering German curse. He jumped from his horse and drew his knife and ran over to the dead Apache. He grabbed his hair and ran the edge of his knife around the head and pulled off the scalp and threw it at the Indian's face. That was another first for the shopkeeper that day.

"Schweinehund!" Zeckendorf shrieked. He kicked the dead body.

"Bastante," Don Jesús said with distaste. Desecration of the dead was Indian business. A dead Indian was meat, unworthy to be touched.

"Look what he did to my face!" Zeckendorf shouted. He kicked the body again, dumping it on its face.

"Bastante," Don Jesús said again. "Bastante, por favor."

The men dismounted and walked over to the body. As Zeckendorf stanched the blood with a kerchief and the other men grinned and made fun of his mishap, the solitary wound of the battle, one of the men knelt and turned over the body and began to count the bullet holes in the Apache's chest. He counted aloud and the other men shouted each number in high glee and he had reached sixteen and was going on when Don Jesús suddenly hunkered down and took the Apache's face in his hands and looked at it closely. As the others gaped in surprise, Don Jesús forced open the dead Apache's mouth.

"I recognize this man," Don Jesús said.

"Who is he?" Bill Oury asked.

"He is one of the Aravaipa Apaches who attacked me that day at Camp Grant."

"How can you be sure of that, Don Jesús?" Oury asked, his pulse quickening. "All these murdering devils look the same."

"Not this one, Don Guillermo." Don Jesús twisted the Apache's face. The mouth was missing an upper front tooth. "This is one of the Camp Grant Indians who tried to kill me."

Don Jesús dropped the bleeding head and got to his feet. While the other men resumed their count of bullet holes he inspected the trail for another fifteen or twenty yards and then returned.

"Let's round up the livestock and start back," he said.

Bill Zeckendorf, still holding a kerchief against his face, asked, "What about the rest of the beeves, and the horses? The man told me there were a hell of a lot more stolen than what we have here."

"The trail is cold," Don Jesús said. "The freshest cattle and the horses are beyond our reach." He put his boot in the stirrup and swung onto his horse. "The Apaches are probably butchering some of those steers at that Aravaipa *ranchería* right now. Perhaps Eskiminzin will invite Lieutenant Whitman over for dinner tonight."

△ 3

"The Apache we killed was a Camp Grant Indian," Bill Oury said in a clear voice. "No question about that. He was identified positively. Not only by Don Jesús, who was attacked by him before my own eyes, but by myself!"

The alarm drum had filled the courthouse this time. The

men shouted and stomped their feet and demanded the total extermination of the entire Apache nation. Don Jesús, dressed in black, his black, flat-crowned hat tilted slightly over his eyes, his hands resting on his cane, listened to the shouting. It did not impress him.

"Old Economy Stoneman refused to lift a finger to help us," Oury went on. "But he did tell us one thing. He told us to go ahead and do the job ourselves!"

Again the men broke into cheers. John Wasson looked around and nodded approval.

"He said we were free men and that we had the right of free men to protect ourselves and our families and our property. Well, friends, the Apaches have been robbing and killing and feeding off us too long. Now we're going to do something about it!"

The men jumped to their feet and shouted hearty agreement. Some of them automatically reached for their guns to express their enthusiasm in the way they knew best, but they remembered in time where they were. Don Jesús remained seated and silent. John Wasson jotted down notes. He felt that he was in the middle of a moment of history.

The men sat down again and the meeting got down to hard business. An argument started immediately over who was going to lead the campaign. The raising of this issue came as a shock to Bill Oury, who had already been unanimously elected to that post. He saw Don Jesús look up at him questioningly and then Don Jesús lowered his eyes and moved his head slowly from side to side. John Wasson looked puzzled.

Oury banged Judge Titus' gavel and brought back order. "The question about who's going to lead this expedition has been settled," he said harshly. "You chose me. You chose me the same night eighty-one of you signed this piece of paper. Now let's not waste any more time on who's going to run the show. If you want to pick somebody else later on, do it. Right now I got this list of names in front of me. Every man who signed up signed up to form a volunteer corps to kill Apaches. Now I call on every man who put his name on this piece of paper to stand up and back his word and his honor."

The room stilled. Men looked at one another. Don Jesús rose to his feet. Sidney DeLong stood up. The other men looked at the men to their right and to their left. John Wasson twisted his head around. No one joined Don Jesús and Delong. Oury sat back in Judge Titus' chair stupefied.

"I think we better talk some more, Bill," a man called out. His voice was oddly subdued.

"He's right," another man said, also in a suppressed voice. "We got to talk about who's best fit to lead this vigilante business."

"We'll be taking our lives into our hands," a third man said. "We don't want to rush into this without working out the last detail."

"The last detail," a man shouted. The shout lacked timbre.

There was more talk and more argument and in the end the sum of $55 was pledged, but no horses, no mules, no provisions, and, apart from Jesús Elías and Sidney Delong, no volunteers.

John Wasson ran out of the courthouse to write a scathing editorial while the fury was still fresh on him. Bill Oury and Jesús Elías left the room without talking to each other, without looking at each other.

△ 4

The isolated settlement of San Pedro, about thirty miles up the valley from Camp Grant, was not unused to the attentions of interested Apaches. Cattle were being raised there and goats and there were some good horses, and the Apaches frequently availed themselves of what the market afforded.

No one in the settlement would have been in any way surprised on wakening that April morning, just three days after the thefts at San Xavier, to have discovered that while they were sleeping Apaches had showed up for work at their normal hour, just before the first light. It would have been nothing out of the ordinary. A steer or two. Some horses. The Apaches would have come and gone without notice.

On that morning one of the farmers, named Alex McKinsey, was up and at his chores a little earlier than usual and he flushed four Apaches and they shot and killed him for that. The Apaches made off with a couple of steers and three horses. Five other farmers, roused by the shooting, gave chase.

The Apaches drove their stolen animals into a constricted arroyo and whooped in behind them and the five Americans closed in behind the Apaches and inside the ragged cut in the desert they discovered they were not involved with four Apaches but with more than one hundred Apaches waiting in ambush for them.

There was little the five settlers could do but fight. Three were killed. The other two managed to get away and report what had happened.

John Wasson, still incensed at the pusillanimous performance of the men in the last meeting at the courthouse, got out the first story two days later, on Saturday, April 15.

ENCOURAGEMENT OF MURDER!!!

As we declared at the time the Camp Grant truce was a cruel farce.

There is not a reasonable doubt but that the Camp-Grant-fed Indians made the raid on San Xavier Monday, and because they were followed, punished and deprived of their plunder, they went to Grant, rested on Wednesday, and in a stronger force on Thursday, attacked the San Pedro settlements.

Judging by results it would have afforded as much protection if Camp Grant during the past twelve months had been located on an obscure East Indian island.

By the time Bill Oury's *Arizonan* got around to going to print, it reached out a little higher than Camp Grant to place the blame. It targeted the President of the United States as the one to be held responsible for all the Indian troubles in Arizona, describing him as the *"most stupid and shamefully ignorant man that ever occupied the presidential chair."*

A few days later, in time for his edition of April 22, John Wasson got his hands on the full report that General Stoneman had made to his superiors some six months before. Although Wasson had already printed excerpts from the report earlier, he now printed the document, with its avowed plan to reduce the number of Army posts in Arizona, in full. Wasson also managed to get his hands on a letter sent by General Stoneman to the Adjutant General of the United States Army.

"Savage, treacherous and cruel as these Indians are," Stoneman wrote, *"they still have enough human nature in their composition to render them controllable through the medium of their bellies."*

Plainly the Government policy was to cut down on troops and forts, John Wasson raged, and then to turn around and spend that money, and more, to maintain the health and well-being of Apaches, so that they could continue their war against the white settlers.

"It is," John Wasson said, "total insanity."

The weather was getting hotter and hotter in Tucson and men read the papers and sweated and talked in the saloons and in the stores and in the streets about everything that was going on and drank and sweated and talked some more. There wasn't much to talk about except the heat and the Apaches.

Bill Oury sat for long hours at his table in the Congress Hall. He sat alone. He invited no one to join him. He sat alone and he drank alone and he listened to the brave words and the boldness and the bragging. All he could do was listen. He had no power now. Only one man could force those drunken braggarts to put their guns where their mouths were. Only Governor Safford had the authority to call out a militia. But Saff wasn't around. Saff had gone on to San Francisco to arrange for the publication of a pamphlet listing Apache depredations in Arizona, and from San Francisco he had gone on to Washington and no man could say when the Governor was coming back.

One afternoon Sidney Delong showed Oury a copy of a telegram he had sent to Richard McCormick, the Territorial Delegate in Washington:

SEND SAFFORD HOME TO CALL TO THE FIELD
ALL ABLE-BODIED MEN AGAINST THE APACHES

Telegram? The message had to go by ordinary stage to San Diego before it became a telegram, if the Apaches let it get there in the first place.

"That's just fine, Sid," Oury said.

He smoked his cigars and poured his drinks and gripped his glass and listened to the fearless, thunderous flatulence in the saloon. He felt he had been gelded.

△ △ △ F I V E

△ 1

About three weeks after Captain Stanwood turned up at Camp Grant he gave Lieutenant Whitman a report he had prepared for General Stoneman.

"Have a look at it, Royal, and if there's nothing there you object to, just send it along," Stanwood said. He hurried out of the office which Whitman had continued to use.

Stanwood always was in a hurry. He exhausted everybody at the post with energy that had no end. But along with the bustle and the bluff and hearty manner, Whitman had learned that Stanwood was a thorough and meticulous officer and he was indefatigable. Whitman had come to know that when Stanwood had told him he wanted to find out about everything going on at Camp Grant, he meant exactly that.

He questioned Miles Wood and Fred Austin and went over their books line by line. He checked the rationing system and verified the Apache names against the tickets issued. He scrutinized the inventories of every pound of beef and corn and salt that passed from the sutler and the contractor and made certain that the books balanced. He went over the accounts of the hay and grama grass brought in by the Indians and amounts paid over to them for their labor. He checked Fred Austin's ledgers on the prices the sutler charged for the manta and sweets and other things the Apaches bought with the money they had earned.

Nothing bothered him, not the heat, not the malaria, to which he seemed impervious. He never stopped moving.

He interrogated Sergeant Clarrity and other noncoms and soldiers and civilians and the women who did the laundry and Oscar Hutton and the Puma and other interpreters and guides. He spoke to nearby ranchers and ascertained that they had no misgivings about having so many Apaches so close, and that, as Whitman had said, they were planning to use the Indians in the fall to gather barley and other grains.

He spent hours in the Aravaipa village, where his red hair startled and then fascinated the Indians. One afternoon when he and Whitman were meeting with Eskiminzin and Little Captain in Eskiminzin's wickiup, Road Runner had touched Stanwood's head and had pretended that he had burned his fingers. Stanwood went along with the joke happily. He inspected the boy's hand and sympathized with him.

In the evenings he and Whitman spoke in their quarters. The two men, from a touchy start, had come to respect each other. When they parted, Stanwood apparently ready to go right on and do another day's work, Whitman went to bed depleted, as much from exposure to this boundless vitality as anything else. He remembered when he had had similar vigor and he thought how pleasant it would be to have it still.

He lit a cigar and began to read Stanwood's letter, addressed, as military protocol prescribed, to the Acting Assistant Adjutant General, Department of Arizona. Stanwood reported on his investigation of conditions at Camp Grant and of his encounters with the Aravaipas.

". . . *They are at work as steadily as you can get Indians to work, in bringing in hay. The hay is received and inspected by the post quartermaster personally. The Indians are paid with checks which they exchange for manta and like goods. The sale of ammunition of any kind whatsoever is forbidden except on an order signed by the post commander. . . .*

"*The post guide, Mr. Hutton, a man of long experience with these Indians, tells me he thinks they are acting in good faith and wish to remain at peace.*

"*This morning I had a count of the Indians on this reservation; they numbered 394. Three days ago they numbered 455. Since that time two parties have left, one to burn mescal, the other hunting; neither party is over ten miles from the post, and they are signaling us with smoke today. . . .*

"*I can say, and in this my reputation as an officer is at*

stake, that these Indians, from the time they first came to Camp Grant up to the time I left to go on scout, did not engage in any depredations upon the people of this Territory."

△ 2

The dispatch rider who took away Captain Stanwood's report to General Stoneman brought a communication from General Stoneman to Lieutenant Whitman. The general returned to the lieutenant the dispatch in which Whitman had informed him of the surrender of the Aravaipa Apaches and had requested instructions as to how to proceed with them.

In returning Whitman's letter the general pointed out that the lieutenant had failed, as regulations required, to brief his communication. There was no other comment from the general.

In the third week of April, Captain Stanwood, fresh from his long leave in California, set out from Camp Grant for a lengthy scout to reacquaint himself with the Territory and with the officers in some of the other outposts. He planned to be gone for several weeks. Before he departed he said to Whitman, "Just keep on doing things exactly as you have been, Royal. I want you to know I am greatly encouraged about the future of these Aravaipa people."

In the expectation of the battles that might lie ahead, Captain Stanwood took with him all the cavalrymen stationed at Camp Grant and all the serviceable horses, as well as Oscar Hutton, who had a trained nose for hostile Indians. He left behind fewer than sixty infantrymen, some of them rookies, some of them down with the fever, just enough of a skeleton garrison to perform basic housekeeping duties.

Captain Stanwood and his cavalrymen shouted a mighty cavalry yell as they rode off the post.

Lieutenant Whitman again was in command of Camp Grant.

Part Five

△ △ △ ONE

△ 1

The land never changed or perhaps it was that it was the last to change or perhaps it was that the change was trifling and that when the feeble hand fell away the land regained itself with a quick and awesome ferocity. The land was always waiting to grab itself back.

The native man had looked on the land as his friend because the land was part of what he was part of and the things that grew on the land and moved on the land were all part of the same thing and each had its place and meaning and purpose and it was all held together.

It is only the white man, Whitman thought, who looks on the land as an antagonist to be defeated. It was the alien man who came to impose alien memories, to make what he found resemble what he had left, to remake the land in his own image.

But he would have his work ahead of him to subdue this land. The land was soaked with blood, old blood and new, and the great rocks were pink in the morning as phylacteries of the blood, but if there was any place anywhere that would resist change longer than any other place surely it was this. For everything was tougher here. The scraggy cactus was tougher than a forest. The animals, the people, the rocks, the hills, were tough; the waterways spit out droplets and then for half the year vanished; and the land itself, land as hard as the obsidian it spawned; land so hard and so imperishable it needed only to be dug and made wet and re-formed into a dwelling and when it dried it was almost as lasting in its new structure as it had been when men's feet trod on it.

Whitman rode along slowly, hearing only the measured rasp of his horse's iron hooves against the shale and stones and scrabble and steplike trap, and the sound of the Puma's horse behind him. The two men reached the top of a small rise and paused and looked out on the vast field that was spread before them and in the field there were men and women and children bent over in the fixed stoop of the worker on the land, the harvester, except here no one had sown what was being reaped. Nobody had planted the grama. The grama had always been there. Once it had nourished animals that had nourished man. Now it would nourish the animals brought by the invader.

The two men watched unnoticed in the blaze of the sun and then Eskiminzin detached himself from the others and walked to them. Whitman and the Puma dismounted and the three men watched the workers in the field.

"It must be a strange sight to you," Eskiminzin said, his face gleaming as though oiled by sweat, "Apaches working like farmers."

"It must seem as strange to you—and to them."

"We have planted before. We have raised corn. We always collect mescal."

"The men?" Whitman asked.

Eskiminzin smiled. He was happy that the other *nantan* was gone and that his friend was chief again, although he knew that the man with the fire hair would be missed. He did not understand how the Army did these things, shuffling leaders around, but he was glad things were as they were before.

"The men?" Whitman asked again.

"Maybe not the men. Maybe not all the men. Maybe some of them thought it was not dignified for men."

"What did they do? When the women were planting corn and gathering food, what did the men do?"

"They hunted. Everybody agreed that was men's work."

"They could not hunt all the time."

"They rested from hunting."

"They could not rest all the time."

"They gambled." Eskiminzin was beginning to sense that Whitman was not chatting idly. "Apaches are great gamblers," he said. He wiped the sweat from his eyes and looked directly at Whitman. "We gamble now."

"Yes."

"We work with our backs bent and our eyes on the ground. That is the biggest gamble we ever made, maybe."

"The backs are protected."

"Yes, I believe that. We never exposed our backs before. It is something the people in Tucson should see."

"The people in Tucson are seeing something else."

"You have something to tell me," Eskiminzin said quietly.

"There have been more killings."

"And they say we did them." He looked at the crouching people.

"There was a raid at San Xavier," Whitman said. "There was a chase. An Indian was killed. They say that he was a Camp Grant Indian."

"How do they know that?"

"They say he was recognized."

"Do the white men of Tucson know Apaches that well?"

"They say that they recognized him because he had an upper front tooth missing."

Eskiminzin looked at Whitman astonished. "Who says that?"

"Many. Elías. Bill Oury."

"Elías? The Mexican who was here? The Mexican who attacked us that time?"

"Yes."

Eskiminzin spat. "It would be easier to keep peace with Americans if it also did not mean keeping the peace with Mexicans." He spat again.

"There was another raid in the San Pedro settlement. There were four Americans killed. Those who gave chase found themselves facing a large force of Apaches."

"How many?" Eskiminzin asked.

"A hundred."

"Half that number, maybe." Eskiminzin smiled.

Whitman turned his head swiftly. "You know about that fight?"

"No."

"You knew the number of Apaches."

"I know nothing. I know that Americans exaggerate. If they said a hundred, it was half, less, maybe."

Whitman asked, "None of them were Aravaipas?"

"None."

"You are certain of that?"

"Yes."

"Would you know if any of your people went off?"

"I have told the *nantan,* we are not a big people. I would know."

"You are certain."

Eskiminzin straightened and something flickered in his eyes, something very old. "I have given my word."

"Goddamn it, I must know!" Whitman said. "I must question you and I must know. And don't, for Christ sake, turn Indian on me. There's enough of that around as it is."

After a little while what there was in Eskiminzin's eyes went away. "You have taken a great risk for us."

"The hell with the damned risk!" Whitman clamped his lips. He took off his hat and wiped his forehead. When he spoke it was in a low, controlled voice. "I will ask it again. I must be sure. You must make me sure. Were any of your men involved in either of those attacks? If they were, they can be punished, as individuals. Nothing else has to change."

"There were none. I do not lie."

Whitman breathed out hard. "All right."

"You believe it?"

Whitman nodded.

"Those hundred Apaches . . ." Eskiminzin said.

"That you said were fifty . . ."

"Those hundred men, those fifty men, what did they fight with?"

"Guns."

"We have no guns."

"There have been other raids before. Guns could have been stolen."

Eskiminzin lowered his head and then he raised it and stared at the people working in the field. "I can understand this. I can understand it from the people in Tucson and I can understand it from you. Something is always what it is." He pointed. "For an Apache to change is like for that rock to change."

"Your people have changed."

"They have returned to what they were."

"Perhaps. But to my eyes they have changed. But there is something else. It is not enough that they have changed. They must believe they have changed. That is almost as important as making the people in Tucson understand they have changed."

"My people have not gone out to kill," Eskiminzin said. "I cannot swear that a man here or a man there, or two men here or there, have not done bad things since we have come here. I do not walk around every night and count the faces. But as I have said, we are a small people, and as I told you before, nothing much can be done without someone knowing about it, and when somebody knows something, then I know it. I can swear to you that nothing you have described to me has been done by my warriors." Eskiminzin paused and looked at the field again. "It is the one thing, whether or not you believe me."

Presently Whitman said, "I believe you."

"And if you found that any of my men had gone out and had done bad things, what would you do?"

"I would arrest them."

"You would come among us?"

"Yes."

"And if they had done very bad things? If they had killed?"

"I would order them hanged."

"And if I killed?"

"If that were proved true, I would order you hanged," Whitman said.

Eskiminzin nodded peacefully. "It is as it should be. You still offer me no white man's presents."

The people started back to their village. The grass had been tied into bundles and they carried the bundles on their shoulders. As the people passed, Eskiminzin muttered something to one man and then another. They looked at their chief puzzled and stepped aside and remained. Soon there were six or more, all waiting patiently for they knew not what.

Small Woman and Child Mother and Melana approached and Fawn and Road Runner chugged along behind them. Small Woman's belly was so distended Whitman was positive parturition would take place now, before him. But he had thought that before.

The women had sweated with the men and there were small pieces of grass stuck to their arms and necks and faces. They paused and Whitman, who was taking a swallow from his canteen, offered it to the women.

Small Woman and Child Mother, holding their bundles of grass on their shoulders, touched the mouth of the canteen to their lips and passed it along to Melana. Melana put down her bundle of grass and took the canteen in both hands and drank deeply. Her face was flushed from her work and the sun and it glistened with sweat and she looked strong and of the land. The angle of her head lifted her breasts and they filled the loose manta shift.

She lowered the canteen from her lips and wiped her mouth with the back of her hand and gave the canteen to Fawn. Eskiminzin's daughter took a sip and then held out the canteen to Road Runner. Road Runner, his small bundle on his shoulder, shook his head angrily and took a step backward.

Whitman, conscious of Melana and the things she was making him feel, asked, "What's wrong with him?"

"He is a man," Eskiminzin said. "He will wait with the other men to wash the dust out of his mouth."

Fawn returned the canteen to Whitman and Melana picked up her bundle of grass and swung it over her shoulder and the women and children walked on and Whitman thought Melana was splendid and he thought it would be good to sleep with her.

"Nantan Whitman," Eskiminzin said.

Whitman, watching the departing Melana, watching how the damp manta clung to her back and to her behind, turned his head quickly. He saw that Eskiminzin was eying him and he thought the Indian could make no mistake about what was passing through his mind. He made a business of fastening the canteen to his belt.

"Nantan Whitman," Eskiminzin said again.

Whitman nodded. He had been away from a woman for a very long time.

"These men," Eskiminzin said. He gestured to the men he had spoken to as they were passing and who were still standing there.

"What about them?" Whitman asked.

Eskiminzin said something to the men. The men, more puzzled than before, opened their mouths. Each was missing an upper front tooth.

△ △ △ TWO

△ 1

It was called the White Dove of the Desert. It was not so old, as Spanish missions went, less than a century, but it seemed to have been there forever. No one could say for certain who had designed it or who had painted the murals or why one of the towers was left unfinished, but everyone knew of its beauty. It was said that of all the mission churches that were built from San Antonio, in Texas, to the Presidio in San Francisco, none was more beautiful than the church of the Papagos, Mission San Xavier del Bac, nine miles below Tucson on the Santa Cruz.

There were legends about the uncompleted east tower. One was that one of the builders fell to his death while working on the tower, and that after that no one could be made to continue. Another story held that the fathers deliberately left the building unfinished so they would not have to pay taxes.

It was a busy place for many years but now the men in the brown cowls who had carried the cross beyond the sword were gone. Now, except for occasional visits by priests from Tucson, the only occupants of the church were birds. The doors of the church were always left open and the birds had made it into a sanctuary of their own. Birds built nests on the heads of saints. Birds built nests in the crown of thorns that circled the brow of the image of Christ. Birds sang all day, from the west tower, from the eaves, from the fingers of saints, from the hands of Christ.

The priests who came down from Tucson were horrified. They called the infestation of birds sacrilege. The Papagos did not. The singing of the birds to them was nothing other than the singing of praises to the Lord the old fathers had taught them to worship.

The Papagos believed that the church had been left to them as a sacred trust and they believed that one day the men in the cowls would return. They believed they were a fortunate people. They had the religion of their ancestors and they had the religion of the powerful white man. They had their old reliable gods and the Figure in the church. They had double protection against their ancient enemies, the Apaches.

On this day late in April the three men met in the Rain House as was required. The Keeper of the Smoke lit the small ceremonial fire. Francisco, the patriarch, opened several holy esoteric fetishes and deposited them carefully in front of the fire.

Francisco was very old. His face was shrunk with the years that rested on it, and it was lined and ridged like desert earth after rain has fallen on it and then the sun has dried it and it crinkles and puckers and seams. He wore denim trousers and a checkered shirt. A turquoise amulet dangled from his neck.

"It will be religious," Francisco said. He spoke in Spanish. He spoke in a whisper but he was clear. But the sounds came from elsewhere, from the ceremonial fire, from beyond that.

"Yes," Jesús María Elías said, "it will be religious."

"They are not yet Enemy Killers," Francisco said.

"It is understood," Don Jesús said.

It was a hot day and they had to sit close to the ceremonial fire. Bill Oury took out a large kerchief and wiped his face.

"They must prepare for it," Francisco said. He was too old to sweat. He was too old and there was no juice in him.

"How long will that take?" Oury asked.

Francisco closed his eyes and went away from the group. He sat still by the ceremonial fire and looked inside himself. He opened his eyes and gazed at the fire.

"It will take days," Francisco said.

"How long?" Oury asked.

"There are words that have to be said and words that have to be heard. Their hearts must come to understand what they are to do or it will not be pure."

"How long?" Oury asked.

"There must be ceremonies," Francisco said. "It cannot be performed without preparation."

Oury was about to speak again, perhaps impatiently, when Don Jesús touched his arm lightly.

"They must be only the youngest and the bravest," Don Jesús said.

"Their hearts must know," Francisco said.

"Perhaps they will need seven days," Don Jesús said.

"Perhaps," Francisco said.

"Perhaps only six."

"Perhaps."

"Don Francisco, let us say five," Don Jesús said.

"It is agreed."

"And we are agreed about all else as well, Don Francisco?" Oury asked.

"Yes, Don Guillermo."

"There is no question?"

"One."

"What is that?"

"Weapons. We have no weapons. We have had no weapons but the ones we make for a long time."

"There will be weapons," Oury said.

"We will need weapons," Francisco said.

Again Don Jesús touched Oury's arm. "Old friend," he said gently, "there will be weapons. Of this you have my word."

"We have had none for a very long time," Francisco said. "The Americans and the Mexicans have said no Indians are to be permitted weapons. We have had no weapons for a long time."

"There will be weapons," Don Jesús said.

"White man's weapons?"

"Yes."

"To become Enemy Killers the young men must use clubs. But they must have weapons, too."

"I have given my word," Don Jesús said. "Do you know of my word?"

"Yes, Don Jesús."

"I have given it. This is what must be done. You must send runners to the different villages. You will inform the people that we are going to mount a campaign against our common enemy. Tell them to be here on the fifth day."

"Yes, Don Jesús."

"It is understood?"

"Yes."

"Clearly?"

"Clearly, Don Jesús."

"When the young men arrive here you must give them a good meal, Don Francisco," Don Jesús said. "There will be a hard march ahead and long and then hard work and they must be prepared for that."

"Their strength will be in their hearts," Francisco said.

"True. But it must be in their arms and legs as well."

"They will be fed."

"As soon as they are finished eating move them over to the Rillito and send a message to me at once," Oury said.

"I will do so with pleasure, Don Guillermo," Francisco said.

The headman put away the fetishes and the three men went outside. The Keeper of the Smoke went inside immediately to put out the ceremonial fire. The sun was bright outside but there were many shade trees along the Santa Cruz and it was pleasant, and the Papagos, dressed in spotless white cotton, walked back and forth immersed in their chores and as they passed their headman they lowered their faces.

Bill Oury took a deep breath. The air was pure and sweet. He was getting smothered in Tucson. He felt good now. He liked the Papagos and they trusted him. They would follow him as they would no other.

Jesús Elías gave Francisco a long, thin cigar and struck a match. He held the light for the Papago and for Oury and lit a cigar for himself.

"There will be weapons," Francisco said tranquilly, breathing out smoke. "You have said that."

"I have said that," Don Jesús said.

Francisco fingered his amulet. The fingers were long and brown and thin and looked like the cigar they were holding.

"There is no question, Don Francisco," Oury said. "They will be here."

"They will be here," the headman said. "The young men must use clubs or it will have no meaning. But they must have weapons."

"They will have weapons," Don Jesús said.

The three men walked to the shaded side of the church where the horses were tied. Francisco raised his eyes and gazed at the lovely building with its finished tower and its unfinished tower and its tenancy of Jesus Christ and saints and birds.

His eyes brightened and his face looked not so old. "It will be religious. That is true, is it not?" he asked no one.

Don Jesús nodded and his eyes shone as did those of Francisco and some of his years departed from his face.

"But they are not men, as we understand men," Don Jesús said softly. "They are not His children, as He speaks of His children."

"No," Francisco agreed. "It is true, Don Jesús, they are not." The cigar smoke drifted upward. "Don Guillermo."

"Yes," Oury said. He was feeling better all the time. The grit was working out from his teeth.

"There is another thing," Francisco said.

Oury looked up sharply. "What other thing? Everything has been settled."

"There is another thing, Don Guillermo," Francisco said. "What of the American military?"

"This will not involve the military," Oury said.

"The young men will not fight against soldiers," Francisco said.

"There will be no soldiers to fight," Don Jesús said.

"If there are soldiers the young men will turn back," the headman said.

"There will be no soldiers, Don Francisco," Don Jesús said. "I give you my word on that too."

"What of the soldiers at Camp Grant?" Francisco asked. "The *comandante* there gives protection to those Apaches."

"He will know nothing until it is finished," Don Jesús said.

"The young men will not fight soldiers," Francisco said.

"Do you believe in me as one on the trail, Don Francisco?" Don Jesús asked.

"There is none such as you."

"No one at Camp Grant will get wind of anything until after we are finished."

"Don Guillermo?" Francisco said.

"It is as Don Jesús has promised," Oury said. "There will be nothing with the soldiers."

"The young men will not fight the soldiers," Francisco said. "If the soldiers see them they will turn back."

"I will lead the young men," Oury said. "Tell them there will be nothing with the soldiers."

Collecting the reins of his horse Oury noticed scratched on the burned brick wall of the church the names of men, fortune hunters seeking gold almost a quarter of a century earlier, men who had followed the trail of the Mormon Battalion past San Xavier on their way to the new discoveries in California. The Papagos had never removed the graffiti.

"Why don't you have that wall cleaned, Don Francisco?" Oury asked. "Those names deface the church."

"Those names are part of the church, Don Guillermo," Francisco said. "To remove them would be defacement."

Oury and Elías mounted their horses. "In five days," Oury said.

"*Dios te bendiga,* Don Francisco," Don Jesús said.

"*Vaya con Dios,*" the headman said.

Francisco watched the two men ride off toward Tucson and then he turned to the church and touched his fingertips to the names carved on the wall. It was almost the same thing as the names scratched on the stones in the church graveyard.

△ △ △ THREE

△ 1

When Surgeon Brierly became excited he talked faster and the black spade beard jumped up and down as though it were trying to fly off his face. The Aravaipas enjoyed seeing that. It made them laugh. Surgeon Brierly had not been around very long but by now almost all the Apaches at Camp Grant knew about the new medicine man at the post with the hair sticking out of his chin and none on his head. The people still missed the *nantan* with the fire hair but they were finding the man they called Moon Head was almost as much fun to have around.

Surgeon Brierly was having a big talk with Little Captain just outside Fred Austin's store. Little Captain had just picked up his ration of beef and corn and salt and he wanted to get back to the village, but Surgeon Brierly was not going to let him get away that easily. Brierly had plans for Little Captain and the new post surgeon never gave up his plans.

"Hate the damned Papagos as much as you please but don't be such a blasted fool!" Brierly jabbed his forefinger under Little Captain's nose.

Victor Ruiz was hard put to keep up with the rapid way the new surgeon talked. It was not usual for the post surgeon to have his own personal interpreter, but Conant Bodoin Brierly, graduate of Toland Medical College in San Francisco, was not the middling workaday surgeon the Army was shifting around these days. When he reported for duty, replacing Surgeon Sumner, who was trotted off to some other military post for no reason other than someone somewhere had a compulsion to do some paper work, Brierly made it clear to Whitman at the outset that the profession that paid his salary was a convenience, something that enabled him to get around and find out about people, primitive people.

"I'm a damned good surgeon, Lieutenant, make no mistake about that," Brierly had said. "But my true vocation is anthropology. And I want to find out all I can about these aborigines." He jabbed a forefinger almost under Whitman's nose. "I want someone who can translate around me full time. You have to catch the bird on the wing, Lieutenant."

Whitman, amused, detailed Victor Ruiz, another escaped Apache captive, for the assignment.

"Another thing, Mr. Whitman," Brierly had said at their first meeting, "you're taking too damned much quinine. You look like a blasted canary. And washing it down with whiskey, I presume."

"That was the prescription, Surgeon," Whitman had said.

"Well, as of this very moment the prescription is changed," Brierly had said. "The malaria season has just about run its course. You now have a choice. Stop the quinine or stop the whiskey."

"Would you care to come to my quarters and have a drink, Surgeon?"

Brierly had tugged on his beard. "I'm never wrong, Lieutenant. The moment I put my eyes on you I knew you were an eminently sensible man."

Now, Little Captain, who had backed away from that forefinger, stood his ground. Others were gathering around and he was, after all, a chieftain second only to Eskiminzin.

"Who is a fool?" Little Captain demanded to know in a voice he made as loud as Brierly's.

"You are a fool. Hate the Papagos all you damned please but take advantage of what they have learned."

"This man wants to learn nothing a Papago has learned. A Papago man is not a man. A Papago woman is not a woman. This man wants to have nothing to do with them."

Just about every Apache agreed with Little Captain one hundred percent, and those who were standing around listening grunted that.

"You are going to raise squash if I have to shove the seeds down your throat," Brierly said.

"Because the Papagos raise squash," Little Captain said with disdain.

"Because it's good for you, you blasted fool. I'm going to get seeds for you and you are going to plant them. You can go on hating the Papagos all you like but you are going to eat squash. It's good food and it's good for you."

Along with every other Apache Little Captain was interested in anything that could be eaten, with the exception of fish, which were nothing but the bodies of dead women, and snakes, which, as even a child knew, gave shelter to the spirits of dead enemies.

"What does this food taste like?" he asked Brierly.

"You'll find out when you grow it and eat it."

Little Captain nodded and then he had the notion that he might seem to be capitulating too easily and in front of people who looked upon him with respect. "If it is good for the Papagos it is not good for us!" he said loudly.

"Damn it, you are being a blasted fool!" The forefinger went into action again.

Little Captain had learned long ago when it was useless, even foolish, to continue battle. "Bring me the seeds," he commanded in the voice of a man who has just won a victory.

"I will order them from Tucson," Brierly said. Not being in any way stupid he made himself sound as though he were obeying orders.

Little Captain climbed on his pony and rode off the post. Brierly went to his infirmary. He had Apache patients along with the soldiers, more Apaches than Surgeon Sumner had ever had. But then Surgeon Sumner did not have a jumping black beard and a head that looked like White Painted Lady up there in the sky.

△ 2

"You must be aware by now that these are astonishing people, Royal," Brierly said. "By the way, you do look better, you know. Not so much the heathen Chinee these days."

"I feel better," Whitman said. He did. Whether it was

because it was off-season for the fever or because things seemed to be working out well with the Aravaipas or simply because he had someone new to talk to he couldn't say. Probably all three. But he did feel well and he had not for a long time.

"They are of extraordinary interest," Brierly said.

"I think I've found that out."

It was a quiet, cool evening near the end of April. The two men were in Whitman's quarters. They had just finished dinner and were smoking cigars and taking a little whiskey.

"I didn't quite mean it that way, Royal," Brierly said. "I don't mean the way you've gotten involved with them as individuals. By the way, may I mention in passing that I think you are rather extraordinary yourself?"

"I never take seriously a compliment from a man who is drinking my whiskey," Whitman said.

"I'm considering the Apaches as a people," Brierly said. "Here were Stone Age people with no command or knowledge of metal whatsoever, landed up on as ungodly a terrain as can be found anywhere on earth, and they mastered their environment. Until we showed up they had defeated all comers. It will turn up as a footnote in history one day that the Apache was able to win out against all his enemies except the white man. Do you realize that, Royal? We have managed in a very few years to accomplish what nature and thirst and heat and hunger and all other natural enemies never were able to do."

Whitman refilled the glasses. "Except that we haven't quite managed that yet."

Brierly shook his head and stuck out a finger. It was part of the hand that was holding the lighted cigar. He withdrew it.

"But we have, Royal. We've destroyed these people. They are already dead. Oh, Cochise and some of the others will fight on a little longer but the mortal wound has already been inflicted and the message just hasn't as yet reached the brain. These people—as they know themselves—are dead." The surgeon contemplated his glass of whiskey and brackish water. "If we manage to turn up some kind of intelligence in our official circles—which, I may add, I very much doubt—perhaps there may be a rebirth. But even if that unlikely event transpires, the phoenix will be quite a different bird."

△ 3

It was another hot morning. Whitman and Brierly were having coffee at Fred Austin's store. Whitman said he had heard something about the surgeon and Little Captain and squash. He wondered what that was about.

"A small experiment, Royal," Brierly said. He peered at the coffee. It undoubtedly was the worst coffee he had ever drunk, fouled beyond redemption by the local water, but that was part of it all, wasn't it?

"Why squash?" Whitman asked. He had long since gotten used to the coffee and the water.

"I chose squash because it is one of the staples of the Papago diet," Brierly said. "I'm most interested to see how Little Captain reacts when he finally tastes it. Eating the food of the hated enemy."

"He'll probably think he's been poisoned," Fred Austin commented. He sucked on a lemon drop. He never drank his own coffee.

"That would be interesting," Brierly said. "And brave." He took out a small note pad and scribbled in it. "You won't forget to order those seeds for me, Mr. Austin?"

"Why Little Captain?" Whitman asked.

"I would have preferred Eskiminzin," Brierly said, but I simply can't manage to be overbearing with him. Damn it to hell, Royal, that man intimidates me! He just goes about his blasted business and he doesn't raise his voice and he damned well intimidates me. No occasion for you to smile, Royal. I'll analyze it one day and explain it to you. In any case, in lieu of the poo-bah himself, I picked Number Two. Little Captain will consider himself the spokesman for the entire tribe and I'm curious to see just what he does."

"Conant, I'm delighted that you have this intellectual interest in the Aravaipas," Whitman said solemnly.

"Thank you, Royal," Brierly said. "That's very decent of you to put it that way. Thank you very much."

"Yes," Whitman said in the same grave voice. "You're about the only one around this place who hasn't told me to get rid of them."

"Get rid of them!" Brierly was aghast. "What a disservice to science that would be!" He struck the table with his fist. "There is a whole body of information to be gathered from these people. Get rid of them indeed!"

The surgeon would have said more but the men looked up at that moment as Eskiminzin galloped into the post with Road Runner under his arm. They rushed out to learn that Road Runner had been fanged in his left leg by a rattlesnake. Brierly grabbed the boy and ran to the infirmary. Whitman and Eskiminzin followed.

Eskiminzin's face was set. He didn't have much hope for his only son. Road Runner had been out gathering mescal with Small Woman when the snake bit him and by the time the distraught mother got him to Eskiminzin some time had passed . Eskiminzin had looked at his son's leg and had decided the bite was beyond the power of Santo's songs. He thought the bite might be beyond any power. It was believed that the snake's poison was not so deadly after the snake had eaten but how could he know when last the snake had taken food?

Brierly laid the boy on the examining table and looked at the bite. The puncture was just under the calf of the left leg. It was swollen and turning black but it appeared to the surgeon that the fang had not penetrated very deeply. He washed his hands with strong soap and then cleaned the wound with alcohol. He made two crossing incisions with his scalpel and suctioned the opened flesh.

Road Runner made no sound. He knew he was going to die and he kept his mouth shut. He was afraid of dying but he was more afraid to open his mouth. He might cry out and that would disgrace his father. He kept his mouth shut and looked at his father so that his father's face would be the last thing he saw when he died.

Surgeon Brierly's hands worked swiftly and expertly. When he was satisfied that he had extracted the venom he washed the wound with alcohol again. He cut away some of the necrotic flesh and cleaned the opening again and then bandaged the leg.

"There," the surgeon said. "There. Ruiz, please tell the boy he is going to be as good as new."

Eskiminzin's eyes widened slightly as the surgeon's interpreter spoke to the boy. Road Runner looked confused.

"He asks is he not going to die," Ruiz said.

"Tell him he certainly is not going to die, not this time anyway," Brierly said. "Tell him he has to be more alert. That's the way Apaches are supposed to be, aren't they? And tell Eskiminzin I'll be around later today to have a look at the boy."

When Ruiz translated this Eskiminzin nodded and picked up Road Runner and left.

Brierly washed his hands again. "Curious."

"What's curious?" Whitman asked. "The fact that Eskiminzin didn't thank you?"

"I might have saved that child's life. Eskiminzin didn't seem in any way grateful."

"Apaches never thank anyone."

"Why? Do they think they are entitled to everything that's done for them? What gall."

"It's not that at all, Conant. It's quite simple. They believe people are intelligent enough to realize they are grateful when something is done for them. To express their gratitude openly is the same as telling you that you're too stupid to know how they must feel."

"I'll be damned," Brierly said. He took out his note pad and entered that information. He looked up. "And yet, it does make sense, you know." He was silent for a moment. He shook his head. "Extraordinary—did you notice that the child never made a sound, not a whimper, while I was slashing away. And he must have been in considerable pain when he left. And I didn't dare give him a morphine tablet. With people unused to medication other than their own the results of some of our drugs are unpredictable. Particularly with a child."

△ 4

Bonita was small and the stethoscope covered a large part of her chest. Fawn waited tensely. There were not many expressions that came to Fawn's face. There usually was only one, a sad, solemn fixing, surrounding eyes that seemed to have seen more than her years could have permitted.

But now she watched and there was a tautness in her lips and Eskiminzin and Small Woman looked at each other and smiled and Road Runner's nose was out of joint because he was the true hero of the day and he felt he had been shoved off into a corner.

Finally Surgeon Brierly straightened. He pursed his lips and looked for a long time at the small doll made of buckskin. "She's going to be just fine," the surgeon pronounced.

When Victor Ruiz put the words into Apache, Fawn looked at her mother and father and then at Bonita and she took the doll from the surgeon's hands and she smiled. It was the first time in a while that anyone had seen her smile. That was something that worried Eskiminzin and Small Woman. Apache children laughed a great deal. Even when the people were running away from the soldiers the children found time to laugh and play. Fawn seemed to have been born old.

It had surprised and pleased Eskiminzin and Small Woman when Fawn accepted the doll from them originally. Fawn didn't play much with things like other children did. The doll was not Bonita then, that came later. It was just a buckskin doll that Eskiminzin had made. Small Woman had sewed the soft skins together, true, but Eskiminzin made it into a doll by mixing colors he used to paint his own deerskins. He painted on the eyes and the nose and the mouth and then he painted small markings on the rest of the doll. These were the kind of markings Eskiminzin painted on his own ceremonial clothing.

Perhaps that was why Fawn adopted and named the doll. She loved her father and she was in awe of him and she kept the doll with her all the time. She had noticed there was something wrong with Bonita lately but she didn't know what to do about it and she was a little afraid to show it to her mother and father because they might think she had not taken care of Bonita. But the visit to the village by Nantan Whitman and the new post shaman straightened everything out.

That took place several hours after Brierly had treated Road Runner. Whitman had remarked after the evening meal at the post that he had to go over to the Apache village to discuss some matters with Eskiminzin and the surgeon said immediately that he wanted to go along to have a look at his little patient.

Small Woman welcomed Whitman and Brierly to her wickiup, and hurriedly made coffee for her guests—coffee that Brierly considered infinitely superior to Fred Austin's. He examined Road Runner's leg. The wound looked clean and uninfected. He wiped it with a little more alcohol and then put on a fresh bandage. Again Road Runner made no sound. He did not look at his father. He was convinced now that he was not going to die. Instead he looked into the surgeon's black bag.

Eskiminzin appeared peaceful and calm. He did not know whether it was the skill of the white medicine man or the fact that the snake must have had a hearty meal just before he bit Road Runner that had saved his son from death, but believed that in any case he was lucky. He believed being lucky was worth more than anything.

When Brierly finished bandaging the leg he put the alcohol and scissors into the bag. When his hand emerged it contained lemon drops. He offered them to the boy.

Road Runner glanced at his father. Eskiminzin nodded. The boy accepted the lemon drops and popped one into his mouth. He was happy he was not going to die but he was glad something had happened to him to make him so important. His sister, Fawn, was sulking in a far part of the wickiup and that was perfectly all right with him.

After Small Woman refilled the coffee mugs, Whitman said, "Fawn, why don't you let the doctor have a look at Bonita."

"Who is Bonita?" Brierly asked. He was pleased that there was more work for him.

Fawn hesitated.

"Do as the *nantan* asks," Eskiminzin said to her.

She went to her part of the dwelling and picked up something from her pallet and went to Brierly with what appeared to him to be a shapeless piece of stuffed buckskin. He looked questioningly at Whitman and then took it from Fawn and saw that it was not shapeless but that it was in the form of a human being, a little battered, perhaps. That it was, in fact, a doll. The surgeon was so dumbfounded to discover that an Apache child possessed a doll he could not for a moment say anything.

"Surprise you, Con?" Whitman asked.

Brierly realized his mouth was open. He closed it.

"Her name is Bonita," Whitman said. "Could you give her your professional attention? She seems to have gotten wounded too."

Brierly was examining the doll, noticing the markings, now somewhat faded.

"The side, Surgeon," Whitman said.

Brierly saw that the stitching on one side of the doll had come apart and that definitely was a wound. He opened his bag again and took out some catgut and a needle and stitched up the wound. He did a neat, professional job, and he felt a little foolish. Even the doll, Brierly thought with cheery inanity, does not make any sounds of pain.

Finished with suturing the wound, Brierly felt the moment called for going the whole way. He took out his stethoscope and pressed it against the doll's chest where the heart surely must be. He listened. "She's going to be just fine," he said, returning the doll to Fawn. He glanced again at Whitman. He saw something on Whitman's face and he didn't feel foolish at all.

Small Woman was bending over to pick up the coffeepot when she straightened suddenly and said something and hurried out of the wickiup. Eskiminzin leaped to his feet.

"What's that about?" Whitman asked.

"She said she is going to have the baby," the Puma said.

"Just like that," Brierly said.

Eskiminzin spoke rapidly and rushed out of the wickiup.

"He just remembered he has important business to talk over with Little Captain," the Puma said with a straight face.

"I'll go along with him," Whitman said.

Brierly said if nobody minded he would hang around. "I might be of some use."

"Never," Whitman said, thinking about Marcus Whitman. "Watch, if you like, but for God's sake, don't interfere."

"All right," Brierly said. Unless, he added to himself, it is absolutely necessary.

Small Woman was kneeling on the ground with her legs spread apart. She clung to a wooden post for support. Her skirt had been pulled up above her distended belly. Child Mother and Melana bathed her thighs with water. Some people were watching but others passed by without turning their heads.

"Do you know what they're putting on her thighs?" Brierly asked.

"The water contains some special herbs," Victor Ruiz said. "I do not know what they are."

"Do they mind my watching?"

"No. You are a famous medicine man because of what you did for Road Runner. They are proud you are interested."

"They are?" Brierly smiled. "Isn't that nice."

By now Santo had appeared and he was singing songs. He had started singing the songs as soon as he had received word Small Woman had gone into labor.

"Why did Eskiminzin run away?" Brierly asked Ruiz. "I wouldn't have thought he would be that squeamish."

"It would embarrass him to see his wife in pain," Ruiz said. "Sometimes men feel so embarrassed they feel the pain themselves and roll around on the ground."

The minutes passed. Santo kept singing. It sounded to Brierly to be the same song sung over and over. The tune seemed remotely Oriental. Small Woman clutched the pole. Her face was glassy with perspiration. Her mouth was clamped shut. The midwives rubbed more of the herbed water on her thighs.

Surgeon Brierly was twitching to get in there and help. He remembered, inconsequentially, that his wife, back in Oregon, was just about due to deliver their own baby.

As the delivery was getting prolonged, Child Mother ran

into her wickiup and returned with a basket containing some greenery. She put some in Small Woman's mouth. Small Woman chewed on it.

In the interest of science Brierly took some of the leaves out of the basket and examined them. They appeared to be yucca leaves. He tasted one. The leaves seemed to have been flavored with salt and some other herbs.

He stepped back and took his pad from his pocket. Ruiz, a short man with a pencil-thin mustache, put his hand on the pad instantly and closed over it.

"Put it away, Señor Cirujano," he said.

"I don't want to forget any of this," Brierly said.

"Remember it in your head until you get back to the post and write it down there. If they see you doing it here they will think you are putting some power over them."

"Thank you, Ruiz," Brierly said, pocketing the pad.

Child Mother and Melana continued to rub the special water on Small Woman's thighs. Santo kept singing. Brierly saw Fawn come out of the wickiup, holding the doll against her chest. Road Runner limped out a few moments later. He looked around. He appeared bored and out of sorts.

Presently Brierly realized that more than two hours had passed since Small Woman had made her announcement and rushed out of the wickiup. Santo was getting hoarse. Fawn drifted off. Road Runner sat down against the wickiup and fell asleep. His dog curled up against him. Little by little the people who had gathered to watch the birth wandered away.

Increasingly conscious of the fact that he was highly esteemed by these people for his professional skills, as Victor Ruiz had informed him, Brierly rapidly was reaching the point where, despite Whitman's warnings, he would feel compelled to offer his talents. He leaned forward slightly as Small Woman said something to Child Mother in what appeared to Brierly to be a perfectly normal manner, which in itself, under the circumstances, he considered astounding, and Child Mother got down on her knees and pressed the flats of her hands on the bulging belly and pushed down with what seemed to Brierly to be excessive force. Melana ran off to her wickiup.

Brierly yanked at his spade beard in outrage and frustration. He saw Melana emerge from her wickiup, accompanied by Eskiminzin's mother, Daya. The first appearance of the old woman appeared significant. Daya walked to where Child Mother was still bearing down on Small Woman's belly and at that same moment, as though Daya commanded it, the baby was delivered. Daya severed the cord and Small Woman let go of the post and slumped down on the ground. Apart from her few words to Child Mother she had not made a sound during the entire course of her labor.

Brierly moved in a little closer. He saw that the baby was a girl, that she seemed whole and well formed and of a respectable size. Daya held up the infant and Melana and Child Mother and Small Woman and those few who had remained watched and waited with what Brierly interpreted as a kind of anxiety. He questioned Ruiz.

"They are waiting to see if the baby cries," Ruiz explained. "If she does not cry she will be strong."

After a little while, while the infant remained mute, everybody agreed that she had passed her first test on earth. They all congratulated Small Woman, who lowered her head modestly. She also pulled down her skirts. She appeared to be recovering quickly. Daya tied a rawhide rope around Small Woman's belly for support.

"None of these people express pain," Brierly said.

"What good would it do?" Ruiz asked.

"Relief. That's what crying out provides."

Ruiz stroked his thin mustache and smiled. He had lived a long time with the Apaches before he had gotten away from them. "They look on that as a waste of effort."

"To obtain relief from pain?"

"Mexicans cry out," Ruiz said. He was Mexican himself, of course, but he was in a position to know of certain differences between his own people and the Apaches. "Mexicans cry out for help. Even when they know they will not be helped, not by anyone in this world anyway, they cry out, to Señor Jesucristo, to the Virgen, to all the saints. An Apache will not cry out."

"Not even the women, obviously," Brierly said.

"The women are Apaches, too."

By this time Child Mother was rubbing a mixture of grease and red ocher over the infant's body. This, Ruiz said, was to prevent the baby's skin from inflaming. Daya gathered the afterbirth and wrapped it in a piece of deerskin and tied it securely and put the package into a juniper bush.

"What's that for?" Brierly asked. This day had been encyclopedic for him.

That was a question Ruiz could not answer. He questioned Melana. "The bush has berries every year," he reported to Brierly. "The women do this so that the new life in the bush each year will be given to the infant."

Eskiminzin, having been notified that it was all over, now returned with Whitman. He looked his wife over closely to make sure no permanent damage or change had been effected and then he glanced very briefly at the child. If he wished it had been a second son he did not show it. He walked back and forth in the clearing with what was very close to a strut. Brierly would not have been surprised if the Apache chief had produced cigars. One thing the surgeon noted: Eskiminzin refused to hold the baby himself. When Child Mother offered the infant to him he backed away in what Brierly would have adjudged, if Eskiminzin was not what he was, to be fear.

Road Runner woke at this time. He made up his mind instantly that something had to be done. Too much attention had been paid to his stupid sister and her stupid doll and now everybody was making such a fuss over this birth of another sister, who undoubtedly would be as stupid as the first one. And he was the hero. He was the only one in the village with a bandage around his leg. And he had lemon candies.

He stood up. He said nothing. He walked back and forth with a very serious limp. He walked so that everyone could see him.

Brierly frowned as he watched Road Runner. Something was wrong. Then he said to Whitman, "But he's limping on the wrong leg."

"I know," Whitman said. "But we won't tell him."

△ △ △ FOUR

△ 1

The Papago young men, who could not as yet be called Enemy Killers, were gathered along the bank of the Rillito when Bill Oury rode up. They were dressed in white cotton. They were sitting on the ground, their legs crossed under them, their faces turned toward the morning sun, their heads bowed.

Oury cast his eyes over them. He reckoned there were about a hundred. On the ground next to each man was his club. The club was carved into a large ball at one end and sharpened to a point at the other end. A leather thong was attached near the sharpened end. The young man's hand could slip through the thong and grip the club and then use either end, the one for the bludgeoning, the other for the stabbing.

Sitting apart from the young men was Chief Francisco. For the event he, too, was dressed in pure white. His head was lowered with the others. No one talked. No one looked up when Bill Oury's horse brought him to the pleasant riverbank.

The Papagos, Oury understood well enough, were meditating. He supposed they would call it that. What they were doing, he knew, was firing themselves up. They were brave enough, he guessed, but they were scared to hell of Apaches. The Papagos were always scared to hell of Apaches and they always had to build up their courage. An Apache had that built into him from the start. Bill Oury had to give the Apache that. Not courage, exactly, since the Apache made his move only when he thought he had an advantage and ran when he figured he had lost, but the instinct to kill. The Apache had that.

The Apache could kill in reflex, the way a rattler, a puma, a wolf, could kill, without thought, without any kind of thought, kill as normally as he breathed and ate and drank and pissed

352

and shit. The Papagos didn't have that in their blood. Maybe they never had it but they certainly didn't have it now. They were a damned decent breed and they worked hard and they could be trusted and when they had to kill they had to work up to it and get their gods involved. They had to find a muscle they hadn't used in a long time, find it and work on it and make it strong.

Watching the Papagos facing the sun and getting their strength from their mysteries, Bill Oury hoped they made the muscle good and strong. They would need it. He counted on surprise but that would take care of only the beginning.

Oury loosened the cinch on his horse and then let the horse drink from the Rillito. He scooped some handfuls of water into his own mouth. He picketed the horse under a paloverde tree, laden with its yellow spring blossoms. He saw that there were about twenty other horses grazing in the shade. That would make it about one horse for every five Papagos.

He sat down and leaned back against a tree and lit a cigar. It was cool and quiet. Whatever prayers the Papagos were saying they were saying inside themselves. The only sound was the splash of the water and the birds and the rustling now and again from the breeze. It was restful and pleasant.

For the first time in a very long time Bill Oury felt good. He felt very good. He didn't need to say prayers. He knew what he was doing was right. It made him feel strong. Things were moving and he was a man of action and all the talking was finished now. The weeks, the months, had soured him until he hardly knew himself, but on this bright spring morning he felt good again.

He thought about what Doña Inez had said before he had left the house that morning. He had tried to move around quietly but she had come into the kitchen while he was waiting for the coffee to boil.

"I believe I know what you plan to do," she said in Spanish.

"I believe you do," Oury said. He had told her nothing but he had long ago become accustomed to the truth that whatever entered his mind generally, sooner or later, entered hers as well.

"Are there many who ride with you?" she asked.

"Yes."

"Don Jesús?"

"Yes."

"All that concerns me is the danger to you."

"I think there will be no more than is around a man any time here."

She went to the stove and picked up the coffeepot and poured the strong black brew. "You know what I feel about those people."

"Yes."

"I still see the child."

He raised his eyes. She almost never spoke of the son who had died that night. She had worked that out with her religion.

"I am happy Don Jesús will be with you," she said.

"Yes."

"I will pray."

As he rode away he saw her slip off to church.

△ 2

He dozed off and when he opened his eyes it was to hear laughter from Mexican throats and he sat up and saw that Mexicans were arriving in twos and threes and they were in very good humor. They were laughing and joking and more and more of them were riding up and they were all in good humor.

The Papagos had not stirred. They were in their own stillness yet. But the Mexicans acted as though they were on holiday. They were bright and happy, as though they were making a fiesta. Oury would not have been surprised to see guitars.

"Don Guillermo."

Oury turned to see Jesús María Elías riding in. Don Jesús dropped lightly to the ground and extended his hand. Oury got up and shook it.

"It is a beautiful day, Don Guillermo," Don Jesús said. He breathed in deeply. His eyes were happy. He looked this way and that. He watched the Papagos for a while and he crossed himself. He understood better than Oury what was going on with the Indians. But then his old friend was not a Catholic and beyond that not a Spaniard.

Now Don Jesús twisted his head this way and that again and when he finished this new surveillance he turned to Oury and there was a sly question in his eyes. Bill Oury had done some looking around himself since he woke from his nap and he damned well knew what Elías was looking for and what he did not see.

"They'll be here," Oury said. He realized it had come out a little louder than he intended and that several Mexicans had turned and were looking at him. Then he said, "There! There's one!" Again it came out resoundingly. Good old Sidney DeLong He could always count on Sid.

"We maybe take a little longer," he said to Elías.

Don Jesús looked at him blandly. "I always was told it was the Mexicans who move slowly."

DeLong dismounted and looked around. He pushed back his hat and wiped his brow. "Where are the others?" he asked.

Both Oury and Elías knew that DeLong was not inquiring about Mexicans, who were there in numbers, or about Papagos, whose numbers were even greater.

"They'll be here," Oury said. He kept his voice down and he hoped he sounded convincing.

He hoped so. He had worked hard. He had not let up. He had twisted arms and bent ears and made threats and promises. He had appealed to honor and pride. He did not expect all of the eighty others. But he expected quite a few.

By one o'clock in the afternoon about twenty-five more men had ridden in. Four of them were Americans. That made, with Oury and DeLong, a total of six. And Bill Oury had a hunch that was it, and he believed his hunches, and at that moment he would have been willing to turn the expedition on Tucson to take care of those arrant cowards. All the good feeling was gone. He was back there in the courthouse and the saloons and the bluster and the bullshit. Those bastards, he thought, his stomach knotted, those bastards.

Don Jesús came to the conclusion that the six men represented the American contingent at just about the same time. Holding a thin cigar between his long, aristocratic fingers, he strolled over to Oury. "Well, Don Guillermo?"

Bill Oury shook his head. More of the Mexicans walked over. This was a rare pleasure.

Don Jesús eased out a drift of smoke. "Your countrymen are grand on resoluting and speechifying, Don Guillermo, but when it comes to action they show up exceedingly thin."

Don Jesús spoke quietly and his face was without expression but other Mexicans smiled and some chuckled and Oury flushed with rage, rage at the men who had pledged their word and then reneged, rage at his oldest friend, rage at everyone who had listened to him and had laughed. His fists clenched. For a moment he was on the verge of doing the unthinkable. He turned away and walked to the river to be alone with his fury. He soon realized it was not to him alone that Don Jesús had spoken.

Don Jesús had spoken against all those Americans in all the meetings and all the other places who had spoken with gringo contempt of Mexican courage. Don Jesús had spoken at this one time, at this one single time, against all the years of gringo contempt of Mexican courage. And he had a right to that.

Oury turned and started back to Don Jesús and the other Mexicans, to extend his hand, to admit what was right and what was wrong, when he saw and heard approaching them something that helped make up for the absent, craven, chicken-hearted defaulters.

The others saw it and heard it, too, and now everyone was looking at the big freight wagon drawn by mules and at the skinner cracking his whip, not to make the mules move any faster but because he was a mule skinner and he could not arrive anywhere, not in the hottest corner of hell, without announcing himself in the proper way, he was a skinner, was he not, and by God he was going to skin mules!

The rumble of the wagon wheels on the hard alkali, the thumping of the mules' hooves, the cracking of the whip like gunfire, the yelling of the skinner, all of it now was the most glorious music Bill Oury had ever heard. All the Mexicans and Americans started yelling and cheering as the wagon thundered up and the skinner pulled on the reins and jerked the brake and even the Papagos rose from their consultations and stood and looked at what had come upon them all.

Oury walked over to the wagon and now his head was high again and the good feeling was there and the hell with men who were all mouth and no balls. The driver, a slab-sided man with a mouth that seemed all on one corner of his face, jumped down grinning and shook hands with Oury.

"Here I am, Uncle Billy, on time, as guaranteed," the driver, a man named Lum Skettle, said proudly.

"Right on time," Oury agreed.

Skettle waggled his fingers and then started untying the ropes holding the canvas down. With flare, with the same kind of grand flourish that he had driven his wagon, he swept back the canvas. Stacked neatly on the wagon bed were long wooden boxes. Lum Skettle lifted out one of the boxes and set it on the ground. He opened it. He took out a rifle. He handed the piece to Bill Oury as though it were an emperor's scepter.

"Compliments of Sammy Hughes, Uncle Billy," Lum Skettle said. "And there's plenty more where that came from."

Bill Oury held the rifle high. He turned to the others and held it high and that was where his spirits were and his eyes caught the eyes of Don Jesús and Don Jesús smiled and it was all right between them again. The rifles and the ammunition said something. They didn't say as much as fifty or sixty or seventy Americans, but they said something.

Bill Oury looked more closely at the rifle. Stamped on the stock were the initials A.T. The rifles were Arizona Territory government rifles, compliments, as Skettle had said, of Adjutant General Sam Hughes. Oury thanked God for Sammy Hughes.

"There's plenty of ammunition to go with them, of course," Lum Skettle said. "And Sammy wanted me special to tell you that his little wife, Mrs. Hughes, made a lot of them bullets in her house herself with her own hands."

The men cheered. It was a touching picture. Little Atanasia Santa Cruz Hughes pouring molten lead into bullet molds with her tiny, well-bred fingers. It was a real frontier feeling and the Mexicans were happy because if the guns came from the gringos at least some of the shot came from the hands of a Mexican woman.

"Sammy Hughes wants me to tell you that he is with you with all his heart," Skettle announced. "He says to tell you that he wishes he could be with you in person, with one of these guns in his hands, but that can't be, as you know. But he says his heart is with all of you."

There were more cheers and then the men set to work to empty the wagon and open the boxes. The rifles were stacked in little pyramids, military style, and soon the cool, pastoral bank of the Rillito had the appearance of a barracks yard. The ammunition was removed next and distributed evenly. But weapons and ammunition were not all. There was more in the wagon. Adjutant General Sam Hughes, who also was a butcher in Tucson, knew the need for food for the stomachs of men on an arduous task. Sam Hughes had missed nothing. He knew how to cater a party.

The empty gun boxes were stacked back in the wagon and the canvas was drawn tight again and the wagon appeared to be the same as when it had arrived, although the mules would now not have the same heavy load to haul and the wheels would not dig ruts quite as deep.

"There's one more thing, Uncle Billy," Skettle said as he climbed back to his seat and took hold of his whip. "Sammy said to be sure and remind you that it's against the law to give any of them guns to Injuns." He gave Bill Oury a broad wink and pulled his mouth almost up to his ear.

"Of course," Oury said. He didn't bother to wink back.

"Sure as hell wish I was going along," Skettle shouted. He waved his big, black hat and most of the men, including some of the Papagos, waved back and then he cracked his whip and the wagon lumbered away on its return to Tucson.

"Wait a minute!" Oury shouted suddenly.

The skinner pulled up. The mules, resigned to motion again, came to a grateful halt.

While the others looked on curiously, Oury groped in his pocket and found a pad but couldn't locate a pencil. Don Jesús had one and gave it to him. Oury wet the tip and scribbled a few words on the paper. He showed what he had written to Don Jesús and the Mexican nodded and patted Oury on the arm.

Oury folded the paper and handed it to Lum Skettle. "Lum, you find Hiram Stevens and give him this."

Skettle took the paper and put it in his shirt pocket.

"It's important, you hear?" Oury said. "Make sure the minute you get back into town you hunt him down. You put that paper in Hiram's hands, you hear?"

"Depend on it, Uncle Billy."

The wagon moved off again and the dust rose and the dust fell.

△ 3

The guns were given to the Mexicans and to the Papagos. The six Americans had their own weapons. During the course of the distribution a head count was made. It came to ninety-four Papagos, forty-eight Mexicans and the six Americans, one hundred and forty-eight men in all.

"We're a motley-looking army," Oury said, trying to make a joke. The tallying of the troops had reminded him anew of the disastrous showing of the Americans and he was starting to smart all over again. "Well," he said jovially, "I thing everything's taken care of. I reckon we're ready to move out." He started for his horse.

"Don Guillermo," Jesús said softly.

"Yes, my friend."

"There is one thing yet to be done.

"Is there? There is? What is that, Don Jesús?"

"We must decide on a commander," Don Jesús said.

For a while nobody said anything. Then the men, Mexicans and Americans, looked at one another in surprise. The most surprised perhaps was Bill Oury and then after a moment he was not surprised at all.

"I've always considered Bill Oury as our leader," Sidney

DeLong said. "He was elected that." The other Americans agreed.

"That was before," Don Jesús said. "We are told this is a democratic country. Let us put it to a new vote."

Bill Oury started to say something and then he did not. There was a lot of making up Don Jesús had to do and he guessed Elías wouldn't be human if he didn't exact the last pound to the last ounce. And it was too late to start quarreling now. And in any case, there was little question who the men would choose, even if almost all of them were countrymen of Don Jesús.

And so on that afternoon on the bank of the Rillito a vote was taken to name the commander in chief of the campaign. The Papagos took no part in the voting. The Papagos were not in the least interested in who would have the title of commander.

All of the Americans voted for Bill Oury and some of the Mexicans voted for him as well, but all the other Mexicans raised their hands for Don Jesús.

"I accept the decision without reservation," Oury said immediately. "And I will obey without question whatever orders Don Jesús sees fit to give."

Don Jesús clasped Oury by the shoulders. "A thousand thanks, old friend. I know why I have been chosen. It is not that I am in any way superior to you as leader, Don Guillermo. Far from it! I am certain I was elected only because most of the men know that I am familiar with the area around Aravaipa Canyon, that I was in a fight there before." Don Jesús turned to the others. "But we will not lose the wisdom and experience and zeal of Don Guillermo. I ask him to serve as my second in command."

"Willingly," Oury said in a clear voice, tasting bile.

Don Jesús extended his hand and Oury took it and the men clasped each other for a long time.

Then Don Jesús began to give orders crisply and swiftly. He laid out the line of march in such an organized manner that Oury understood Elías had known from the start that he would be chosen leader and had made plans long before. Elías said he would ride at the head of the column and that the

Americans and Mexicans would follow him and that Oury would ride behind them at the forefront of the Papagos. Although Don Jesús had been elected *comandante*, the Papagos would follow only Don Guillermo. Chief Francisco would ride at Don Guillermo's side.

A little after six o'clock Don Jesús struck the trail of the Indians who had attacked San Xavier. The trail led through Cebadilla Pass and then down the slopes of the San Pedro. In the early evening they came upon the remains of the Apache with the missing tooth. The carcass, what was left of it, was against the rock where the Apache had been shot down. Vultures and coyotes had feasted. The scalp, which Bill Zeckendorf had hacked off in his pique, had been gnawed on by the carrion eaters.

Each man looked down soberly as he passed the slain Apache. The mutilated body seemed a kind of symbol. The Papagos, most of them on foot, looked at Enemy more intently than the others. The glaring skull became one with their own dead through the many years. The empty eyeholes told them they were on course. They gripped their clubs. They held rifles in their other hands but the clubs gave them their power.

Don Jesús led the column down the slope under the light of the moon. Shortly after midnight the moon set. Don Jesús announced that he could not follow the trail in darkness and he called a halt to the march.

Bill Oury thought it was hardly necessary for Don Jesús to maintain the fiction that he was actually following a trail that might lead anywhere. Everybody knew where he was going. The reason they were traveling this roundabout way was not to follow a trail that was more than a week old and was almost obliterated. They were going along this circuitous route instead of taking the direct Camp Grant Road from Tucson because it was necessary that they move in secrecy. The last thing anybody wanted was to be intercepted by a military patrol.

But if Don Jesús wanted to make it appear that he was following a trail, that was his business. Bill Oury ate cold rations with his Papago section and then unrolled his blanket and made himself comfortable. There were benefits at that at not having to run the show. He soon was in deep and untroubled sleep.

△ 4

At first light Don Jesús got the men up and on the way. He rode back and forth, driving the men along.

"*Vámanos! Vámanos!*" he cried out. "*Pronto, pronto, amigos, por amor de Dios!*"

He was very nervous. He wanted the men off the slope as quickly as possible. On that bare and shaley incline in the bright and clear Arizona daylight they were exposed for any eyes to see. The dust they raised was a signal that went out for miles. It could be picked up by bands of roving Apaches who would use their own infernal smoke signals to report to anyone who might be interested the size and direction of the armed detachment. Word could reach the Aravaipas and that meant word would reach Whitman. And if they were lucky enough to avoid Apache discovery there was always the military riding around.

"*Pronto, pronto, compañeros!*" he shouted.

He got the last of the men off the slope and down on the San Pedro bottoms before the sun was very high and there he called another halt. He gathered the Mexicans and the Americans and Chief Francisco around him. He knew the rest of the Papagos were not interested.

"By my estimate, we are approximately fifteen miles from the Aravaipa village," Don Jesús said in Spanish. "We will remain here during the hours of daylight, taking as much cover as possible, and move again after dark. We should reach our destination just about midnight."

This intelligence that they were so close to their foes stirred the men. Every man there had lost someone or something to the Apaches. Men were scarred, men limped. Everyone remembered.

They made themselves comfortable and accommodated themselves in their own ways on that clear Saturday, the twenty-ninth day of April, along the waters of the San Pedro. They talked and napped and ate Sammy Hughes' food and some of them had had the foresight to bring along decks of playing cards. There were games of monte and poker. Don Jesús had ordered that no fires be built, of course, but none was needed. It was pleasant whiling away the warm hours under the blanketing shade of the trees that lined the river. The Aravaipa village was waiting for them like a waiting woman.

The Papagos kept themselves apart from the others. They ate a little food and drank a little water. They were frugal with both. They would have preferred to have fasted. This was not the time to indulge in food, although the white man's food was good and there was much of it. The time for feasting and the other things would come later.

The Papagos who had marched on foot were no more tired than those who had ridden. The men on the horses had offered to change with the marchers many times but the marchers had refused. It was part of the discipline. And they were sustained more durably than by horses in the still rapture of the obligation they owed to every one of their blood who had ever died at Apache hands.

For each one of them, those who had ridden and those who had walked, this was to be just the latest battle, the newest date and story to record on the calendar sticks. The war with the Enemy had gone on for centuries, antedating even the war between the Spaniards and the Enemy. The Papagos had been fighting the Enemy longer than anybody and they had the most complete memories.

The war with the Enemy had lasted so long it was ancient history and it was at the same time today. There no longer were names. There were only numbers. Each Enemy killed was a cipher to be put on the calendar stick to be totaled against the sum of Papago dead and the account was so lopsided it would not be balanced if every Apache who walked the earth of Apacheria was on the instant put to death.

Off to one side, as indifferent to where they were at that

moment as they were to the minutes and the hours passing, or to the shine of the sun or the leafing of the trees or to the desert opening itself in its spring flowering, they sat quietly and held rifles in one hand, and that was a new feeling, and gripped their clubs in the other, and that was an old feeling, the oldest.

The clubs now were just artfully fashioned pieces of mesquite but they would be consecrated. When the triumphant young men, those who survived, all were prepared to die, returned to their villages they would be consecrated as well. Each man had left his village untried, untested, unknown even to himself. They would return Enemy Killers.

The comeliest girls would greet them as they returned in new austerity and would take the sanctified clubs from the hands of each Enemy Killer. The Enemy Killer had by decree and inviolable ceremony to purify himself and then he must find a suitable gift and redeem from the sightly maiden the club that had created him Enemy Killer.

It was all worked out long ago. Chief Francisco knew of it and all of the young men knew of it almost as fully. The instructions, to the final detail, were known to have come from the Spirit who guides everyone and everything, the Rule Maker, who makes plants grow and birds fly and animals run, who provides life for the River People and the Desert People and the Thirst Enduring People.

Soon after they were settled down Don Jesús said he would make a brief scout ahead to verify certain landmarks he would need to guide him in the dark. This was true. Don Jesús was meticulous on trail. He was as good as the Apache but he was different from the Apache. The Apache trailed by instinct as wolves trail and vultures trail from the air. Don Jesús had not that primitive, rooted skill. Don Jesús trailed successfully because he worked at it with the mind of a clever, civilized man.

But while it was correct for him to look a little ahead on the land, that was not the deep reason why he rode on and refused any company. He wanted no companion.

Don Jesús was in a state of exaltation. He had never before felt so pure and so open and so filled with life and his blood.

He needed to know all of it and by himself. He had felt something of this when he was a boy and first went to confession and felt in his hand the hand of God.

And he knew that God's hand was in his now. Each step in this crusade, from the time he had spoken to Chief Francisco, had proven that. His election as leader over the redoubtable Bill Oury, surely that was divinely arranged. The gathering on the Rillito, the passage over the trail through Cebadilla Pass, and then the skeletonized Apache to refresh each man, down the naked slopes unseen—each instance had worked in a perfection that could not have been achieved without the concurrence of God.

Even the heretical gringos had felt the pressure of His hand this time. The government of the Territory had itself sanctioned and given assistance to the crusade. And then, riding slowly, as alone as he might have been alone on earth, there came to Don Jesús a blinding revelation. The force was so great he reined his horse and trembled.

It came to him there that it was God's will that this cleansing should be done by True Believers, and that was why He had turned strong men into poltroons and had inspirited only enough heretics to serve as witnesses.

This truth stunned him and he remained in the saddle because he could not move. He was filled with his soul. It was a little while later that he dismounted and was alone with God. He knelt and prayed.

He prayed for the success of His undertaking and he prayed that there would not be many deaths among His people. There would be deaths. Whitman had said the Aravaipas had no guns but the latest Apache outrages belied him. The savages who had raided at San Xavier were armed with guns, and Alex McKinsey and the others were killed not by arrows but by bullets. Whitman either was lying or had been taken in. And he would lie to protect those Apaches. And he could be fooled by Eskiminzin.

There would be deaths among his countrymen but they could die in worse ways and he prayed to God to be merciful and to receive the souls of those whom He selected to die.

He prayed to Señor Jesucristo, he prayed to the Santa Madre de Dios, he prayed to the Santa Virgen de Guadalupe. He spoke the names of his martyred father and brothers and uncle. He spoke their names, Don Juan Bautista, Don Ramón, Don Cornelio, Don Ramón, again, and he prayed for their souls and he knew that their eyes as well as the eyes of God were on him.

△ 5

Don Jesús sought out Bill Oury when he returned to where the men were encamped. Don Jesús had come to know the loneliness of leadership and the distance it separated him from other men, but he did not forget that Bill Oury was an old friend.

He found Oury talking to DeLong and he dismounted and hunkered down with them. "We are on the right trail," he said. His eyes still glowed from the disclosure on the desert. "I followed it for more than two miles. I am confident that it will lead us to the Camp Grant Apaches and that we have fifteen miles to go, no more."

"And what if the trail leads away from Camp Grant?" DeLong asked.

"It will not," Don Jesús said.

"But if it did?"

Bill Oury looked at DeLong curiously. DeLong had been very quiet since they left the Rillito. DeLong was not much given to talk, true. He was into himself a great deal. But he had seemed to be quieter than usual.

"Anything on your mind, Sid?" Oury asked.

"Many things."

"Anything you want to talk about?"

"No."

Don Jesús, looking first to one and then the other, had no need to ask questions or to listen to what was going on in DeLong's mind. He knew what was going on in DeLong's mind. Gringos did not know how to hate. Gringos could get mad but they knew nothing about long hate. Gringos got violent, more violent than anyone, but it was of the moment. Gringos felt guilty about hating. Gringos knew nothing of the sweetness of hate. Don Guillermo came closer than anybody, perhaps, but then Don Guillermo spent a great deal of his time with Mexicans and he was married to one.

Don Jesús stood up and went among his own people.

The desert was in bloom. The cactus seemed almost ashamed of itself. All during the winter months the cactus was harsh, as though filled with anger. The land was forbidding and malevolent and fierce in its defense against encroachment, any encroachment, man, animal, bird. The cholla threw out its needles against anything that touched it. Cactus was thorny against all life that moved, as though protesting viciously at being rooted and bound.

But now the desert from its winter days and nights of execration turned girlish. Almost monochromatic during the winter, grays, dull whites, flat tans, it now was yellow and red and purple, and although the thorns were still there, the cactus appeared enticing and soft. The thorns were there, the jagged points were there, but they were camouflaged now as though this was a time of peace or at least armistice.

But all of the one hundred and forty-eight men there had seen this miracle many times and no one took any notice of the splendor around him.

Sidney DeLong walked off a little way to empty his bladder. Oury got up and followed him.

"You want to talk, Sid?" Oury asked.

DeLong shook his head.

"You want to say anything?"

"No."

"You asking yourself anything?" Oury asked. DeLong was a character. Had the idea he wanted to write books someday. People like Sid DeLong always made problems for themselves.

DeLong buttoned up his pants. "I don't know, Bill." He looked at Oury. "Bill, you feel sure we're doing the right thing." He made it a statement.

"This is a hell of a time to come up with that," Oury said.

DeLong nodded and started to walk back.

"Wait a minute," Oury said. "Sid, what the hell is eating you?"

"I don't know. Maybe it's just the way we're going about this."

"What way is that?"

"I don't know. The whole business seems—underhanded."

"Underhanded! For the love of God, Sid, what would you like us to do? Send them advance warning?"

DeLong shook his head.

"It's never right to take the law into your own hands," Oury said. "Not a man here but wishes the damned cavalry was out doing its proper job, and not us."

△ △ △ FIVE

△ 1

The long, narrow retail establishment of Tully & Ochoa was noisy and jammed on that Saturday shopping day. Everything was in its normal happy mess. Clothing, boots, hardware, liquor, tobacco, ribbons, materials for dresses and petticoats, and everything else for sale had been dumped as usual on the counters in a masterpiece of disarrangement. After the customers picked up things and examined them and put them down again the store looked as though it had accommodated a tornado.

Everybody in the Old Pueblo loved it just that way. Everybody loved to go to the big stores and poke around. In the delightful confusion everybody met everybody they knew and for a time people could forget about the Apaches and imagine they were leading ordinary civilized lives.

People, mostly women and youngsters that day, pushed past Captain Dunn coming and going. He felt like a top spinning around.

"What do you think, dear?" Harriet Dunn held up the white dress.

Captain Dunn brushed his neat mustache and executed a tactical maneuver to avoid an enormous woman barreling down the tight aisle. He made a business of inspecting the white dress.

"Please, Thomas," Harriet said. "Please look at it properly. Do you prefer this to the pink?"

"Yes, Daddy, please take this seriously," Lizzie Dunn pleaded. "You always have that funny look on your face."

Captain Dunn could hardly hear them in the talking and shouting but he made a determined effort to concentrate on the two dresses. He knew it was important. Lizzie, turning eighteen, her face as pretty as an opening rose, wasn't exactly an Army brat any more. She was a young woman and he knew that in a dismal, filthy, end-of-the-line place like Tucson a ball was an important matter. As a point of fact he knew he ought to thank the good Lord there were these diversions. There was precious little else.

"Well," Harriet stated politely.

Harriet, Lord Love her, knows the drill, Captain Dunn thought. She had been an Army wife a long time and she never would raise her voice, not in public, not in front of civilians.

"Well, Daddy?" Lizzie said.

Captain Dunn pursed his lips and considered. He backed away as a man walked past him. The man tipped his hat to the captain's lady and to the captain's daughter and nodded to the captain.

Then the man said to a wildly harassed clerk, "Tell Mr. DeLong I'm here." He spoke with a rolling Scottish burr.

"Mr. DeLong isn't here, Mr. MacKenzie," the clerk said, defending himself against three customers. "Several people have been asking for him."

MacKenzie looked around as though an ill-considered joke were being played on him. "What do you mean he's not here, lad? This is Saturday, is it not, now?"

The clerk, involved with a woman holding an armful of ribbon, twisted his head and nodded.

"Sent word to me more than a week ago to come in to see him this morning," MacKenzie said, scratching his chin. "He said it was very important. This is Saturday, April the twenty-ninth, is it not, laddie?"

"All day, Mr. MacKenzie," the clerk said brightly.

"When do you expect him then?"

"I don't know, sir. He was not here yesterday either." The clerk was dragged off by a woman with a cluster of children.

MacKenzie turned to Captain Dunn. "Now I've come all the way up from Calabasas. Mr. DeLong never did anything like this before. He is reliable." He shrugged. "Well, lad," he called out to the clerk, "I'll be over to Charlie Brown's." He winked at Captain Dunn. "No reason to make the journey altogether for naught, now is there, Captain?" He ambled out of the store.

"Thomas," Harriet said. She had the patient patience in her voice now, one step beyond plain patience.

Captain Dunn made the command decision. "The white. Without question, the white." He smiled gently at his daughter. "You'll look like an angel in the white dress. I think I'll pop into Charlie Brown's myself."

"Thomas," Harriet said.

"There's a good girl," Dunn said. "Just tell them to put the dress on our account. The white one, now, absolutely the white. And white shoes to go with it."

Dunn walked out of the store. He knew he could depend on Harriet. Another wife might have started arguing with him but Harriet would choke before she did anything unseemly.

Out in the street he saw the tall figure of MacKenzie headed for the Congress Hall. Curious. DeLong had integrity. Quiet sort of man. People respected him. Some said he was going to be the next mayor. Why would he bring in a man from his ranch and then not show up?

Dunn walked down the street to Jake Mansfeld's news store. He had the odd feeling that the men there were talking about something when he walked in, and then stopped. Not that there were many men there, few of the familiar faces. Were they looking at him in a quirky way? The people in this benighted town always were complaining about the Army but he generally got along. Maybe it was in his mind. He picked up a copy of the *Arizonan* and left. The men were civil enough in bidding him goodbye.

Dunn walked to the Congress Hall, the dust settling on his boots, shined to brilliance that morning by his striker. The town felt like Sunday. Now why would he think that? The stores were open.

"Petra said Hiram was out of town somewhere," a man at the bar was saying when Dunn entered the Congress Hall. "Didn't say where."

The man next to him opened his mouth to say something

and saw Dunn and shut it. All the men at the bar turned and looked at the captain. He said hello and some of them said hello and then they turned back to the bar. MacKenzie, having just downed a glass, waggled a finger at him and Dunn waggled back. Dunn took his own drink to a table and sat down. It seemed a lot of faces were missing at the Congress Hall, too. There was a big hole in the air that Bill Oury usually filled. Dunn looked at the *Arizonan*. His eye was caught by a story that had to do with the Aravaipas at Camp Grant. It was a crime against decent people that those bloody savages were being coddled. ". . . *Would it not be well for the citizens of Tucson to give the Camp Grant wards a slight entertainment to the music of about a hundred double-barreled shotguns?*"

Dunn sipped a little of his whiskey and lit a cigar. He wondered how Whitman was progressing with his "wards."

A man entered the saloon. "Where the hell is everybody around here?" he demanded of the entire room. He started to say more and spotted Dunn and went to the bar without another word.

Captain Dunn looked at the story in the *Arizonan* again and then it occurred to him just what it was that might be going on. He finished his drink and left the saloon. He thought he knew why the town felt like Sunday and why DeLong hadn't kept his appointment and why Petra Stevens' husband was off somewhere.

He went back to Tully & Ochoa. Harriet looked up, pleased. She had not expected him back so soon.

"You can help decide on the shoes, Thomas," she said.

"I have to go to the post."

Tucson, A.T., April 29, 1871

CAPTAIN:

I am informed that a body of citizens have organized for the purpose of *massacring* all Indians at your post. *You have it*—attend to it.

(Sgd) THOS. S. DUNN
Capt. 21 Infantry
Comdg. Camp Lowell

Dunn folded the note and handed it to Sergeant Clarke. "Take another man and get out to Camp Grant as quickly as you can. Give this to the commanding officer. If Captain Stanwood isn't there, give it to Lieutenant Whitman."

"Yes, sir."

"Fast, Clarke."

"Yes, sir."

The sergeant, a burly, wide-shouldered man, rushed out of the office and Dunn sat back and lit a fresh cigar. With everything that had been going on in Tucson why had it taken him so damned long to figure it out?

△ 2

Sergeant Gregory Clarke didn't like to sweat horses that way. Sergeant Clarke was an Irishman with an Irishman's love of horses and these were good horses, he'd picked the best, and he didn't like to work them this way, not in this heat. This was no day for pushing horses this way.

But Captain Dunn had been explicit and Sergeant Clarke was an experienced trooper and he would ride the horses until they fell dead from under them both and if that happened they would go on foot.

He didn't think that Trooper Kennedy would make it on foot, not very far. Trooper Francis Kennedy was the first man Clarke had seen after he ran out of the captain's office, and he grabbed him. Kennedy was scared to hell riding in the open country with just one other man. Kennedy was still a recruit. This would be good for him. Only Sergeant Clarke did not believe Kennedy would go very far on foot if that was how it had to be.

The sun was turned on all the way now and the slaver and sweat whipped back on them and the dust kicked up a storm and Sergeant Clarke knew they were sending out invitations to Apaches.

The earth was pulverized rock, harder than a proper road,

and the hooves made sounds like little cracked bells and the heat lay on all of them, men and horses. All Sergeant Clarke hoped was that if they were jumped by Apaches the Indians' ponies would be jaded, too.

The two soldiers entered Cañada del Oro and then Sergeant Clarke thought, Oh, Holy Mother of God, because he saw men ahead of him and they held rifles and the sun was in his eyes and he couldn't make them out right away, and then he saw that they were Americans and he thought, thank you, Lord, thank you.

There were about eight of the men and they were lined up facing the oncoming troopers and they held their guns as though they planned to use them, which puzzled Sergeant Clarke and made Trooper Kennedy want to turn around and go home.

When they pulled up in front of the men, one of them stepped forward. Sergeant Clarke recognized him immediately. He was Hiram Stevens, one of the important merchants in Tucson.

Stevens smiled pleasantly. "Get down, gentlemen," he said. Nobody who ever heard that resonant voice forgot it.

"Can't do that, Mr. Stevens," Sergeant Clarke said. "We're on our way to Camp Grant."

"Yes, I know, Sergeant. But I think you'll take a little rest first."

"We're under orders, Mr. Stevens," Sergeant Clarke said. "Captain Dunn said to get there as fast as we could."

"Not for a while, Sergeant." The smile never left Stevens' face.

Sergeant Clarke looked to the right and to the left. The men looked like they meant business.

"Get down," Stevens said again.

For a moment Sergeant Clarke thought about breaking through that line but he had never known a horse that could outrun a bullet. He dismounted. Trooper Kennedy, who looked as though he didn't know whether to feel intercepted or rescued, dropped down, too.

"I'll take your guns," Stevens said.

Again Sergeant Clarke hesitated. "What's all this for, Mr. Stevens?"

"The guns, please."

"You know we're under orders, Mr. Stevens."

"You said that."

"You know you're breaking the law, stopping us this way."

"The guns, please."

Sergeant Clarke took out his revolver and handed it, grip forward, as was proper, to Stevens. Kennedy did the same. Some of the other men had already taken care of the rifles in the saddle holsters.

"You going to tell me why you're doing this, Mr. Stevens?" Sergeant Clarke asked.

"It's only what you know that can hurt you, Sergeant," Hiram Stevens said affably. "Now both you gentlemen just make yourselves comfortable."

Sergeant Clarke sat down with Trooper Kennedy. Kennedy was blissful. Sergeant Clarke had no idea what this was all about. He had no idea what was in the message Captain Dunn had given him. It had to be important because Captain Dunn didn't like to break down horses either. He wondered what he would do if Mr. Stevens and the others decided to search him. What could he do?

Hiram Stevens made himself comfortable in another shady place in the canyon. He had to hand it to Bill Oury. When Lum Skettle gave him the note he thought Uncle Billy was going a little too far. He thought this vigilante business must be going to Uncle Billy's head.

"*Send a party to Cañada del Oro, the main road from Tucson to Camp Grant, with orders to stop any and all persons going toward Camp Grant until 7 o'clock A.M. of April 30th.*" That was what Bill Oury had written and by God, Uncle Billy had hit it right on the nose, hadn't he?

Mr. Stevens and all the other men had been friendly enough and they had shared food and coffee and afterward whiskey, and since Sergeant Clarke worked it out that he was in fact not on duty now, he had accepted the whiskey. Kennedy said he didn't drink, which caused Sergeant Clarke to have grave doubts as to both his sanity and his future. There was no unpleasantness of any kind, and Mr. Stevens had sat up with his rifle across his knees and then he had wakened another man to stand guard. Nobody had any idea of tying Sergeant Clarke and Trooper Kennedy. Nobody would go that far against an American uniform.

But it was funny anyway to Sergeant Clarke. To be guarded like that as though he had been captured by the enemy. And these were all Americans like himself. He had seen most of them around town in Tucson. It was funny. He pondered on it.

It wasn't funny to Kennedy. It wasn't anything to Francis Kennedy. Kennedy was sound asleep. Kennedy felt safe and protected and lucky and he fell asleep before anybody else.

The second man to stand guard walked back and forth in the moonlight and smoked a cigar and kept his eyes bright and active, turning his head this way and that, taking a snort now and again against the chill night air, and then he sat down, and that was his mistake, Sergeant Clarke saw right away. Walking would have kept him awake; any soldier who had ever done guard duty could have told him that. Soon the man's head fell and then jerked up again. The man got up and shook himself awake but then after a little he sat down again and his head fell again and then he was snoring along with all the others, including Trooper Francis Kennedy.

Sergeant Clarke got to his feet slowly. He thought about waking Kennedy and rejected that out of hand. He thought about lifting the guard's rifle. He thought about that a little longer. He didn't much fancy riding alone and unarmed in Apacheria. He gazed for a long time at the sleeping guard.

In the end he rejected pinching the rifle, too, and he walked as lightly as his bulk and the darkness allowed toward where the horses were tethered and he prayed to God and to His Mother and to a saint or two who came to mind that none of the horses would whinny. There would be no problem putting his hands on his own big bay. He had noticed earlier that while his captors had removed the saddles from their own horses they had merely loosened the Army cinches. Sergeant Clarke had had it in mind to raise an objection to this rampant demonstration of antimilitary prejudice but then for a reason not at the time clear to him he did not.

Now he located his horse almost immediately. None of the animals made any sound. They spooked only at Indian smell, not at the decent scent, mixed with a little nervousness and a little whiskey, of a good, God-loving Irishman.

He tightened the girth and led his horse away from the other horses, aware that in this season of the year the rattlers, unable to adjust to the heat of the day, roamed at night. When he decided he was far enough away from the camp he climbed aboard and kicked the bay and the horse bolted forward and he heard a shout behind him. He ducked his head so close to the horse's strong neck that the mane whipped at his face and he kicked the bay again and when no shots were fired and no bullets caught up with him he knew nothing was going to catch up, not now, not with this animal after five or six hours' rest.

Sergeant Clarke rode fast into the night on the rejuvenated mount and he didn't hear anybody in back of him and he wondered, as he had wondered all evening, what the hell was going on, why he had been stopped by other Americans and held prisoner. No matter. Now he was again obeying orders. He was so relieved to be doing what he had for years been trained to do it escaped his mind entirely that he had nothing to do battle with against any new adversaries but the good, strong hands his Irish father had bequeathed to him.

△ △ △ S I X

△ 1

The ceremony had not been performed for a long time. A big
fire had to burn for three days and three nights before the
ceremony. For many seasons the people couldn't stay in one
place and hang around a fire for all that time. That was over
with now.

Santo chose Delchan to be in charge of the fire. Delchan
ordered men to gather wood. Delchan told the men how to
arrange the wood. Delchan never let go of his rifle as he supervised the men. Naco was his assistant policeman now and he
saw to it that the men brought in enough wood. The fire was
started and after that Delchan had to stay there and keep it
going.

When the fire was burning in a good, healthy way, Santo
took the ritual shirts and moccasins out of the parfleche and
gave them to the four young men he had selected to enact the
ceremony. The buckskin shirts and moccasins had been in the
parfleche so long people had forgotten they were there. The
young men Santo had picked out had to be very careful with
them. The garments were stiff and creased. The men unfolded
them with reverence. They were excited but they did not show
it. They were to become important men and they had to be
modest.

Santo watched little patches of dried paint flake off the
shirts as the men spread them out. He did not like to see that.
It was not very good. Things had to be a certain way and had
to be kept that way. He would have to repaint the shirts when
the ceremony was over. Now that the people were settled, the
ceremony would be made more often. Maybe he would make
new shirts.

Santo was feeling good. While he had had reservations about the move Eskiminzin had made he now was getting to think maybe it might work out after all. Maybe they could have more of the old ceremonies. The puberty rite, for instance. That took four days and there was hardly anyone who remembered it anymore.

As the men flattened out the shirts and Delchan stood guard with his rifle cradled in his arms, Santo rolled a leaf of tobacco into a tight, stringy cigar. He lit the cigar with a brand from the fire and puffed smoke to the Directions. He had not gone through these preparations in a very long time but he had forgotten nothing.

He watched and approved the delicacy with which the men handled the shirts. There was a lot of talk that the young people didn't believe in the old customs, that they laughed at them. These four men were not laughing now. They had just the right expressions on their faces. They looked proud and modest and Delchan looked as though he believed he was performing the most important duty of his life.

Each man picked up his shirt and moccasins and followed Santo. Delchan stayed at the fire. He walked all around the fire and made sure it was burning evenly. Naco told men to collect more wood.

Santo led the four young men across the creek and up the bluff on the other side. He instructed them exactly how to spread out the shirts on the ground and how to place the moccasins below them. Then he instructed them how to build the wickiup. After the men put the dwelling together Santo rolled and lit another cigar and puffed smoke to the Directions. Then he told the men how to make the masks. The masks could not be preserved the way the shirts and moccasins were. The masks of one ceremony could never be used again. The masks had to be made new each time and destroyed right after the ceremony.

The masks were helmets. The skins had been kneaded with deer brains by Santo and were soft and pliable. The men threaded drawstrings to tighten the masks around their necks and then cut slits for the eyes. Under Santo's guidance the men made slats into a frame. Some of the slats jutted upright and some at angles and they were held in place by horizontal slats and the frame was fixed into the top of the mask. The slats were more than a foot long. The men tied little pieces of wood to the slats. The little pieces of wood dangled and rattled.

After all that was done Santo told the men just what to paint on the masks. That was the most important part. Santo was still worried about how the paint had come off the shirts and he didn't want anything else to go wrong with the markings. He watched over the men carefully.

When the men were finished with the masks Santo told the men to put on the shirts and moccasins. He was gratified to see that they were still in awe of the shirts and they put them on mindfully and very little more paint fell off.

Santo lit another cigar he had twisted thin. He told the men to face east. He puffed smoke to that Direction.

"The great Black Mountain Spirit lives inside the Star Mountain," Santo said. *"He can be seen to the East under the heavens. The design of his body is fixed and unchanging and the big stars have created the uprights of his headdress. The Mountain Spirit rattles his headdress as he dances around the fire and drives away diseases. He sends away all evil and brings good."*

The four men listened. They were affected. This pleased Santo. The old words still had power. He hadn't liked to see the little bits of the symbols floating off the shirts. Each little fleck diminished the power by just that amount. But there was enough left in the shirts and the words had power and now there was peace and the people didn't have to run from here to there and fires could be lit day and night. He decided at that moment that he would not try to refurbish the shirts. He would make the new ones.

From then on, until the time of the ceremony, the four men were kept in the wickiup, isolated from everybody else. They had to eat special food and they could not speak, not even among themselves.

On the night of the ceremony, Santo instructed the four men how to paint their arms and legs. There were the signs of

Lightning and the moon sign of White Painted Lady and there was Holos, the sun. There were other designs, the meanings of which only Santo knew and which he would not impart to any man because they formed much of his power.

"*The Holy Mountain,*" Santo sang, "*the Holy Mountain, there it is and in its middle, in its body, there stands a brush-built hut. This brush-built hut is for the Mountain Spirit. This is what he says.*"

The four men were transfixed. The words were going into them and the words had all their power.

Santo looked down from the bluff to which he had brought the four men. He could see the village. He could see the big fire that Delchan had tended without sleeping. He could see Delchan circling the fire with his rifle in his arms and he could see the people moving about. The people were excited. They had not started drinking *tiswin* yet. They were not allowed to until the ceremony was over. But they were all a little drunk on what it all meant and what they remembered of it and what it promised them for today and tomorrow.

"*This is what the Mountain Spirit in his brush-built hut in the Holy Mountain says,*" Santo chanted. " '*In these moccasins flash Lightning. I am Lightning, flashing and blazing. There is life here in this headdress, in the noise of its pendants there is life. The noise is heard and it sounds and my song is around these dancers and protects them.'* "

A little distance away a fifth man was getting ready for his part in the ceremony. He was the clown and the devil and the enemy all at the same time. Santo had given him his instructions briefly and had left him. Santo knew he did not have to hang around with Evil. Santo knew that Evil knew how to take care of himself.

△ 2

On that Saturday, the next to the last day of April of that year, Ghost Face was gone from the land but at night his memory hung around. The wind from the Galiuros carried his cold teeth. Little Eagles had arrived but at night the old man's memory hung around.

But on that night the Dark Canyon People felt good. They felt good because the big fire made fun of Ghost Face and took away his strength. They felt good because they were back on the bank of Little Running Water and because of what had happened to them. They felt good because the women and the children and the old people were safe now.

The fire told the big story, of course. Fires always told the horse soldiers where they were out on the desert or up in the mountains and where they slept. Fires asked the horse soldiers to come and kill them. Now the horse soldiers knew where they were and there was no fighting and for some time there had been no killing.

And—and this was something some of the people still could not get used to—there was the chief of the horse soldiers right there with their own chief, sitting right there by the fire, waiting for the ceremony to start. Not even the oldest person there could remember anything like that.

Eskiminzin said, "You are making a joke. Nothing can be so big." Eskiminzin laughed heartily so that everybody would understand he could take a joke played on himself.

"It is bigger than that," Whitman said.

Eskiminzin laughed again. "Days and nights and days and nights and the land is still there?" He was glad the *nantan* was poking fun at him. Only close friends did that.

"It is more than that," Whitman said. "For the people who travel in the covered wagons from the East it takes many months."

As the Puma translated the words Eskiminzin began to believe that perhaps the soldier chief was not teasing him after all. But it was hard to believe there was so much land. And if there was all that land, what had made the white people come here?

The whole family was sitting there getting warm from the fire, waiting to see something they had not seen in a long time. Small Woman was nursing the new baby, who had been named

Chita. Chita was a healthy baby with a good appetite. By then her ears had been pierced so that she would always have good hearing and tiny turquoise earrings hung from them. Fawn and Road Runner were with their mother. Road Runner was in high spirits. Even though too much attention had been paid to the stupid new sister, he had not been ignored. The white medicine man had come around to look at his wound every day and had changed the bandage every day. Road Runner's dog was there but it was not lying around sleeping as usual. It sensed the excitement in the air and it moved around sniffing.

Child Mother was there with her two daughters. Ria was crawling around. Star was a happy little girl. She laughed a lot, especially tonight. Child Mother was making a buckskin jacket for Chita. She had sewed on quail heads, arrow points, quartz crystals, shell beads and pine twigs, all good things to ward off bad luck and disease. Eskiminzin had made himself a necklace charm—cholla, to make the baby healthy; corn for good luck; and spots of red paint to make Chita grow up strong.

Surgeon Brierly studied the little jacket and the necklace charm. He would have given a great deal to be able to write each detail down in his pad. But he remembered Victor Ruiz's warning and he respected it, so he just looked and tried to memorize what he saw.

Melana and Daya were there. Daya was bright-eyed as usual. She looked at everything. She didn't miss anything. Melana looked most of the time at Whitman. She watched him when he was not looking. She knew that some white men took on Indian women and some loved them and some even married them. She wondered what Whitman thought about her. She knew she was not good enough for such an important man to want to marry.

"Are there other places as big as Tucson?" Eskiminzin asked.

Now it was Whitman's turn to laugh. "Tucson is a small village. There are places where Americans live in which a hundred Tucsons would be lost."

Eskiminzin said nothing. He was getting to think that maybe Whitman was poking fun at him, as he had thought at the beginning. He hoped the *nantan* was making jokes. That would mean he had peace of mind and was relaxed and that in turn would mean that he was not being criticized by the star *nantan* for what he was doing with the Aravaipas.

"I see you believe every word I have said," Whitman said.

Eskiminzin looked startled and then he smiled and then he stopped smiling. He did not know what to say or how to look.

"In some of these places we call cities many times one hundred thousand people live together." Whitman had by then learned that the Apaches had invented a sophisticated system of counting that went as high as 100,000 but no higher.

Eskiminzin looked polite. He decided that was the best response to the *nantan's* jokes.

Melana leaned forward. "Please speak again of the houses that float on water." Her voice was low as always and musical and she gazed directly at Whitman, which she could do without embarrassment because she was asking something of him. Whitman had become the most important thing in Melana's life. She worshiped him. Child Mother had explained to her that Whitman had done all those things for the people because within himself he was a greater chief than he appeared to be. Melana knew that no one so important would have anything to do with an Indian girl.

"The ships?" Whitman looked at Melana, at the shadows and lights from the fire passing over her face. He thought how comely she was and how womanly and how good it would be to sleep with her. Her hair glowed and her full lips were parted and she smelled of fresh mint.

"Yes," Melana said. She saw the expression on Whitman's face and she thought it was tender. She lowered her eyes. She had rubbed the mint under her arms and between her breasts, which was what women did to please their husbands. Although Aravaipa men had spoken to her she was able to see no man since the first time she had looked on Whitman.

"They are like great floating houses," Whitman said. The Puma had told him he knew of no word in the Apache language for a ship. "They are built of wood and they float on the water and hundreds of people live in them as they cross the great water."

"How many days does it take to cross this water?" Melana asked.

"Many. Many, many days."

"Is there so much water?"

"Yes."

"Always?"

"Always?" Whitman was puzzled.

"Even during the dry times?" Melana was blushing. She had never before dominated the conversation with Whitman.

"The dry times." Whitman understood now. "There are no dry times on this great water."

Road Runner stood up and walked over to Whitman. He was so fascinated that he neglected to limp. "What is on the other side of the water?"

"Another land," Whitman said. "As great as this land, greater. It is where the white people came from originally."

Eskiminzin thought how much better it would have been if they had remained there. "Where does that land end?"

"In more water, in that direction." Whitman waved his hand toward the west. "One can travel toward the rising sun and cross our land and then get into one of the floating houses and cross the great water to the other land and then travel across the other land and then cross a new great water and come back here."

Eskiminzin laughed even more robustly. Of course this was the biggest joke of all. He had not known white men had this humor, so much like Apache humor. He was glad they had. If people laughed with each other they usually did not kill. He had not been familiar with any white man.

"It is where I come from," Whitman said, staring into the fire. "I was born on land near this great water. One can stand on rocks at the edge of this land and look out on the water and see nothing beyond it, just water to the place where the water joins the sky."

He was not surprised that they listened to this in wonderment and only half believed. After all this time in the West he was beginning to wonder too and almost to half believe. Had he ever truly walked along the edge of the sea, with the horizon like a whip-crack, and listened to the squawking gulls and smelled the biting brine that tingled in his nose like champagne?

"The water stretches away like the desert, all the way to the meeting with the sky, and sometimes there are great storms and the water rises and smashes against the rocks at the edge of the land and it makes a great noise and the little houses on the water are tossed forth and back and some of them are smashed against the rocks."

Surgeon Brierly could see the patent dubiety on the faces of the Apaches and to support Whitman he nodded his head vigorously. Eskiminzin and his family were glad to see that. They always liked to see the black spade beard bobbing up and down. And the white medicine man had removed his hat so that his great bald dome was showing and that made it even better.

Road Runner was staring at Whitman. His eyes were so wide they seemed to take up most of the space on his face. "What happens to the big houses on the water, those that are far away from the rocks?"

"If the storm is bad enough sometimes they break into pieces and sink into the water," Whitman said.

"What happens to the people in them?"

"Some of them may be saved in smaller water houses attached to the big water house. Some may drown."

The Puma was hard put to get all this into a language that didn't have the suitable words. He managed as best he could and Eskiminzin began to have the feeling that Whitman was not making jokes after all. Because plainly this great water the *nantan* had spoken of was disturbed by nothing less than Spirits. What else would have the power to make water stand up and break houses and make noise? And since Eskiminzin knew no intelligent man would talk carelessly about Spirits or make up stories about them, he concluded that Whitman must be telling the simple truth.

Whitman picked up Road Runner and sat him on his lap, making a business of showing great care for the wound. "One day perhaps some of you will see all that," Whitman said, his eyes on the fire again, seeing it again there, smelling the sea in the smell of mesquite. He turned his eyes to Road Runner, who was gazing at him adoringly. "Perhaps it will be you," he said. "Perhaps when you are a man the world will be different. Perhaps there will not be so much hate. Perhaps everybody will be able to travel everywhere and there will be no killing. Perhaps you can journey to the East and see all the things I have told you about, the big villages and the great water and the houses that float."

Eskiminzin knew for certain now that Whitman was not joking in the slightest. No man would lie to a child. And when he came to that judgment he sat back stunned at the wonder of the world.

Surgeon Brierly jumped up then, surprising everybody. Surgeon Brierly had been looking around for Little Captain all evening and now he spotted him. He ran over to Little Captain. Victor Ruiz pulled himself to his feet and followed. Little Captain was not happy to see the surgeon. Little Captain knew what that was all about.

"I have those squash seeds," Surgeon Brierly said.

"I will get them from you one day," Little Captain said.

"I have them with me now," Brierly said, reaching into his pocket.

"I will take them later," Little Captain said.

Brierly took the packet of seeds out of his pocket. "Take them now and plant them tomorrow!"

Everybody was watching. Everybody liked to see the *nantan* medicine man get excited. They started to laugh and some of them clapped their hands. Little Captain knew they were laughing not at him but at the white medicine man but still he did not relish being part of any situation where people laughed so he grabbed the packet from Brierly's hand and hoped that would quiet Brierly down. He looked at the little bag and considered throwing it into the fire but the fire was not an ordinary one that night. He slipped it into the pocket made by the fold in one of his knee-high moccasins. Maybe if he walked around a lot the thing would fall out and get lost.

"Stubborn man," Brierly muttered to Whitman as he sat down again.

Melana wanted to go on talking with Whitman. She had never been so happy. There were all kinds of little things flying around inside her. She started to say something and she hoped the little things would not fly out and embarrass her but she was arrested by a shriek. It came out of the dark like the scream of a wild bird.

Everybody stopped talking. Brierly and Whitman were jolted erect. Road Runner got off Whitman's lap and scurried over to his father, who took him in his arms. Ria and Star looked petrified. Then the screech came out of the night a second time and the people began to scream back.

Small Woman and Child Mother and Melana and Daya rose on their knees and Whitman and Brierly listened to them make sounds that were not words, that were not human sounds. The sounds could have come from anywhere and anything. The sounds could have been the wind or the rain.

Whitman looked at Eskiminzin. The Apache now held Road Runner close to his chest and he was not making any of the sounds but his face had changed.

Now the hooded men were in front of the fire. They came out of the night as if they had on that instant been conjured into being. There was no approach. They were there. They had not been there and now they were there.

The masked dancers leaped into the air. They contorted and twisted their bodies so that they lost human form. The loose pendants of wood on their latticed headdresses clattered like hail on a wall. The people watched. The light from the fire, moving around, making unmoving things move, gave a sense of delirium. The people kept crying out. They cried out their fears and the way they wanted things to be.

The hooded men vaulted upward. They defied natural law. At the highest points in their leaps their hoods lost themselves in the night and for a moment each time they were headless bodies and the rattling of the pendants came from elsewhere.

Whitman received the sight and the sounds as a personal assault. He was under a bombardment. He told himself in reflex defense that he was no part of this, that this was a rite of a primitive people, that he was a spectator. It was no good to remind himself of his name and his uniform and his origin. It was too strong. He gave up and let what was happening to him have its way.

He glanced at Brierly. The surgeon was spellbound. Whitman knew that Brierly would not have been able to collect himself and put down notes on his pad even if he were given permission to do so.

Now there was a new element. The man who was the clown and the devil and the Enemy all in one leaped into the firelight swinging a long stick with its own rattles. He mocked the hooded men. He made as though to attack them. He defied them and he defied the people. The people shouted at him because he was peril. Although there were four of the hooded men and only one of him, he had the power of evil and the question that had to be settled was who was going to win. Who was going to be defeated and driven away?

The masked dancers and the evil one jumped around and rasping sounds tore out of their throats and the people screeched and Whitman wondered how much more of this anyone could take. His nerves felt as though they were being sandpapered. His ears ached and he wanted to cup them with his hands. His eyes had seen enough.

It was all there in front of him in the light from the fire, all of it, good and evil in their most ancient form, the old fight that started when the angel Satan rebelled against God and tumbled from heaven to eternal damnation. It was that, the root, the source, the naked beginning, and it was prayer and it was exorcism and it was all the violence he had ever known, war and the sea in its greatest anger and the merciless nor'easter that scourged the place where he was born. It was all there in the Arizona night in the firelight and the moon watching from the middle of the stars and he wondered how much longer it could go on before something else happened, before people came apart, and then the four hooded dancers found their joint power and they descended on Evil and Evil fought back with his rattling stick and then Evil curled his neck and turned and ran away like a whipped cur and the people sobbed and gave thanks for their deliverance.

Whitman sagged. There didn't seem to be enough air around. He looked at Brierly. The surgeon was pale and drained. His head was moving slowly from side to side as though he was remembering what he had seen and felt and did not believe it. Whitman turned his eyes to Eskiminzin. The Apache's face seemed to have been purified by a kind of personal suffering. Road Runner clung to him, his back to what had been going on. Whitman looked at the women. They were emptied. It was all out of them. Melana's face was heavy and spent and her eyes had nothing behind them.

But it was not yet over, not quite. The story had been told and the victory had been won and the evil one had been reconsigned but there was a final note. As the four hooded men worshiped the fire from the four Directions, marking the victory of the Aravaipas against all their enemies and the enemies to come, there came from the darkness that had birthed everything that night a new sound, a beating of drums and gourds, a sound as simple and natural and inexplicable as the rumble of thunder.

And over that new sound Santo appeared and there was a long, slow sigh from the people like a rush of surf and Santo took his position among the four standard-bearers and he chanted the solemnization of the defeat and the salvation and then none of the men was there, not the masked dancers, not Santo. They went back into the dark air from which they had come and the beating of the drums and the gourds and the clacking of the wooden pendants went with them.

They were gone, all of them, until that day when the people needed them again.

△ 3

The social dancing got under way after a while. The men started filling up with *tiswin*. Delchan, who had not lain down on his pallet for three nights, stalked around on patrol to make sure nobody got out of hand. Naco assisted him but Naco had no rifle and he was nowhere as big as Delchan.

Small Woman and Child Mother had recovered quickly from the emotion of the masked dancers. Daya was livelier than Whitman had ever seen her. The children were all themselves again and the baby, Chita, slept.

Melana was taking longer to find herself, Whitman saw. Her eyes were wide and she blinked like a child. She looked around as though she were just learning how to see. She looked at Whitman as though he were the first thing she had ever seen.

She was still on her knees and she swayed a little and Whitman reached over and took her hand. Her hand was not soft. Her hand was firm from the work in the fields and all the other work, but it was small and he held it. He held it and her eyes became even larger and then he released it and she no longer swayed. He looked away. He felt he had held a small bird in his hand.

Somewhere out of the light of the fire men now started scraping Apache fiddles and twanging Jew's harps and beating rhythm on drums. Other men with them sang old songs. The sounds came out of the desert emptiness like a wind, like the ruffle of wings of unseen birds, like the ripple and splash of Little Running Water. It was big all around out there and the sounds came in.

The dancing men and women faced one another in long lines. They held their arms folded across their chests. They moved back and forth slowly, coming close to one another and then backing away, the way people live their lives. When they came close they smiled a little but they did not touch, not in front of the others. The men were putting away plenty of *tiswin* but they kept their arms folded and they never touched the women.

Eskiminzin rolled a cigarette. He was worried about the drinking. Everything was all right now but from old habit he did not like to see the men drink too much. But they had worked hard for a long time gathering grass for the soldiers' horses and this was a large night and maybe it was not too bad. But many of them would have stones rolling in their heads tomorrow.

Eskiminzin lit his cigarette with one of the matches Whitman had given him. Eskiminzin smoked cigarettes one after the other but he rarely wasted a match. He lit cigarettes from cigarettes or he took a brand from a fire or used flint. But he wanted to mark the importance of this night and he was extravagant with a match. When he finished lighting the cigarette he flipped away the match as though it were nothing, as though he used matches all the time.

Now Little Captain and his family joined them. Little Captain sat as far away as he could from Surgeon Brierly. Little Captain had moved around a lot that evening but the seeds had not fallen out of his moccasin pocket. Well, maybe they still would.

Santo joined them. The old man didn't appear to be tired at all, after everything that had happened and after all his arduous preparations. He looked refreshed. He looked like he wanted to have ceremonies all the time.

Eskiminzin gestured toward the dancers. "This is the way the people know who they are," he said to Whitman.

Whitman nodded. Surgeon Brierly leaned closer to listen. Small Woman and Child Mother nodded their agreement, too. Little Captain grunted. Santo took his pipe out of his mouth and put it back again. Daya's shoulders twitched in time to the music. She would have liked to be dancing but that would not be fitting. Melana just kept her eyes on Whitman. Her hand never would feel the same again.

Whitman felt very good. He looked around and it made him feel good to see how the people looked. Eskiminzin was in his deer hides, of course. But the women all wore new clothing made of manta, cloth they had earned working in the fields, and the men looked good, too, and some of them wore new shirts and pants they had bought from the sutler. The people looked as though they had forgotten about rags and starvation.

"Do white people dance?" Eskiminzin asked Whitman.

"Yes."

"Does it teach them who they are?"

"I don't believe so."

"Because they know who they are and they do not need that?"

"Some of the people know who they are, or think they do," Whitman said. "But those who don't—I don't believe dancing could tell them."

While Eskiminzin talked and listened he watched the dancing. The sight of the people filled his eyes and the sounds of the musicians and singers filled his ears and he could scarcely see or hear anything else. Maybe he should not worry so much about the drinking. The men were happy and even with sore heads tomorrow they would believe it had been worthwhile. And there was Delchan, walking around with his rifle. It was hard to worry very much when Delchan was around with his gun, even though it was the only gun in the village.

"Even in the old days, before we had to run from the soldiers, when we had the same villages all the time, and moved around only for the seasons and hunting and gathering mescal, even then the dance taught us," Eskiminzin said. "The dancing brought us together and we made jokes with each other and we faced each other, just as they are facing each other now. And we told each other by what we were doing who we were."

Road Runner, who had fallen asleep against Whitman, woke up. He shivered in the chill. He rubbed his eyes and then huddled against Whitman to get warm. His dog stood up and shook itself and then curled up and went back to sleep.

"We never were afraid when we danced," Eskiminzin said.

Whitman put his arm around Road Runner. "People would be surprised to find out Apaches get afraid."

"People would be surprised to find out we have any feelings."

Little Captain turned his head and spat. Santo took his pipe out of his mouth and put it back again, illuminating his chieftain's statement with silence.

"We fear," Eskiminzin said, his eyes on the dancers. "We fear many things. We have feeling for one another, our women and children and the old people, so we fear." He made a new cigarette. "But we are not afraid when we dance. We know it has been done that way from the beginning, and it is something we have together with those who walked before us. Dancing is sending signals back to the grandfathers and their grandfathers and their grandfathers. The white man has paper to keep memories. We have this. That is why the people feel good. They felt good in the old days and they feel good now. They need it more now."

"I suppose they do." Road Runner was burrowing into Whitman and he held him closer.

"When the people spend their days gathering grass to feed Army animals they need very much to remind themselves who they are," Eskiminzin said.

Road Runner woke up again and sat up and Whitman got to his feet. He rubbed his side. He took out his watch and held it toward the firelight. Whitman knew that Melana hated the little metal box filled with noisy spirits that told him when he must leave. The noisy spirits said it was past midnight.

"I have to get up very early," Whitman said, "I have to finish the report on the events of the month."

He put on his hat and touched his fingers to the brim. Little Captain stood up and grunted. Santo raised himself and took the pipe out of his mouth and did not put it back.

Surgeon Brierly stood up. He did not want to leave. But then he reminded himself that the sooner he returned to his quarters the sooner he could start making notes on what he had seen and heard.

Whitman glanced at Melana and raised his hand slightly and then he waved farewell to all the others and with Brierly started for their horses. Eskiminzin went along with them and Road Runner, wide-awake now, tagged along. The Puma and Victor Ruiz followed noiselessly.

"Your people worked hard," Whitman said. "In this short time they have gathered three hundred thousand pounds of hay."

"Will you report to the star *nantan?*" Eskiminzin asked.

"Yes."

"What else will you tell him in your report of events?"

"The happiest event of all—no event." Whitman turned his back as he tightened the saddle cinch. "Unless you have something to tell me."

"Nothing."

"My neck is riding on this."

"Your neck is as valuable to me as my own."

Whitman remained with his back to Eskiminzin for a moment or two and then he reached into the saddle holster and took from it a rolled-up sheet of paper. He handed the roll to Eskiminzin.

"I have given you few presents, Eskiminzin," Whitman said. "Almost none."

Eskiminzin gazed at him and then he took the paper and unrolled it and held it up so that he could see what it was. He saw instantly what it was.

"The picture writing," Eskiminzin said.

He looked at the map, a duplicate of the map in Whitman's office, the map that had filled him with awe and dread the first time he saw it, the map that he had seen many times since and still feared. And now that power was in his hands. He looked at it and he could not talk. He looked away. He had to find someplace to put his eyes.

Road Runner yawned. Eskiminzin bent down and scooped him up. The bandage had slipped down on Road Runner's leg and Eskiminzin fixed it in place. He was glad to have something to do.

Whitman climbed onto his horse. Brierly and the Puma and Ruiz already were mounted. Whitman looked at Eskiminzin.

"It seems to me that the arroyos are all smoothed over," Eskiminzin said at last. "It seems to me there are no more thorns to rip us open. It seems to me there are no more snakes to poison us." Eskiminzin peered up at Whitman. "A long time ago Cochise said something to me. He said a man was lucky in his lifetime if he found one friend."

Whitman and Brierly and the two interpreters rode off to Camp Grant. After a while Whitman looked back. Eskiminzin was still standing where he had left him, the rolled-up map in his hand, Road Runner asleep on his shoulder. Beyond Eskiminzin, Whitman could see in the light of the great fire the Aravaipa people dancing.

△ △ △ SEVEN

Darkness trickled across the belly of the San Pedro Valley. The thin air chilled as the sun abandoned it and the darkness took over and in the dwindling light the flowery frills around the cactus disappeared and only the stern shapes remained to stand vigil.

Don Jesús María Elías had been watching the endless passage of the sun for a long time. He watched the day expire as he might have stood over the last breathing of a human being. He had kept to himself and had had very little to eat during the deathwatch. He had taken no part in the joking and fun. The Americans had led in the joking and fun, of course, and Don Jesús understood that, because that was the manner of gringos and in this particular time they had to make up in noise and laughter for their lack of numbers.

Some of the Mexicans joined with the Americans but not many and Don Jesús was pleased to see that most of his countrymen had decency now that the moment was getting close. None of the Papagos took part in the jollity. The Papagos stayed by themselves all the day. Sometimes they listened to Chief Francisco. Mostly they just sat and meditated.

Don Jesús heard heavy footsteps as Bill Oury walked over to join him. Don Jesús looked up and nodded. It was fitting that he and Don Guillermo should have this moment alone. There was no need to talk.

Presently Don Jesús stood up and he gave out word that it was time to move on. When the men were again mounted and the foot Papagos were lined up for march, Don Jesús addressed them. He spoke again in Spanish.

"Friends, our task should not take long." He remembered the deep fear of the Papagos. "We shall be protected by darkness. We shall not be seen by the military at Camp Grant." He paused and said in a low voice, "Each of us knows why we are here and what it is we must do. Let us proceed, with the blessings of God."

Don Jesús crossed himself and many of the other men did the same. Then Don Jesús sent three men, a Mexican, a Papago and one of the Americans, to scout ahead. Don Jesús touched the side of his horse with the rowels of his great Spanish spurs.

Bill Oury walked his horse slowly. The column was gaited to the pace of the walking Papagos. He sat easily and now and again rinsed his mouth with water from the canteen slung around the saddle horn. In the silence his mind roved in his head.

He would be fifty-four in a few months and it seemed longer than that. The boy who had sneaked out of the Alamo surely was not this man. Surely that boy was only someone he had heard of somewhere, had not known of well. This man could touch on none of the feelings of that boy. This man was bearded and the beard was almost white and had nothing to do with that scared youth who had slipped out under Mexican guns —how many years ago? This man was scarred outside and in and that boy was just peeking into fear and the wonder of life.

Oury looked up to see that the riders ahead had halted. He waved down his own men and looked at his watch. He twisted the face this way and that to read it in the moonlight. It was a little after midnight and the moon was almost gone. And at that moment a rider came down from the head of the line and told him that Don Jesús wanted to see him.

When the Papagos heard that Oury was being called away they started to mutter and mill around. Oury spoke to them. "It is only that it is the time," he said in Spanish. And knowing the fragility of courage, he said, "I do not forsake you. Before we continue I shall be back to lead you. I give you my word."

The Papagos quieted and Oury rode to the head of the line. He heard low talking among the Mexicans and felt a tension. Some of the Mexicans whispered his name as he passed, as though touching a lucky piece. The Mexicans were proud that it was one of their own who led the expedition but they were happy that Don Guillermo was there.

Oury took his own strength from those contacts with the Mexicans and when he reached the van of the column he was feeling good and he sensed immediately that something had gone wrong. He saw Don Jesús talking to the Mexican he had sent out to reconnoiter with the American and the Papago and he saw that the Mexican's horse was breathing hard and was lathered.

Don Jesús looked up at Oury. Even in the faint light of the moon that was slipping away Oury could see the shame and disgrace on the drawn face of his old friend.

"I have miscalculated, Don Guillermo," Elías said. His voice was dead. "I estimated that the Apache village was about fifteen miles from where we camped today. I now am informed the distance is double that. I now am informed we still have fifteen miles to journey."

"We will have to go back," a Mexican said.

"We will just have to move faster," Oury said quickly.

"Impossible, Don Guillermo," another Mexican said. "We can never get there before daylight. The troops from Camp Grant would jump us before we could fire one shot."

The other Mexicans who heard him called out their agreement.

"Stop!" Oury said. "All of you, stop!" The voice had thunder in it and the babbling died down. "It is not impossible. We have come this far and we will prevail." Oury looked around defying anyone to gainsay him.

The talking started again and now Oury heard that some of the men agreed with him and he saw too that his words also had had an animating effect on Don Jesús and he realized with a shock that his friend too had resigned himself to calling off the venture.

"The question is the Papagos," Don Jesús said, gnawing on his mustache, groping for encouragement. In all his years of working on trails he had never before gone so far off the mark and he was discountenanced.

"Have no concern about the Papagos, Don Jesús," Oury said, loudly enough for the others to hear.

"You are certain?" Don Jesús asked with little certainty.

"I am certain," Oury said. *"Cuerpo de Cristo, Don Jesús, vámanos!* We waste time!"

Oury galloped off immediately to preclude any more talk. When he got back to the Papagos the word had already reached them and they were close to panic.

"It is nothing," Oury said to Chief Francisco. "It changes nothing. Give your people heart."

"The soldiers," Chief Francisco said.

That summed it up. The Papago courage was to kill Apaches and not to fight soldiers. That courage was slipping away like sand through open fingers.

"There will be no soldiers," Oury said, cursing the luck that caused Don Jesus, of all times, to blunder.

"It will be light before we reach there," Chief Francisco said.

"The soldiers will kill us," a Papago cried.

The Papagos babbled about the soldiers and Oury saw that they were ready to bolt.

"Listen to me!" he said. "All of you, listen to me!"

The chattering in the Papago language, the shifting of feet in the sliding scree, held and then tapered off. Oury wondered how many of them had slipped away.

"Listen to me," he said again.

He tried to make out the faces but he could not. How many faces were left out there? How many of them had slipped away with the magic that was good against Apaches but useless against soldiers?

"Nothing is changed," Oury said. "We go on to kill our enemies. The soldiers will not find out until we are finished and gone. Now the venture lies in your hearts. We must double the rate of march. That will not be hard for the men on horses. But you men on foot must keep pace. You men must run!"

There was no response from the Papagos. Oury wondered whether any had fled, how many? Would any of the Papagos believe they still had their magic? He had no doubt they were capable of trotting the rest of the way but to do that they had to believe they still had their magic.

There now was the sound of the Mexicans and the Americans moving on, but there still was no response from the Papagos. Oury wondered whether he should speak to them again.

Chief Francisco said, "Don Guillermo, we will follow you."

△ 2

The moon favored them and took its leave as they followed along the course of the San Pedro and each moment of the night was treasured as a jewel and was yielded with reluctance. No one of them had ever before so raptured himself with darkness. No one of them had ever before found such comfort in riding or loping on foot with the earth unseen, against sharp stones that bruised, stumbling into the pockets of holes, tripping on root growths that reached out and seized like traps. A sudden whipping of mesquite or paloverde branch or sharp-needled cactus brought forth curses and then thanks. The hurt was a reminder. They had not seen what struck them or their horses and so they could not be seen and the night still gave shelter.

The river led them. The river joined the Aravaipa Creek. The river would not fail them.

The riders in front of Bill Oury drew to a halt again. The Papagos immediately became nervous. They had been moving on their own momentum and when the momentum was gone they were ready to fall. They called out to Oury. They asked him whether they had reached their destination or whether they had come on trouble. Oury could give them no answer. He wanted to ride ahead to find out what was happening but he was afraid to leave the Papagos. He was the only thing holding them there.

A few moments later Sidney DeLong rode back from the van. He reported that the other two scouts, the American and the Papago had returned.

"They say we're about two miles from Camp Grant," DeLong said. "The Apache village is about four miles beyond that."

Oury looked at the sky. "We have about an hour."

Don Jesús shifted the line of march. He swung the column away from the fort. It added distance. In the east there was a grayness, a coloration not as black as night.

About a half hour later Don Jesús sent word down the line for Bill Oury to join him and to bring the Papagos with him. Oury and the Papagos knew what that must mean and the Papagos knew they still had their magic. They gripped their clubs and their rifles and they trotted behind Oury. They still had their magic and they were entering into themselves again.

Oury saw that Don Jesús had brought the column to the bank of the dried-out Aravaipa Creek. Don Jesús was looking at the sky.

"In my estimation we are at a point midway between the post and the *ranchería*," Don Jesús said. He was taut and exultant and still fearful that the daylight at this last moment might still snatch away his prize and he remembered his mistake.

"There's enough darkness left," Oury said. His throat was dry. He unscrewed the cap of his canteen and rinsed his mouth.

"I would have liked to have had enough time to reconnoiter the village," Don Jesús said. "I don't know what side of the wash it's on. Now, what I propose is that I will take my men up the left bank and you take the right. Whoever finds the enemy first will strike. Agreed?"

"Agreed."

"*Vaya con Dios*, Don Guillermo," Don Jesús said. He pressed his friend's arm.

"And you, Don Jesús," Oury said.

Don Jesús and the Mexicans and the Americans crossed Aravaipa Creek. Tightening the cap on his canteen, Oury slung it over the saddle horn and kicked his horse's side. The animal leaped forward and the canteen swung around and fell to the ground. Oury cursed and jerked on the reins and jumped down to retrieve it. The Papagos ran past him in the darkness as he groped around on the ground.

A few moments later a Mexican, one of the last riders in Don Jesús' column, galloped up. "*En el nombre de Cristo,* Don Guillermo," he called out in a hoarse whisper, "get back to your Indians!"

Oury grabbed the canteen and jumped back on his horse and dashed forward. He found the Papagos chattering in terror and confusion.

"I am here," Oury said. "I have not forsaken you."

When the Papagos understood that Oury was again among them they cried out their relief and clustered around his horse and called his name to reclaim their talisman.

Oury pulled his rifle out of its holster and waved the Papagos on. The ecstatic men sprang forward like deer. The men on foot had to hold themselves back so they would not outrun the horses.

It was about fifteen minutes later when Oury drew rein and held up his rifle again. The Papagos, already engaged in their dance of death, were hard put to stop. Men piled up on other men and blinked their eyes in consternation, as though a religious service had been interrupted.

Oury stood in his stirrups and squinted his eyes. It was the most hellish of times. It was not dark and not yet light and what could be seen, what little could be made out, played tricks on a man's eyes.

He thought he saw a light. Perhaps a campfire. He could not be certain. Reflections jested.

He jumped down and bade Chief Francisco and the riding Papagos to do the same. He ordered three men to watch the horses. He waved aside their protests at being denied their birthright. He raised his rifle.

"*Silencio, compañeros,*" he said in a low voice. "*Vámanos.*"

Following the left bank of the wash Don Jesús and his men found themselves trodding on sharply rising ground. They knew they had lost their gamble. They knew the Apaches would build their village on the other side of the creek in the shelter of high ground.

Don Jesús gave orders to dismount. He and the other men eased their rifles out of the holsters. He left men to take care of the horses and led the others on. Presently, from the bluff where a few hours earlier Santo had sent forth the masked mountain dancers, they could see below them in the glimmering twilight of the morning the wickiups of the Apache village.

Don Jesús hunkered down and rested his rifle across his knees and looked down at the pustules on the land.

△ △ △ EIGHT

△ 1

The faded markings on the cards made of stiff deerhide were hard to see. The little fire was burning down and there was not yet enough morning light. It was chilly and there was a wind. Naco thought about gathering more wood but it was almost day and his tour of duty would be over.

Naco played the monte game without interest. He was still annoyed that his mother had insisted on sitting up with him. What would the others say?

Not that there even was need for a sentry, not anymore. But Delchan had finally reached the limit of his strength and had to sleep and he had ordered Naco to stand watch over the village where the men had drowned in *tiswin* during the social dancing. Unnecessary as the guard duty was, Naco felt he should have been able to spend it in manly solitude.

Naco turned a card with three spots. It matched his mother's card. The old woman cackled with pleasure. Naco's brains splattered on the card. His mother's cackles were driven back down her throat by the shattered fragments of her skull.

Two Papagos had become the first Enemy Killers.

It was several moments before the new warriors recalled themselves and turned to where Bill Oury was waiting with Chief Francisco and the other Papagos. The two newest Enemy Killers raised their clubs, the first that morning to be consecrated with Enemy blood.

Oury unleashed the rest of the Papagos. They rushed forward in a tidal wave. Don Guillermo had cautioned them to use their clubs first, to kill as many of the Enemy as possible before the village was aroused. The Papagos took that as a needless command. Bullets were impersonal. What joy was there in slaying an Enemy from a long way away?

The Papagos entered the first of the Apache wickiups at about the same time. Their acts became almost a single act. They bludgeoned and then they stabbed and then they hacked with their knives. They worked silently. They were hunters. The only sounds in the beginning were the crunching of heads and the padding of feet.

Some of the Aravaipas woke in time to see death descending and the manner of it. Others slept through and passed over without the benefit of that knowledge. Some of the more attractive young Aravaipa women won a respite of a kind.

The avengers worked unangrily. They were drugged with dedication. Age and sex and size meant nothing. Each Enemy counted the same as every other Enemy in the tabulation on the calendar sticks. A small head gave less reward perhaps but only because the bone was softer or thinner and crushing it proved no true substantiation of zeal. A small head was no harder than a squash.

As the Papagos moved through the village they seized brands from what remained of the ceremonial fire and set ablaze wickiups they had done with. The early submission to the mandatory arson gave the game away. The dogs heralded the first warnings and then the ponies in the tribal corral whickered and moved around uneasily and then, as the flames spread, their eyes bulged and they neighed wildly and stampeded.

People were waking up by then, those whom the avengers had not yet visited. Women and children screamed and men rolled out of sleep still groggy from *tiswin* and they ran out of their dwellings and they saw what was happening and who was doing it but they did not know where to run. The Papagos were everywhere. The clubs were raised and brought down and the Papagos were everywhere.

Old people came out of their huts and looked around as though asking for directions. The Papagos helped along as many as they could reach. The ponies were running all over the place now. They didn't know where to go either. The Papagos didn't bother with the ponies or the dogs. There was no honor in opening the head of an animal.

Some of the people who won clear of the Papago clubs

and the Papago knives and the Papago guns, which were being used now, were kicked and trampled by the unshod hooves of their own maddened ponies and some of their skulls were staved in as effectively as those smitten by the clubs.

Bill Oury and Chief Francisco stood at the edge of the village not far from where Naco and his mother were slain. Oury wished that the Papagos had waited a little longer before spreading the flames. But he knew that immolation by fire was as ancient a prescript as the clubs and the Papagos now were in no way to be denied. And in any case the fires allowed them to watch the avengers perform their ordained act of extermination.

Bill Oury's blood was boiling. It had taken a long time. And for a long time it was as though it could never be. He supposed that was the way it had had to be. He had waited it out and then he had brought it about.

He saw Apaches escaping the avalanching clubs and the guns and the hysterical ponies. They were his prey. He did not want to risk hitting any of the Papagos and he had to wait until the fleeing Apaches were almost out of the village before he could shoot at them. It was dark on the periphery of the village and he could not tell how many of his slugs found their targets.

Chief Francisco rested on a long staff and watched. In his white clothes he looked like a Biblical shepherd. His blood was too old to boil. And that was not the way. His face was peaceful. There was no anger in any of his flock. The beautiful, burgeoning Enemy Killers were following Instructions. There was sublime beatitude on his face and there was no anger.

From their excellent position on the bluff on the other side of the wash Don Jesús and his men watched. At the onset they were bitter and frustrated. They had not journeyed to the Aravaipa village to be spectators.

But then some of the Apaches who had managed to break through the storm of Papagos and crazed ponies waded across Little Running Water to get to the bluff and then to the mountains. The mountains always meant safety.

The fires behind the Apaches served nicely. Don Jesús and his men leisurely shot the Apaches down.

Eskiminzin ran out of his wickiup. He had only to see the Papagos. He shouted to Aravaipa men to come to him and make a stand but it was too late to rally anybody. By the time the Papagos reached Eskiminzin's end of the village they were almost finished with their labors.

Eskiminzin ran back into the wickiup. He and Child Mother got Ria and Star out of the dwelling and Eskiminzin sent them off and then ran over to Small Woman's wickiup. Half of it was in flames. The wall on one side was caving in. Eskiminzin started around to the other side. He was sent reeling by a roundhouse clout from a Papago club. He tumbled over and the Papago pressed in for the coup. Eskiminzin rolled closer to the burning hut and the club struck the earth instead and made an indentation greater than his head.

The Papago raised his club again. Flames flared from the wickiup. The Papago covered his face and ran away. Eskiminzin lurched to his feet. His hands were burned and he was in dizzying pain. He kicked in the smoking hide wall. He pushed his way through the brush pole supports. The wickiup was full of smoke. He could make out nothing. He tried to get in farther. Part of the burning roof fell on him. He choked and staggered out. He heard a small cry. He filled his lungs and clawed his way inside. He found Chita. Another piece of roof fell in. He sheltered Chita with his arms and backed out.

He set the baby down and started back into the wickiup. The rest of the roof caved in. He tried to kick aside the burning hide and brush. He heard Chita wail again. He saw Papagos come out of the wickiup shared by his mother and Melana. The Papagos started for him. He picked up Chita and ran toward the desert. He heard shots. He heard bullets go past him. He heard screams behind him and the thudding of clubs and rifle fire and the barking of dogs and the whinnying of ponies.

At the edge of the village he looked back. He saw his image of hell.

It was a picture of hell to Don Jesús. It filled his eyes. It filled his ears. It filled his soul. He could have sat there through eternity.

Apaches of all ages, men and women and babies and children, panicked in magnificent terror, shrieking, shot, clubbed, stabbed, stomped on by their own ponies—glorious irony— chased in the lurid light of the conflagration by relentless club-swinging wraiths whose white clothing now was enriched and decorated by Enemy blood.

Don Jesús María Elías, the dispossessed Spanish *hidalgo,* wanted never to forget that scene. He would die with that scene before his eyes. He watched icily, as a scientist might observe an experiment. He had thought his blood would surge so that it could not be held but he was icy. Of the avengers that Sunday morning, Don Jesús had waited longest. The Papagos had tribal memories and an obligation to their calendar sticks. He had names. He had names and he, too, could bring on no anger.

Again and again, almost with melancholy, he raised his rifle and fired at Apaches trying to cross the creek. It was as though they were struggling toward him to be killed. Some of the Apaches fell on land and some on water. The dead released their hold on children. Babies floated away and went under. Children wandered about and some of them were shot and some fell on land and some on water and some who were only wounded drowned.

After a while there were no more Apache adults to kill. There were children drifting around in shock and the Papagos collected twenty-seven of them. Apache children were saleable in Sonora.

The Papagos and their captives went back to where Bill Oury and Chief Francisco were waiting. What had been done had been done in less than thirty minutes.

△ 2

The desert was a flamboyant garden without end. The sun sparkled. The sky was flawless.

On the bank of the San Pedro a few miles from Camp

Grant the victorious rejoined forces relaxed from their work. The Mexicans and the Americans congratulated one another and refreshed themselves. Uncle Billy Oury and Don Jesús embraced and men cheered. On this Lord's day some men did not forget to kneel and give thanks.

Oury dispatched a message to Adjutant General Samuel Hughes:

"It is eight o'clock. Our tired troops are resting in the full satisfaction of work well done. The red devils have been killed or captured or driven off. Not a man in our party has been hurt to mar the full measure of our triumph."

The twenty-seven captured red devils sat huddled together. None of them was crying. In the last hour they had ended their lives as children.

The Papagos kept to themselves once more. The newly fledged Enemy Killers, too, discovered that not one of them was wounded, not in the smallest way. So great was their magic. They gazed at their purified clubs with awe and Chief Francisco spoke a few words to the Giver of Instructions.

The Enemy Killers neither ate nor drank. They had feasted.

Whitman set down his coffee cup. He wiped his lips with his napkin, picked up his cigar and rose to his feet.

Fred Austin said, "Coffee ain't that bad."

"I'm late with that damned report," Whitman said.

"That's right, tomorrow's the first of the month."

"And I'm going to have one of the old man's riders waiting on my doorstep at the crack of dawn, a-twitching and a-quivering to go." Whitman bulged his eyes. "And glaring."

"When you finish that report don't forget to brief it," Austin said.

"Funny," Whitman said.

He stepped outside. It was just after seven-thirty on that Sunday morning. It was still cool from the night but as soon as the sun got moving it would attend to that.

Whitman stared across the parade ground to his office. The post had the feeling of Sunday. Under one of the *ramadas* some of the men were standing with bared heads listening to another soldier read from the Bible. Whitman wondered when the Army would get around to sending a chaplain to Camp Grant.

He turned his head sharply as a rider clattered onto the parade ground from off the Tucson Road. The uniformed rider pulled up, jumped down, saluted Whitman.

"Sergeant Clarke, sir," the man said. "I have an urgent message from Captain Dunn, commanding officer, Camp Lowell, for the commanding officer of Camp Grant."

Sergeant Clarke announced all that in a loud, clear voice. What he was telling everybody who was gathered around was that he had made his way through Apacheria alone and unarmed.

Whitman accepted the dispatch and opened it, noting automatically that Sergeant Clarke's horse appeared uncommonly fresh for having just completed the hard fifty-five-mile ride from Tucson. He saw, too, that the sergeant appeared to be without a weapon.

He read the message and ordered a horse and sent for the Puma. "Ride out to the Indian village as fast as you can. Tell Eskiminzin to get everybody inside the post limits immediately."

The Puma galloped down the parade ground, scattering pebbles and dust. Whitman informed Sergeant Clarrity what was in the message and Sergeant Clarke finally understood why he had been stopped and held captive by Americans from Tucson. Whitman ordered Sergeant Clarrity to double the guard and to issue arms and ammunition to every able-bodied man on the post.

"Against Americans?" Fred Austin asked.

"Against anybody," Whitman said. He ordered Sergeant Clarke to follow him into his office to answer some questions.

The post leaped to life. The soldier stopped reading the Bible. The feeling of Sunday was gone.

The troops at Camp Grant were armed and ready and were waiting when the Puma returned half an hour later. Whitman was standing outside the camp on the bank of the dried-up creek. He was taut with fury. He had listened to Sergeant Clarke.

The Puma pulled his horse to a stop. "The village is burning. All the people there are dead."

△ 2

The fires still burned all over the village. Far down the canyon the air was filled with the smell.

An Aravaipa man and two Aravaipa women stood on the bluff overlooking Little Running Water. Whitman called to them and held out his hand. They fled. Whitman rode on.

The horses got it first. They nickered and shied. The soldiers brought them under control. Then the soldiers caught it. The wind was blowing down Dark Canyon and carried the smell of the burned flesh of the Dark Canyon People and the smell of the burned hides of their dwellings. The smell was strong. Some of the young soldiers swallowed hard.

After the smell came the whining of dogs, aimless and continuous and from everywhere and from nowhere. The horses, old horses and half passed over, became nervous again and the soldiers had to hold them hard and to hold themselves hard as well.

The troopers, carrying shovels and spades along with their carbines, led by Whitman with Surgeon Brierly riding at his side, made the last turn in the canyon to where Little Running Water deepened and now flowed under smoke. Smoke was everywhere. The smoke lay low on the land and on the wash. The smoke drifted up in tendrils and caught and twisted in eddies. The smoke lay heavy and oily. The smoke mixed with the smell of roasted flesh. The young soldiers quieted their horses and fought down the vomit in their throats.

The first bodies Whitman and Brierly came upon were Naco and his mother. Whitman did not recognize the woman, who had no face to recognize. The youth doubled up next to her could not at first be identified either. The side of his face exposed to the world presented bones and flesh and brains and flies. Whitman got down and turned the body over.

"It's Naco," Duncan shouted. "Excuse me, sir."

Naco was still holding his deerhide cards. The undamaged side up, there was nothing to show how he had met his death. There was no expression of surprise or fear.

Whitman straightened. He looked across the flat ground where the village had lived. There were a few wickiups still standing. The rest were burned or burning. The air now lay still over the village. The smoke went straight up. Dogs collected around the soldiers. They lamented. There were dead dogs, shot not clubbed.

Whitman ordered the troopers to dismount and they entered the village. Whitman peered closely at the dead. At first he saw only women. Some of the women had been stripped. Their legs were spread apart. Their thighs and bellies were mottled with globs of sperm. Whitman could make out only a few of them. The clubs had made almost all of them anonymous.

Whitman came upon Delchan. There was no mistaking Delchan, although he no longer possessed a face. The giant Indian's hand gripped his rifle. The hand was smashed to tatters and the stock of the rifle was smashed. A woman lay next to Delchan. Two children were close by. The woman was naked and spread-eagled. Her face was pulp. Her body was punctured with stab wounds. One of the boys was a torso without a head. The head was in another part of the wickiup. The other child's arms had been hacked off.

Whitman walked on. From the moment he had heard what had taken place in the Aravaipa village he had tried not to see faces. Now there were no faces to see.

He walked straight through the village, pausing to look at one body and then another. He walked in a straight line. Brierly knew where he was going.

"Women and children," Whitman said. "They're almost all women and children. Have you counted, Conant?"

"No."

"Nor have I. We should have kept count, Conant."

Whitman was almost at the far side of the village when he came upon the body of Child Mother. He believed he would have recognized her sooner or later but he did so immediately because she had Ria in one arm and Ria had been stabbed to death and still had features. And nearby was Star. She had been strangled and she, too, still had a face.

Whitman walked to a wickiup that had burned partly. In the ravaged village it looked like a tall building. He pushed aside the door and entered. He stumbled over Daya's body. He knew where he was so he knew the crumpled heap was the mother of Eskiminzin. Melana was lying in the back of the wickiup. She was naked. Her head was crushed. Her thighs were streaked with blood and sperm. There was gray sperm on her belly. Not far from her was a bundle of hay tied neatly for delivery.

"It's quite interesting," Surgeon Brierly said. "There must

have been primitives involved in this. They raped the women but they considered them unworthy to receive their seed." He saw the look on Whitman's face. "Sorry, Royal."

Whitman and Brierly went to the third wickiup in what had been Eskiminzin's compound. It was still smoldering. Small Woman had been clubbed and raped. Fawn had been stabbed and thrown into the fire pit. Her buckskin doll, Bonita, was in her hand. The doll had come apart again but not in the place where Surgeon Brierly had sutured it.

Whitman looked around for Road Runner. He could not find him. He went outside. He took off his cap and wiped his face.

Close to the edge of the village, close to the place where the desert started, Whitman saw a dog that looked familiar. He walked to the dog. The dog was silent. Behind a clump of cactus was the body of Road Runner. He had almost gotten away. His body was full of stab wounds. His right arm was torn off. The arm lay about three feet from the body.

Whitman picked up the arm and the small body. The bandage on Road Runner's leg fell off. Whitman picked up the bandage and slipped it back on the leg. It was hard to find the place where the snake had bitten.

Whitman held Road Runner in his arms and he raised his eyes and looked around, around the destroyed village, beyond the village to the desert and the hills. He did not know what he was looking for. Whatever it was, it was not there.

△ 3

Whitman set some of the soldiers to work digging a single grave in the dance ground. He sent others to collect bodies. The day was steaming. The soldiers stripped to the waist. The soldiers who searched out and picked up the charred and bleeding and dismembered and violated and beheaded bodies soon had to change places with those who dug in the ground. And those who took their places soon had to change back.

It went that way that brilliant and very hot Arizona Sunday, men carting as many bodies as their senses would allow, collecting arms and legs and heads, some men pausing to retch, and then changing with the diggers, and then changing again, until all the bodies and all the parts of bodies that could be found were in the grave.

The job of finding the dead in the village, in the char of the wickiups, on the land under the bluff, in the wash, caught on stones and brush, started a little after ten o'clock that day and it was almost three o'clock when the last Aravaipa body anybody could find was put into the ground. The young, un-tried soldiers were soaked with sweat and covered with soot and blood and dirt. These men, who had done no more than paper work and housekeeping at the post, had worked without pause, with nothing more than a swallow of water against the heat and the nausea and the smell.

Whitman knelt and put Road Runner's body and the severed arm with the bodies of his mother and sister and he thought how he had betrayed them, how he had betrayed them all. He had disarmed them and had made them helpless and then he had failed to protect them and what greater betrayal could there be than that? He was filled with sorrow and a rage greater than any he had ever known. He raged against the men who had done this, but he raged more greatly against himself. He was the betrayer.

"I make the body count about one hundred and twenty-five, sir, give or take a few," Sergeant Clarrity said.

"About a quarter of the tribe." Whitman said.

"Only eight men, sir, the rest women and children."

When the last body was in the grave the men stepped back and removed their hats and looked at Whitman.

"Say something, Royal," Brierly said.

"I don't know anything to say." .

"You must know something." Brierly pulled out a large kerchief and blew his nose. "Damn it, man, how the devil were you brought up!"

"I used to know. I've forgotten."

"I've forgotten, too. My God, and we call ourselves Christians." Brierly shoved the kerchief into his pocket.

Whitman cast his eyes over the men. They stood bare-headed, waiting. He was proud of them and he would think of them always as men, not as boys who had never fired a shot in anger, not as raw and green and unformed. And yet he thought fleetingly, fleetingly, of the cavalrymen and the cavalry horses Stanwood had taken away with him and what he might have done with those men and those horses now. He thought of Oury and some of the other faces in the courthouse. He wanted to kill.

"Is there any man here who can say a prayer?" Whitman asked.

Nobody responded. Sergeant Clarrity pushed Colin Duncan forward. "I've listened to you," Clarrity said.

"Go ahead then," Whitman said.

Duncan looked at Whitman and then at the other soldiers and he walked closer to the open grave. He looked at the bodies. He closed his eyes and cleared his throat.

" 'The Lord is my shepherd; I shall not want. He maketh me to lie down in green pastures: he leadeth me beside the still waters. . . .' "

Whitman looked at Little Running Water rippling itself free from the pall of smoke. He felt cold under the sun. He saw that some of the soldiers were crying and that they were not ashamed to be crying and made no effort to hide their crying or to stop it. My God, Whitman thought, they are young but they are not that young.

" 'Yea, though I walk through the valley of the shadow of death, I will fear no evil: for thou art with me; thy rod and thy staff they comfort me. . . .' "

In the high, clear tenor voice of Colin Duncan Whitman heard the deep voice of his father and he closed his eyes and he was away and it was long ago and he opened his eyes and looked at Brierly. The surgeon's face was cast. The spade beard jutted in challenge. The surgeon's lips were compressed against his teeth in a line. Brierly, Whitman thought, will always have some of that in his face from this time on.

" '. . . My cup runneth over—' " Duncan stopped short and stared past Whitman.

Whitman turned his head swiftly. He saw Eskiminzin

standing about ten yards away. Eskiminzin carried Chita in his arms. He was covered with grime. His hands and arms were burned. He seemed to see everything around him and nothing at all. Road Runner's dog caught his scent and ran to him whimpering.

"Go on," Whitman said to Duncan. How long had Eskiminzin been there? Where had he come from?

Duncan kept looking at the Aravaipa chief.

"Go on," Whitman said harshly. "Finish it."

Duncan could not take his eyes away from Eskiminzin. He wet his lips. " '. . . Surely goodness and mercy shall follow me all the days of my life: and I will dwell in the house of the Lord forever.' Amen."

As the other men echoed the last word Eskiminzin raised his head slightly as though he understood that the prayer was ended and he walked slowly to the grave. The troopers parted and made way for him. He passed Whitman without looking at him. Road Runner's dog followed at his feet. Eskiminzin walked to the edge of the grave and looked into it. Chita started to cry. He patted her.

Eskiminzin stood at the graveside for about five minutes. No one spoke and no one moved. Then Eskiminzin turned his back to the open hole. His shoulders bent and shook.

Whitman gave a curt order. The soldiers picked up their shovels and covered the dead.

△ △ △ TEN

△ 1

The victorious army found a pleasant surprise awaiting them when they reached that point along the Rillito where first they had formed. Adjutant General Sammy Hughes was there with a hayrack loaded with food and drink.

"The people of Arizona will never forget what you have done," General Hughes said.

The Americans and the Mexicans ate and drank and celebrated. The Papagos still waited to celebrate.

The guns were cleaned and returned to the Adjutant General, who took possession of them in the name of the Territorial Government of Arizona.

Bill Oury pronounced the final benediction of the day. "We may return to our homes with the satisfaction of work well done."

The Papagos collected the Aravaipa children and went on to San Xavier. Chief Francisco rode over to Bill Oury and Don Jesús. Chief Francisco's face was serene.

"It was religious," Chief Francisco said.

"It was religious, Don Francisco," Elías said.

"It was religious," Chief Francisco said, nodding his head slowly. He raised his hand as though in blessing, then lowered it and rode off to the mission, his head still nodding slowly.

The Americans and the Mexicans returned to Tucson. In front of Bill Oury's house, Oury and Don Jesús clasped hands.

"God was with us, Don Jesús," Oury said.

Don Jesús, who had not prayed on the bank of the San Pedro when other men prayed, continued on to the San Augustin cathedral. He went inside and in his private fashion gave his personal thanks to God.

Part Six

△ △ △ ONE

△ 1

"The people of Tucson and San Xavier must be crazy. They acted as though they had neither heads nor hearts. They must have a thirst for our blood."

Whitman made no reply. He could think of no words to say. He had a New Englander's distrust of easy words. But he was glad Eskiminzin was starting to talk. It was Tuesday, two days after the massacre, and Eskiminzin had said almost nothing since he had come back to what was left of his village.

The two men were sitting in front of a small fire near Little Running Water. The night was cold. It was after midnight. Some of the people were sleeping, almost all children. Most of the men and women were walking around. Some of them had not slept since those thirty minutes the morning before.

People had drifted back to the village that day. The women commenced mourning before they got there. They started their shrill keening while they were still in the hills and out on the desert. The dogs in the village had been quiet until then but when they heard the wailing of the women they started to bark and howl and yipe.

The people looked changed as Whitman watched them return. They looked the way they would look for a long time. Some of them would always look that way. They walked around finding out who was alive but it didn't seem to matter very much. They were not surprised and they showed no joy when they came upon a relative or a friend. They showed no grief when they decided they never again would find whoever it was they were looking for.

The big mound where the dead were buried did not seem to interest them very much either. They couldn't help see it;

it was new and the earth was a different color and it was rounded on the old, flat desert, and next to it was the pile of desert earth that was left over after the dead Aravaipas were put into the hole. They couldn't help but see all that and some of them walked over and had a closer look, but they were not much interested either.

They walked past Whitman and Brierly and Sergeant Clarity and the other white soldiers as though they did not see them, as though they were not there with them in their world. They were not angry. They were not bitter. Nothing mattered.

Brierly had a lot of work to do with all the wounds and burns and broken bones, and he had so many volunteers from among the soldiers he had to turn most of them away. Brierly set fractures and cleaned stab wounds and did what he could to patch up bruised heads and arms and legs. Most of the people didn't look at him as he worked on them. Some of them seemed a little embarrassed at having been damaged, but most of them just gazed off elsewhere as though what was happening was not happening to them at all. For a long time now the only thing they would remember happening to them was what had happened that Sunday morning during that half hour.

The people had not eaten since that time and Whitman had sent off to the post for food. He was surprised to see Fred Austin and Miles Wood riding back with the loaded ambulance wagon and then he wondered why he should be surprised. No matter how they had felt in the beginning, the sutler and the beef contractor had gotten to know the Aravaipas in the last months. Maybe they didn't feel about the Aravaipas the way Whitman did but they had some respect for them. They had told Whitman that more than once.

The people took the food but they did not look at the men who gave it to them. Fred Austin and Miles Wood tried to make the Aravaipa men understand how bad they felt about what had happened. The Aravaipa men listened politely without looking at the beef contractor or the sutler and then they turned away and some of the shoulders shook as Eskiminzin's shoulders had shaken.

Whitman expected that. How else could it have been? He blamed himself but he knew the Apaches didn't blame him.

He had expected the children would be different too. He expected they would be just about the way they were when the Aravaipas first were brought in by Eskiminzin, when it had all started. He expected they would be timid as deer and that they would shy away from him. Why did his heart hurt him so much then?

During the second day Little Captain showed up. Little Captain went over to Surgeon Brierly and started to talk rapidly to the surgeon in Apache as though Brierly could understand him. The Puma went over and listened.

"His wife is in the mountains, he says," the Puma said. "She was shot in the chest. There is another woman who is also shot. He says he tried to bring the women down but he could not." Without pausing, the Puma said, "I would like the permission of the *teniente* to ride out and get them."

Duncan said instantly, "I'd like to go along, sir."

Whitman looked at his striker. "Permission granted."

Santo turned up at the end of the second day. He was bewildered. People sat him down and made him comfortable and gave him food. He didn't understand very much.

Eskiminzin rolled a cigarette and watched the fire burn. "We know there are a great many white men and Mexicans who do not want us to live in peace. We know that the Papagos would not have come here unless they were persuaded."

The Puma, who, with Duncan and Little Captain, had brought in the wounded women and had found several children as well, gave over Eskiminzin's words.

Whitman smoked his cigar and listened. It was important that Eskiminzin was talking. It was important that Eskiminzin was opening up, even though he spoke of things both men knew. What he was saying was probably important to him, personally and as the leader of his people. But Whitman wished that Eskiminzin would talk a little about Small Woman and Child Mother, about Road Runner and Star and Ria and Fawn, about his mother, about Melana. Whitman thought again how he had last seen them and he thought it was a good thing that Eskiminzin had not seen all the things he had seen. What Eskiminzin had looked on in the grave was enough. The Puma had explained to Whitman that Apaches almost never spoke the names of the dead and Whitman accepted that taboo, and yet it grieved him that Eskiminzin could not talk about his family and get out of him a little of what must be inside, and that he, Whitman, could say nothing as well. The taboo worked both ways.

"When we first talked to you you told us you could not make a treaty of peace," Eskiminzin said, "but if we would turn ourselves in as prisoners of war and give up our arms you would issue rations and write to the star *nantan* and he would send someone to make the peace.

"I then placed a stone on the earth and said as long as that stone would last I would keep the peace. Two nights ago while my people slept, the people of Tucson, white men, Mexicans, Papago Indians, stole in, hoping to kill us all. We heard them in time for our men, who are swift of foot, and for most of our women and children to get away. They knew we had no arms or they would not have come. They killed more than a hundred of my people, almost all of them women and children." Eskiminzin stopped abruptly. He said in a whisper, as though he were not truly saying it, "Among them my wives and four of my children and my mother." And then quickly, as though he had sinned and was ashamed, "I ask you, what shall we do?"

Whitman remained silent at this first mention of Eskiminzin's personal loss. He hoped the Apache would say more. He thought how agonizing it must be for Eskiminzin to hold it in.

"We saw you with your people bury our dead and we do not think you knew of their coming or we would not be here together." Eskiminzin looked away.

"By my word as a man I knew nothing about this," Whitman said. "And I had no means to overtake them—nor was I authorized to take punishment in my own hands."

"If we were white people?" Eskiminzin asked.

"I could still not on my own deal punishment."

Eskiminzin raised his head. "If Indians massacred whites?"

Whitman's jaw tightened. "Yes," he agreed. "That's the way it is."

The two men were silent for a while. Eskiminzin looked into the fire as though it could inform him, as though secrets were there for him to discover.

"Tell us what to do," Eskiminzin said again.

"If I thought anything like this could have happened I would not have allowed you to build your village so far from the post. I think now that you must bring what is left of your people back to the first camp. We can arrange about getting water." As his Maine farmer father would have said, locking the stable door afterward.

"And then?" Eskiminzin asked.

"I will make a full report on what has happened." Whitman was aware of how bootless his words must sound. "Since your people were prisoners of war they were under the protection of the American flag. What took place was out-and-out murder. The guilty must pay."

Eskiminzin turned away his head and Whitman knew him well enough to know that the Apache was averting his face because there was disbelief and scorn on it and he did not want to insult Whitman by revealing it.

Presently Eskiminzin said, "We believe in you. But we know that no white man will ever be hanged or punished for killing an Indian. But the dead are dead. Now the only thing that matters is the children who were stolen." The firelight found sockets where the eyes were lost. "Can you get back our children?"

"I do not know. I will try."

"I am glad you do not make easy promises. I am glad you do not lie."

"I have never lied to you. I will try to get back the children but I cannot promise it."

Eskiminzin looked away from the fire, away into the night. "Do you know what will happen to them?"

"I think so."

"Our little boys will grow up as slaves. Our little girls— as soon as they are large enough—will be diseased prostitutes to get money for whoever owns them."

Whitman nodded slowly.

"Our women work hard and they are good women and they and our children have no diseases," Eskiminzin said. "Our dead you cannot bring back to life but those who are living we give to you. We look to you who can write and talk and have soldiers to get them back."

"I will try," Whitman said. "The rest of you, the rest of your people, what will you do with them in the future?"

"I? I have done enough. I have brought this on my people. The dead are dead because they trusted me."

"And because they trusted me," Whitman said.

"They trusted you because I trusted you," Eskiminzin said gratingly. "What has been done I have done." The firelight played havoc with his face. "The dead are on my conscience." He stood up abruptly, his arms rigid, his hands clenched at his sides. "I look at the people and I think, 'I have killed your women, I have killed your relatives, I have killed your children.'"

And to yourself, Whitman asked silently, what must you say to yourself about your own dead?

And what could he say to himself? Whitman asked. Who had given him the right to have brought this about?

Eskiminzin asked, "What will I do?"

He tried to say more but for a few moments he could not. His head shifted from side to side but no words would come out, only sounds that strangled before they left his throat. He was like a mute, fighting hopelessly to utter a word.

Whitman turned away. He had never before witnessed such naked anguish. He had no right to look on it.

"I no longer want to live," Eskiminzin said.

Whitman stared at the fire.

"My women and my children have been killed before my face," Eskiminzin said. The face in the reflections from the fire looked as though it were cut out of rock. "Most Indians in my place would take a knife and cut their throats."

Now it was Whitman's time to try to find answers in the flames. If only he could find words. If only he could say something of some value. Promises were obscenities.

In a little while in a voice so low it sounded like nothing more than murmuring in the night, Eskiminzin said, "But I will live to show these people that all they have done, all they can do, shall not make me break faith with you—so long as you will stand by us and defend us in a language we know nothing of to a great *nantan* we have never seen and never will."

It was not far from dawn and there was the sound of Little Running Water close by and the sound of the walking people who could not sleep.

△ △ △ T W O

△ 1

Bloody Retaliation!!!

The So-Called Camp Grant Massacre

The policy of feeding and supplying hostile Indians has brought its bloody fruits. To say this instance shows a spirit of barbarism in our people would be gross slander. While the killing is a matter for regret, the necessity for it is still more to be deplored.

The wonder is not so much that this killing occurred—and as it did—as that it was so long delayed. . . .

Whitman tossed the copy of the *Citizen* over to Brierly. The editorial was printed in the edition of Saturday, May 6, the first since the attack on the Aravaipa village.

"He was right," Whitman said. "Eskiminzin was right."

"But then he's had a little more experience with this sort of thing, hasn't he?" Brierly picked up the newspaper.

"Eskiminzin said nobody would be punished," Whitman said. "Punished! Oury, Elías, all of them, have been made into goddamned heroes!" He got up and walked to the window. Once again he could see the Aravaipas from his window. "Conant, what kind of people are we?"

Brierly glanced through the editorial. "What kind of people are we, Royal?" Brierly scratched the underside of his beard. "What kind of people? Ordinary, everyday, selfish people. Like all people everywhere. There are no saints anymore. Eskiminzin is no saint. He has put people below the ground in his time and so have many of the others—on both sides."

Whitman walked back to the desk. "I'm not talking about the past. I'm not talking about what Eskiminzin once did or did not do. Everybody's done something. We did it by coming out here in the first place. I'm talking about one thing, this one thing." He slapped the paper. "About a hundred and twenty-five people were killed and almost all of them were women and little children and babies and this son of a bitch says that the only thing strange about that was that it wasn't done long ago. What kind of a mind is that?"

"Have you heard from General Stoneman?"

"Have I heard from General Stoneman! Ever since I came here it seems all I've been asked is have I heard from General Stoneman. No, Conant, I have not heard from General Stoneman. I wrote him a full report but I have not heard from General Stoneman."

"Have you heard from anybody?"

"No. It's as though it never happened." Whitman sat down heavily. "I don't even know where to locate Captain Stanwood. He's still out there somewhere looking for Apaches to kill. And look what happened in his own backyard. And I cannot get anybody to do a goddamned thing about it."

"These things take time, Royal."

"Tell me about it, Conant. Tell me about General George Stoneman taking his time."

"Has Eskiminzin spoken to you about it?"

"There is no need. And he doesn't want me to lose face. But it's in his eyes. He told me right after it happened that nobody would be punished. It's in his eyes."

△ 2

Most of the people who still were alive returned to where the third Aravaipa village was being built across Little Running Water close to Camp Grant. Little Running Water was still in summer sleep there and Whitman established a shuttle service using the post's water wagons.

The soldiers were deeply into what had happened to the Aravaipas. The soldiers blamed themselves, too. They felt they had let the Aravaipas down. They drove the wagons back and forth from the place where Little Running Water still flowed freely. Each time they went there they were reminded of what had taken place. The grave mound was a long way from settling and the pile of leftover dirt was not going to get blown away for a while.

When the soldiers were not running the water shuttle and were not occupied with duties at the post, they spent as much time as they could helping to get the surviving Aravaipas settled again. They didn't much know how to do that. The Aravaipas let them help but that was more to please the soldiers than anything else. Eskiminzin told the people how he had seen soldiers weep when they prayed over the dead and the people felt they owed something to the soldiers for that.

The soldiers tried to help erect wickiups. They were clumsy. The people found it strange to have soldiers working with them. The people were not quick at accepting changes but Eskiminzin had told them the soldiers had cried so the people made the best of it.

Whitman knew that the one thing all the Aravaipas, from Eskiminzin on down, were waiting for was word on the missing children. Whitman felt like a trapped animal. He wrote to Captain Dunn at Camp Lowell about the children. "*Owing to the absence of Captain Stanwood with the Cavalry Company, I am unable to go, or send any sufficient force to take back those prisoners . . .*" He pleaded with Captain Dunn to take immediate steps "*to save these children from a life of debauched servitude.*" He concluded, "*I have the honor, therefore, to request that you will use your authority as an officer of the United States Army and as a Post Commander in the accomplishment of the above object.*"

The days passed. Most of the ponies that had bolted on the morning of the killing were collected. The new village got itself finished despite the assistance of the soldiers. The people worked in the fields and gathered hay and some of the old women started making *tiswin* again and sewed clothing and watched over the younger children while their parents were out cutting food for the post animals. The ration system was set up again and the Aravaipas came to the post more often now because they were close again. After a while the children did not run away when they saw Whitman and other white soldiers.

Whitman, balked on all sides, confined to his post as though imprisoned there, wrote again to Captain Dunn about the missing children. Nothing had been heard about them. Nobody seemed to be doing anything to find them.

In his frustration, Whitman began to wonder about Sergeant Clarke. Sergeant Clarke had told him everything that had happened to him and Trooper Kennedy and Sergeant Clarke had had the manner of a man who was to be believed, and at the time Whitman had not doubted his story, but as days passed, Whitman wondered about that, too, and he had a dark suspicion.

". . . *Whether your dispatch was forcibly detained or its bearer an accessory before the fact in this murder is a question I have the honor to request you to immediately cause to be investigated,*" he wrote to Captain Dunn.

The days passed and Whitman knew Eskiminzin and his people were waiting. Nobody thought any of the men in the killing would be punished but the people were waiting. They were waiting to know for certain that nobody was going to be called to account. They expected that. But they waited to know that and more than anything else they waited for word of the missing children.

△ 3

The days followed the days. There was no word from General Stoneman. There was no word from Dunn. There was no word from the Bureau of Indian Affairs. Nobody wanted to know.

As far as the Army and the Bureau were concerned the attack on the Aravaipa village officially never took place at all.

△ △ △ THREE

△ 1

It was different in Tucson. The Old Pueblo was in celebration. The Old Pueblo was in fiesta. If, in the eyes of the Army and the Indian Bureau, the massacre of the Aravaipas had never happened, it happened over and over again in Tucson.

It was relived every time one of the heroes could be cornered in a saloon. Every detail was told and retold and when the men ran out of facts they made up new facts. Before very long there was not a child in Tucson who could not give a blow-by-blow account of the historic march and victory.

The men Bill Oury had begged to join him were kicking themselves now that they knew how safe the venture had been. Some of those sorry men turned wishful thought into reality and started saying they had been on the expedition. That was a little hard for Americans to do. There were only six Americans involved and they all knew who they were. The men who now were including themselves in the attack and who were telling their cronies how many Indians they had personally killed had to be careful who was in the saloon when they started to brag.

It was simpler for the Mexicans. There had been forty-eight Mexicans in the little army and it was hard for every one of them to remember everyone else. Mexicans all over Tucson claimed they had taken part in the illustrious event and won favors of the fair for it. In a spirit of high fun John Wasson wrote that if all the men who said they were in on the kill at Camp Grant actually had been there the citizen army would have outnumbered the regular troops in the Territory two to one.

Uncle Billy Oury became instant living legend. All his exploits from the days of the Alamo on were recalled and repeated

432

with awe. Uncle Billy was held to be the star of the show despite the fact that Don Jesús Elías was the actual commander and only four per cent of the troops were Americans.

In a public meeting in the courthouse not ever to be forgotten, Uncle Billy announced that the strike against the Camp Grant Apaches was a "memorable and glorious morning when swift punishment was dealt out to those red-handed butchers and they were wiped from the face of the earth."

Uncle Billy was generous with his old friend Don Jesús. Don Jesús, he proclaimed, "followed the highest traditions of nobility and chivalry in avenging the honor of his renowned family." The audience, made up largely of those Americans who had volunteered and then welshed and who now, some of them, were going around saying they had been there, cheered and yelled, but Don Jesús did not rise to take a bow. These were not the people to whom he wanted to be a hero.

Uncle Billy and Don Jesús got most of the kudos but there was enough glory around for everybody. Largely because of his involvement in the massacre, on May 17, less than three weeks after the event, a grateful citizenry elected Sidney DeLong mayor of Tucson.

△ △ △ FOUR

On that same seventeenth of May, still with no word from General Stoneman, Whitman did receive a dispatch from Captain Dunn. It was not in connection with the missing Aravaipa children; there was no word about them. Captain Dunn wrote that he had investigated Sergeant Clarke's story and that he had verified the fact that the sergeant and the other courier had been intercepted by armed citizens and had been detained, as the sergeant had reported. Far from denying it, the citizens involved were proud of their part in the adventure.

"Since we are not under martial law there is no action I can take against these offenders," Captain Dunn wrote. *"And taking into consideration the emotional climate of Tucson at this time, an attempt to punish any of the men connected with the attack on the Camp Grant Indians would in my opinion bring about nothing less than an armed uprising."*

Whitman sat at his desk for a long time in a deepening sense of despondency and futility. After a while he picked up his pen and wrote to Colonel James Lee. Colonel Lee was still in command of the Quartermaster Depot in Tucson and one of Whitman's responsibilities was that of commissary and he had had occasion to exchange ideas with Colonel Lee before.

He wrote rapidly and he wrote with a passion he had not yet known. He wrote that he was finding it difficult to make the Aravaipas believe he was trying to do anything for them when they saw so little done.

". . . I have pledged my word to them that I never would rest easily, day or night, until they should have justice, and just now I would as soon leave the Army as to be ordered away from them, or to be obliged to order them away from here.

"But you well know the difficulties in the way. You know that parties who would engage in murder like this could and would (and already have) make statements and multiply affidavits without end in their justification. I know you will use your influence on the right side.

"As to the Aravaipas, I believe with Eskiminzin, that this may be made either a means of making good citizens of them and their children, or drive them out to a hopeless war of extermination. They ask to be allowed to live here in their old home, where nature supplies nearly all their wants. They ask for a fair and impartial trial of their faith, and they ask that all their captive children be returned to them. Is their demand unreasonable?

"Unless some action is taken to convince them that the Government means kindness and justice, and they are driven away desperate and disappointed, blinded by ignorance, rage and superstition, I assure you that I could hardly command men to fire upon them. And if I fail to do for them now everything in my power, I should expect it to be remembered against me when I am finally called to account as my gravest offense and my greatest life responsibility. . . ."

△ △ △ FIVE

△ 1

First Sergeant Harry Ralston would not admit that he was lost. He would not admit it to himself and he certainly was not going to admit it to his sixteen men. Most of them were rookies, this was the first scout for some of them, and he didn't know how they would take it if he told them he had gotten them lost.

Sergeant Ralston didn't know what had gone wrong exactly after they left Camp Apache. The patrol had cut an Indian trail and they had followed that and then they lost it and then Sergeant Ralston didn't know where he was. Sergeant Ralston was not very seasoned himself. He was not a recruit, naturally, but this was the first scout he had undertaken without an officer.

Now it was late morning and the sun was boiling on that day early in June and the men were drinking up their water and he couldn't keep an eye on every one of them all the time because there was too much else he had to keep his eyes out for. The land told him nothing. The mountains looked like all other mountains and the arroyos and the canyons and the cactus with their silly flowers all looked the same no matter where he turned.

Sergeant Ralston called a halt and he leaned on his saddle horn and tried to figure out just where the hell he was. He had to do that with a certain expression on his face. The men might not know very much but they sure as hell knew when somebody looked like he was lost, when somebody looked like he didn't know where the hell he was going to head next.

He ordered the men to get moving again, making it sound decisive and knowledgeable. Stood to reason, Sergeant Ralston told himself. If he kept moving in one direction he was bound to come to somewhere.

Damned if he'd let these men find out he didn't know where on God's green earth he was, although this earth wasn't exactly green. And how was he going to explain his incompetence to the colonel when they got back to the post?

The patrol moved through the early afternoon, through a long canyon, up onto a bluff, down another ravine, and then Sergeant Ralston saw something moving and he saw right after that that what was moving were Apaches and that was something Sergeant Ralston did know about and he gave the order to charge.

The men opened fire. The Indians fled. The ponies scattered. The Indians and the ponies went off in all directions and Sergeant Ralston knew there was no point trying to follow them.

Sergeant Ralston rested his men. They all looked curiously at the dead Apache. He was an old man. He hadn't been able to run very fast.

Sergeant Ralston knew that other Apaches had been wounded. He reckoned some of them would die. One thing he didn't have to worry about anymore. When they turned up late at the post the old man wouldn't eat his ass out now that he could report he had attacked and killed Apaches.

△ 2

The Apaches remained in hiding for about an hour. Eskiminzin had no watch and he could not have said it was an hour but an old instinct told him when it was safe for him to summon the others.

There were about ten of them, including a man and his wife and two children, and a very old man. They had all been wandering around in the mountains since the massacre. Eskiminzin had gotten word about them and had taken some men out to find them and bring them back to the new village.

The woman was wounded now. Eskiminzin had found her in the mountains half crazed with hunger and fear and he had reassured her that everything was all right now and that it was safe to come down from the mountains. On the way back to the village Eskiminzin had stopped to gather mescal. That was to make the woman know that everything was ordinary again and now she had an Army slug in her side.

Eskiminzin and the others rounded up the ponies and went back to where the soldiers had attacked them. Eskiminzin picked up the body of the old man. He threw the body over his pony and they all started back for Camp Grant.

△ 3

Some of Eskiminzin's ceremonial skins were charred and some of the markings could not be read. His hair was plaited in two braids and he wore his turquoise and silver jewelry and around his neck was a string of silver coins.

Whitman had heard about the latest attack and he had expected Eskiminzin and when he saw that Eskiminzin was in ceremonial dress he knew what the Apache would say.

Eskiminzin spoke without waiting out his Indian time.

"The peace you have promised to the Aravaipas has been broken not once but twice, and each time by Americans. We now go back to the mountains to avenge our people."

Eskiminzin stood stiffly until the Puma translated the last word and then he turned and walked out of Whitman's office.

Whitman went to the window. He watched Eskiminzin walk unhurriedly down the length of the parade ground. He saw that soldiers under the *ramadas* were watching. The soldiers had learned of the latest killing and they, too, knew what was taking place.

Whitman saw Eskiminzin pause and then bend down and pick up the stone that had marked his peace. He saw Eskiminzin hold the stone in his hand and he prayed that the Apache would put it back. He saw Eskiminzin cast it away and walk on to the village.

Whitman watched Eskiminzin until he could no longer see him.

Whitman turned away from the window.

The Aravaipa village would disappear as a mirage on the desert.

He would have the years of his life to abide with what he had done.

△ △ △ S I X

△ 1

Lieutenant Whitman rode up the dry bed to the place where Little Running Water splashed into the open.

There was not much left of the village. There were burned parts of wickiups and burned ground. The grave mound was settling and soon the earth there would be the same as other earth. The wind had whittled away at the pile of leftover dirt and soon that landmark would be gone as well.

Before long the desert would reclaim all of its own and tidy up the land and then it would be part of the desert again and no different from any other part.

Lieutenant Whitman saw something white caught on a cactus. He rode over to it. It was a bandage.

Lieutenant Whitman started back for Camp Grant. His horse's hooves beat a soft, slow tattoo. Otherwise it was quiet.

The Aftermath

Not long after the attack on the Aravaipa village General Stoneman was removed from his command. Weeks later, when word of this reached Tucson, John Wasson expressed the feelings of just about every settler in the Territory.

EXIT STONEMAN!!!

Georgie, we see the curtain hides you with unalloyed pleasure and the most jovial contempt.

The joy of everybody was made even greater when it was learned that the general to whom Stoneman handed over his command at Los Robles was the redoubtable George Crook. General Crook, known to the settlers as Gray Wolf, was an exterminator of Indians. All now would be well.

The massacre at Camp Grant, however, outraged the country. President Grant called it "purely murder" and let it go at that. The affair might have died of official indifference. Lieutenant Whitman again emerged as a point of pivot. His letter to Colonel Lee found its way to Washington and to the front page of *The New York Times*. It was picked up and reprinted all over the country. Under great pressure President Grant ordered that the men involved be brought to trial.

With Stoneman out of the picture, John Wasson turned his attention to Whitman, labeling him "The Most Hated Man in Arizona," and set out to destroy his credibility. This officer, he wrote, "*signalized his entry into Tucson by a round of beastly drunkenness and dishonorable gambling.*" "*The royal Whitman*" had reason to be fond of Indians since he consorted with beautiful "*dusky maidens*" and additionally was a "*drunkard both off duty and on.*" General Crook ordered a Departmental Investigation of Whitman.

The grand jury enjoined to investigate the massacre was taking its time. It was not until November, 1871, seven months after the slaughter, that it started its work. President Grant finally issued an order that if indictments were not drawn up in the next three days he would place the entire Territory of Arizona under martial law. That would mean that any defendants would be tried not by their peers and friends but by military officers. The grand jury immediately indicted six Americans, including Oury and DeLong; twenty Mexicans, including Elías; and seventy-five Papagos, including Chief Francisco.

And on November 20, a military court was detailed to try Whitman on one charge of "conduct unbecoming an officer," which, if sustained, meant mandatory dismissal from the service; and also a second and lesser charge of "conduct to the prejudice of good order and military discipline." In addition to having to defend himself against these charges, Whitman also was scheduled to be one of the chief witnesses against Oury, Elías and the others.

At this point General Crook suggested to Whitman that he modify his testimony against the indicted citizens. Whitman was only too aware that if he was found guilty by the military court, his case would automatically come up for review by the Departmental Commander—General Crook—and that General Crook had the authority to reduce Whitman's sentence and save his career.

Additionally, Whitman knew the trial of Oury and Elías and the others was little more than a face-saving farce, that no matter what he or anybody else testified to, the result was foreordained. Nobody ever was going to be punished in Arizona for killing Apaches.

But that very stiff, stubborn, Yankee sense of principle that had gotten him involved in the first place would not release its hold on him now. The lieutenant told the general that he would testify under oath as his memory and conscience dictated.

The trial of Oury and the others began on December 6 and lasted five days. The jurors took nineteen minutes to bring in a verdict of not guilty for all defendants.

Five days later Whitman was on trial. Whitman acted as his own defense and charged that the statements made against him were made by John Wasson, a civilian, "in vindictive spirit," and that if they had had any basis in fact they would have been acted on earlier by the Army itself. The court agreed and threw the case out. General Crook was enraged and felt insulted.

On March 12, 1872, almost a year after the massacre, after having conducted three separate investigations into Whitman's conduct, and having received three satisfactory reports, General Crook ordered Whitman arrested and sent to Camp Crittenden, in an isolated part of the Territory, and to remain there until a second military trial. While there Whitman called Crook "a son of a bitch."

On May 27, 1872, Whitman went on trial again. He was accused of disobeying orders in connection with the Aravaipas, with drunkenness, with allowing "three disreputable Mexican women" to occupy Government quarters at Camp Grant, and with spending the night with one of them. The second court dismissed all the charges and exonerated Whitman.

Whitman was transferred to San Francisco, where he again was brought before a military court. He was convicted this time of calling General Crook "a son of a bitch." He was sentenced to be "reprimanded in General Orders; to be suspended from rank and command for six months; and to be confined to the limits of the Post where his company is serving."

Soon after relinquishing his command, General Stoneman retired from the Army for "disability contracted in the line of duty." He entered California politics and in 1882 was elected governor. He served one term and then returned to his ranch and devoted himself full time to raising grapes for wine and brandy. His health began to fail and he returned to New York State, where he was born, and he died in Buffalo on September 5, 1894.

William Sanders Oury was elected sheriff of Pima County in 1873, was re-elected and held office until 1877. He remained hale and hearty to the end, never denying his part in the attack at Camp Grant, holding always that it was justified. While going about routine business on March 31, 1887, he was stricken with severe pains and died minutes later.

Not too many years after the Camp Grant incident the Apaches were rounded up and sent to reservations and the railroad came to Tucson and things quieted down. Don Jesús Elías seemed no longer to have a reason for being. With Apaches no longer at large he had no mission. He lived through his quiet years with dignity and died as quietly on January 10, 1896.

The Aravaipas, along with other Apaches, were settled by the Government on the San Carlos Reservation in Arizona. Only six of the twenty-seven stolen children ever were recovered. Eskiminzin took as wives two of Santo's daughters, cleared land and planted corn. Some drunken Chiricahuas killed two American teamsters one day and returned to the reservation boasting of it. Eskiminzin, fearing reprisals, took what was left of his people to Mexico. Early in 1874, tired of running and hiding, he brought them back to San Carlos. The commanding officer at Camp Apache riveted leg irons on him and sentenced him to six months at hard labor.

After completing his sentence he went back to work for himself again. He prospered as a farmer and rancher. He dealt with merchants in Tucson and his accounts ran into thousands of dollars. He and his new family ate off white linen with silver tableware.

His daughter, Chita, whom he had rescued from the massacre, married the notorious outlaw the Apache Kid, and a rumor was started that Eskiminzin provided a hideout for the Apache Kid in his own home. With no formal charges brought, in 1890 Eskiminzin was arrested as a "prisoner of war" and was sent to Mount Vernon Barracks, a prison in Alabama. On the way there he saw some of the cities Whitman once had described to him.

Eskiminzin went to work as a gardener, eventually becoming head gardener. In 1895 there was nobody at Mount Vernon

Barracks who knew why he was there and he was released. In December of that year, soon after his return to San Carlos, he turned on his side in bed and died. He was about sixty-seven.

On that day the Indian Agent sent a telegram to the Commissioner of Indian Affairs:

THE NOTED CHIEF ESKIMINZIN DIED HERE DAYLIGHT THIS MORNING CHRONIC STOMACH TROUBLE STOP MYER AGT.

Lieutenant Whitman's health, broken at Camp Grant (the post was abandoned at the end of 1872 because it was "*so extremely malarious and unhealthy*"), declined steadily, and in February, 1879, he reported to the Adjutant General that doctors had informed him it was "useless to attempt any further frontier duty." On March 29 of that year he was formally severed from the service. At age forty-six, Whitman now was a retired lieutenant with a monthly pension of $120.

His marriage broke up and he remarried and then he worked on something that had occupied his mind for some time. The man who had ridden for many years in constant pain invented a saddletree that was designed to be easier both on the rider and the horse. The Whitman Saddle Company flourished and the saddle itself came within a hair of being adopted by the Army. Financially secure, Whitman moved to Washington, where he lived the rest of his life.

In 1904, many retired officers of the regular Army who had served in the Civil War were advanced a grade. Twenty-five years after his retirement Whitman achieved a captaincy.

Although he lived a long life, he was in broken health most of the time. In reply to a Circular of Query in his later years, he wrote to the War Department, "... *I can hardly realize the loss of a limb, but would gladly give one for the Vigorous health I had when I went to Old Camp Grant in Arizona.*"

Captain Royal Emerson Whitman, 3rd Cavalry, died on February 12, 1913. He was buried in Arlington National Cemetery.